Praise for the novels of
#1 *New York Times* bestselling author
Debbie Macomber

"Macomber is a skilled storyteller."
—*Publishers Weekly*

"This heartwarming story sweetly balances friendship and mother-child bonding with romantic love."
—*Kirkus Reviews* on *Window on the Bay*

"Romantic, warm, and a breeze to read—one of Macomber's best."
—*Kirkus Reviews* on *Cottage by the Sea*

"Exudes Macomber's classic warmth and gentle humor."
—*Library Journal* on *Three Brides, No Groom*

"Debbie Macomber tells women's stories in a way no one else does."
—*BookPage*

"Popular romance writer Debbie Macomber has a gift for evoking the emotions that are at the heart of the genre's popularity."
—*Publishers Weekly*

"Debbie Macomber is one of the most reliable, versatile romance writers around."
—*Milwaukee Journal Sentinel*

"Bestselling Macomber...sure has a way of pleasing readers."
—*Booklist*

DEBBIE MACOMBER

Finding You Again

mira

ISBN-13: 978-0-7783-8817-3

Finding You Again

Recycling programs
for this product may
not exist in your area.

Mira
22 Adelaide St. West, 40th Floor
Toronto, Ontario M5H 4E3, Canada
www.Harlequin.com

Printed in Lithuania

MIX
Paper from
responsible sources
FSC® C021394

Also available from Debbie Macomber and MIRA

Blossom Street

The Shop on Blossom Street
A Good Yarn
Susannah's Garden
Back on Blossom Street
Twenty Wishes
Summer on Blossom Street
Hannah's List
"The Twenty-First Wish"
  (in *The Knitting Diaries*)
A Turn in the Road

Cedar Cove

16 Lighthouse Road
204 Rosewood Lane
311 Pelican Court
44 Cranberry Point
50 Harbor Street
6 Rainier Drive
74 Seaside Avenue
8 Sandpiper Way
92 Pacific Boulevard
1022 Evergreen Place
Christmas in Cedar Cove
  (*5-B Poppy Lane* and
  A Cedar Cove Christmas)
1105 Yakima Street
1225 Christmas Tree Lane

The Dakota Series

Dakota Born
Dakota Home
Always Dakota
Buffalo Valley

The Manning Family

The Manning Sisters
  (*The Cowboy's Lady* and
  The Sheriff Takes a Wife)

The Manning Brides
  (*Marriage of Inconvenience* and
  Stand-In Wife)
The Manning Grooms
  (*Bride on the Loose* and
  Same Time, Next Year)

Christmas Books

A Gift to Last
On a Snowy Night
Home for the Holidays
Glad Tidings
Christmas Wishes
Small Town Christmas
When Christmas Comes
  (now retitled *Trading
  Christmas*)
There's Something About Christmas
Christmas Letters
The Perfect Christmas
Choir of Angels
  (*Shirley, Goodness and Mercy,
  Those Christmas Angels* and
  Where Angels Go)
Call Me Mrs. Miracle

Heart of Texas

Texas Skies
  (*Lonesome Cowboy* and
  Texas Two-Step)
Texas Nights
  (*Caroline's Child* and
  Dr. Texas)
Texas Home
  (*Nell's Cowboy* and
  Lone Star Baby)
Promise, Texas
Return to Promise

Midnight Sons

Alaska Skies
(*Brides for Brothers* and
The Marriage Risk)
Alaska Nights
(*Daddy's Little Helper* and
Because of the Baby)
Alaska Home
(*Falling for Him,
Ending in Marriage* and
Midnight Sons and Daughters)

This Matter of Marriage
Montana
Thursdays at Eight
Between Friends
Changing Habits
Married in Seattle
(*First Comes Marriage* and
Wanted: Perfect Partner)
Right Next Door
(*Father's Day* and
The Courtship of Carol Sommars)
Wyoming Brides
(*Denim and Diamonds* and
The Wyoming Kid)
Fairy Tale Weddings
(*Cindy and the Prince* and
Some Kind of Wonderful)
The Man You'll Marry
(*The First Man You Meet* and
The Man You'll Marry)
Orchard Valley Grooms
(*Valerie* and *Stephanie*)
Orchard Valley Brides
(*Norah* and *Lone Star Lovin'*)
The Sooner the Better
An Engagement in Seattle
(*Groom Wanted* and
Bride Wanted)
Out of the Rain
(*Marriage Wanted* and
Laughter in the Rain)

Learning to Love
(*Sugar and Spice* and
Love by Degree)
You...Again
(*Baby Blessed* and
Yesterday Once More)
Three Brides, No Groom
Love in Plain Sight
(*Love 'n' Marriage* and
Almost an Angel)
I Left My Heart
(*A Friend or Two* and
No Competition)
A Man's Heart
(*The Way to a Man's Heart* and
Hasty Wedding)
North to Alaska
(*That Wintry Feeling* and
Borrowed Dreams)
On a Clear Day
(*Starlight* and
Promise Me Forever)
To Love and Protect
(*Shadow Chasing* and
For All My Tomorrows)
Home in Seattle
(*The Playboy and the Widow*
and *Fallen Angel*)
Together Again
(*The Trouble with Caasi* and
Reflections of Yesterday)
The Reluctant Groom
(*All Things Considered* and
Almost Paradise)
A Real Prince
(*The Bachelor Prince* and
Yesterday's Hero)
Private Paradise
(in *That Summer Place*)

*Debbie Macomber's
Cedar Cove Cookbook*
*Debbie Macomber's
Christmas Cookbook*

CONTENTS

WHITE LACE
AND PROMISES

To Maggie Osborne
With deep respect and affection

One

Maggie Kingsbury ground the gears of her royal-blue Mercedes and pulled to a screeching halt at the red light. Impatient, she glanced at her wristwatch and muttered silently under her breath. Once again she was late. Only this time her tardiness hadn't been intentional. The afternoon had innocently slipped away while she painted, oblivious to the world.

When Janelle had asked her to be the maid of honor for the wedding, Maggie had hesitated. As a member of the wedding party, unwelcome attention would be focused on her. It wasn't until she had learned that Glenn Lambert was going to be the best man that she'd consented. Glenn had been her friend from the time she was in grade school: her buddy, her co-conspirator, her white knight. With Glenn there everything would be perfect.

But already things were going badly. Here she was due to pick him up at San Francisco International and she was ten minutes behind schedule. In the back of her mind, Maggie realized that her tardiness was another symptom of her discontent.

The light changed and she roared across the intersection, her back tires spinning. One of these days she was going to get a well-deserved speeding ticket. But not today, she prayed, please not today.

Her painting smock was smudged with a full spectrum of rainbow colors. The thick dark strands of her chestnut hair were pinned to the back of her head, disobedient curls tumbling defiantly at her temples and across her wide brow. And she had wanted to look so good for Glenn. It had been years since she'd seen him—not since high school graduation. In the beginning they had corresponded back and forth, but soon they'd each become involved with college and had formed a new set of friends. Their texts and emails had dwindled and as often happens their communication became a chatty note on a Christmas card. Steve and Janelle had kept her updated with what had been going on in Glenn's life, and from what she understood, he was a successful stockbroker in Charleston. It sounded like a job he would manage well.

It surprised Maggie that in all those years, Glenn hadn't married. At twenty-nine and thirty they were the only two of their small high school graduation class who hadn't. Briefly she wondered what had kept Glenn away from the altar. As she recalled, he had always been easy on the eyes.

Her mind conjured up a mental picture of a young Glenn Lambert. Tall, dark, athletic, broad shouldered, thin—she smiled—he'd probably filled out over the years. He was the boy who lived next door and they had been great friends and at times the worst of enemies. Once, in the sixth grade, Glenn had stolen her diary and as a joke made copies and sold them to the boys in their class. After he found her crying, he had spent weeks trying to make it up to her. Years later his patience had gotten her a passing grade in

chemistry and she had fixed him up with a date for the
Junior-Senior prom.

Arriving at the airport, Maggie followed the freeway
signs that directed her to the passenger-pickup area. Almost immediately she sighted Glenn standing beside his
luggage, watching the traffic for a familiar face. A slow
smile blossomed across her lips until it hovered at a grin.
Glenn had hardly changed, and yet he was completely
different. He was taller than she remembered, with those
familiar broad shoulders now covered by a heather-blue
blazer instead of a faded football jersey. At thirty he was
a prime specimen of manhood. But behind his easy smile,
Maggie recognized a maturity—one he'd fought hard for
and painfully attained. Maggie studied him with fascina-
tion, amazed at his air of deliberate casualness. He knew
about her inheritance. Of course he knew; Steve would
have told him. Involuntarily, her fingers tightened around
the steering wheel as a sense of regret settled over her. As
much as she would have liked to, Maggie couldn't go back
to being a carefree schoolgirl.

She eased to a stop at the curb in front of him and leaned
across the seat to open the passenger door. "Hey, handsome, are you looking for a ride?"

Bending over, Glenn stuck his head inside the car.
"Muffie, I should have known you'd be late."

As she climbed out of the vehicle, Maggie grimaced
at the use of her nickname. Glenn had dubbed her Muffie
in junior high, but it had always sounded to Maggie like
the name of a poodle. The more she'd objected the more
the name had stuck until her friends had picked it up. The
sweet, innocent Muffie no longer existed.

After checking the side-view mirror for traffic to clear,
she opened her door and stepped out. "I'm sorry I'm late,

I don't know where the time went. As usual I got carried away."

Glenn chuckled and shook his head knowingly. "When haven't you gotten carried away?" He picked up his suitcase and tucked it inside the trunk Maggie had just opened. Placing his hands on her shoulders, he examined her carefully and gave her a brief hug. "You look fantastic." His dark eyes were somber and sincere.

"Me?" she choked out, feeling the warmth of many years of friendship chase away her earlier concerns. "You always could lie diplomatically." Maggie had recognized early in life that she was no raving beauty. Her eyes were probably her best feature—dark brown with small gold flecks, almond shaped and slanting upward at the corners. She was relatively tall, nearly five foot eight, with long shapely legs. Actually, the years hadn't altered her outwardly. Like Glenn's, the changes were more inward. Life's lessons had left their mark on her as well.

Looking at Glenn, Maggie couldn't hide the feeling of nostalgia she experienced. "The last time I looked this bad I was dressed as a zucchini for a fifth-grade play."

He crossed his arms and studied her. "I'd say you were wearing typical Muffie attire."

"Jeans and sneakers?"

"Seeing you again is like stepping into the past."

Not exactly. She didn't stuff tissue paper in her bra these days. Momentarily, she wondered if Glenn had ever guessed that she had. "I've got strict instructions to drop you off at Steve's. The rehearsal's scheduled at the church tonight at seven." This evening he'd have the opportunity to see just how much she had changed.

Of all the people Maggie knew, Glenn would be the one to recognize the emotional differences in her. She might have been able to disguise them from others, but not from Glenn.

"With you chauffeuring me around there's little guarantee I'll make the wedding," Glenn teased affectionately.

"You'll make it," she assured him and climbed back into the car.

Glenn joined her and snapped the seat belt into place. Thoughtfully he ran his hand along the top of the dashboard. "I heard about your inheritance and wondered if it'd made a difference in your life."

"Well, I now live in a fancy beach house, and don't plan to do anything with the rest of my life except paint." She checked his profile for a negative response and finding none, she continued. "A secretary handles the mail, an estate planner deals with the finances, and there's a housekeeper and gardener as well. I do exactly as I want."

"Must be nice."

"I heard you haven't done so shabbily yourself."

"Not bad, but I don't lounge around in a beach house." He said it without censure. "I've had dealings with a lot of wealthy people the past few years. As far as I can see, having money can be a big disappointment."

The statement was open-ended, but Maggie refused to comment. Glenn's insight surprised her. He was right. All Great-aunt Margaret's money hadn't brought Maggie or her brother happiness. Oh, at first she had been filled with wonderful illusions about her inheritance. But these days she struggled to shroud her restlessness. To anyone else her life-style was a dream come true. Only Maggie knew differently.

"Money is supposed to make everything right. Only it creates more problems than it solves," she mumbled and pulled into the flow of traffic leaving the airport. Glenn didn't respond and Maggie wasn't sure he heard her, which was just as well, because the subject was one she preferred to avoid.

"It's hard to imagine Steve and Janelle getting married after all these years." A lazy grin swept across his tanned face.

Maggie smiled, longing to keep things light. "I'd say it was about time, wouldn't you?"

"I've never known two people more right for each other. The surprising part is that everyone saw it but them."

"I'm happy for those two."

"Me, too," he added, but Maggie noted that Glenn's tone held a hint of melancholy, as if the wedding was going to be as difficult for him as it was for her. Maggie couldn't imagine why.

"Steve's divorce devastated him," Maggie continued, "and he started dating Janelle again. The next thing I knew they decided to march up the aisle." Maggie paused and gestured expressively with her right hand.

Glenn's eyes fell on Maggie's artistically long fingers. It surprised him that she had such beautiful hands. They looked capable of kneading the stiffest clay and at the same time gentle enough to soothe a crying child. She wore no rings, nor were her well-shaped nails painted, yet her hands were striking. He couldn't take his eyes from them. He had known Maggie most of her life and had never appreciated her hands.

"Are you going to invite me out to your beach house?" he asked finally.

"I thought I might. There's a basketball hoop in the gym and I figured I'd challenge you to a game."

"I'm not worried. As I recall the only slam dunk you ever made was with a doughnut into a cup of coffee."

Hiding her laugh, Maggie answered threateningly, "I'll make you pay for that remark."

Their families had shared a wide common driveway, and Maggie had passed many an hour after school playing ball with Glenn. Janelle and Steve and the rest of the gang from the neighborhood had hung around together. Most of the childhood friendships remained in place. Admittedly, Maggie wasn't as trusting of people nowadays. Not since she had inherited the money. The creeps had come crawling out of the woodwork the minute the news of her good fortune was out. Some were obvious gold diggers and others weren't so transparent. Maggie had gleaned valuable lessons from Dirk Wagner and had nearly made the mistake of marrying a man who loved her money far more than he cared for her.

"I don't suppose you've got a pool in that mansion of yours?"

"Yup."

"Is there anything you haven't got?" Glenn asked suddenly serious.

Maggie didn't know where to start, the list was so long. She had lost her purpose, her ambition, her drive to succeed professionally with her art. Her roster of friends was meager and consisted mainly of people she had known most of her life. "Some things," she muttered, wanting to change the subject.

"Money can't buy everything, can it?" Glenn asked so gently that Maggie felt her throat tighten.

She'd thought it would at first, but had learned the hard way that it couldn't buy the things that mattered most: love, loyalty, respect or friendship.

"No." Her voice was barely above a whisper.

"I suppose out of respect for your millions, I should call

you Margaret," Glenn suggested next. "But try as I might, you'll always be Muffie to me."

"Try Maggie. I'm not Muffie anymore." She smiled to take any sting from her voice. With his returning nod, her hand relaxed against the steering wheel.

She exited from the freeway and drove into the basement parking lot of Steve's apartment building. "Here we are," she announced, turning off the engine. "With a good three hours to spare."

While Glenn removed his suitcase from the car trunk, Maggie dug in the bottom of her purse for the apartment key Steve had given her. "I have strict instructions to personally escort you upstairs and give you a stiff drink. You're going to need it when you hear what's scheduled."

With his suitcase in tow, Glenn followed her to the elevator. "Where's Steve?"

"Working."

"The day before his wedding?" Glenn looked astonished.

"He's been through this wedding business before," she reminded him offhandedly.

The heavy doors swished closed and Maggie leaned against the back wall and pulled the pins from her hair. It was futile to keep putting it up when it came tumbling down every time she moved her head. Stuffing the pins in her pocket, she felt Glenn's gaze studying her. Their eyes met.

"I can't believe you," he said softly.

"What?"

"You haven't changed. Time hasn't marked you in the least. You're exactly as I remember."

"You've changed." They both had.

"Don't I know it." Glenn sighed, leaned against the side

of the moving elevator and pinched the bridge of his nose. "Some days I feel a hundred years old."

Maggie was mesmerized by him. He was different. The carefree, easygoing teen had been replaced by an introspective man with intense, dark eyes that revealed a weary pain. The urge to ask him what had happened burned on her lips, but she knew that if she inquired into his life, he could ask about her own. Instead she led the way out of the elevator to the apartment.

The key turned and Maggie swung open the door to the high-rise that gave a spectacular view of San Francisco Bay.

"Go ahead and plant your suitcase in the spare bedroom and I'll fix us a drink. What's your pleasure?"

"Juice if there's any."

Maggie placed both hands on the top of the bar. "I'll see what I can do." Turning, she investigated the contents of the refrigerator and brought out a small can of tomato juice. "Will this do?"

"Give it to me straight," he tossed over his shoulder as he left the living room.

By the time he returned, Maggie was standing at the window holding a martini. She watched him take the glass of juice from the bar and join her.

"Are you on the wagon?" she asked impulsively.

"Not really. It's a little too early in the afternoon for me."

Maggie nodded as a tiny smile quirked at the corners of her mouth. The first time she had ever tasted vodka had been with Glenn.

"What's so amusing?"

"Do you remember New Year's Eve the year I was sixteen?"

Glenn's brow furrowed. "No."

"Glenn!" She laughed with disbelief. "After all the trouble we got into over that, I'd think you'd never forget it."

"Was that the year we threw our own private party?"

"Remember Cindy and Earl, Janelle and Steve, you and me and...who else?"

"Brenda and Bob?"

"No... Barb and Bob."

"Right." He chuckled. "I never could keep the twins straight."

"Who could? It surprises me he didn't marry both of them."

"Whatever happened to Bob?"

Maggie took a sip of her martini before answering. "He's living in Oregon, going bald, and has four kids."

"Bob? I don't believe it."

"You weren't here for the ten-year reunion." Maggie hadn't bothered to attend either, but Janelle had filled in the details of what she'd missed.

"I'm sorry I missed it," Glenn said and moved to the bar. He lifted his drink and finished it off in two enormous swallows.

Mildly surprised at the abrupt action, Maggie took another sip of hers, moved to a deep-seated leather chair, sat and tucked her long legs under her.

Glenn took a seat across from her. "So what's been going on in your life, Maggie? Are you happy?"

She shrugged indolently. "I suppose." From anyone else she would have resented the question, but she'd always been able to talk to Glenn. A half hour after being separated for years and it was as if they'd never been apart. "I'm a wealthy woman, Glenn, and I've learned the hard way about human nature."

"What happened?"

"It's a long story."

"Didn't you just get done telling me that we had three hours before the rehearsal?"

For a moment Maggie was tempted to spill her frustrations out. To tell Glenn about the desperate pleas for money she got from people who sensed her soft heart. The ones who were looking for someone to invest in a sure thing. And the users, who pretended friendship or love in the hopes of a lucrative relationship. "You must be exhausted. I'll cry on your shoulder another time."

"I'll hold you to that." He leaned forward and reached for her hand. "We had some good times, didn't we?"

"Great times."

"Ah, the good old days." Glenn relaxed with a bittersweet sigh. "Who was it that said youth was wasted on the young?"

"Mark Twain," Maggie offered.

"No, I think it was Madonna."

They both laughed and Maggie stood, reaching for her purse. "Well, I suppose I should think about heading home and changing my clothes. Steve will be here in an hour. That'll give you time to relax." She fanned her fingers through her hair in a careless gesture. "I'll see you tonight at the rehearsal."

"Thanks for meeting me," Glenn said, coming to his feet.

"I was glad to do it." Her hand was on the doorknob.

"It's great to see you again."

The door made a clicking sound as it closed and Glenn turned to wipe a hand over his tired eyes. It was good to be with Maggie again, but frankly, he was glad she'd decided to leave. He needed a few minutes to compose his thoughts before facing Steve. The first thing his friend was bound to ask him about was Angie.

Glenn stiffened as her name sent an instant flash of pain through him. She had married Simon two months earlier, and Glenn had thought that acceptance would become easier with time. It had, but it was far more difficult than he'd expected. He had loved Angie with a reverence; eventually he had loved her enough to step aside when she wanted to marry Simon. He'd been a fool, Glenn realized. If he had acted on his instincts, he'd have had a new bride on his arm for this trip. Now he was alone, more alone than he could ever remember. The last place he wanted to be was a wedding. Every part of it would only be a reminder of what could have been his, and what he'd allowed to slip through his fingers. He didn't begrudge Steve any happiness; he just didn't want to have to stand by and smile serenely when part of him was riddled with regrets.

Maggie shifted into third gear as she rounded the curve in the highway at twenty miles above the speed limit. Deliberately she slowed down, hating the urgency that forced her to rush home. The beach house had become her gilded cage. The world outside its door had taken on a steel edge that she avoided.

Although she had joked with Glenn about not being married, the tense muscles of her stomach reminded her of how much she envied Janelle. She would smile for the wedding pictures and be awed at all the right moments, but she was going to hate every minute of it. The worst part was she was genuinely happy for Janelle and Steve. Oh, Janelle had promised that they'd continue to get together as they always had. They'd been best friends since childhood, and for a time they probably would see each other regularly. But Janelle wanted to start a family right away, and once she had a baby, Maggie thought, everything would change. It had to.

Automatically Maggie took the road that veered from the highway and a few minutes later turned onto the long circular driveway that led to her waterfront house. The huge structure loomed before her, impressive, elegant and imposing. Maggie had bought it for none of those reasons. She wasn't even sure she liked it. The two-story single-family dwelling on Eastwood Drive where she had grown up was far more appealing. Even now she couldn't bring herself to sell that house and had rented it for far less than market value to a retired couple who kept the yard and flower beds meticulously groomed. Sometimes during the darkest hour of a sleepless night, Maggie would mull over the idea of donating her money to charity. If possible, she would gladly return to the years when she had sat blissfully at her bedroom window, her chin resting on her crossed arms as she gazed into the stars and dreamed of the future. Childhood dreams that were never meant to come true.

Shaking herself from her reverie, Maggie parked the fancy sport car in front of the house. For this night she would put on her brightest smile. No one would ever know what she was feeling on the inside.

Janelle's mother looked as if she were preparing more for a funeral than a wedding. Flustered and worried, she waved her hands in five different directions, orchestrating the entourage gathered in the church vestibule.

"Girls, please, please pay attention. Darcy go right, June left and so on. Understand?"

The last time anyone had called Maggie a girl was in high school. Janelle, Maggie, the bridesmaids, the flower girl, and the ring bearer were all positioned, awaiting instructions. Maggie glanced enviously to the front of the church where Steve and Glenn were standing. It didn't seem fair that they should get off so lightly.

"Remember to count to five slowly before following the person in front of you," Janelle's mother continued.

The strains of organ music burst through the church and the first attendant, shoulders squared, stepped onto the white paper runner that flowed down the center aisle.

"I can't believe this is really happening," Janelle whispered. "Tomorrow Steve and I will be married. After all the years of loving him it's like a dream."

"I know," Maggie whispered and squeezed her friend's forearm.

"Go left, go left." Mrs. Longmier's voice drifted to them and Maggie dissolved into giggles.

"I can't believe your mother."

"The pastor assured her he'd handle everything, but she insisted on doing it herself. That's what I get for being the only girl in a family of four boys."

"In another twenty years or so you may well be doing it yourself," Maggie reminded her.

"Oops." Janelle nudged her. "Your turn. And for heaven's sake don't goof up. I'm starved and want to get out of here."

Holding a paper plate decorated with bows and ribbons from one of Janelle's five wedding showers, Maggie carefully placed one foot in front of the other in a deliberate, step-by-step march that seemed to take an eternity. The smile on her face was as brittle as old parchment.

Standing in her place at the altar, Maggie kept her head turned so she could see Janelle's approach. The happiness radiating from her friend's face produced a curious ache in Maggie's heart. If these feelings were so strong at the rehearsal, she couldn't help wondering how she'd react during the actual wedding. Maggie felt someone's eyes on her and glanced up to see Glenn's steady gaze. He smiled briefly and looked away.

The pastor moved to the front of the young couple and cracked a few old jokes. Everyone laughed politely. As the organ music filled the church, the bride and groom, hands linked, began their exit.

When it came time for Maggie to meet Glenn at the head of the aisle, he stiffly tucked her hand in the crook of his elbow.

"I never thought I'd be marching down the aisle with you," she whispered under her breath.

"It has all the makings of a nightmare," Glenn countered. "However, I'll admit you're kinda cute."

"Thanks."

"But so are lion cubs."

Maggie's fingers playfully bit into the muscles of his upper arm as she struggled not to laugh.

His hand patted hers as he whispered, "You're lovely."

"Is that so?" Maggie batted her eyes at him, blatantly flirting with him. "And available. I have a king size bed too."

They were nearing the back of the church. Glenn's dark eyes bored holes into her. "Are you looking for a lover?"

The question caught Maggie by surprise. The old Glenn would have swatted her across the rump and told her to behave. The new Glenn, the man she didn't know, was dead serious. "Not this week," she returned, deliberately flippant. "But if you're interested, I'll keep you in mind."

His gaze narrowed slightly as he tilted his head to one side. "How much have you had to drink?"

Maggie wanted to laugh and would have if not for a discouraging glare from Mrs. Longmier. "One martini."

The sound of a soft snort followed. "You've changed, Maggie." Just the way he said it indicated that he wasn't pleased with the difference.

Her spirits crashed to the floor with breakneck speed. Good grief, she thought angrily, it didn't matter what Glenn thought of her. He had made her feel like a teenager again and she'd behaved like a fool. She wasn't even sure why she was flirting with him. Probably to cover up how miserable the whole event made her.

Casually, Glenn dropped her arm as they entered the vestibule and stepped aside to make room for the others who followed. Maggie used the time to gather her light jacket and purse. Glenn moved in the opposite direction and her troubled gaze followed him.

A flurry of instructions followed as Steve's father gave directions to the family home, where dinner was being served to the members of the wedding party.

Maggie moved outside the church. There wasn't any need for her to stay and listen. She knew how to get to the Grants' house as well as her own. Standing at the base of the church steps, Maggie was fumbling inside her purse for her keys when Glenn joined her.

"I'm supposed to ride with you."

"Don't make it sound like a fate worse than death," she bit out, furious that she couldn't do what she needed.

"Listen, Maggie, I'm sorry. Okay?"

"You?" Amazed, Maggie lowered the purse flap and slowly raised her dark eyes to his. "It's me who should apologize. I was behaving like an idiot in there, flirting with you like that."

He lifted a silken strand of hair from her shoulder. "It's

rather nice to be flirted with now and then," he said with a lazy smile.

Maggie tore her gaze from his and withdrew her car keys. "Here," she said, handing the key chain to him. "I know you'll feel a whole lot safer driving yourself."

"You're right," he retorted, his mood teasing and jovial. "I still remember the day you wiped out two garbage cans and an oak tree backing out of the driveway."

"I'd just gotten my learner's permit and the gears slipped," she returned righteously.

"Unfortunately your skills haven't improved much."

"On second thought, I'll drive and you can do the praying."

Laughing, Glenn tossed an arm across her shoulders.

They chatted easily on the way to the Grants' home and parked behind Steve and Janelle in the driveway. The four car doors slammed simultaneously.

"Glad to see you still remember the way around town," Steve teased Glenn. The two men were nearly the same height, both with dark hair and brown eyes. Steve smiled lovingly at Janelle and brought her close to his side. "I hope everyone's hungry," he said, waiting for Glenn and Maggie to join them. "Mom hasn't stopped cooking in two days."

"Famished," Glenn admitted. "The last time I ate was on the plane."

"Poor starving baby," Maggie cooed.

Glenn was chuckling when the four entered the house. Immediately Janelle and Maggie offered to help Steve's mother and carried the assorted salads and platters of deli meats to the long table for the buffet. Soon the guests were mingling and helping themselves.

Maggie loaded her plate and found an empty space beside Glenn, who was kneeling in front of the coffee table with several others. He glanced up from the conversation he was having with a bridesmaid when Maggie joined them.

"Muffie, you know Darcy, don't you?" Glenn asked.

"Muffie?" Darcy repeated incredulously. "I thought your name was Maggie."

"Muffie was the name Glenn gave me in junior high. We were next-door neighbors. In fact, we lived only a few blocks from here."

"I suppose you're one of those preppy, organized types," Darcy suggested.

Glenn nearly choked on his potato salad. "Hardly."

Maggie gave him the sharp point of her elbow in his ribs. "Glenn thought he was being cute one day and dubbed me something offensive. Muffie, however, was better than Magpie—"

"She never stopped talking," Glenn inserted.

"—or Maggie the Menace."

"For obvious reasons."

"For a while it was Molasses." Maggie closed her eyes at the memory.

"Because she was forever late."

"As you may have guessed, we fought like cats and dogs," Maggie explained needlessly.

"The way a lot of brothers and sisters do," Glenn inserted.

"So where did the Muffie come in?"

"In junior high things became a bit more sophisticated. We couldn't very well call her Magpie."

Darcy nodded and sliced off a bite of ham.

"So after a while," Glenn continued, "Steve, Janelle, the whole gang of us decided to call her Muffie, simply because she talked so much we wanted to muffle her. The name stuck."

"Creative people are often subjected to this form of harrassment," Maggie informed her with a look of injured pride.

"Didn't you two...?" Darcy hesitated. "I mean Steve and Janelle obviously had something going even then."

"Us?" Maggie and Glenn shared a look of shock. "I did ask you to the Sadie Hawkins dance once."

Glenn nodded, a mischievous look in his eyes. "She'd already asked five other guys and been turned down."

"So I drastically lowered my standards and asked Glenn. It was a complete disaster. Remember?"

Their eyes met and they burst into fits of laughter, causing the conversational hum of the room to come to an abrupt halt.

"Hey you two, let me in on the joke," Darcy said. "What's so funny?"

Maggie composed herself enough to begin the story. "On the way home, Glenn's beat up car stalled. We learned later it was out of gas. Believe me, I wasn't pleased, especially since I'd sprung for new shoes and my feet were killing me."

"I don't know why you're complaining; I took you to the dance, didn't I?"

Maggie ignored him. "Since I didn't have a driver's license, Mr. Wonderful here insisted on steering while I pushed his car—uphill."

"You?" Darcy was aghast.

"Now, Maggie, to be fair, you should explain that I helped push, too."

"Some help," she grumbled. "That wasn't the worst part.

It started to rain and I was in my party dress, shoving his car down the street in the dead of night."

"Maggie was complaining so loud that she woke half the neighborhood," Glenn inserted, "and someone looked out the window and thought we were stealing a car. They phoned the police and within minutes we were surrounded by three patrol cars."

"They took us downtown and phoned Glenn's dad. It was the most embarrassing moment of my life. The Girls' Club had sponsored the dance and I was expecting roses and kisses in the moonlight. Instead I got stuck pushing Glenn's car in the rain and was darn near arrested."

"Believe me, Maggie made me pay for that one." Glenn's smiling eyes met hers and Maggie felt young and carefree again. It'd been so long since she had talked and laughed like this; she could almost forget. Almost. The present, however, was abruptly brought to her attention a few minutes later when Steve's cousin approached her.

"Maggie," he asked, crowding in next to her on the floor, "I was wondering if we could have a few minutes alone? There's something I'd like to ask you."

A heavy sensation of dread moved over her. It had happened so often in the past that she knew almost before he spoke what he would say. "Sure, Sam." As of yet, she hadn't found a graceful way of excusing herself from these situations.

Rolling to her feet, she followed Sam across the room to an empty corner.

"I suppose Steve's told you about my business venture?" he began brightly with false enthusiasm.

Maggie gritted her teeth, praying for patience. "No, I can't say that he has."

"Well, my partner and I are looking for someone with

a good eye for investment potential who would be willing to lend us a hundred thousand dollars. Would you happen to know anyone who might be interested?"

Maggie noticed Glenn making his way toward them. As she struggled to come up with a polite rejection to Sam, Glenn stopped next to her.

"Sam," he interrupted, taking Maggie by the arm, "excuse us for a minute, will you?" He didn't wait for a response and led her through the cluttered living room and into the kitchen.

"Where are you taking me?" Maggie asked when he opened the sliding glass door that led to the patio.

"Outside."

"That much is obvious. But why are you taking me out here?"

Glenn paused to stand under the huge maple tree and looked toward the sky. "There's only a half-moon tonight, but it'll have to do."

"Are you going to turn into a werewolf or something?" Maggie joked, pleased to be rescued from the clutches of an awkward conversation.

"Nope." He turned her in his arms, looping his hands around her narrow waist and bringing her against the hard wall of his chest. "This is something I should have done the night of the Girls' Club dance," he murmured as he looked down at her.

"What is?"

"Kiss you in the moonlight," he whispered just before his mouth claimed hers.

Two

Maggie was too amazed to respond. Glenn Lambert, the boy who had lived next door most of her life, was kissing her. And he was kissing her as if he meant to be doing exactly that. His lips moved slowly over hers, shaping and fitting his mouth to hers with a gentleness that rocked her until she was a churning mass of conflicting emotions. This was Glenn, the same Glenn who had teased her unmercifully about "going straight" while she wore braces. The Glenn who had heartlessly beaten her playing one-on-one basketball. The same Glenn who had always been her white knight. Yet it felt so right, so good to be in his arms. Hesitantly, Maggie lifted her hands, sliding them over his chest and linking her fingers at the base of his neck, clinging to him for support. Gently parting her lips, she responded to his kiss. She savored the warm taste of him, the feel of his hands against the small of her back and the tangy scent of his after-shave. It seemed right for Glenn to be holding her. More right than anything had felt in a long time.

When he lifted his head there was a moment of stunned silence while the fact registered in Glenn's bemused mind that he had just kissed Maggie. Maggie. But the vibrant woman in his arms wasn't the same girl who'd lived next door. The woman was warm and soft and incredibly feminine, and he was hungry for a woman's gentleness. Losing Angie had left him feeling cold and alone. His only desire had been to love and protect her, but she hadn't wanted him. A stinging chill ran through his blood, forcing him into the present. His hold relaxed and he dropped his arms.

"Why'd you do that?" Maggie whispered, having difficulty finding her voice. From the moment he had taken her outside, Maggie had known his intention had been to free her from the clutches of Steve's cousin—not to kiss her. At least not like that. What had started out in fun had become serious.

"I'm not sure," he answered honestly. A vague hesitancy showed in his eyes.

"Am I supposed to grade you?"

Glenn took another step backward, broadening the space between them. "Good grief, no; you're merciless."

Mentally, Maggie congratulated him for recovering faster than she. "Not always," she murmured. At his blank look, she added, "I'm not always merciless."

"That's not the way I remember it. The last time I wanted to kiss you, I got a fist in the stomach."

Maggie's brow furrowed. She couldn't remember Glenn even trying to kiss her and looked at him with surprise and doubt as she sifted through her memories. "I don't remember that."

"I'm not likely to forget it," he stated and arched one brow arrogantly. "As I recall, I was twelve and you were eleven. A couple of the guys at school had already kissed a girl and said it wasn't half-bad. There wasn't anyone I wanted to kiss, but for a girl you weren't too bad, so I offered you five of my best baseball cards if you'd let me kiss you."

Maggie gave him a wicked grin as her memory returned. "That was the greatest insult of my life. I was saving my lips for the man I planned to marry. At the time I think it was Billy Idol."

"As I recall you told me that," he replied with a low chuckle. He tucked an arm around her waist, bringing her to his side. "Talking about our one and only date tonight made me remember how much I took you for granted all those years. You were great."

"I know," she said with a complete lack of modesty.

A slow, roguish grin grew across his features. "But then there were times…"

"Don't go philosophical on me, Glenn Lambert." An unaccustomed, delicious heat was seeping into her bones. It was as if she'd been standing in a fierce winter storm and someone had invited her inside to sit by the cozy warmth of the fire.

"We've both done enough of that for one night," Glenn quipped, looking toward the bright lights of the house.

Maggie didn't want to go back inside. She felt warm and comfortable for the first time in what seemed like ages. If they returned to the house full of people, she'd be forced to paint on another plastic smile and listen to the likes of Steve's cousin.

"Do you ever wonder about the old neighborhood?"

Grinning, Glenn looked down on her. "Occasionally."

"Want to take a look?"

He glanced toward the house again, sensing her reluctance to return. The old Maggie would have faced the world head-on. The change surprised him. "Won't we be missed?"

"I doubt it."

Glenn tucked Maggie's hand in the crook of his arm. "For old times' sake."

"The rope swing in your backyard is still there."

"You're kidding!" He gave a laugh of disbelief.

"A whole new generation of kids are playing on that old swing."

"What about the tree house?"

"That, unfortunately, was the victim of a bad windstorm several years back."

His arm tightened around her waist and the fragile scent of her perfume filled his senses. She was a woman now, and something strange and inexplicable was happening between them. Glenn wasn't sure it was right to encourage it.

"How do you keep up with all this?" he asked, attempting to steer his thoughts from things he shouldn't be thinking, like how soft and sweet and wonderfully warm she felt.

"Simple," Maggie explained with a half smile. "I visit often." The happiest days of her life had been in that house in the old neighborhood. She couldn't turn back the clock, but the outward symbols of that time lived on for her to visit as often as needed. "Come on," she said brightly and took his hand. She was feeling both foolish and fanciful. "There probably won't be another chance if we don't go now."

"You'll freeze," Glenn warned, running his hands down the lengths of her bare arms and up again to cup her shoulders.

"No," she argued, not wanting anything to disturb the moment.

"I'll collect your jacket and tell Steve what we're up to," Glenn countered.

"No," she pleaded, her voice low and husky. "Don't. I'll be fine. Really."

Glenn studied her for an instant before agreeing. Maggie was frightened. The realization stunned him. His bubbly, happy-go-lucky Maggie had been reduced to an unhappy, insecure waif. The urge to take her in his arms and protect her was nearly overwhelming.

"All right," he agreed, wrapping his arms around her shoulder to lend her his warmth. If she did get chilled he could give her his own jacket.

With their arms around each other, they strolled down Ocean Avenue to the grade school, cut through the play yard and came out on Marimar near Eastwood Drive.

"Everything seems the same," Glenn commented. His smile was filled with contentment.

"It is."

"How are your parents doing?" he inquired.

"They retired in Florida. I told them they ought to be more original than that, but it was something they really wanted. They can afford it, so why not? What about your folks?"

"They're in South Carolina. Dad's working for the same company. Both Eric and Dale are married and supplying them with a houseful of grandchildren."

A chill shot through Maggie and she shivered involuntarily. She was an aunt now, too, but the circumstances weren't nearly as pleasant. Her brother, Denny, had also discovered that his inheritance wasn't a hedge against unhappiness. Slowly shaking her head, Maggie spoke. "Do you realize how old that makes me feel? Dale married—I'd never have believed it. He was only ten when you moved."

"He met his wife the first year of college. They fell in love, and against everyone's advice decided not to wait to get married. They were both nineteen and had two kids by the time Dale graduated."

"And they're fine now?"

"They're going stronger than ever. The boys are in school and Cherry has gone back to college for her degree." There wasn't any disguising the pride in his voice.

"What about Eric?"

"He married a flight attendant a couple of years ago. They have a baby girl." His hand rested at the nape of her neck in a protective action. "What about your brother?"

"Denny was already married by the time you moved, wasn't he? He and Lisa have two little girls."

"Is he living in San Francisco?"

"Yes," she supplied quickly and hurried to change the subject. "The night's lovely, isn't it?"

Glenn ignored the comment. "Is Denny still working for the phone company?"

"No," she returned starkly. "I can't remember when I've seen so many stars."

They were silent for a moment while Glenn digested the information. Something had happened between Denny and Maggie that she was obviously reluctant to discuss.

"Do you realize that there's never been a divorce in either of our families?" she said softly with sudden insight. She knew what a rarity that was in this day and age. Nearly thirty percent of their high school class were on their second marriages.

"I doubt that there ever will be a divorce. Mom and Dad believe strongly in working out problems instead of running from them and that was ingrained in all three of us boys."

"We're in the minority then. I don't know how Janelle is going to adjust to Steve's children. It must be difficult."

"She loves him," Glenn countered somewhat defensively.

"I realize that," Maggie whispered, thinking out loud. "It's just that I remember when Steve married Ginny. Janelle cried for days afterward and went about doing her best to forget him. Every one of us knew that Ginny and Steve were terribly mismatched and it would only be a matter of time before they split."

"I wasn't that sure they couldn't make a go of it."

Maggie bristled. "I was, and anyone with half a brain saw it. Ginny was pregnant before the wedding and no one except Steve was convinced the baby was his."

"Steve was in a position to know."

Maggie opened her mouth to argue, glanced up to see Glenn's amused gaze and gingerly pressed her lips tightly closed. "I don't recall you being this argumentative," she said after several moments.

"When it comes to the sanctity of marriage, I am."

"For your sake, I hope you marry the right woman then."

The humor drained from his eyes and was replaced with such pain that Maggie's breath caught in her throat. "Glenn, what did I say?" she asked, concern in her voice.

"Nothing," he assured her with a half smile that disguised none of his mental anguish. "I thought I had found her."

"Oh, Glenn, I'm so sorry. Is there anything I can do? I make a great wailing wall." From the pinched lines about his mouth and eyes, Maggie knew that the woman had been someone very special. Even when Maggie had known him best, Glenn had been a discriminating male. He had dated only a few times and, as far as she could remember, had never gone steady with one girl.

The muscles of his face tightened as he debated whether to tell Maggie about Angie. He hadn't discussed her with anyone over the past couple of months and the need to purge her from his life burned in him. Perhaps someday, he thought, but not now and not with Maggie, who had enough problems of her own. "She married someone else. There's nothing more to say."

"You loved her very much, didn't you?" Whoever she was, the woman was a fool. Glenn was the steady, solid type most women sought. When he loved, it would be forever and with an intensity few men were capable of revealing.

Glenn didn't answer. Instead he regarded her with his pain-filled eyes and asked, "What about you?"

"You mean why I never married?" She gave a shrug of indifference. "The right man never came along. I thought he might have once, but I was wrong. Dirk was more interested in spending my money than loving me."

"I'm sorry." His arm tightened around her as an unreasonable anger filled him over the faceless Dirk. He had hurt Maggie, and Glenn was intimately aware of how much one person could hurt another.

"Actually, I think I was lucky to discover it when I did. But thirty is looming around the corner and the biological clock is ticking like Big Ben. I'd like to get married, but I won't lower my standards."

"What kind of man are you looking for?"

He was so utterly blasé about it that Maggie's composure slipped and she nearly dissolved into laughter. "You mean in case you happen to know someone who fits the bill?"

"I might."

"Why not?" she asked with a soft giggle. "To start off, I'd like someone financially secure."

"That shouldn't be so difficult."

He was so serious that Maggie bit into her bottom lip to hide the trembling laughter. "In addition to being on firm financial ground, he should be magnanimous."

"With you he'd have to be," Glenn said in a laughter-tinged voice.

Maggie ignored the gibe. "He'd have to love me enough to overlook my faults—few as they are—be loyal, loving, and want children."

She paused, expecting him to comment, but he nodded in agreement. "Go on," he encouraged.

"But more than simply wanting children, he'd have to take responsibility for helping me raise them into worthwhile adults. I want a man who's honest, but one who won't shout the truth in my face if it's going to hurt me. A special man to double my joys and divide my sorrows. Someone who will love me when my hair is gray and my ankles are thick." Realizing how serious she'd become, Maggie hesitated. "Know anyone like him?" Her words hung empty in the silence that followed.

"No," Glenn eventually said, and shook his head for emphasis. Those were the very things he sought in a wife. "I can't say that I do."

"From my guess, Prince Charmings are few and far between these days."

They didn't speak again until they paused in front of the fifty-year-old house that had been Glenn's childhood home. Little had altered over the years, Glenn realized. The wide front porch and large dormers that jutted out from the roof looked exactly as they had in his mind. The house had been repainted, and decorative shutters were now added to the front windows, but the same warmth and love seemed to radiate from its doors.

Maggie followed Glenn's gaze to the much-used basketball hoop positioned above the garage door. It was slightly crooked from years of slam dunks. By the look of things, the hoop was used as much now as it had been all those years ago.

"I suppose we should think of heading back. It's going to be a long day tomorrow." Maggie's gaze fell from the house to the cracked sidewalk. It hit her suddenly that in a couple of days Glenn would be flying back to Charleston. He was here for the wedding and nothing more.

"Yes," Glenn agreed in a low, gravelly voice. "Tomorrow will be a very long day."

The vestibule was empty when Maggie entered the church forty minutes before the wedding. Out of breath and five minutes late, she paused to study the huge baskets of flowers that adorned the altar, and released an unconscious sigh at the beauty of the sight. This wedding was going to be special. Hurrying into the dressing room that was located to her right, Maggie knocked once and opened the door. The woman from The Wedding Shop was helping Janelle into her flowing lace gown. Mrs. Longmier was sitting in a chair, dabbing the corner of her eye with a tissue.

"Oh, Maggie, thank goodness you're here. I had this horrible dream that you showed up late. The wedding was in progress and you ran down the aisle screaming how dare we start without you."

"I'm here, I'm here, don't worry." Stepping back, Maggie inspected her friend and could understand Mrs. Longmier's tears. Janelle was radiant. Her wedding gown was of a lavish Victorian style that was exquisitely fashioned with ruffled tiers of Chantilly lace and countless rows of tiny pearls. "Wow," she whispered in awe. "You're going to knock Steve's eyes out."

"That's the idea," Janelle said with a nervous smile.

Another woman from the store helped Maggie don her blushing-pink gown of shimmering taffeta. Following a common theme, the maid of honor's and the bridesmaids' dresses were also Victorian in style, with sheer yokes and lace stand-up collars. Lace bishop sleeves were trimmed with dainty satin bows. The bodice fit snugly to the waist and flared at the hip. While the woman fastened the tiny buttons at the back of the gown, Maggie studied her mirrored reflection. A small smile played on her mouth as she pictured Glenn's reaction when he saw her. For years she wore tight jeans and sweatshirts. She had put on a dress for the rehearsal, but this gown would amaze him. She was a woman now and it showed.

The way her thoughts automatically flew to Glenn surprised Maggie, but she supposed it was natural after their kisses and walk in the moonlight. He had filled her dreams and she'd slept better than she had in a long while.

After their visit to the old neighborhood, Maggie's attitude toward the wedding had changed. She wouldn't be standing alone at the altar with her fears. Glenn, her friend from childhood, would be positioned beside her. Together they would lend each other the necessary strength to smile their way through the ordeal. Maggie realized her thoughts were more those of a martyr than an honored friend, but she'd dreaded the wedding for weeks. Not that she begrudged Janelle any happiness. But Maggie realized that at some time during the wedding dinner or the dance scheduled to follow, someone would comment on her single status. With Glenn at her side it wouldn't matter nearly as much.

From all the commotion going on outside the dressing room, Maggie realized the guests were beginning to arrive. Nerves attacked her stomach. This wasn't the first time she'd been in a wedding party, but it was the most elaborate wedding to date. She pressed a calming hand to her abdomen and exhaled slowly.

"Nervous?" Janelle whispered.

Maggie nodded. "What about you?"

"I'm terrified," she admitted freely. "Right now I wish Steve and I had eloped instead of going through all this." She released her breath in a slow, drawn-out sigh. "I'm convinced that halfway through the ceremony my veil's going to slip or I'll faint, or something equally disastrous."

"You won't," Maggie returned confidently. "I promise. Right now everything's overwhelming, but you won't regret a minute of this in the years to come."

"I suppose not," Janelle agreed. "This marriage is forever and I want everything right."

"I'd want everything like this, too." Maggie spoke without thinking and realized that when and if she ever married she wanted it to be exactly this way. She yearned for a flowing white dress with a long train and lifetime friends to stand with her.

Someone knocked on the door and, like an organized row of ducklings, the wedding party was led into the vestibule. Organ music vibrated through the church and the first bridesmaid, her hands clasping a bouquet of pink hyacinths, stepped forward with a tall usher at her side.

Maggie watched her progress and knew again that someday she wanted to stand in the back of a church and look out over the seated guests who had come to share her moment of joy. And like Janelle, Maggie longed to feel all the love that was waiting for her as she slowly walked to the man with whom she would share her life. And when she repeated her vows before God and those most important in her life she would feel, as Janelle did, that her marriage was meant to last for all time.

When it was her turn to step onto the trail of white linen that ran the length of the wide aisle, Maggie held her chin high, the adrenaline pumping through her blood. Her smile was natural, not forced. Mentally she thanked Glenn for that and briefly allowed her gaze to seek him out in the front of the church. What she found nearly caused her to pause in midstep. Glenn was standing with Steve at the side of the altar and looking at her with such a wondrous gaze that her heart lodged in her throat. This all-encompassing wonder was what Maggie had expected to see in Steve's eyes when he first viewed Janelle. A look so tender it should be reserved for the bride and groom. The moment stretched out until Maggie was convinced everyone in the church had turned to see what was keeping her. By sheer force of will she continued with short steps toward the front of the church. Every resounding note of the organ brought her closer to Glenn. She felt a throb of excitement as the faces of people she'd known all her life turned to watch her progress. A heady sensation enveloped her as she imagined it was she who was the bride, she who would speak her vows, she who had found her soul mate. Until that moment Maggie hadn't realized how much she yearned for the very things she had tried to escape in life, how much she was missing by hiding in her gilded cage, behind her money.

As they'd practiced the night before, Maggie moved to the left and waited for Janelle and Steve to meet at center front. At that point she would join her friend and stand at Janelle's side.

With the organ music pulsating in her ear, Maggie strained to catch Steve's look when he first glimpsed Janelle. She turned her head slightly, and paused. Her gaze refused to move beyond Glenn who was standing with Steve near the front of the altar. Even when Janelle placed her hand in Steve's, Maggie couldn't tear her eyes from Glenn. The pastor moved to the front of the church and the four gathered before him. Together they lifted their faces to the man of God who had come to unite Steve and Janelle.

The sensations that came at Glenn were equally disturbing. The minute Maggie had started down the aisle it had taken everything within him not to step away from Steve, meet her and take her in his arms. He had never experienced any sensation more strongly. He wanted to hold her, protect her, bring the shine back to her eyes and teach her to trust again. When she had met him at the airport he'd been struck by how lovely she'd become. Now he recognized her vulnerability, and she was breathtaking. He had never seen a more beautiful woman. She was everything he'd ever wanted—warm, vibrant, alive and standing so close that all he had to do was reach out and touch her. He felt like a blind man who had miraculously and unexpectedly been gifted with sight. Maggie needed him. Charleston, with all its painful memories, lay on the other side of the world.

"Dearly beloved, we are called here today to witness the vows between Janelle and Stephen."

The rush of emotion that assaulted Maggie was unlike anything she'd every known. She couldn't keep her eyes from Glenn, who seemed to magnetically compel her gaze to meet his. Their eyes locked and held as the pastor continued speaking. There was no exchange of smiles, no winks, nothing cute or frivolous, but a solemn mood that made that instant, that moment, the most monumental of their lives. Maggie felt a breathless urgency come over her, and an emotion so powerful, so real that it brought brimming tears that filled her vision. In order to keep her makeup from streaking, she held one finger under each eye a hand at a time and took in several deep breaths to forestall the ready flow. The void, the emptiness in her life wasn't entirely due to her money. What she needed was someone to love and who would love her. Desperately, Maggie realized how much she wanted to be needed. Several seconds passed before she regained her composure. The tightening lessened in her chest and she breathed freely once again.

When the pastor asked Steve and Janelle to repeat their vows, Maggie's gaze was again drawn to Glenn's. He didn't speak, nor did Maggie, but together, in unison, each syllable, each word was repeated in their hearts as they issued the same vows as their friends. When the pastor pronounced them man and wife, Maggie raised stricken eyes to the man of God who had uttered the words, needing the reassurance about whom he had meant. It was as if he had been speaking to Glenn and her, as well, and as if the formal pronouncement included them.

The organ burst into the traditional wedding march and Steve and Janelle turned to face the congregation, their faces radiant with happiness. As the newly wedded couple moved down the aisle, Glenn's arm reached for Maggie's, prepared to escort her. At the touch of his hand at her elbow, Maggie felt a series of indescribable sensations race through her: wonder, surprise, joy. Their eyes met and for the first time that day, he smiled. An incredible, dazzling smile that all but blinded her. Their march down the aisle, her arm on his elbow, added to the growing feeling that that day, that moment was meant for them as well.

Family and friends gathered outside the church doors, spilling onto the steps, giving hearty applause as Steve turned Janelle into his arms and kissed her. A festive mood reigned as Janelle was joyously hugged and Steve's hand was pumped countless times. The photographer was busily snapping pictures, ordering the wedding party to pose one way and then another.

For a brief second the fantasy faded enough to frighten Maggie. What game was Glenn playing with her? No. She'd seen the sincerity in his eyes. But pretending was dangerous, far too dangerous.

"Are you all right?" Glenn whispered in her ear.

Maggie didn't have the opportunity to answer. As it was, she wasn't sure how to respond. Under other circumstances, she would have asked him to drive her to the hospital emergency room. Her daydreams were overpowering reality. This wasn't her wedding, nor was the man at her side her husband. She had no right to feel sensations like these.

The next thing she knew, Glenn had disappeared. Maggie hardly had time to miss him when a shiny new Cadillac pulled to the curb. Just Married was painted on the back window. Glenn jumped out and opened both doors on the passenger side. Then, racing up the church stairs, he took Maggie by the hand and following on the heels of Steve and Janelle, pulled her through a spray of rice and laughter as he whisked her toward the car.

Amidst hoots and more laughter, Glenn helped her

gather her full-length skirt inside the automobile before closing the door and running around the front to climb in beside her.

Maggie was still breathless with laughter when he flashed her another of his dazzling smiles and started the engine. A sea of happy faces was gazing in at them. Turning her head to look out the side window, Maggie was greeted with the well-wishes of several boys and girls— children of their friends—standing on the sidewalk and waving with all their might. Glenn checked the rearview mirror and pulled into the steady flow of street traffic.

"Maggie, it was just as wonderful as you claimed it would be," Janelle said softly from the back seat.

"Did you doubt?" Steve questioned, his voice thick with emotion.

"I'll have you know, Mr. Grant, that I nearly backed out of this wedding at the very last minute. The only thing that stopped me was Maggie. Somehow she convinced me everything was going to work out. And it did."

"Janelle, I hardly said anything," Maggie countered, shocked by her friend's admission.

"You said just enough."

"I'm eternally grateful," Steve murmured and from the sounds coming from the back seat he was showing Janelle just how grateful he was that she was his bride.

Glenn's hand reached for Maggie's and squeezed it gently. "You look stunning." He wanted to say so much more and discovered he couldn't. For weeks he had dreaded the wedding and having to stand at the altar with his friend when it should have been his own wedding. The day had been completely unlike anything he'd expected. Maggie alone had made the difference.

"You make a striking figure yourself," she said, needing to place their conversation on an even keel.

Glenn unfastened the top button of the ruffled shirt and released the tie. "I feel like a penguin."

Laughter bubbled up in Maggie. She felt happy, really happy for the first time in a long while. When Glenn held out his arms, she scooted across the seat so that they were as close as possible within the confines of the vehicle.

The sounds of smothered giggles from the back seat assured Maggie that things were very fine indeed. They stopped at a light and Glenn's gaze wandered to her for a brief, glittering second, then back to the road. "Thank you for today," he said, just low enough for her to hear. "You made our friends' wedding the most special day of my life."

"I...felt the same way about you," she whispered, wanting him to kiss her so badly she could almost taste his mouth over hers.

"Maggie," Janelle called from the back seat. "Will you check this veil? I can't walk into the dinner with it all askew. People will know exactly what kind of man I married."

"Oh, they will, will they?" Steve said teasingly, and kissed her soundly.

Maggie turned and glanced over her shoulder. "Everything looks fine. The veil's not even crooked, although from the sound of things back there it should be inside out and backward."

"Maggie," Steve said in a low and somewhat surprised tone as he studied her, "I expected Janelle's mother to cry, even my own. But I was shocked to see you were the one with tears in your eyes."

"You were shocked?" she tossed back nonchalantly.

"Believe me, they were just as much of a surprise to me. Tears were the last thing I expected."

"Count your blessings, you two," Glenn said, tossing a glance over his shoulder. "Knowing Muffie, you should be grateful she didn't burst into fits of hysterical laughter." He glanced over to her and leaned close and whispered, "Actually, they should thank me. It took everything in me not to break rank and reach for you." Glenn hadn't meant to tell her that, but those tears had nearly been his undoing. He had known when he'd seen her eyes bright with unshed tears that what was happening to him was affecting Maggie just as deeply. He had come so close to happiness once, and like a fool, he'd let it slip away. It wouldn't happen again; he wouldn't allow it.

Everything was happening so quickly that Maggie didn't have time to react. Glenn's breath fanned her temple and a shiver of apprehension raced up her spine. They were playing a dangerous game. All that talk in the moonlight about the sanctity of marriage had affected their brain cells and they were daydreaming. No…pretending that this moment, this happiness, this love, was theirs. Only it wasn't, and Maggie had to give herself a hard mental shake to dislodge the illusion.

A long string of cars followed closely behind as the other members of the wedding party caught up with the Cadillac. Watching Glenn weave in and out of traffic, Maggie was impressed with his driving skill. However, everything about Glenn had impressed her today. Fleetingly, she allowed her mind to wander to what would happen when he left on Monday. She didn't want this weekend to be the end, but a beginning. He lived in Charleston, she in San Francisco. The whole country separated them, but they were only hours apart by plane and seconds by phone.

When he turned and caught her studying him, Maggie guiltily shifted her attention out the side window. The way her heart was hammering, one would think she was the bride. She struggled for composure.

Janelle's family had rented a huge Victorian hall for the dinner and dance. Maggie had no idea that there was such a special place in San Francisco and was assessing the wraparound porch and second-floor veranda when the remainder of the wedding party disembarked from the long row of cars that paraded behind the Cadillac. Wordlessly, Glenn took her by the elbow and led her up the front stairs.

Everything inside the huge hall was lushly decorated in antiques. Round tables with starched white tablecloths were set up to serve groups of eight. In the center of each table was a bowl of white gardenias. A winding stairway with a polished mahogany banister led to the dance floor upstairs.

Being seated at the same table as Steve and Janelle added to the continuing illusion. Somehow Maggie made it through the main course of veal cordon bleu, wild rice and tender asparagus spears. Her appetite was nonexistent and every bite had the taste and the feel of cotton. Although Glenn was at her side, they didn't speak, but the communication between them was louder than words. Twice she stopped herself from asking him what was happening to them, convinced he had no answers and the question would only confuse him further.

When Janelle cut the wedding cake and hand-fed the first bite to Steve, the happy applause vibrated around the room. The sound of it helped shake Maggie from her musings and she forced down another bite of her entrée. The caterers delivered the cake to the wedding guests with astonishing speed so that all the guests were served in a matter of minutes.

Glenn's eyes darkened thoughtfully as he dipped his fork into the white cake and paused to study Maggie. He prayed she wasn't as confused as he. He didn't know what was happening, but was powerless to change anything. He wasn't even convinced he wanted anything different. It was as if they were in a protective bubble, cut off from the outside world. And although they sat in a room full of people, they were alone. Not knowing what made him do anything so crazy, Glenn lifted his fork to her mouth and offered Maggie the first sample of wedding cake. His eyes held her immobile as she opened her mouth and accepted his offering. Ever so lightly he ran his thumb along her chin as his dark, penetrating eyes bored into hers. By the time she finished swallowing, Glenn's hand was trembling and he lowered it.

Promptly Maggie placed her clenched fingers in her lap. A few minutes later she took a sip of champagne, her first that day, although she knew that enough was happening to her equilibrium without adding expensive champagne to wreak more damage.

The first muted strains of a Vienna waltz drifted from the upstairs dance floor. Maggie took another sip of champagne before standing.

Together, Steve and Janelle led their family and friends up the polished stairway to the dance floor.

When he saw the bride and groom, the orchestra leader stepped forward and announced: "Ladies and gentlemen, I give you Mr. and Mrs. Stephen Grant."

Steve took Janelle in his arms and swung his young

bride around the room in wide fanciful steps. Pausing briefly, he gestured to Glenn, who swung Maggie into his arms.

Again the announcer stepped to the microphone and introduced them as the maid of honor and best man. All the while, the soft music continued its soothing chords and they were joined by each bridesmaid and usher couple until the entire wedding party was on the dance floor.

As Glenn held Maggie in his arms, their feet made little more than tiny, shuffling movements that gave the pretense of dancing. All the while Glenn's serious, dark eyes held Maggie's. It was as though they were the only two in the room and the orchestra was playing solely for them. Try as she might, Maggie couldn't pull her gaze away.

"I've been wanting to do something from the moment I first saw you walk down the aisle."

"What?" she asked, surprised at how weak her voice sounded. She thought that if he didn't kiss her soon she was going to die.

Glenn glanced around him to the wide double doors that led to the veranda. He took her by the hand and led her through the crowd and out the curtained glass doors.

Maggie walked to the edge of the veranda and curled her fingers over the railing. Dusk had already settled over the city and lights from the bay flickered in the distance. Glenn joined her and slipped his arms around her waist, burying his face in her hair. Turning her in his arms, he closed his eyes and touched his forehead to hers. He took in several breaths before speaking.

"Are you feeling the same things I am?" he asked.

"Yes." Her heart was hammering so loud, Maggie was convinced he'd hear it.

"Is it the champagne?"

"I had two sips."

"I didn't have any," he countered. "See?" He placed the palm of her hand over his heart so she could feel its quickened beat. "From the moment I saw you in the church it's been like this."

"Me too," she whispered. "What's happening to us?"

Slowly, he shook his head. "I wish I knew."

"It's happening to me, too." She took his hand and placed it over her heart. "Can you feel it?"

"Yes," he whispered.

"Maggie, listen, this is going to sound crazy." He dropped his hands as if he needed to put some distance between them and took several steps back.

"What is?"

Glenn jerked his hand through his hair and hesitated. "Do you want to make this real?"

Three

"Make this real?" Maggie echoed. "What do you mean?"

Glenn couldn't believe the ideas that were racing at laser speed through his mind. Maggie would burst into peals of laughter and he wouldn't blame her. But even that wasn't enough to turn the course of his thoughts. He had this compulsion, this urgency to speak as if something were driving him to say the words. "Steve and Janelle are going to make this marriage a good one."

"Yes," Maggie agreed. "I believe they will."

The look she gave him was filled with questions. Surely she realized he hadn't asked her onto the veranda to discuss Steve and Janelle. After Angie, Glenn hadn't expected to feel this deep an emotion again. And so soon was another shock. Yet when he'd seen Maggie that first moment in the church the impact had been so great it was as though someone had physically assaulted him. She was lovely, possessing a rare beauty that had escaped his notice when they were younger. No longer had he been standing witness to his best friends' wedding, but he'd participated in a ceremony with a woman who could stand at his side for a lifetime. Maggie had felt it, too; he had seen it in her eyes. The identical emotion had moved her to tears.

"Glenn, you wanted to say something?" She coaxed him gently, her mind pleading with him to explain. He couldn't possible mean what she thought.

Remembering the look Maggie had given him when Steve and Janelle exchanged vows gave Glenn the courage to continue. "Marriage between friends is the best kind, don't you think?"

"Yes," she answered, unable to bring her voice above a husky whisper. "Friends generally know everything about each other, whether good or bad, and then still choose to remain friends."

They stood for a breathless moment, transfixed, studying each other, hesitant and unsure. "I'd always believed," Glenn murmured, his voice low and seductive, "that it would be impossible for me to share my life with anyone I didn't know extremely well."

"I agree." Maggie's mind was formulating impossible thoughts. Glenn was leading this conversation down meandering paths she'd never dreamed of traveling with him.

"We're friends," he offered next.

"Good friends," she agreed, nodding.

"I know you as well as my own brothers."

"We lived next door to each other for fifteen years," she added, her heart increasing its tempo to a slow drumroll.

"I want a home and children."

"I've always loved children." There hadn't been a time in her life when the pull was stronger toward a husband and family than it was that very moment.

"Maggie," he said, taking a step toward her, but still not touching her, "you've become an extremely beautiful woman."

Her lashes fluttered against her cheek as she lowered her gaze. Maggie didn't think of herself as beautiful. For Glen to say this to her, sent her heart racing. She hardly knew how to respond and finally managed a weak. "Thank you."

"Any man would be proud to have you for his wife."

The sensations that raced through her were all too welcome and exciting. "I... I was just thinking that a woman... any woman would be extremely fortunate to have you for a husband."

"Would you?"

Her heart fluttered wildly, rocketed to her throat and then promptly plummeted to her stomach. Yet she didn't hesitate. "I'd be honored and proud."

Neither said anything for a timeless second while their minds assimilated what had just transpired, or what they thought had.

"Glenn?"

"Yes."

Her throat felt swollen and constricted, her chest suddenly tight as if tears were brewing just beneath the surface. "Did I understand you right? Did you—just now—suggest that you and me—the two of us—get married?"

"That's exactly what I'm suggesting." Glenn didn't hesitate. He'd never been more sure of anything in his life. He had lost one woman; he wasn't going to lose Maggie. He would bind her to him and eliminate the possibility of someone else stepping in at the last moment. This woman was his and he was claiming her before something happened to drive her from his arms.

"When?"

"Tonight."

She blinked twice, convinced she hadn't heard him right. "But the license, and..."

"We can fly to Reno." Already his mind was working out the details. He didn't like the idea of a quickie wedding, but it would serve the purpose. After what they had shared earlier they didn't need anything more than a document to make it legal.

Stillness surrounded them. Even the night had gone silent. No cars, no horns, no crickets, no sounds of the night—only silence.

"I want to think about it," she murmured. Glenn was crazy. They both were. Talking about marriage, running away this very night to Reno. None of it made sense, but nothing in all her life had sounded more exciting, more wonderful, more right.

"How long do you want to think this over?" A thread of doubt caused him to ask. Perhaps rushing her wasn't the best way to proceed, but waiting felt equally impossible.

A fleeting smile touched and lifted Maggie's mouth. They didn't dare tell someone they would do anything so ludicrous. She didn't need time, not really. She knew what she wanted: she wanted Glenn.

"An hour," she said, hoping that within that time frame nothing would change.

The strains of another waltz drifted onto the veranda and wordlessly he led her back to the dance floor. When he reached for her, Maggie went willingly into his arms. His hold felt as natural as breathing, and she was drawn into his warmth. The past two days with Glenn had been the happiest, most exciting in years. Who would have thought that Glenn Lambert would make her pulse pound like a jackhammer and place her head in the clouds where the air was thin and clear thought was impossible? Twenty-four hours after his arrival, and they were planning the most incredible scheme. Their very best scheme, crazy as it sounded.

"This feeling reminds me of the night we stole out of the house to smoke our first cigarette," Glenn whispered in her ear. "Are we as daring and defiant now as we were at fourteen?"

"Worse," she answered. "But I don't care as long as you're with me."

"Oh, Maggie." He sighed her name with a wealth of emotion.

Her hands tightened around his neck as she fit her body more intimately to the contour of his. Her breasts were flattened to his broad chest; and they were melded together, thigh to thigh, hip to hip, as close as humanly possible under the guise of dancing.

Every breath produced an incredible range of new sensations. Maggie felt drugged and delirious, daring and darling, bold and extraordinarily shy. Every second in his arms brought her more strength of conviction. This night, in less than an hour she was going to walk out of this room with Glenn Lambert. Together they would fly to Reno and she would link her life with his. There was nothing to stop her. Not her money. Not her pride. Not her fears. Glenn Lambert was her friend. Tonight he would become her lover as well.

Unable to wait, Maggie rained a long series of kisses over the line of his jaw. The need to experience his touch flowered deep within her.

Glenn's hold at her waist tightened and he inhaled sharply. "Maggie, don't tease me."

"Who's teasing?" They'd known each other all these years and in that time he had only kissed her once. But it was enough, more than enough to know that the loving between them would be exquisite.

Without her even being aware, Glenn had maneuvered her into a darkened corner of the dance floor where the lighting was the dimmest. His eyes told her he was about to kiss her and hers told him she was eager for him to do exactly that. Unhurriedly, Glenn lowered his mouth to hers with an agonizing slowness. His kiss was warm and tender and lingering, as if this were a moment and place out of time meant for them alone. Her soft mouth parted with only the slightest urging and her arms tightened around his neck. Trembling in his embrace, Maggie drew in a long unsteady breath. Glenn's kisses had been filled with such aching tenderness, such sweet torment that Maggie felt tears stinging for release. Tears for a happiness she had never hoped to find. At least not with Glenn. This was a wondrous surprise. A gift. A miracle so unexpected it would take a lifetime to fully appreciate.

"I want you," he whispered, his voice hoarse with desire. His breath warmed her lips.

"Yes" she returned, vaguely dazed. "I want you, too."

His arms tightened and Maggie felt the shudder that rocked him until her ribs ached. Gradually his hold relaxed as his gaze polarized hers. "Let's get out of here."

"Should...should we tell anyone?" *No*, her mind shouted. Someone might try to talk them out of this and she didn't want that to happen. She yearned for everything that Glenn suggested.

"Do you want to tell Steve and Janelle?" Glenn asked.

"No."

Tenderly he brushed his lips across her forehead. "Neither do I. They'll find out soon enough."

"It'll be our surprise." She smiled at him, the warm

happy smile of someone about to embark on the most exciting adventure of her life. And Maggie felt like an adventurer, daring and audacious, dauntless and intrepid, reckless and carefree. There'd be problems; she realized that. But tonight with Glenn at her side there wasn't anything she couldn't conquer.

Glenn raised her fingertips to his lips and kissed each one. "I'm not letting you out of my sight. We're going directly to the airport."

"Fine." She had no desire to be separated from him, either.

"I'll call a taxi."

"I'll get my purse."

The night air brought a chill to her arms, but it didn't sharpen any need to analyze what they were doing. If Glenn expected her to have second thoughts as they breezed through the streets of San Francisco, she found none. Even the busy airport, with its crowded concourses and people who stared at their unusual dress, wasn't enough to cause her to doubt.

Glenn bought their airline tickets, and she found a seat while he used his cell to make hotel reservations. When he returned, the broad smile reached his eyes. Maggie was struck anew with the wonder of what was happening.

"Well?"

"Everything's been taken care of."

"Everything?" It seemed paramount that they get married tonight. If they were forced to wait until morning there could be second thoughts.

"The Chapel of Love is one block from city hall and they're going to arrange for the marriage license." He glanced at his watch and hesitated. "The plane lands at ten-thirty and the ceremony is scheduled for eleven-fifteen."

He sat in the seat beside her and reached for her hand. "You're cold."

"A little." Despite her nerves she managed to keep her voice even. She didn't doubt they were doing the right thing and wanted to reassure Glenn. "I'm fine. Don't worry about me."

Rising to his feet, Glenn stripped the tuxedo jacket from his arms and draped it over her shoulders. "Here. We'll be boarding in a few minutes and I'll get you a blanket from the flight attendants." His dark eyes were full of warmth and he was smiling at her as if they'd been sitting in airports, waiting for planes to fly them to weddings every day.

His strong fingers closed over hers and for the first time she admired how large his hands were. The fingers were long and tapered and looked capable of carving an empire or soothing a crying child. "Are you—" Maggie swallowed convulsively, almost afraid to ask "—are you having any second thoughts?"

"No," he answered quickly. "What about you?"

"None." She was never so positive of anything in her life.

"I'll be a good husband."

"I know." She placed her free hand over the back of his. "And I'll be a good wife."

His returning smile, filled with warmth and incredible wonder, could have melted a glacier.

"My parents are going to be ecstatic." Shocked too, her mind added, but that didn't matter.

"Mine will be pleased as well," Glenn assured her. "They've always liked you."

He bent his head toward her and Maggie shyly lifted her face and met him halfway. His kiss was filled with soft exploration, and they parted with the assurance that everything was perfect.

"After we're married, will you want me to move to Charleston?" Maggie ventured.

"No," he said on a somber note. "I'll move to San Francisco." The time had come to leave Charleston. Glenn wanted to bury the unhappiness that surrounded him there. The brief visit to San Francisco had felt like coming home. With Maggie at his side he'd build a new life in San Francisco. Together they'd raise their family and live in blissful happiness. No longer would he allow the memory of another woman to haunt him.

Maggie felt simultaneously relieved and confused. Her career in art made it possible for her to work anywhere. For Glenn to move to San Francisco would mean giving up his Charleston clientele and building up a new one on the West Coast. It didn't make sense. "I don't mind moving, really. It would be easier for me to make the change. You've got your career."

He slid his hand from her arm to her elbow, tightening his hold. "I'll transfer out here." Turning his wrist he glanced at his watch, but Maggie had the feeling he wasn't looking at the time. "I'm ready for a change," he murmured after a while. "You don't mind, do you?"

Did she? No, Maggie decided, she loved California. "No, that'll be fine. You'll like the beach house."

"I don't doubt that I will."

Their flight number was announced and Maggie returned Glenn's tuxedo jacket before they boarded the plane. The flight attendant came by a few minutes later, after they were comfortably seated, to check their seat belts. She paused and commented that they both looked as if they were on their way to a wedding. Glenn and Maggie smiled politely, but neither of them opted to inform the young woman that it was exactly what they were doing. Maggie feared that if they let someone in on their plan it would somehow shatter the dream. Briefly she wondered if Glenn shared her fears.

The flight touched down on the Reno runway precisely on schedule. With no luggage to collect, Glenn and Maggie walked straight through the airport and outside, where a taxi was parked and waiting.

"You two on your way to a wedding?" the cabdriver asked with a loud belly laugh as he held the door open for Maggie.

"Yes," Maggie answered shyly, dismissing her earlier fears.

"Ours," Glenn added, sliding into the seat next to Maggie and reaching for her hand.

The heavyset cabbie closed the door and walked around to the driver's side. He checked the rearview mirror and merged with the traffic. "Lots of people come to Reno to get married, but then a lot of folks come here to get unmarried, too."

A thundering silence echoed through the close confines of the taxi. "There won't be any divorce for us," Glenn informed him.

The driver tipped back the rim of his cap with his index finger. "Lot of folks say that, too." He paused at the first red light, placed his arm along the back of the seat and turned to look at Glenn. "Where was it you said you wanted to go?"

"Chapel of Love," Glenn said firmly and glanced over to Maggie. "Unless you want to change your mind?" he whispered.

"You're not backing out of your proposal, are you?" The words nearly stuck in her throat.

"No."

"Then we're getting married," she murmured, more determined than ever. "I didn't come this far in a shimmering pink taffeta gown to play the slot machines."

"Good."

"Very good," she murmured, unwilling to let anyone or anything ruin this night.

A half hour later, after arriving at the chapel, Maggie had freshened her makeup and done what she could with her hair. They stood now before the proprietor of the wedding chapel.

"Organ music is fifteen dollars extra," Glenn told her as he reached for his back pocket.

Her hand stopped him. "I don't need it," she assured him with perfect serenity. "I'm still hearing the music from the church."

The impatience drained from his eyes and the look he gave her was so profound that it seemed the most natural thing in the world to lean forward and press her lips to his.

The justice of the peace cleared his throat. "If you're ready we can start the ceremony."

"Are you ready?" Glenn asked with smiling eyes.

"I've been ready for this all night," she answered, linking her arm with his.

The service was shockingly short and sterile. They stood before the justice and repeated the words that had already been spoken in their hearts. The stark ceremony wasn't what Maggie would have preferred, but it didn't diminish any of her joy. This wedding was necessary for legal reasons; their real vows had already been exchanged earlier that day as they stood witnesses for Steve and Janelle. Those few moments in the church had been so intense that from then on every moment of her life would be measured against them. Maggie yearned to explain that to Glenn, but mere words felt inadequate. He, too, had experienced it, she realized, and without analyzing it, he had understood.

Their room at the hotel was ready when they arrived. With the key jingling in Glenn's pocket they rode the elevator to the tenth floor.

"Are you going to carry me over the threshold, Mr. Lambert?" Maggie whispered happily and nuzzled his ear. She felt a free-flowing elation unlike anything she'd ever experienced. That night and every night for the rest of her life would be spent in Glenn's arms.

"I'll see what I can manage," Glenn stated seriously as he backed her into the corner of the elevator and kissed the side of her neck.

Maggie shot him a dubious look. "I'm not that heavy, you know."

"What I suggest we do," he murmured as he nibbled on her earlobe, "is have me lift one of your legs and you can hop over the threshold."

"Glenn," she muttered, breaking free. "That's crazy."

Chuckling, he ignored the question. "On second thought I could probably manage to haul you piggyback."

Deftly her fingers opened his tie and she teased his throat with the moist tip of her tongue. If he was going to joke with her then she'd tease him as well. "Never mind," she whispered. "I'll carry you."

The elevator came to a grinding halt and the doors swished open. Glenn glanced around him, kissed Maggie soundly and with a mighty heave-ho, hauled her over his shoulder fireman fashion.

"Glenn..." she whispered fiercely, stunned into momentary speechlessness. "Put me down this instant."

Chuckling, he slowly rubbed his hand over her prominently extended derriere. "You said you wanted me to carry you over the threshold. Only I can't very well manage you, the key and the door all at once."

Using her arms against his shoulders for leverage, Maggie attempted to straighten. "Glenn, please," she begged, laughing until it was difficult to speak and probably just as impossible to be understood.

He shifted her weight when he fidgeted with the key card. Maggie couldn't see what was happening, but the sound of the door opening assured her all was well. Her eyes studied the same door as it closed and the narrow entryway as he carried her halfway into the room. The next thing Maggie knew, she was falling through space. She gave a frightened cry until the soft cushion of the mattress broke her rapid descent.

Panting and breathless with laughter, Maggie lay sprawled across the bed. She smiled up at Glenn playfully and raised her arms to her husband of fifteen minutes. Glenn knelt beside her, his eyes alive with passion as he lowered his mouth to hers in a deep kiss that sent her world into a crazy tailspin. She clung to him, her fingers ruffling the thick, dark hair that grew at his nape. Wildly, she returned his kiss, on fire for him, luxuriating in the feel of his body over hers. Unexpectedly, he tore his mouth from hers and lifted his head. Without a word, he brushed the soft wisps of hair from her temple and dipped his head a second time to sample her mouth. When he broke away and moved to the long dresser that dominated one side of the hotel room, Maggie felt a sudden chill and rose to a sitting position.

A bottle of champagne was resting in a bed of crushed ice. With his back to her, Glenn peeled off the foil covering and removed the cork. He ached with the need to take her physically, but feared his building passion would frighten her. Silently, Glenn cursed himself for not having approached the subject sooner. He wanted her, but did he dare take her so soon?

The dresser mirror revealed Glenn's troubled frown and Maggie felt a brooding anxiety settle over her. For the first time she could see doubt in his eyes. The breath jammed in her lungs. No, not doubt, but apprehension, even foreboding. Maggie was feeling it, too. Maybe advancing from friends to lovers in the space of a few hours wasn't right for them. Maybe they should think it through very carefully before proceeding with what was paramount on both their minds. As far as she was concerned there wasn't any reason to wait. They were married. They knew each other better than most newlyweds. The certificate in Glenn's coat pocket granted them every right.

With her weight resting on the palm of one hand, she felt her heart throb painfully. "Glenn," she whispered brokenly, not knowing what to say, or how to say it.

The sound of her voice was drowned by the cork, exploding from the bottle. Fizzing champagne squirted across the dresser. Glenn deftly filled the two glasses and returned the dark bottle to its icy bed.

Handing her a goblet, Glenn joined her on the side of the mattress. "To my wife," he whispered tenderly and touched the edge of her glass to his.

"To my husband," she murmured in return. The bubbly liquid tickled her nose and she smiled shyly at Glenn as she took another sip. "I suppose this is when I'm supposed to suggest that I slip into something more comfortable."

"I'm for that." He quickly stood and strode across the room for the bottle, setting it on the floor next to the bed as he sat down again, avoiding her eyes the whole time.

"However, we both seemed to have forgotten something important." She bit her bottom lip in a gesture of uncertainty and laughter.

He glanced up expectantly. "What's that?"

"Clothes," she said and giggled. They had been so afraid to leave one another for fear something would happen to change their minds that they hadn't even stopped to pack an overnight bag.

"We're not going to need them." In that instant Glenn realized that they weren't going to wait. He wanted her. She wanted him; it was in her eyes and the provocative way she regarded him. "We have two days," he murmured, "and I can't see any need we'll be having for clothes."

He was so utterly serious that laughter rumbled in her throat. Where there had once been anxiety there was expectancy. "Maybe we could get away with that sort of thing on the Riviera, but believe me, they arrest people for walking around nude in Reno."

Smiling, he tipped back his head and emptied his glass. "You know what I mean."

Maggie set their champagne glasses aside. "No," she said breathlessly as she lightly stroked the neatly trimmed hair at his temple. "I think you'll have to show me."

Gently, Glenn laid her back on the bed and joined her so the upper portion of his body was positioned over the top of hers. His arms went around her, pressing her to his hard strength until her breasts strained against him. "I have every intention of doing exactly that."

His lips left hers to investigate her ear before tracing their way back across her cheek and reclaiming her mouth.

Maggie buried her face in the hollow of his throat, drawing in a deep shuddering breath as his busy hands fumbled with the effort to locate the tiny buttons at the back of her dress. Every place his fingers grazed her skin, a glowing warmth spread. Again Maggie opened her mouth to explore the strong cord of his neck, savoring his salty-tasting skin. She heard the harsh intake of his breath when she pulled his silk dress shirt free and stroked his muscular back.

"Oh, Glenn," she whispered when she didn't think she could stand it anymore. Her shoulders were heaving when he lifted his weight from her.

He rolled onto his back and she heard him release a harsh breath. "Maggie." His voice was thick and husky. "Listen, are you sure about this? We can wait."

"I'm sure," she whispered and switched positions so that now it was she who was sprawled half atop him. "Glenn, I'm so sure it hurts."

"Maggie, oh, Maggie." He repeated her name again and again in a broken whisper. "She'd spent a lifetime searching for him when all along he'd been so close and she hadn't known.

His arms crushed her then, and his mouth passionately sought hers with a greedy need that seemed to want to devour her. He took; she surrendered. He gave; she received. They were starved for each other and the physical love their bodies could share. With her arms wrapped securely around him, Maggie met his hunger with her own. When he half lifted her from the mattress she was trembling.

"Glenn," she whispered brokenly. "Oh, Glenn, don't ever let me go."

"Never," he promised, sitting on the edge of the bed with her cradled in his lap. "This is forever." His words were a vow. Carefully, in order not to tear her dress, his fingers released each tiny button at the back of her gown. As each one was freed he pressed his lips to the newly exposed skin.

"Forever," she repeated, and twisted so she could work loose the tuxedo tie and the buttons to the ruffled shirt. She pulled the shirt free of his shoulders and slid her hand down his chest to his tightening abdomen.

"Maggie," he warned hoarsely.

"Love me," she whispered. "Oh, Glenn, make me your wife."

Her fingers clutched frantically at his thick dark hair as he continued to stroke her breast.

All too soon she was on fire for him. Consumed with desire, lost in a primitive world, aware of nothing but the desperate need he awoke within her.

Moving quickly he laid her upon the mattress and eased his body over hers.

The loving was exquisite and when they'd finished a long moment passed before he gathered her in his arms. He rolled onto his side, taking her with him. Lying cradled in his embrace, their legs entwined, Maggie closed her eyes and released a contented sigh.

"It was beautiful," she whispered, still overcome with emotion.

Glenn kissed the top of her head. "You're beautiful."

"So are you," she added quickly. "Oh, Glenn, we're going to have such a good life."

"Yes," he agreed and kissed her forehead.

Maggie snuggled closer against him and kissed the nape

of his neck when he reached down to cover them with the sheet and blanket.

Glenn held her close, kissing the crown of her head until her eyes closed sleepily. Her last thought as she drifted into the welcoming comfort of slumber was of warmth and security.

Maggie woke a couple of times in the darkest part of the night, unaccustomed to sharing her bed. Each time she experienced the unexpected thrill of finding Glenn asleep at her side. No longer was she alone. Her joy was so great that she felt ten years old again, waking up on Christmas morning.

She cuddled him spoon fashion, pressing her softness to his backside. Her body fit perfectly to his. Edging her hand over his muscular ribs she felt his strength and knew that this man was as steady as the Rock of Gibraltar. She had chosen her life mate well. Content, she drifted back to sleep.

A low, grumbling sound woke her when morning light splashed into the room from the small crack between closed drapes. Sitting up, Maggie yawned and raised her arms high above her head. She was ravenous, and pressed a hand to her stomach to prevent her rumbling from waking Glenn. A menu for room service sat by the phone and Maggie reached for it, studying its contents with interest, wondering if it would wake him if she ordered anything.

Glenn stirred and rolled onto his back, still caught in the last dregs of sleep. Gloriously happy, Maggie watched as a lazy smile grew on his face. Pride swelled in her heart as she realized their lovemaking was responsible for his look of blessed contentment. Maybe she wasn't so hungry after all.

Her long, tangled hair fell forward as she leaned down

to press her lips to his. As she drew near, he whispered something. At first Maggie couldn't understand his words, then she froze. Stunned, her hand flew to her breast at the unexpected pain that pierced her. The arctic chill extended all the way to her heart and she squeezed her eyes closed to fight back the burning tears. Choking on humiliation, she struggled to untangle herself from the sheet. Her frantic movements woke Glenn from the nether land of sleep to the world of consciousness.

He turned on his side and reached for her hand. "Good morning," he said cheerfully. At the sight of her stricken face, he paused and rose to a full sitting position. "What's wrong?"

"The name is Maggie," she whispered fiercely, shoving his hand away. "And in case you've forgotten, I'm your wife as well."

Four

Tugging the sheet loose from the mattress, Maggie climbed out of bed. Her hands were shaking so badly that she had trouble twisting the material around her. Glenn had mistaken her for another woman. A woman he had obviously once loved...and apparently still did.

Holding it together with one hand she sorted through the tangled mess of clothes on the floor. The tightness in her chest was so painful she could barely breathe. The room swayed beneath her feet and she closed her eyes, struggling to maintain her balance and her aplomb. Everything had been so beautiful. So perfect. How readily she had fallen into the fantasy, believing in each minute with a childlike innocence and trust. She'd been living in a twenty-four-hour dream world. That fantasy had been shattered by the reality of morning and she was shamed to the very marrow of her bones.

Glenn wiped a hand over his face and struggled to a sitting position. He vaguely recalled the contented pleasure of sleeping with a warm body at his side. In his sleep he must have confused Maggie with Angie. He cursed Angie for haunting him in his marriage.

"Maggie, what did I say?"

Straightening, she turned to regard him coolly before speaking. "Enough." *More than enough,* her mind shouted. Clenching the sheet in one hand, her clothes in the other, she marched across the floor, her head tilted at a stately angle. She never felt more like crying in her life. Her pride and dignity remained intact but little else was as it should be.

Once inside the bathroom she leaned against the heavy door, her shoulders sagging. Covering her face with both hands in hurt and frustration, she let the sheet slip to the floor. Equal doses of anger and misery descended on her until she was convinced she'd slump under the force of their weight. She didn't know what do, but taking a bath seemed important.

"Maggie." Glenn stood on the other side of the door, his voice low and confused. "Tell me what I said. At least talk to me."

"No," she shouted, still reeling from the shock. "I don't want to talk. I've heard enough to last me a lifetime." Forcing herself into action, she turned on the faucet and filled the tub with steaming hot water. She had been a fool to believe in yesterday's illusions. The morning had shattered the dream—only she didn't want it to end. Glenn was someone she had thought she could trust. In her heart she knew that he wouldn't be like all the rest.

"Maggie, for the love of heaven give me a chance to explain."

Sliding into the steaming bath, Maggie bit into her bottom lip and forced herself to think. She could demand that they divorce, but she didn't want that and Glenn didn't, either. For twelve hours she had been a happily married woman. Somehow Maggie had to find a way to stretch twelve hours into a lifetime.

In the other room Glenn dressed slowly, his thoughts oppressive. Things couldn't be worse. From the moment Maggie had met him at the airport he had seen how reserved and untrusting her inheritance had made her. Now he had hurt her, and he silently cursed himself for doing the very thing he vowed he never would. He could still see her stricken eyes glaring down at him when he woke. He'd wanted to take her in his arms and explain, but she'd jumped from the bed as if she couldn't get away fast enough. Not that he blamed her. The worst part was that he couldn't guarantee it wouldn't happen again. Angie had been an integral part of his life for nearly two years. He had cast her from his thoughts with an all-consuming effort, but he had no control over the ramblings of his mind while he slept. If only he knew what he'd said. He stroked his fingers through his hair and heaved a disgusted sigh. Whatever it was, he wouldn't allow it to ruin this marriage. Somehow he'd find a way to make it up to Maggie.

The bathroom door opened and Glenn turned anxiously. He studied Maggie's face for evidence of tears and found none. He had forgotten what a strong woman she was and admired her all the more. He vividly recalled the time she was fifteen and broke her arm skateboarding. She'd been in intense pain. Anyone else would have been screaming like a banshee, but not Maggie. She had gritted her teeth, but hadn't shed a tear. He also remembered how the only person she had trusted to help her had been him. The guilt washed over him in dousing waves.

"Can we talk now?" he asked her gently.

"I think we should," she said, pacing because standing

in one spot seemed an impossible task. "We need to make some rules in this marriage, Glenn."

"Anything," he agreed.

"The first thing you have to do is stop loving that other woman right now. This minute." Her voice trembled and she battled for control.

Glenn felt physically ill. Maggie was unnaturally pale, her cheeks devoid of color. Her dark, soulful eyes contained a sorrow he longed to erase and yet he knew he couldn't. His thoughts were in turmoil. "You know I'd never lie to you."

"Yes." Glenn might be a lot of things, she knew, but a liar wasn't one of them.

"Maggie, I want this marriage to work, but what you're asking me to do is going to be hard."

A tingling sensation went through her that left her feeling numb and sick. She wouldn't share this man—not even with a memory.

"In that case," she murmured and swallowed, "I've got some thinking to do." She turned from him and started toward the door.

"Maggie." Glenn stopped her and she turned around. Their eyes met and held. "You don't want a divorce, do you?"

The word hit Maggie with all the impact of a freight train. "No," she said, shaking her head. "I may be mad, Glenn Lambert, but I'm not stupid."

The door made an echoing sound that bounced off the walls as Maggie left the hotel room. Glenn felt his tense shoulder muscles relax. It had taken everything in him to ask her about a divorce. That was the last thing he wanted, but he felt he had to know where Maggie stood after what had happened that morning.

The curious stares that met Maggie as she stepped off the elevator convinced her that the first thing she had to do was buy something to wear that was less ostentatious. A wrinkled pink maid-of-honor gown would cause more than a few heads to turn, and the last thing Maggie wanted was attention. In addition, she couldn't demand that her husband give up his affection for another woman and love and care for her instead, when she looked like something the cat left on the porch.

The hotel had a gift shop where she found a summer dress of pale-blue polished cotton, which she changed into after purchasing it. A walk through the lobby revealed that Glenn was nowhere to be seen. With time weighing heavily on her hands, Maggie pulled a ten-dollar bill from her purse. Already the hotel casino was buzzing with patrons eager to spend their money. Standing in front of the quarter slot machine, Maggie inserted the first coin. Pressing the button, she watched the figures spin into a blur and slowly wind down to two oranges and a cherry. Maggie stared at the fifty cents she won in disbelief. She didn't expect to win. Actually, it was fitting that she was in Reno. She had just made the biggest gamble of her life. The scary part was that Maggie felt like a loser and had felt like one almost from the minute she inherited her Great-aunt Margaret's money. She felt the ridiculous urge to laugh, but recognized that if she gave in to the compulsion tears wouldn't be far behind.

Glenn found her ten minutes later, still playing the slot machine. For several moments he stood watching her, wondering how to approach this woman he had known most of his life. The woman who was now his wife. There were so many issues facing them that had to be settled before he left for Charleston. Maggie's inheritance was one thing he wouldn't allow to hang between them like a steel curtain. It was best to clear the air of that and everything else they could.

A discordant bell clanged loudly and a barrage of celebratory characters danced across the slot machine. She looked stunned and stepped back as the machine finished. Without emotion, she cashed out. As she turned, their eyes clashed. Her breath caught in her throat and she hesitated, waiting for him to speak first. Like her, he had purchased another set of clothes, and again Maggie wondered why she'd never noticed how extraordinarily good-looking Glenn was. He was a man any woman would be proud to call her husband. If he'd come to tell her he wanted out of the marriage, she didn't know what she would say. The time spent in front of the slot machine had given her the perspective to realize that Glenn was as shocked by what had happened as she was. She prayed that he hadn't come for the reason she suspected. Maggie wanted this marriage. She had been so lonely and miserable. The previous day with Glenn had been the most wonderful day of her life. Maybe she was still looking at the situation through rose-colored glasses, but the deed was done. They were married now. The other woman had no claim to him. He might murmur "her" name in his sleep, but he was married to Maggie.

"Our plane leaves in two hours," he said, stepping forward. "Let's get something to eat."

Nodding required a monumental effort. Her body went limp with relief.

The hostess at the restaurant led them to a booth and handed them menus. She gave Glenn a soft, slightly seductive smile, but Maggie was pleased to notice that he didn't pay the woman the least bit of attention. Glenn had never been a flirt. Beyond anything else, Maggie realized, Glenn was an intensely loyal man. For him to whisper another woman's name in his sleep had been all the more devastating for just that reason.

Almost immediately a waitress arrived, poured them each a cup of coffee and took their order.

"I want you to know that I'll do everything in my power to do what you asked," Glenn announced, his eyes holding hers. His hands cupped the coffee mug and there was a faint pleading note shining from his eyes. "About this morning; I suppose you want to know about her."

"Yes," Maggie whispered, hating the way his eyes softened when he mentioned his lost love.

A sadness seemed to settle over him. "Her name is Angie. We were…" He hesitated. "Engaged. She decided to marry her childhood sweetheart. It's as simple as that."

"You obviously cared about her a great deal," Maggie said softly, hoping to take some of the sting from her earlier comments. Talking about Angie, even now, was obviously painful for him.

He held her gaze without hesitation. "I did care for her, but that's over now. I didn't marry you longing for anyone else. You aren't a substitute. This marriage wasn't made on the rebound. We're both vulnerable for different reasons. I want you for my wife. Not anyone else, only you. We've known each other most of our lives. I like you a great deal and respect you even more. We're comfortable together."

"Yes, we are," she agreed. So Glenn regarded her as an old pair of worn shoes. He could relax with her and put aside any need for pretense…as she could. But then she hadn't exactly come into their marriage seeking white lace and promises. Or maybe she had, Maggie didn't know anymore; she was confused.

"We're going to work this out," he said confidently, smiling for the first time that day as he reached for her hand.

"We're going to try," she suggested cautiously. "I'm not so sure we've done the right thing running off like this. We were both half-crazy to think we could make a marriage work on a twenty-four-hour re-acquaintance."

"I knew what we were doing every second," Glenn countered gruffly. "I wanted this, Maggie."

"I didn't know if it was right or wrong. I guess only time will tell if we did the right thing or not."

The flight back to San Francisco seemed to take a lifetime. Maggie sat by the window, staring at the miniature world far below. The landscape rolled and curved from jutting peaks to plunging valleys that reminded her of the first few hours of her marriage. Even now a brooding sense of unreality remained with her.

The days were shorter now that winter was approaching, and dusk had settled by the time the taxi pulled up in front of the beach house. While Glenn was paying the cabdriver, Maggie looked over the house where she'd voluntarily sequestered herself, wondering how Glenn would view the ostentatious showplace. Undoubtedly he would be impressed. Her friends had praised the beach house that seemed to lack for nothing. There was a work-out gym, a sauna, a Jacuzzi, a swimming pool and a tennis court in the side yard that Maggie never used. The house held enough attractions to keep even the most discriminating prisoner entertained.

On the way from the airport they had stopped off at Steve's empty apartment and picked up Glenn's luggage. Seeing it was a vivid reminder that he was scheduled to leave in the morning. "What time is your flight tomorrow?" she asked, wondering how long they'd be in Charleston. They had already decided to make their home in San Francisco, but arrangements would need to be made in Charleston.

His mouth hardened. "Are you so anxious to be rid of me?"

"No." She turned astonished eyes to him, stunned at his sharp tongue. He made it sound as though she wouldn't be going with him. She should. After all, she was his wife. She could make an issue of it now, or wait until she was certain she'd read him right. They had already experienced enough conflict for one day and Maggie opted to hold her tongue. Her fingers fumbled with the lock in an effort to get inside the house. "I have to phone my brother," she announced once the door was open.

"Denny?"

"Yes, Denny, or is that a problem, too?"

He ran his fingers through his hair and expelled an angry breath. "I didn't mean to snap at you."

Maggie lowered her gaze. "I know. We're both on edge. I didn't mean to bite your head off, either." They were nervous and unsure of each other for the first time in their lives. What had once been solid ground beneath their feet had become shifting sand. They didn't know where they stood…or if they'd continue to stand at all.

Glenn placed a hand at the base of her neck and gently squeezed it. "My flight's scheduled for three. We'll have some time together."

He didn't plan to have her travel with him! That was another shock. Fine, she thought angrily. If he didn't want her, then she wouldn't ask. "Good," she murmured sarcastically. Fine indeed!

The house foyer was paved with expensive tiles imported from Italy, and led to a plush sunken living room decorated with several pieces of furniture upholstered in white leather. A baby grand piano dominated one corner of the room. As she hung up Glenn's coat he wandered into the large living room, his hands in his pockets.

"Do you like it?"

"It's very nice" was all he said. He stood, legs slightly apart while his gaze rested on an oil painting hung prominently on the wall opposite the Steinway. It was one of Maggie's earlier works and her favorite, a beachscape that displayed several scenes, depicting a summer day's outing to the ocean. Her brush had captured the images of eager children building a sand castle. Another group of bikini-clad young girls were playing a game of volleyball with muscle-bound he-men. A family was enjoying a picnic, their blanket spread out on the sand, shaded by a multicolored umbrella. Cotton-candy clouds floated in a clear blue sky while the ocean waves crested and slashed against the shore. Maggie had spent hours agonizing over the minute details of the painting. Despite its candor and realism, Maggie's beachscape wasn't an imitation of a snapshot recording, but a mosaiclike design that gave a minute hint at the wonder of life.

"This is a marvelous painting. Where did you ever find it?" Glenn asked without turning around. "The detail is unbelievable."

"A poor imitation of a Brueghel." A smile danced at the corners of her mouth.

"Who?"

"Pieter Brueghel, a sixteenth-century Flemish painter."

"A sixteenth-century artist didn't paint this," Glenn challenged.

"No. I did."

He turned with a look of astonished disbelief. "You're not teasing, are you?" The question was rhetorical. His eyes narrowed fractionally as if reassessing her.

"It's one of my earliest efforts after art school. I've done better since, but this remains one of my favorite."

"Better than this?" His voice dipped faintly as though he doubted her words. "I remember you scribbling figures as a kid, but I never suspected you had this much talent."

A shiver of pleasure raced up her arm at the pride that gleamed from his eyes as he glanced from the painting back to her. "I had no idea you were this talented, Maggie."

The sincerity of the compliment couldn't be doubted. Others had praised her work, but Maggie had felt a niggling doubt as to the candidness of the comments. "Thank you," she returned, feeling uncharacteristically humble.

"I'd like to see your other projects."

"Don't worry, you'll get the chance. Right now, I've got to phone Denny. He'll wonder what happened to me."

"Sure. Go ahead. I'll wait in here if you like."

Maggie's office was off the living room. She hesitated a moment before deciding, then walked to the telephone on a table next to the couch. Her back was to Glenn as she picked up the receiver and punched out the number.

"Denny, it's Maggie."

"Maggie," he cried with obvious relief. "How was the wedding? You must have been late. I tried to get hold of you all day."

It was on the tip of Maggie's tongue to tell him about her marriage, but she held back, preferring to waylay his questions and doubts. She would tell him soon enough.

Her brother's voice softened perceptibly. "I was worried."

"I'm sorry, I should have phoned." Maggie lifted a strand of hair around her ear.

"Did you get the money transferred?"

Maggie sighed inwardly, feeling guilty. Denny knew all the right buttons to push with her. "The money will be ready for you Monday morning."

"Thanks. You know Linda and I appreciate it." His voice took on a honey-coated appeal.

"I know."

"As soon as I talk to the attorney about my case I'll let you know where we stand."

"Yes, Denny, do that." A large portion of Denny's inheritance had been lost in a bad investment and Maggie was helping him meet expenses. She didn't begrudge him the money: how could she when she had so much? What she hated was what it was doing to him. Yet she couldn't refuse him. Denny was her brother, her only brother.

After saying her goodbye, she replaced the receiver and turned back to Glenn. "I gave the housekeeper the weekend off. But if you're hungry, I'm sure I'll be able to whip up something."

"How's Denny?" Glenn ignored her offer.

"Fine. Do you want something to eat or not?"

"Sure." His gaze rested on the phone and Maggie realized that he'd probably picked up the gist of her conversation with Denny. More than she had intended. As a stockbroker Glenn would know what a foolish mistake her brother had made and she wanted to save her brother the embarrassment if possible.

Determined to avoid the subject of her brother, Maggie strolled past Glenn, through the dining room and into the expansive kitchen that was equipped with every conceivable modern cooking device. The double-width refrigerator/freezer was well stocked with frozen meals so that all that was required of her was to insert one into the microwave, push a button and wait.

The swinging doors opened as Glenn followed her inside. He paused to look around the U-shaped room with its oak cabinets and marble countertops. His hands returned to his pockets as he cocked his thick brows. "A bit large, wouldn't you say? One woman couldn't possibly require this much space."

Of course the kitchen was huge, she thought, irritated. She hadn't paid an exorbitant price for this place for three drawers and a double sink. "Yes," she returned somewhat defensively. "I like it this way."

"Do you mind if I take a look outside?" he asked and opened the sliding glass doors that led to a balcony overlooking the ocean.

"Sure. Go ahead."

A breeze ruffled the drape as he opened and closed the glass French door. Maggie watched him move to the railing and look out over the beach below. If she paused and strained her ears, she could hear the the ocean as the wild waves crashed upon the sandy shore. A crescent moon was barely visible behind a thick layer of clouds.

Leaning a hip against the counter, Maggie studied his profile. It seemed incomprehensible that the man who was standing only a few feet from her was her husband. She felt awkward and shy, even afraid. If he did head back to Charleston without her, their marriage would become increasingly unreal. Before Glenn turned to find her studying him, Maggie took out a head of lettuce from the refrigerator and dumped it into a strainer, and then placed it under the faucet.

Rubbing the chill from his arms, Glenn returned a few minutes later.

"Go ahead and pour yourself a drink," Maggie offered, tearing the lettuce leaves into a bowl. When he hesitated, she pointed to the liquor cabinet.

"I'm more interested in coffee if you have it."

"I'll make it."

"I'll do it."

Simultaneously they moved and somehow Maggie's face came sharply into contact with the solid mass of muscle and man. Amazingly, in the huge kitchen, they'd somehow managed to collide. Glenn's hand sneaked out to steady Maggie at the shoulders. "You okay?"

"I think so." She moved her nose back and forth a couple of times before looking up at him. "I should have known this kitchen wasn't big enough for the two of us."

Something warm and ardent shone from his eyes as his gaze dropped to her mouth. The air in the room crackled with electricity. The hands that were gripping her shoulders moved down her upper arms and tightened. Every ticking second seemed to stretch out of proportion. Then, very slowly, he half lifted her from the floor, his mouth descending to hers a fraction of an inch at a time. Maggie's heart skipped a beat, then began to hammer wildly. He deliberately, slowly, left his mouth a hair's space above hers so that their breaths mingled and merged. Holding her close, he seemed to want her to take the initiative. But the memory of that morning remained vivid in her mind. And now it seemed he intended to leave her behind in San Francisco as well. No, there were too many questions left unanswered for her to give in to the physical attraction between them. Still his mouth hovered over hers, his eyes holding her. At the sound of the timer dinging, Glenn released her. Disoriented, Maggie stood completely still until she realized Glenn had moved away. Embarrassed, she turned, making busywork at the microwave.

"That smells like lasagna," Glenn commented.

"It is." Maggie's gaze widened as she set out the dishes. What an idiot she'd been. The bell she heard hadn't been her heart's song from wanting Glenn's kisses. It had been the signal from her microwave that their dinner was ready. The time had come to remove the stars from her eyes regarding their marriage.

Maggie noted that Glenn's look was thoughtful when they ate, as if something was bothering him. For that matter, she was unusually quiet herself. After the meal, Glenn silently helped her stack the dinner plates into the dishwasher. "Would you like the grand tour?" Maggie inquired, more in an effort to ease the tension than from any desire to show off her home.

"You did promise to show me some more of your work."

"My art?" Maggie hedged, suddenly unsure. "I'm more into the abstract things now." She dried her hands on a terry-cloth towel and avoided looking at him. "A couple of years ago I discovered Helen Frankenthaler. Oh, I'd seen her work, but I hadn't appreciated her genius."

"Helen who?"

"Frankenthaler." Maggie enunciated the name slowly. "She's probably the most historically important artist of recent decades and people with a lot more talent than me have said so."

Glenn looped an arm around her shoulders and slowly shook his head. "Maggie, you're going to have to remember your husband knows absolutely nothing about art."

"But you know what you like," she teased, leading him by the hand to the fully glassed-in upstairs studio.

"That I do," he admitted in a husky whisper.

No one else had ever seen the studio, where she spent the vast majority of her time. It hadn't been a conscious oversight. There just had never been anyone she'd wanted to show it to. Not even Denny, who, she realized, only gave lip service to her work. She led Glenn proudly into her domain. She had talent and knew it. So much of her self-esteem was centered in her work. In recent years it had become the outpouring of her frustrations and loneliness. Her ego, her identity, her vanity were all tied up in her work.

Glenn noted that her studio was a huge room twice the size of the kitchen. Row upon row of canvases were propped against the walls. From the shine in her eyes, Glenn realized that Maggie took her painting seriously. She loved it. As far as he could see it was the only thing in this world that she had for herself.

He hadn't been pleased by what he'd overheard in her telephone conversation with Denny. He had wanted to ask Maggie about it over dinner, but hesitated. He felt that it was too soon to pry into her relationship with her brother. As he recalled, Denny was a decent guy, four or five years older than Maggie. From the sounds of it, though, Denny was sponging off his sister—which was unusual since he had heard that Denny was wealthy in his own right. It was none of his affair, Glenn decided, and it was best that he keep his nose out of it.

Proudly Maggie walked around the studio, which was used more than any other room in the house. Most of the canvases were fresh and white, waiting for the bold strokes of color that would bring them to life. Several of the others contained her early experiments in cubism and expressionism. She watched Glenn as he strolled about the room, studying several of her pictures. Pride shone in his eyes and Maggie basked in his approval. She wanted to hug him and thank him for simply appreciating what she did.

He paused to study a large ten-foot canvas propped at an angle against the floor. Large slashes of blue paint were smeared across the center and had been left to dry, creating their own geometric pattern. Maggie was especially pleased with this piece. It was the painting she had been working on the afternoon she was late meeting Glenn at the airport.

"What's this?" Glenn asked, his voice tight. He cocked his head sideways, his brow pleated in concentration.

"Glenn," she chided, "that's my painting."

He was utterly stupefied that Maggie would waste her obvious talent on an abstract mess. The canvas looked as though paint had been carelessly splattered across the top. Glenn could see no rhyme or pattern to the design. "Your painting," he mused aloud. "It's quite a deviation from your other work, isn't it?"

Maggie shrugged off his lack of appreciation and enthusiasm. "This isn't a portrait," she explained somewhat defensively. This particular painting was a departure from the norm, a bold experiment with a new balance of unexpected harmony of different hues of blues with tension between shapes and shades. Glenn had admitted he knew nothing about art, she thought. He wouldn't understand what she was trying to say with this piece, and she didn't try to explain.

Squatting, Glenn examined the large canvas, his fingertips testing the texture. "What is this material? It's not like a regular canvas, is it?"

"No, it's unprimed cotton duck—the same fabric that's used for making sails." This type of porous material allowed her to toss the paint across the canvas; then point by point, she poured, dripped and even used squeegees to spread the great veils of tone. She spent long, tedious hours contemplating each aspect of the work, striving for the effortless, spontaneous appeal she admired so much in Helen Frankenthaler's work.

"You're not into the abstract stuff, are you?" she asked with a faint smile. She tried to make it sound as if it didn't matter. The pride she'd seen in Glenn's eyes when he saw her beachscape and her other work had thrilled her. Now she could see him trying to disguise his puzzlement. "Don't feel bad, abstracts aren't for everyone."

A frown marred his smooth brow as he straightened and brushed the grit from his hands. "I'd like to see some more of the work like the painting downstairs."

"There are a couple of those over here." She pulled a painting out from behind a stack of her later efforts in cubism.

Glenn held out the painting and his frown disappeared. "Now this is good. The other looks like an accident."

An accident! Maggie nearly choked on her laughter. She'd like to see him try it. "I believe the time has come for me to propose another rule for this marriage."

Glenn's look was wary. "What?"

"From now on everything I paint is beautiful and wonderful and the work of an unrecognized genius. Understand?"

"Certainly," he murmured, "anything you say." He paused to examine the huge canvas a second time. "I don't know what you're saying with this, but this is obviously the work of an unrecognized and unappreciated genius."

Maggie smiled at him boldly. "You did that well."

Five

Glenn muttered under his breath as he followed Maggie out of her studio. Her dainty back was stiff as she walked down the stairs. She might have made light of his comments, but he wasn't fooled. Once again he had hurt her. Twice in one day. The problem was that he was trying too hard. They both were. "I apologize, Maggie. I didn't mean to offend you. You're right. I don't know a thing about art."

"I'm not offended," she lied. "I keep forgetting how opinionated you are." With deliberate calm she moved into the living room and sat at the baby grand piano, running her fingers over the ivory keys. She wanted to be angry with him, but couldn't, realizing that any irritation was a symptom of her own insecurity. She had exposed a deeply personal part of herself. It had been a measure of her trust and Glenn hadn't known or understood. She couldn't blame him for that.

"I don't remember that you played the piano." He stood beside her, resting his hand on her shoulder.

His touch was oddly soothing. "I started taking lessons a couple of years ago."

"You're good."

Maggie stopped playing; her fingers froze above the keys. Slowly, she placed her hands in her lap. "Glenn, listen, the new rule to our marriage only applies to my painting. You can be honest with my piano playing. I'm rotten. I have as much innate rhythm as lint."

Glenn recognized that in his effort to make up for one faux pas he had only dug himself in deeper. He didn't know anything about music. "I thought you played the clarinet."

"I wasn't much better on that, if you recall."

"I don't."

"Obviously," she muttered under her breath, rising to her feet. She rubbed her hands together in a nervous gesture. "It's been a long day."

Glenn's spirits sank. It had been quite a day and nothing like he'd expected. Yet he couldn't blame Maggie—he had brought everything on himself. His hand reached for hers. "Let's go to bed."

Involuntarily, Maggie tensed. Everything had been perfect for the wedding night, but now she felt unsure and equally uneasy. Glenn was her husband and she couldn't give him the guest bedroom. But things were different from what they had been. Her eyes were opened this time, and white lace and promises weren't filling her mind with fanciful illusions.

"Is something wrong?" Glenn's question was more of a challenge.

"No," she murmured, abruptly shaking her head. "Nothing's wrong." But then not everything was right, either. She led the way down the long hallway to the master bedroom, feeling shaky.

The room was huge, dominated by a brick fireplace, with two pale-blue chairs angled in front of it. The windows were adorned with shirred drapes of a delicate floral design that had been specially created to give a peaceful, easy-living appeal. The polished mahogany four-poster bed had a down comforter tossed over the top that was made from the same lavender floral material as the drapes. This room was Maggie's favorite. She could sit in it for hours and feel content.

If Glenn was impressed with the simple elegance or felt the warmth of her bedroom, he said nothing. Maggie would have been surprised if he had.

His suitcase rested on the thick carpet, and Glenn sighed, turning toward her. "We have a lot to do tomorrow." Frustrated anger filled Glenn at his own stupidity. Everything he had done that day had been wrong. From the moment he had opened his eyes to the time he'd mentioned going to bed. He couldn't have been more insensitive had he tried. He didn't want to argue with Maggie and yet, it seemed, he had gone out of his way to do exactly that. There would be a lot of adjustments to make with their marriage and he had gotten off on the wrong foot almost from the moment they'd started. Maggie was uncomfortable; Glenn could sense that. He could also feel her hesitancy. But he was her husband, and by heaven he'd sleep with her this and every night for the remainder of their lives.

The mention of the coming day served to remind Maggie that Glenn was planning on returning to Charleston alone. That rankled. Sometime during the evening, she had thought to casually bring up the return trip. But with what had happened in her studio and afterward, the timing hadn't been right. Crossing her arms over her breasts, she met his gaze.

"Oh. What are we doing tomorrow?" She couldn't think

of anything they needed to do that couldn't be handled later.

"First we'll see a lawyer, then—"

"Why?" she asked, her voice unnaturally throaty. Alarm filled her. Glenn had changed his mind. He didn't want to stay married. And little wonder. She kept making up these rules and—

"I want to make sure none of your inheritance money is ever put in my name." With all the other problems they were facing, Glenn needed to assure Maggie that he hadn't married her for her wealth. If anything, he regretted the fact she had it. Her Great-aunt Margaret's money had been a curse as far as he was concerned. And judging by the insecure, frightened woman Maggie had become, she might even have realized that herself.

"I... I know you wouldn't cheat me." The odd huskiness of her voice was made more pronounced by a slight quiver. Of all the men she had known in her life, she trusted Glenn implicitly. He was a man of honor. He might have married her when he was in love with another woman, but he would never deliberately do anything to swindle her.

Their gazes melted into each other's. Maggie trusted him, Glenn realized. The heavy weight that had pressed against him from the moment she had turned her hurt, angry eyes on him that morning lessened. Surely there'd been a better way to handle that business with her paintings, he thought. She had talent, incredible talent, and it was a shame that she was wasting it by hiding it away.

"After the lawyer we'll go to a jeweler," he added.

"A jeweler?"

"I'd like you to wear a wedding ring, Maggie."

The pulse in her neck throbbed as she beat down a rush of pure pleasure. "Okay, and you too."

"Of course," he agreed easily. His gaze did a sweeping inspection of the room as if he'd noticed it for the first time. It reminded him of Maggie. Her presence was stamped in every piece of furniture, every corner. Suddenly, a tiredness stole into his bones. He was exhausted, mentally and physically. "Let's get ready for bed."

Maggie nodded, and some of her earlier apprehension faded. She wasn't completely comfortable sleeping with him after what had happened. Not when there was a chance he would take her in his arms, hold her close, kiss her, even make love to her, with another woman's name on his lips. "You go ahead, I've got a few odds and ends to take care of first."

Sitting at the oak desk in her office, Maggie lifted her long hair from her face and closed her eyes as weariness flooded her bones. She was tired—Glenn was tired. She was confused—Glenn was confused. They both wanted this marriage—they were both responsible for making it work. All right, there wasn't any reason to overreact. They'd share a bed and if he said "her" name in his sleep again, Maggie refused to be held responsible for her actions.

By the time Glenn returned from his shower, Maggie had gone back to the bedroom and changed into a sexless flannel pajama set that would have discouraged the most amorous male. She had slipped beneath the covers, and was sitting up reading, her back supported by thick feather pillows. Behind her book, she followed Glenn's movements when he reentered the bedroom.

He paused and allowed a tiny smile of satisfaction to touch his lips. He had half expected Maggie to linger in her office until he was asleep and was greatly pleased that she hadn't. Although she looked like a virgin intent on maintaining her chastity in that flannel outfit, he knew that this night wasn't the time to press for his husbandly rights. Things had gone badly. Tomorrow would be better, he promised himself.

Lifting back the thick quilt, Glenn slid his large frame into the king-size bed and turned off the light that rested on the mahogany nightstand on his side of the bed.

"Good night." His voice was husky and low with only a trace of amusement. He thought she would probably sit up reading until she fell asleep with the light on.

"Good night," she answered softly, pretending to read. A few minutes later, Maggie battled to keep her lashes from drooping. Valiantly she struggled as her mind conjured up ways of resisting Glenn. The problem was that she didn't want to resist him. He would probably wait until she was relaxed and close to falling asleep, she theorized. When she was at her weakest point, he would reach for her and kiss her. Glenn was a wonderful kisser and she went warm at the memory of what had happened their first night together. He had held her as if he were dying of thirst and she was a cool shimmering pool in an oasis.

Gathering her resolve, Maggie clenched her teeth. By heaven, the way her thoughts were going she'd lean over and kiss him any minute. Her hand rested on her abdomen and Maggie felt bare skin. Her pajamas might be sexless, but they also conveniently buttoned up the front so he had easy access to her if he wanted. Again she recalled how good their lovemaking had been and how she had thrilled to his hands and mouth on her. Her eyes drooped shut and with a start she forced them open. Lying completely still she listened, and after several long moments discovered that Glenn had turned away from her and was sound asleep.

An unexpected rush of disappointment filled her. He hadn't even tried to make love to her. Without a thought, he had turned onto his side and gone to sleep! Bunching up her pillow, Maggie rolled onto her stomach, feeling such frustration that she could have cried. He didn't want her, and as unreasonable as it sounded, Maggie felt discouraged and depressed. Her last thought as she turned out her light was that if Glenn reached for her in the night she would give him what he wanted...what she wanted.

Sometime in the middle of the night Maggie woke. She was sleeping on her side, but had moved to the middle of the bed. Her eyes fluttered open and she wondered what had caused her to wake when she felt so warm and comfortable. Glenn's even breathing sounded close to her ear and she realized that he was asleep, cuddling his body to hers. Contented and secure, she closed her eyes and a moment later a male hand slid over her ribs, just below her breasts. When he pulled her close, fitting his body to hers, Maggie's lashes fluttered open. Not for the first time, she was amazed at how perfectly their bodies fit together. Releasing a contented breath, Maggie shut her eyes and wandered back to sleep.

Glenn woke in the first light of dawn with a serenity that had escaped him for months. That morning he didn't mistake the warm body he was holding close. Maggie was responsible for his tranquility of spirit, Glenn realized. He needed Maggie. During the night, her pajama top had ridden up and the urge to move his hand and trace the soft, womanly curves was almost overpowering. Maggie was all the woman he would ever want. She was everything he had ever hoped to find in a wife—a passionate, irresistible mistress with an intriguing mind and delectable body, who surrendered herself willingly. Her passion had surprised and pleased him. She hadn't been shy, or embarrassed, abandoning herself to him with an eagerness that thrilled him every time he thought about it. She was more woman than he'd dared hope and he ached to take her again.

In her sleep, Maggie shifted and her breasts sprang free of the confining top. For an eternity he lay completely still until he couldn't resist touching her any longer. In his mind he pictured turning her onto her back and kissing her until her lips opened eagerly to his. With inhuman patience he would look into those dark beautiful eyes and wait until she told him how much she wanted him.

Groaning, he released her and rolled onto his back, taking deep breaths to control his frantic frustration. He had no idea how long it would be before he would have the opportunity to make love to his wife again. Two weeks at least, maybe longer. Almost as overwhelming as the urge to make love to her was the one to cherish and protect her. She needed reassurance and he knew she needed time. Throwing back the blankets he marched into the bathroom and turned on the cold water.

Maggie woke at the sound of the shower running. Stirring, she turned onto her back and stared at the ceiling as the last dregs of sleep drained from her mind. She had been having the most pleasant erotic dream. One that caused her to blush from the roots of her dark hair to the ends of her toenails. Indecent dreams maybe, but excruciatingly sensual. Perhaps it was best that Glenn was gone when she woke, she thought. If he had been beside her she didn't know what she would have done. She could well have embarrassed them both by reaching for him and asking him to make love to her before he returned to Charleston...alone.

Taking advantage of the privacy, she dressed and hur-

Debbie Macomber

riedly made the bed. By the time she had straightened the comforter across the mattress, Glenn reappeared.

"Good morning," he said as he paused just inside the bedroom, standing both alert and still as he studied her. "Did you sleep well?"

"Yes," she responded hastily, feeling like a specimen about to be analyzed, but a highly prized specimen, one that was cherished and valued. "What about you?" she asked.

The hesitation was barely noticeable, but Maggie noticed. "Like a rock."

"Good. Are you hungry?" Her eyes refused to meet his, afraid of what hers would tell him.

"Starved."

"Breakfast should be ready by the time you've finished dressing," she said as she left the room. Glenn had showered last night, she remembered; she couldn't recall him being overly fastidious. Shrugging, she moved down the long hall to the kitchen.

The bacon was sizzling in the skillet when Glenn reappeared, dressed in dark slacks and a thick pullover sweater. Maggie was reminded once again that he was devastatingly handsome and experienced, and with a burst of pride, she remembered that he was married to her. At least legally, he was hers. However, another woman owned the most vital part of him—his heart. In time, Maggie trusted, she would claim that as well.

The morning swam past in a blur; such was their pace. They began by contacting Maggie's attorney and were given an immediate appointment. Together they sat in his office, although it was Glenn who did the majority of the talking. Maggie was uncomfortable with the rewording of her will, but Glenn was adamant. He desired none of her money and he wanted it stated legally. When and if they had children, her inheritance would be passed on to them.

From the attorney's they stopped off at a prominent San Francisco jeweler. Maggie had never been one for flashy jewels. All too often her hands were in paint solvent or mixing clay and she didn't want to have to worry about losing expensive rings or valuable jewels. Knowing herself and her often thoughtless ways, Maggie was apt to misplace a diamond and she couldn't bear the thought of losing any ring Glenn gave her.

"You decide," Glenn insisted, his hand at the back of her neck. "Whatever one you want is fine."

Sensing a sure sale, the young jeweler set out a tray of exquisite diamonds, far larger than any Maggie had dreamed Glenn would want to purchase. Her gaze fell on a lovely marquise and her teeth worried her bottom lip. "I... was thinking maybe something with a smaller stone would be fine," she murmured, realizing that she should have explained her problems about a diamond to Glenn earlier.

He pinched his mouth closed with displeasure, resenting her concern that he couldn't afford to buy her a diamond large enough to weight her hand.

"Try on that one," he insisted, pointing to the marquise solitaire with the wide polished band that she had admired earlier. The diamond was the largest and most expensive on the tray.

Maggie paled, not knowing how to explain herself. The salesman beamed, exchanging pleased glances with Glenn.

"An excellent choice," the jeweler said, lifting Maggie's limp hand. The ring fit as if it was made for her slender finger. But the diamond was so heavy it felt bulky and unnatural. In her mind Maggie could picture the panic of looking for it once it was mislaid...and it would be.

"We'll take it."

"Glenn." Maggie placed her hand on his forearm. "Can I talk to you a minute? Please."

"I'll write up the sales order," the jeweler said, removing the tray of diamonds. "I'll be with the cashier when you've finished."

Maggie waited until the salesman was out of earshot before turning troubled eyes to Glenn. Her heart was in her eyes as she recognized the pride and irritation that glared back at her.

"What's the matter, Maggie?" he growled under his breath. "Are you afraid I can't afford a wedding ring for my wife? I may not own a fancy beach house, but be assured, I can afford a diamond."

Glenn's words smarted and it was all Maggie could do to bite back a flippant reply. "It's not that," she whispered fiercely, keeping her voice low so the jeweler wouldn't hear them arguing. "If you'd given me half a chance, I'd have explained. I'm an artist, remember? If you buy me that flashy diamond, I'll be constantly removing it for one reason or another."

"So? What are you suggesting? No ring at all?"

"No… I'm sorry I said anything. The ring is fine." Maggie backed down, aware that anything said now would be misconstrued. Somehow she would learn to be careful with the diamond. Purchasing it had become a matter of male pride and Maggie didn't want to cause any more problems than the ones already facing them.

"Would a plain gold band solve that?" he asked unexpectedly.

"Yes," she murmured, surprised. "Yes, it would." To her delight, Glenn also asked the jeweler to size a band for her. Maggie felt wonderful when they stepped outside.

The question of the ring might have been only a minor problem, but together they had settled it without wounding each other's sensitive pride. They were making progress and it felt good.

They ate lunch in Chinatown, feasting on hot, diced chicken stir-fried with fresh, crisp vegetables. All the time they were dining, Maggie was infinitely aware of two pressing items: the heavy feel of the ring on the third finger of her left hand, and the time. Within hours Glenn would be leaving for Charleston. A kaleidoscope of regrets and questions whirled through her mind. She wanted to go with him, but didn't feel she could make the suggestion. Glenn had to want her along, yet he hadn't said a word. Silence hung heavy and dark between them like a thick curtain of rain-filled clouds. He was going back to his lost love. Dread filled Maggie with each beat of her heart.

Glenn made several attempts at light conversation during their meal, but nothing seemed to ease the strained silence that had fallen over them. A glance at his watch reminded him that within a few hours he would be on a plane for Charleston. He didn't want to leave, but in some ways felt it was for the best. Maggie seemed to assume that she wouldn't be going with him and he was disappointed that she hadn't shown the willingness to travel with him. He might have made an issue of it if he hadn't thought a short separation would help them both become accustomed to their marriage without the issue of sleeping together. Those weeks would give Maggie the opportunity to settle things within her own mind. When he came back to her they would take up their lives as man and wife and perhaps she'd come to him willingly as she had that first night. That was what he wanted.

The drive back to the house and then on to the airport

seemed to take a lifetime. With each mile, Maggie felt her heart grow heavier. She was apprehensive and didn't know how to deal with it. She and Glenn had been together such a short time that separating now seemed terribly wrong. Unreasonable jealousy ate at her and Maggie had to assure herself repeatedly that Glenn probably wouldn't even be seeing the other woman. She was, after all, married to another man or so Glenn had told her. But Maggie didn't gain a whit's comfort from knowing that. For the first time in memory, she found herself in a situation where money wasn't part of the solution.

As they left the airport parking garage, Glenn's hand took hers. "I won't be long," he promised. "I'll need to get everything settled at the office, list the condominium with a Realtor and settle loose business ties—that kind of thing. I can't see it taking more than two weeks, three at the most."

"The weeks will fly by," she said on a falsely cheerful note. "Just about the time I clean out enough closet space for you, you'll be back."

"I wouldn't leave if it wasn't necessary," Glenn assured her as they approached the ticketing desk to check in his luggage.

"I know that." Maggie hugged her waist, feeling a sudden and unexpected chill. "I'm not worried about...you know." *Liar,* her mind tossed back.

Their shoes made a clicking sound as they walked together toward security. Maggie had the horrible feeling she was about to cry, which, she knew, was utterly ridiculous. She rarely cried, yet her throat felt raw and scratchy and her chest had tightened with pent-up emotion. All the things she wanted to say stuck in her throat and she found that she couldn't say a thing.

"Take care of yourself," Glenn murmured, holding her by the shoulders.

"I will," she promised and buried her hands deep within the pockets of her raincoat. Even those few words could barely escape.

Glenn fastened the top button of her coat and when he spoke his voice was softly gruff. "It looks like rain. Drive carefully."

"I always do. You'll note that you're here on time." She made a feeble attempt at humor.

Tiny laugh lines fanned out from his eyes. "Barely. I don't suppose you've noticed that by now my flight's probably boarding. Married two days and I'm already picking up your bad habits."

His observation prompted a soft smile. "You'll phone?" She turned soft, round eyes to him.

"Yes," he promised in a husky murmur. "And if you need me, don't hesitate to call." He had written down both his work and home numbers in case she had to get in touch with him.

"You'll phone tonight." It became immensely important that he did. She pulled her hands from her pockets and smoothed away an imaginary piece of lint from his shoulder. Her hand lingered there. "I'll miss you." Even now if he hinted that he wanted her with him, she'd step on that plane. If necessary she'd buy the stupid plane.

"I'll phone, but it'll be late because of the time change," Glenn explained.

"I don't mind.... I probably won't sleep anyway." She hadn't meant to admit that much and felt a rush of color creep up her neck and into her cheeks.

"Me either," he murmured. His hands tightened on her upper arms and he gently brought her against his bulky sweater. With unhurried ease his mouth moved toward hers. The kiss flooded her with a swell of emotions she had tasted only briefly in his arms. She was hot, on fire and cold as ice. Hot from his touch, cold with fear. His kiss sent a jolt rocketing through her and she fiercely wrapped her arms around his neck. Her mind whirled and still she clung, afraid that if Glenn ever released her she'd never fully recover from the fall. Dragging in a deep breath, Maggie buried her face in his neck.

Glenn wrapped his arms around her waist and half lifted her from the floor. "I'll be back soon," he promised.

She nodded because speaking was impossible.

When he released her his gaze was as gentle as a caress and as tender as a child's touch. Maggie offered him a feeble smile. Glenn turned up the collar of her coat. "Stay warm."

Again she nodded. "Phone me."

Glenn claimed Maggie's lips again in a brief but surprisingly ardent kiss. "I'll call the minute I land."

With hands in her pockets for fear she'd do something silly like reach out and ask him not to go, or beg him to ask her to come. "Hurry now, or you'll miss the flight."

Glenn took two steps backward. "The time will go fast."

"Yes," she said, not exactly sure what she was agreeing to.

"You're my wife, Maggie. I'm not going to forget that."

"You're my husband," she whispered and choked back the tears that filled her eyes and blurred her vision.

Then tossing a glance over his shoulder, he hurriedly handed the TSA agent his boarding pass and identity.

Maggie pushed her. "Go on," she encouraged, not wanting him to see her cry. For all the emotion that was raging through her one would assume that Glenn was going off to war and was unlikely to return. Her stomach was in such tight knots that she couldn't move without pain. Rooted to the spot close to security, Maggie stood as she was until Glenn turned and ran toward his gate. When she could, she stepped to the window and whispered, "New rules for this marriage...don't ever leave me again."

The days passed in a blur. Not since art school had Maggie worked harder or longer. Denny phoned her twice. Once to thank her for the "loan" and later to talk to her about the top-notch lawyer he had on retainer. The attorney was exactly who he had hoped would pursue his case, and his spirits were high. Maggie was pleased for Denny and prayed that this would be the end of his problems.

Without Glenn, sound sleep was impossible. She'd drift off easily enough and then jerk awake a couple of hours later, wondering why the bed seemed so intolerably large. Usually she slept in the middle of the mattress, but she soon discovered that she rested more comfortably on the side where Glenn had slept. She missed him. The worst part was the unreasonableness of the situation. Glenn had spent less than twenty-four hours in her home, yet without him the beach house felt like a silent tomb.

As he promised, Glenn had phoned the night he arrived back in Charleston and again three days later. Maggie couldn't recall any three days that seemed longer. A thousand times she was convinced her mind had conjured up both Glenn and their marriage. The marquise diamond on her ring finger was the only tangible evidence that the whole situation hadn't been a fantasy and that they really were married. Because she was working so hard and long she removed it for safekeeping, but each night she slipped it on her finger. Maggie didn't mention the wedding to her parents or any of her friends, and Denny didn't notice anything was different about her. She didn't feel comfortable telling everyone she was married, and wouldn't until Glenn had moved in with her and they were confident that their marriage was on firm ground.

Glenn phoned again on the fifth day. Their conversation was all too brief and somewhat stilted. Neither of them seemed to want it to end, but after twenty minutes, there didn't seem to be anything more to say.

Replacing the receiver, Maggie had the urge to cry. She didn't, of course, but it was several minutes before she had composed herself enough to go on with her day.

Nothing held her interest. Television, music, solitaire—everything bored her. Even the housekeeper lamented that Maggie had lost her appetite and complained about cooking meals that Maggie barely touched. Glenn filled every waking thought and invaded her dreams. Each time they spoke she had to bite her tongue to keep from suggesting she join him; her pride wouldn't allow that. The invitation must come from him, she believed. Surely he must realize that.

As for Angie, the woman in Glenn's past, the more Maggie thought about the situation, the more angry she became with herself. Glenn hadn't deceived her. They both were bearing scars from the past. If it wasn't love that cemented their marriage then it was something equally strong. Between them there was security and understanding.

The evening of the eighth day the phone rang just as Maggie was scrounging through the desk looking for an address. She stared at the telephone. Instantly she knew it was Glenn.

"Hello," she answered, happily leaning back in the swivel chair, anticipating a long conversation.

"Hi." His voice sounded vital and warm. "How's everything?"

"Fine. I'm a little bored." Maggie was astonished that she could sound so blasé about her traumatic week. "A little bored" soft-pedaled all her frustrations. "What about you?"

Glenn hesitated, then announced, "I've run into a small snag on my end of things." A small snag was the understatement of the century, he thought. Things had been in chaos from the minute he had returned. The company supervisor had paid a surprise visit to him Thursday afternoon and had suggested an audit because of some irregularity in the books. The audit had gone smoothly enough, but Glenn had worked long hours and had been forced to reschedule several appointments. In addition, the Realtor who listed the condominium offered little hope that it would sell quickly.

And worse, Glenn was miserable without Maggie. He wanted her with him. She was his wife, yet pride dictated that he couldn't ask her. The suggestion would have to come from her. Even a hint would be enough. He would pick up on a hint, but she had to be one to give it.

"A small snag?" Her heart was pounding so hard and strong that she felt breathless.

"I've got several accounts here that have deals pending. I can't leave my clients in the lurch. Things aren't going as smoothly as I'd like, Maggie," he admitted.

"I see." Maggie's vocabulary suddenly decreased to words of one syllable.

"I can't let them down." He sounded as frustrated as she felt. A deafening silence grated over the telephone line, and it was on the tip of Glenn's tongue to cast his stupid pride to the wind and ask her to join him.

"Don't worry, I understand," she said in an even tone,

congratulating herself for maintaining firm control of her voice. On the inside she was crumbling to pieces. She wanted to be with him. He was her husband and her place was at his side. Closing her eyes she mentally pleaded with him to say the words—to ask her to come to Charleston. She wouldn't ask, couldn't ask. It had to come from Glenn.

"In addition there are several loose ends that are going to require more time than I originally planned." He sounded almost angry, an emotion that mirrored her own frustration.

"I think we were both naive to think you could make it back in such a short time."

"I suppose we were." *Come on, Maggie,* he pleaded silently. *If you miss me, say something. At least meet me halfway in this.*

The line went silent again, but Maggie didn't want to end the conversation. She waited endless hours for his calls. They would talk for ten minutes, hang up and immediately she'd start wondering how long it would be before he phoned again.

"The weather's been unseasonably cold. There's been some talk of freezing tempratures," Maggie said out of desperation to keep the conversation going.

"Don't catch cold." *Damn it, Maggie, I want you here, can't you hear it in my voice?*

"I won't," she promised. *Please,* she wanted to scream at him, *ask me to come to Charleston.* With her eyes shut, she mentally transmitted her need to have him ask her. "I've been too busy in the studio to venture outside."

"Brueghel or Frankenthaler?" Glenn questioned, his voice tinged with humor. "However, I'm sure that either one would be marvelous and wonderful." He smiled as he said it, wanting her with him all the more just to see what other crazy rules she'd come up with for their marriage.

"This one's a Margaret Kingsbury original," she said proudly. Maggie had worked hard on her latest project and felt confident that Glenn would approve.

"It can't be." Glenn stiffened and tried to disguise the irritation in his voice.

Maggie tensed, wondering what she had said wrong. He hadn't approved of her art, but surely he didn't begrudge her the time she spent on it when he was away.

"Your name's Lambert now," Glenn stated.

"I...forgot." *Remind me again,* she pleaded silently. *Ask me to come to Charleston.* "I haven't told anyone yet.... Have you?"

"No one," Glenn admitted.

"Not even your parents?" She hadn't told hers, either, but Glenn's family was in South Carolina. It only made sense that he'd say something to them before moving out west.

"That was something I thought we'd do together."

The sun burst through the heavy overcast and shed its golden rays on Maggie. He had offered her a way to Charleston and managed to salvage her pride. The tension flowed from her as her hand tightened around the receiver. "Glenn, don't you think they'll be offended if we wait much longer?"

"They might," he answered, unexpectedly agreeable. "I know it's an inconvenience, but maybe you should think about flying...."

"I'll be on the first flight out tomorrow morning."

Six

Glenn was in the terminal waiting when Maggie walked off the plane late the following afternoon. He was tall, rugged and so male that it was all Maggie could do not to throw her arms around him. He looked wonderful and she wanted to hate him for it. For nine days she had been the most miserable woman alive and Glenn looked as if he'd relished their separation, thrived on it. Renewed doubts buzzed about her like swarming bees.

Stepping forward, Glenn took the carry-on bag from her hand and slipped an arm around her waist. "Welcome to Charleston."

Shamelessly, Maggie wanted him to take her in his arms and kiss her. She managed to disguise the yearning by lowering her gaze. "I didn't know if you'd be here."

She tried to call to give him her flight number, but his phone had gone directly to voice mail. She'd left a message and then later sent him a text. If he hadn't gotten her message Maggie wouldn't have had a way of getting into Glenn's condominium.

"Of course I'm here. Where else would I be?"

"I'm so glad to see you." *Very glad,* her heart sang.

"How was the flight?"

"Just the way I like 'em," she said with a teasing smile. "Uneventful."

Glenn's features warmed and he grinned at her answer. Captivated by the tenderness in his eyes, Maggie felt her heart throb almost painfully. His eyes were dark, yet glowing with a warm light. Although he hadn't said a word, Glenn's gaze told her he was pleased she was with him.

"Your luggage is this way," he commented, pressing a hand to the middle of her back as he directed her toward baggage claim.

"I didn't bring much."

"Not much" constituted two enormous suitcases and one large carry-on. Maggie had spent half the night packing, discarding one outfit after another until her bedroom floor was littered with more clothes than a second-hand store. She wanted everything perfect for Glenn. She longed to be alluring and seductive, attractive without being blatant about it. She wanted his heart as well as his bed and only she realized how difficult that was going to be if Glenn was still in love with "her."

The more Maggie thought about the other woman who had claimed his heart the more she realized what an uphill struggle lay before her. Glenn wouldn't ever give his love lightly, and now that he had, it would take a struggle to replace her in his heart. Maggie yearned to know more of the details, but wouldn't pry. In the meantime, she planned to use every womanly wile she possessed and a few she planned to invent.

The leather strap of her purse slid off her shoulder and Maggie straightened it. As she did, Glenn stopped in midstride, nearly knocking her off balance.

"Where's your diamond?" he asked, taking her hand.

Surprise mingled with disappointment and disbelief. "I thought you said the only time you wouldn't wear it was when you were working. You aren't painting now."

Maggie's mind whirled frantically. She had removed the diamond the morning before the phone call and placed it in safekeeping the way she always did. Then in her excitement about flying out to be with Glenn, she had forgotten to put it back on her finger.

"Maggie?"

Her fingers curled around the strap of her purse. "Oh, Glenn…"

He took her hand and examined the plain gold band that he had bought her with the marquise.

Maggie wanted to shout with frustration. From the moment they'd ended their phone conversation she had been carefully planning this reunion. Each detail had been shaped in her mind from the instant he picked her up until they dressed for bed.

"Maggie, where is the diamond?" he repeated.

"I forgot it, but don't worry… I have it with me." Her voice rose with her agitation. They hadn't so much as collected her luggage and already they were headed for a fight.

"You mean to tell me you packed a seven-thousand-dollar diamond with your underwear?" His voice was a mixture of incredulity and anger.

"I didn't do it on purpose, I…forgot I wasn't wearing it." Somehow that seemed even worse. "And furthermore it isn't in the suitcase, I have it in my carry-on."

Glenn's stride increased to a quick-paced clip that left Maggie half trotting in an effort to keep up. "Glenn," she protested, refusing to run through airports.

He threw an angry glare over his shoulder. "Forgive me for being overly concerned, but I work hard for my money."

The implication being, she thought, that she didn't work and the ring meant nothing to her. Little did he realize how much it did mean.

Maggie stopped cold as waves of anger hit her. Few words could have hurt her more. She was outraged he would say such a thing to her. For several minutes she found herself unable to speak. Nothing was going as she had planned. She'd had such wonderful images of Glenn sweeping her into his arms, holding her close and exclaiming that after the way he'd missed her, they'd never be separated again. He was supposed to tell her how miserable he'd been. Instead, he'd insulted her in a way that would hurt her the most.

Apparently he was angry because she had forgotten to slip on the diamond ring he'd gotten her, finding her casualness with the diamond a sign of irresponsibility. She had the ring; she knew where it was.

Glenn was standing outside the baggage-handling system, waiting for it to unload the luggage from her flight, when she joined him.

"If you'd give me a second I'll…"

"Talk to me after you've gotten your ring, Maggie. At the moment I'm worried about losing an expensive diamond."

"And you work hard for your money. Right? At least that's what you claim. I don't doubt it. It's said that those who marry for it usually do."

Although he continued to look straight ahead, a nerve jumped convulsively in his clenched jaw, and Maggie was instantly aware of just how angry that remark had made him. Good, she meant it to do exactly that. If he wanted to hurl insults at her, then she could give as well as take.

"Can I have my carry-on?"

Without a word, he handed it to her. He studied the baggage conveyor belt as if it were the center of his world. Maggie wasn't fooled. Glenn was simply too outraged to look at her.

Maggie knelt down on the floor and flipped open the lid. Her small jewelry case was inside and the ring was tucked safely in that. With a brooding sense of unhappiness, Maggie located the marquise diamond and slipped it on her finger beside the plain gold band. Snapping the suitcase closed, she stood.

"I hope to hell you didn't mean that about me marrying you for your money."

Maggie regarded him coolly before answering. "I didn't," she admitted. "I was reacting to your implication that I didn't have to work hard for my money."

He exhaled slowly. "I didn't mean it like that."

"I hope not."

They stood side by side, silent for several moments before his hand claimed hers. Right away he noticed the diamond was on her ring finger, he arched one brow expressively. "You had it with you all the time?"

"Yes."

He groaned inwardly. He had been wanting Maggie for days, longing for her. And now things were picking up right where they'd left off, with misunderstandings and sharp words. He had wanted everything perfect for her, and once again this bad start had been his own doing.

His fingers tightened over hers. "Can I make a new rule for this marriage?" he asked her with serious eyes.

"Of course."

"I want you to wear your wedding set all the time."

"But…"

"I know that may sound unreasonable," he interrupted, "and I'm not even entirely sure why my feelings are so strong. I guess it's important to me that your wedding bands mean as much to you as our marriage."

Slowly, thoughtfully, Maggie nodded. "I'll never remove them again."

Looking in her eyes, Glenn felt the overwhelming urge to take her in his arms and apologize for having started on the wrong foot once again. But the airport wasn't the place and now wasn't the time. From here on, he promised himself, he'd be more patient with her, court her the way he should have in the beginning.

They didn't say a word until the luggage was dispensed. Maggie pointed out her suitcases.

He mumbled something unintelligible under his breath and Maggie realized he was grumbling about the fact she claimed to have packed light for this trip. But he didn't complain strenuously.

The deafening quiet in the car was one neither seemed willing to wade into. Maggie wanted to initiate a brilliant conversation, but nothing came to mind and she almost cried with frustration. Their meeting wasn't supposed to happen this way. She sat uncomfortably next to a man she'd known most of her life and whom, she was discovering, she didn't know at all.

Glenn's condominium was situated just outside historic Charleston with a view of Colonial Lake. Maggie knew little about the area. Her head flooded with questions about the city that Glenn had made his home for a decade, but she asked none. While he took care of her luggage, she wandered into the living room to admire the view. The scenery below revealed magnificent eighteenth-century homes, large public buildings and meticulously kept gardens. The gentle toll of church bells sounded, and Maggie strained to hear more. Charleston was definitely a city of grace, beauty and charm. Yet Glenn was willing to sacrifice it all—his home, his family, his job, maybe even his career to move to San Francisco.

He must have suffered a great deal of mental anguish to be willing to leave all this, Maggie determined, experiencing an attack of doubt. Glenn had told her so little about this other woman, and Maggie had the feeling he wouldn't have told her anything if it hadn't been for the unfortunate scene the morning after their wedding. He was an intensely personal man.

The condominium was far more spacious than what Maggie had assumed. The living room led into a formal dining area and from there to a spacious kitchen with plenty of cupboards and a pantry. A library/den was separated from the living room by open double-width doors that revealed floor-to-ceiling bookcases and a large oak desk. She hadn't seen the bedrooms yet, but guessed that there were three, possibly four. The condo was much larger than what a single man would require. Her eyes rounded with an indescribable ache that came over her when she realized Glenn had purchased this home for Angie.

"Are you hungry?" he asked, halfway into the living room, standing several feet from her.

Maggie unbuttoned her coat and slipped the scarf from her neck. "No thanks, I ate on the plane, but you go ahead." The lie was a small, white one. The flight attendant had offered her a meal, but Maggie had declined. She'd been too anxious to eat when she was only a few hours from meeting Glenn.

He hesitated, turned, then whirled back around so that he was facing her again. "I regret this whole business with the ring, Maggie."

A shiver of gladness came over her at his offhand apology. "It's forgotten."

Something close to a smile quirked his mouth. "I'm glad you're here."

"I'm glad to be here."

He leaned around the kitchen door. "Are you sure you're not hungry?"

A small smile claimed her mouth. "On second thought, maybe I am at that."

A sense of relief flooded through Glenn's tense muscles. He hadn't meant to make such an issue of the diamond. For days he'd been longing for Maggie, decrying his earlier decision to leave her in San Francisco. They had so few days together that he'd thought the separation would give her the necessary time to adjust mentally to her new life. Unfortunately, it was he who had faced the adjustment...to his days...and nights without her. Now that she was here, all he wanted was to take her in his arms and make love to her. The level of physical desire she aroused in him was a definite shock. He hadn't expected to experience this intensity. All he had thought about since he'd known she was coming was getting her into his bed. He'd dreamed of kissing her, holding her and making love to his wife. She was the woman he'd married and he'd waited a long time for the privileges due a husband. He doubted that Maggie had any conception of how deep his anger had cut when she had suggested that he'd married her for her money. That was a problem he had anticipated early on and it was the very reason he had insisted they see a lawyer as soon as possible.

Working together they cooked their dinner. Maggie made the salad while Glenn broiled thick steaks. Glenn didn't have a housekeeper to prepare his meals and for that matter, Maggie surmised, he might not even have someone in to do the housework. Now that she was here, she decided, she would take over those duties. Surprisingly, Maggie discovered she looked forward to being a wife. Glenn's wife.

Later, while he placed the few dirty plates in the dishwasher, Maggie decided to unpack her bags. She located the master bedroom without a problem and gave a sigh of relief when she noticed that Glenn fully intended that she would sleep with him. It was what she wanted, what she had planned, but after their shaky beginning, Maggie hadn't known what to think. A soft smile worked its way across her face, brightening her dark eyes. Glenn longed for their marriage to work as much as she did, she thought. What they both needed to do was quit trying so hard.

When Maggie had finished unpacking, she joined Glenn in the living room. It amazed her how unsettled they were around each other still. Glenn suggested they turn on the last newscast of the evening. Readily, Maggie agreed. She supposed that this time could be thought of as their honeymoon. They were probably the only couple in America to watch television when they could be doing other…things.

After the news, Glenn yawned. Once again Maggie was reminded that his daily schedule was set with the routine of his job. Staying awake until two or three in the morning, watching a late late movie or reading would only cause problems the following morning. She would need to adjust her sleeping habits as well, although she had become a night person these past few years, often enjoying the peace and tranquility of the early-morning hours to paint. Glenn didn't live a life of leisure and she couldn't any longer, either.

Funny, Maggie thought, that the realization that she must now live according to a clock didn't depress her. She was willing to get up with him in the morning and cook his breakfast and even do the dishes. She didn't know how long this "domesticated" eagerness would continue, and vowed to take advantage of it while it lasted. In the morning, she would stand at the front door, and send him off to the office with a juicy kiss. But from the frowning look he was giving the television, Maggie had the impression the goodbye kiss in the morning would be all the kissing she was going to get.

Glenn's thoughts were heavy. Maggie was sitting at his side and he hadn't so much as put his arm around her. He felt as though he were stretched out on a rack, every muscle strained to the limit of his endurance. It was pure torture to have her so close and not haul her into his arms and make love to her. If she could read only half of what was going through his mind, she would run back to California, he thought dryly. No, he wouldn't take her that night. He'd bide his time, show her how empty his life was without her, how much he needed a woman's tenderness. Then, in time, she would come to him willingly and desire him, maybe even as keenly as he did her.

"Don't you think we should go to bed? It's after eleven." Maggie broached the subject with all the subtlety of a locomotive. Sitting next to him was torture. They had hardly said two words all night. The thick, unnatural silence made the words all the more profound.

Smoothly rolling to his feet, Glenn nodded. He hadn't noticed that the news was over. For that matter, he couldn't recall the headlines or anything that had been reported.

Not even the weather forecast, which he listened for each night. "I imagine you're tired," he finally answered.

"Dead on my feet," she confirmed, walking with him toward the hallway and the master bedroom. *You're wide awake,* her mind accused. She was on Pacific time and it was barely after eight in San Francisco.

Following a leisurely scented bath, Maggie joined him wearing a black nightshirt that buttoned up the front and hit her at midthigh with deep side slits that went halfway up to her hip. The satin top was the most feminine piece of sleepwear Maggie owned. The two top buttons were unfastened and she stretched her hands high above her head in a fake yawn, granting him a full glimpse of her upper thighs.

Glenn was in bed, propped against thick feather pillows, reading a spy thriller. One look at her in the black satin pajama top and the book nearly tumbled from his hands. Tension knotted his stomach and he all but groaned at the sight of his wife. Still wanting her was torture he endured willingly.

The mattress dipped slightly as she lifted back the blankets and slipped into the bed. Glenn set his novel aside and reached for the lamp switch. The room went dark with only the shimmering rays of the distant moon dancing across the far walls.

Neither moved. Only a few inches separated them, but for all the good it did to be sleeping with her husband, Maggie could well have been in San Francisco, she decided.

"Good night, Glenn," Maggie whispered after several stifled moments. If he didn't reach for her soon she'd clobber him over the head. Maybe she should say something to encourage him—let him know her feelings. But what?

Listen, Glenn, I've reconsidered and although I realize that you may still be in love with another woman I've decided it doesn't matter. We're married. I'm your wife.... Disheartened, Maggie realized she couldn't do it. Not so soon, and not in a condominium he probably bought with "her" in mind.

Glenn interrupted Maggie's dark thoughts with a deep, quiet voice. "Good night." With that he rolled onto his side away from her.

Gallantly, she resisted the urge to smash the pillow over the top of his head, pull a blanket from the mattress and storm into the living room to sleep. She didn't know how any man could be so unbelievably dense.

Maggie fell easily into a light, untroubled slumber. Although asleep, lying on her side, her back to him, she was ever conscious of the movements of the man who was sharing the bed. Apparently, Glenn was having more difficulty falling asleep, tossing to one side and then to another, seeking a comfortable position. Once his hand inadvertently fell onto her hip and for a moment he went completely still. Content now, Maggie smiled inwardly and welcomed the calm. Sleeping with him was like being in a rowboat wrestling with a storm at sea.

With unhurried ease the hand that rested against her bare hip climbed upward, stopping at her ribs. Shifting his position, Glenn scooted closer and gathered her into his embrace. As if he couldn't help himself, his hand sought and found a firm breast. His touch was doing insane things to her equilibrium and she was encompassed in a gentle, sweet warmth. Savoring the moment, Maggie bit into her bottom lip as he slowly, tantalizingly, caressed her breasts until she thought she'd moan audibly and give herself away.

Glenn was in agony. He had thought that he would wait

and follow all the plans he'd made for courting his wife. But each minute grew more torturous than the one just past. He couldn't sleep; even breathing normally was impossible when she lay just within his grasp. He hadn't meant to touch her, but once his hand lightly grazed her hip he couldn't stop his mind from venturing to rounder, softer curves and the memory of the way her breast had fit perfectly into the palm of his hand. Before he could stop, his fingers sought to explore her ripe body. Maggie remained completely still, waiting patiently for him to roll her onto her back and make love to her. When he didn't move and she suspected that he might not ease the painful longing throbbing within her, she rolled onto her back and linked her arms around his neck.

"Kiss me," she pleaded.

"Maggie." He ground out her name like a man possessed, and hungrily devoured her lips with deep, slow, hot kisses that drove him to the brink of insanity. Groaning, he buried his face in her hair and he drew deep gulps of oxygen into his parched lungs. Again he kissed her, tasting her willingness, reveling in her eagerness. Her hands rumpled the dark thickness of his hair while she repeated his name again and again. Hungry for the taste of him, Maggie urged his mouth to hers, but his devouring kiss only increased her aching need.

"I want you," he groaned, breathing in sharply.

"Yes," she murmured, kissing the hollow of his throat and arching against him.

"Oh, Glenn," Maggie groaned in a harsh whisper. "What took you so long?" The sensation was so blissfully exultant that she felt she could have died from it.

"Took me so long?" he repeated and groaned harshly. "You wanted me to make love to you?"

Looping her arms around his neck, Maggie strained upward and planted a long, hot kiss on his parted mouth. "How can any man be so blind?"

"Next time, hit me over the head." He arched forward then, and buried himself deep within her.

Maggie moaned. "I will. Oh, Glenn, I will," she cried. He took her quickly, unable to bear slow torture. Their bodies fused in a glorious union of heart with soul, of man with woman, of Maggie with Glenn. They strained together, giving, receiving until their hearts beat in a paired tempo that left them breathless, giddy and spent.

Glenn gathered her in his arms and rolled onto his side, taking her with him. Her head rested in the crook of his shoulder, their legs entwined as if reluctant to release the moment.

Maggie felt the pressure of his mouth on her hair and snuggled closer into his embrace, relishing the feel of his strong arms wrapped securely around her.

Brushing a wayward curl from her cheek, Glenn's hand lingered to lightly stroke the side of her face. Maggie smiled gently up at him, the contented smile of a satisfied woman.

"Do you think you'll be able to sleep now?" she teased.

Glenn chuckled, his warm breath fanning her forehead. "Did my tossing and turning keep you awake?"

"Not really.... I was only half-asleep." Maggie lowered her chin and covered her mouth in an attempt to stifle a yawn. "Good night, Mr. Lambert," she whispered, dragging out the words as she swallowed back another yawn.

"Mrs. Lambert," he murmured huskily, kissing the crown of her head.

Maggie's last thought before slipping into an easy slumber was that she wasn't ever going to allow another woman's ghost to come between them again. This man was her husband and she loved him…yes, loved him with a ferocity she was only beginning to understand. Together they were going to make this marriage work. One hundred Angies weren't going to stand in the way of their happiness. Maggie wouldn't allow it.

Within minutes Maggie was asleep. Still awake, Glenn propped up his head with one hand and took delight in peacefully watching the woman who had become everything to him in such a shockingly short amount of time. She was his friend, his lover, his wife, and he had the feeling he had only skimmed the surface of who and what Maggie would be in his life. His finger lightly traced the line of her cheek and the hollow of her throat. As impulsive as their marriage had been, there wasn't a second when Glenn regretted having pledged his life to Maggie. She was fresh and warm, a loving, free spirit. And he adored her. She had come to him with an ardor he had only dreamed of finding in a woman. She was stubborn, impulsive, headstrong: a rare and exquisite jewel. His jewel. His woman. His wife.

The low, melodious sound of a ballad slowly woke Maggie.

"Good morning, Sleeping Beauty," Glenn said as he sat on the edge of the mattress and kissed her lightly. He finished buttoning his shirt and flipped up the collar as he straightened the silk tie around his neck.

"You're dressed," she said, struggling to a sitting position and wiping the sleep from her eyes. She had wanted to get up with him, but must have missed the alarm.

"Would you like to undress me?"

Leaning against the down pillow, Maggie crossed her

arms and smiled beguilingly up at him. "What would you do if I said yes?"

Glenn's fingers quit working the silk tie. "Don't tempt me, Maggie, I'm running late already."

"I tempt you?" He'd never said anything more beautiful.

"If only you knew."

"I hope you'll show me." She wrapped her arms around her bent knees and leaned forward. "It...it was wonderful last night." She felt shy talking about their lovemaking, but it was imperative that he realize how much he pleased her.

"Yes it was," he whispered, taking her hand and kissing her knuckles. "I never expected anything so good between us."

"Me neither," she murmured and kissed his hand. "I wish you'd gotten me up earlier."

"Why?" He looked surprised.

Tossing back the covers, Maggie climbed out of bed and slipped into a matching black satin housecoat that she hadn't bothered to put on the night before—for obvious reasons. "I wanted to do the wifely thing and cook your breakfast."

"I haven't got time this morning." He paused, thinking he'd never seen any woman more beautiful. Her tousled hair fell to her shoulders, her face was free of any cosmetics, but no siren had ever been more alluring.

"Is there anything you'd like me to do while you're gone?" she offered. The day stretched before her and they hadn't made plans.

"Yes, in fact there are several things. I'll make a list." He reached for a pad and paper on his nightstand and spent the next few minutes giving her directions and instructions. "And don't plan dinner tonight," he added. "I phoned my parents yesterday and told them I had a surprise and to expect two for dinner."

Maggie sat on the bed beside him and unconsciously her shoulders slouched slightly. This was the very reason she'd come to Charleston, yet she was afraid. "Will they think we've gone crazy?"

"Probably," he returned with a short chuckle. "But they'll be delighted. Don't worry about it; they know you and have always liked you. Mom and Dad will be happy for us."

"I'm happy, Glenn." She wanted to reassure him that she had no regrets in this venture.

The smile faded from his dark eyes and his gaze held her immobile. "I am, too, for the first time since I can remember. We're going to make it, Maggie."

A grandfather clock in the den chimed the hour and reluctantly Glenn stood. "I've got to leave."

"Glenn." Maggie stopped him, then lowered her gaze, almost afraid of what she had to say. Waiting until the last minute to tell him wasn't the smartest thing to do.

"Yes?" he prompted.

"I'm… Listen, I think you should probably know that I'm not using any birth control."

His index finger lifted her chin so that her uncertain gaze met his. "That's fine. I want a family."

A sigh of relief washed through her and she beamed him a brilliant smile. "I probably should warn you, though, my mother claims the Kingsbury clan is a fertile one. We could be starting our family sooner than you expect."

"Don't worry about it; I'm not going to. When a baby comes, you can be assured of a warm welcome."

Maggie experienced an outpouring of love far too powerful to be voiced with simple words. Nodding demanded an incredible effort.

"I'll leave the car keys with you and I'll take public transportation. If you're in the neighborhood around noon stop into the office and I'll introduce you and take you to lunch."

"Maybe tomorrow," she said, stepping onto her tiptoes to kiss him goodbye. There was barely enough time to do everything she had to and be ready for dinner with his parents that evening.

A minute later Glenn was out the door. The condo seemed an empty shell without him. Maggie wandered into the kitchen with her list of errands, then poured a cup of coffee and carried it to the round table. She pulled out a chair and sat, drawing her legs under her. The first place she needed to stop was the bank to sign the forms that would add her name to the checking account. When she was there, Glenn had asked her to make a deposit for him.

She glanced at the front page of the paper he had left on the table and worked the crossword puzzle, then finished her coffee and dressed. The day held purpose. If she was going to see his parents it might not be a bad idea to find someplace where she could have her hair done.

With a jaunty step, Maggie found the deposit envelope Glenn had mentioned on the top of his desk. The room emanated his essence and she paused to drink it in. As she turned, Maggie caught a glimpse of a frame sticking above the rim of his wastepaper basket. What an unusual thing to do to a picture, she thought. As an artist, her sense of indignation rose until she lifted the frame from out of the basket and saw the multitude of small pictures with faces smiling back at her. Her breath came to an abrupt halt and the room crowded in on her, pressing at her with a strangling sensation. *So this was Angie.*

Seven

The first thought that came to Maggie was how beautiful Angie was. With thick, coffee-dark hair and intense brown eyes that seemed to mirror her soul, Angie had the ethereal look of a woman meant to be cherished, loved and protected. There was an inner glow, a delicate beauty to her that Maggie could never match. Angie was a woman meant to be loved and nurtured. It was little wonder that Glenn loved her. One glance at the woman who claimed his heart told Maggie that by comparison she was a poor second.

The frame contained a series of matted pictures that had obviously been taken over a period of several months. There was Angie on a sailboat, her windblown hair flying behind her as she smiled into the camera; Angie leaning over a barbecue, wearing an apron that said Kiss The Cook; Angie standing, surrounded by floral bouquets, in what looked like a flower shop, with her arms outstretched as though to signal this was hers. And more…so much more. Each picture revealed the rare beauty of the woman who claimed Glenn's heart.

A sickening knot tightened Maggie's stomach and she placed a hand on her abdomen and slowly released her breath. Although most of the photos were of Angie alone, two of them showed Glenn and Angie together. If recognizing the other woman's inner and outer beauty wasn't devastating enough, then the happiness radiating from Glenn was. Maggie had never seen him more animated. He seemed to glow with love. In all the years Maggie had known Glenn, she had never seen him look more content. He was at peace with his world, and so in love that it shone like a polished badge from every part of him. In comparison, the Glenn who had arrived in San Francisco was a sullen, doleful imitation.

Pushing the hair off her forehead, Maggie leaned against a filing cabinet and briefly closed her eyes. As early as the night before, she'd thought to banish Angie's ghost from their marriage. She had been a fool to believe it would be that easy. With a feeling of dread, she placed the frame back where she'd found it. Building a firm foundation for their marriage wasn't going to be easy, not nearly as easy as she'd thought. But then, nothing worthwhile ever was. Maggie loved her husband. Physically, he wanted her and for now that would suffice. Someday Glenn would look at her with the same glow of happiness that Angie evoked. Someday his love for her would be there for all the world to witness. Someday...

Glancing at her wristwatch, Maggie hurried from the bathroom into the bedroom. In a few hours she and Glenn were having dinner with his parents, Charlotte and Mel, people she'd known and liked all her life. Family friends, former neighbors, good people. Yet Maggie had never been less sure of herself. Already she had changed outfits twice. This one would have to do, she decided. There wasn't time to change her mind again. As she put the finishing touches on her makeup, Maggie muttered disparaging remarks over the sprinkling of freckles across the bridge of her nose; wanted to know why her lashes couldn't be longer and her mouth fuller. Mentally she had reviewed her body: her breasts looked like cantaloupes, her hips like a barge; her legs were too short, her arms too long. Maggie could see every imperfection. Finally she had been forced to admit that no amount of cosmetics was going to make her as lovely as Angie. She had to stop thinking of Charlotte and Mel as the mother-and father-in-law who would compare her to their son's first choice. She had to force herself to remember them instead as the friends she knew they were.

Perhaps if she'd had more time to prepare mentally for this dinner, she thought defensively. As it was, the list of errands had taken most of the day and Maggie had been grateful to have something to occupy her time and her mind. Instead of concentrating on being bright and witty for her meeting with Glenn's parents, her thoughts had returned again and again to the discarded series of photographs. If she had found those photos, she reasoned, then there were probably other pictures around. The realization that Angie could be a silent occupant of the condominium was an intolerable conjecture.

When Glenn had walked in the door that afternoon and kissed her, Maggie had toyed with the idea of confronting him with the pictures. Sanity had returned in the nick of time. He had obviously intended to throw them away, but surely must have realized that she would stumble upon them. Maybe it was cowardly of her, but Maggie had decided to ignore the fact that the pictures were in the other room, and pretended she hadn't seen them. For the first time since their marriage, things were going right and she didn't want to ruin that.

"Maggie, are you ready?" Glenn sauntered into the bedroom and hesitated when he saw her. "I thought you were wearing a blue dress."

"I...was," she answered slowly, turning and squaring her shoulders. "Do I look all right?"

"You're lovely." He placed a hand on each of her shoulders. "Maggie, I wish you'd stop worrying. Mom and Dad are going to be thrilled for us."

"I know." Absently she brushed her hand across the skirt of her black-and-red-print dress and slowly released her breath. "I've always been Muffie to them and I'm... I'm not sure they'll be able to accept me as your wife."

Glenn's chuckle echoed through the bedroom. "Maggie, how can they not accept you? You're my wife. Mother's been after me for years to marry and settle down. She'll be grateful I finally took the plunge."

"That's encouraging," she mumbled sarcastically. "So you were desperate to placate your mother and decided I'd do nicely as a wife. Is that supposed to reassure me?"

The muscles of his face tightened and a frown marred his wide brow as he dropped his hands to his side. "That's not true and you know it."

Ashamed, Maggie lowered her head and nodded. "I'm sorry, I didn't mean that. My stomach feels like a thousand bumblebees have set up camp. Even my hands are clammy." She held them out, palms up, for him to inspect. "Wait until we visit my parents, then you'll know how I feel."

Slipping an arm around her waist, Glenn led her into the living room. "If you're worried, stick to my side and I'll answer all the questions."

"I had no intention of leaving your side," she returned, slightly miffed.

A faint smile touched his mouth.

The ride to Glenn's parents' did little to settle her nerves. Maggie thought she would be glad when this evening was over. When Glenn turned off the main road and into a narrow street lined with family homes, Maggie tensed. Two blocks later he slowed and turned into a cement driveway.

Before Maggie was out of the car the front door opened and Mel and Charlotte Lambert were standing on the wide porch. Maggie was surprised by how little they'd changed. Glenn's father's hair was completely gray now and his hairline had receded, but he stood proud and broad shouldered just as Maggie remembered him. Glenn's mother was a little rounder, and wearing a dress. As a child, Maggie knew she was always welcome at the Lamberts' kitchen. Charlotte had claimed it was a pleasure having another woman around since she lived with a house full of men. Maggie had dropped over regularly when Dale, the youngest Lambert, was born. She had been at the age to appreciate babies and had loved to help feed and bathe him.

"Muffie!" Charlotte exclaimed, her bright eyes shining with genuine pleasure. "What a pleasant surprise. I had no idea you were in town."

Glenn joined Maggie and draped his arm around her shoulders as he boldly met his parents' gaze. To be honest, he had been dreading this confrontation himself. His parents would be pleased for him and Maggie, and do their best to hide their shock. But his father was bound to say something about Angie when they had a private moment. He might even suspect that Glenn had married on the rebound. He hadn't. Glenn tried not to think of Angie and ignored the nip of emotional pain associated with her name. His parents had loved her and encouraged him to marry her. Their disappointment had been keen when he told them she'd married Simon.

"Are you visiting from California?" Charlotte asked with a faint tinge of longing. "I do miss that old neighborhood. If we had a hundred years, we'd never find any better place to raise our family." Taking Maggie by the elbow, she led her into the house. "What's the matter with us, standing on the porch and talking when there's plenty of comfortable chairs inside."

Maggie tossed a pleading glance over her shoulder to Glenn, hoping he wouldn't leave the explaining to her.

The screen door closed with a bang as they entered the house. The small living room managed to hold a recliner, a sofa and an overstuffed chair and ottoman. In addition, a rocking chair sat in one corner. The fireplace mantel was lined with pictures of the three sons and the grandchildren.

"Mom, Dad," Glenn began, his expression sober as he met their curious faces. His arm slipped around Maggie as he stood stiffly at her side. He didn't know any better way to say it than right out. "Maggie is my wife. We've been married nearly two weeks."

"Married? Two weeks?" Charlotte echoed in a stunned whisper.

Mel Lambert recovered quickly and reached across the room to pump Glenn's hand. "Congratulations, son." Cupping Maggie's shoulders he gently kissed her cheek. "Welcome to the family, Muffie."

"Thank you." Her voice was both weak and weary. This was worse than she'd thought. Glenn's mother stood with a hand pressed over her heart and an absurd look of shock written across her face, which she was trying desperately to disguise.

"You two...are married," Charlotte whispered, apparently having recovered. "This is wonderful news. Mel, you open that bottle of wine we've been saving all these years and I'll get the goblets." Within seconds they had both disappeared.

Glenn took Maggie's hand and led her to the sofa where they both sat. "See, I told you it wouldn't be so bad." His hand squeezed hers and his eyes smiled confidently into hers. He smoothed a strand of hair from her temple with his forefinger in a light caress.

"How can you say that?" she hissed under her breath. "Your mother nearly fainted." To further her unease she could hear hushed whispers coming from the kitchen. The barely audible word "rebound" heightened the embarrassed flush in Maggie's red cheeks. She pretended not to hear, as did Glenn.

Glenn's handsome face broke into a scowl. It was a mistake not to have said something to his parents earlier. His better judgment had prompted him to tell them. But he had made such an issue of the necessity of Maggie and him confronting them together that he couldn't very well change plans. Informing his parents of their marriage had been what it took to get Maggie to join him in Charleston, and he would never regret that.

Mel and Charlotte reappeared simultaneously. Charlotte carried four shining crystal goblets on a silver tray and Mel had a wine bottle and corkscrew in one hand.

"Before leaving California," Mel explained as he pulled open the corkscrew, "Charlotte and I took a drive through the Napa Valley and bought some of the finest wines available. That was thirteen years ago now and we only open those bottles on the most special occasions."

"Let me see, the last time we opened our California

wine was..." Charlotte paused and a network of fine lines knitted her face as she concentrated.

Glenn tensed and his hand squeezed Maggie's so tightly that she almost yelped at the unexpected pain. Gradually he relaxed his punishing grip, and Maggie realized that the last special occasion in the Lambert family had been shared with Angie and Glenn.

"Wasn't it when Erica was born?" Mel inserted hastily.

"No, no," Charlotte dismissed the suggestion with an impatient wave of her hand. "It was more recent than that... I think it was..." Flustered, she swallowed and reached for a wineglass to hide her discomfort. "I do believe you're right, dear, it was when Erica was born. It just seems more recent is all."

The tension left Glenn, and even Maggie breathed easier. Mel finished opening the bottle and nimbly filled the four goblets. Handing Maggie and Glenn their wineglasses, he proposed a toast. "To many years of genuine wedded happiness."

"Many years," Charlotte echoed.

Later Maggie helped Charlotte set the table, carrying out the serving dishes while Glenn and his father chatted companionably in the living room. At dinner, the announcement that Glenn would be moving to San Francisco was met with a strained moment of disappointment.

"We'll miss you, son," was all that was said.

Unreasonably, Maggie experienced a flood of guilt. It hadn't been her idea to leave Charleston. She would make her home wherever Glenn wished, but apparently he wanted out of South Carolina.

"We'll visit often," Glenn assured his parents and catching Maggie's eye, he winked. "Especially after the children come."

Mel and Charlotte exchanged meaningful glances, making Maggie want to jump up and assure them she wasn't pregnant...at least she didn't think so.

The meal was saved only because everyone felt the need to chat and cover the disconcerting silence. Maggie did her share, catching the Lamberts up on what had been happening with her parents and skimming over Denny's misfortunes, giving them only a brief outline of his life. In return, Charlotte proudly spoke of each of her three grandchildren, and while they cleared the table the older woman proudly brought out snapshots of the grandkids. Maggie examined each small smiling face, realizing for the first time that these little ones were now her nieces and nephew.

While Maggie wiped off the table, Charlotte ran sudsy water into the kitchen sink. "There was a time that I despaired of having a daughter," Charlotte began awkwardly.

"I remember," Maggie responded, recalling all the afternoons she had sat with Mrs. Lambert.

"And now I have three daughters. Each one of my sons have married well. I couldn't be more pleased with the daughters they've given me."

Maggie's hand pushed the rag with unnecessary vigor across the tabletop. "Thank you. I realize our marriage must come as a shock to you, but I want you to know, Mrs. Lambert, I love Glenn and I plan to be a good wife to him."

The dark eyes softened perceptively. "I can see that, Muffie. No woman can look at a man the way you look at Glenn and not love him." Hesitantly, she wiped her wet hands on her apron and turned toward Maggie. Her gaze drifted into the living room and she frowned slightly. "Are you free for lunch tomorrow? I think we should talk."

"Yes, I'd enjoy that."

Maggie didn't tell Glenn of her luncheon arrangement

with his mother until the following morning. She woke with him and put on the coffee while he showered. When he joined her in the kitchen, Maggie had fried bacon and eggs, which was about the limit of her breakfast skills. Learning to cook was something she planned to do soon. Rosa, her housekeeper at the beach house, would gladly teach her. Thoughts of California brought back a mental image of her brother, and Maggie sighed expressively. "I'll need the car again today; do you mind?" Maggie asked Glenn, turning her thoughts from the unhappy subject of Denny.

Glenn glanced up from the morning paper. "Do you want to do some shopping?"

"No... I'm meeting your mother for lunch." With a forced air of calm she scooted out the chair across from him. Her hands cupped the coffee mug, absorbing its warmth. She was worried about letting Glenn know she was meeting his mother. "You don't mind, do you... I mean, about me using the car?"

"No." He pushed his half-eaten breakfast aside, darting a concerned look toward Maggie. "I don't mind." Great! he thought vehemently. He could only imagine what his mother was going to tell Maggie. If Maggie heard the details of his relationship with Angie, he'd prefer that they came from him, not his mother.

"Good." Despite his aloofness, Maggie had the impression that he wasn't altogether pleased. He didn't have to be—she was going and she sensed they both knew what would be the main subject of the luncheon conversation.

"Would you like to meet me at the health club afterward?" Glenn asked, but his attention didn't waver from the newspaper. "I try to work out two, sometimes three times a week."

It pleased Maggie that he was including her. "Sure, but let me warn you I'm terrible at handball, average at tennis and a killer on the basketball court."

"I'll reserve a tennis court," Glenn informed her, a smile curling up one side of his mouth. "And don't bother about dinner tonight. We'll eat at the club."

The morning passed quickly. Since she was meeting Glenn later, Maggie dressed casually in white linen slacks and a pink silk blouse, checking her appearance several times. All morning, Maggie avoided going near Glenn's den. She wouldn't torment herself by looking at the pictures again; stumbling upon them once had been more than enough. For all she knew, Glenn could have tossed them out with the garbage, but Maggie hadn't the courage to look, fearing that he hadn't.

Allowing herself extra time in case she got lost, Maggie left early for her luncheon date with Charlotte. She had some difficulty finding the elder Lamberts' home, and regretted not having paid closer attention to the route Glenn had taken the night before. As it turned out, when she pulled into the driveway it was precisely noon, their agreed time.

Charlotte met her at the door and briefly hugged her. "I got to thinking later that I should have met you someplace. You hardly know your way around yet."

"It wasn't any problem," Maggie fibbed, following the older woman into the kitchen. A quiche was cooling on the countertop, filling the room with the delicious smell of egg, cheese and spices.

"Sit down and I'll get you a cup of coffee."

Maggie did as requested, not knowing how to say that she didn't want to be thought of as company. Charlotte took the chair beside her. "The reason I asked you here today is to apologize for the way I behaved last night."

"No, please." Maggie's hand rested on her mother-in-law's forearm. "I understand. Our news must have come as a shock. Glenn and I were wrong not to have told you earlier."

"Yes, I'll admit that keeping it a secret for nearly two weeks was as much of a surprise as the deed." She lifted the delicate china cup to her mouth and took a sip. Glenn had always been close to his family; for him to have married without letting them know immediately was completely out of character. For that matter, their rushed marriage wasn't his style either. Maggie didn't need to be reminded that Glenn was a thorough person who weighed each decision, studied each circumstance. It was one reason he was such an excellent stockbroker.

"You have to understand," Maggie said, wanting to defend him. "We were as surprised as anyone. Glenn arrived for Steve and Janelle's wedding and everything seemed so right between us that we flew to Reno that night."

"The night of the wedding?" Charlotte did a poor job of hiding her astonishment. "Why, he'd only arrived in San Francisco…"

"Less than twenty-four hours before the wedding." Maggie confirmed her mother-in-law's observation. "And we hadn't seen each other in twelve—thirteen years. It sounds impulsive and foolish, doesn't it?" Maggie wouldn't minimize the circumstances surrounding their marriage.

"Not that… Glenn's never done anything impulsive in his life. He knew exactly what he was doing when he married you, Maggie. Don't ever doubt that."

"I don't. But I know that Glenn was engaged to someone else recently and that he loved her a great deal."

Obviously flustered, Charlotte shook her head, her face reddening. "You don't need to worry any about her."

"I have, though," Maggie confirmed, being frank and honest. "Glenn hasn't told me much."

"He will in time," Charlotte said confidently. The older woman's brow was furrowed with unasked questions, and Maggie nearly laughed aloud at how crazy the situation must sound to someone else. Glenn and Maggie had grown up fighting like brother and sister, had moved apart for more than a decade and on the basis of a few hours' they'd decided to get married.

"I think I always knew there was something special between you and Glenn. He wasn't too concerned about girls during high school. Sports and his grades took up the majority of his energy. But he was at ease with you. If there was something troubling him, it wasn't me or his father he discussed it with; instead he talked it over with you. I suppose a few people will be surprised at this sudden marriage, but don't let that bother you. The two of you are perfect together."

"I won't." Maggie swallowed, the words nervously tripping over her tongue. "Neither of us came into this marriage the way normal couples do, but we're both determined to make it work. I'd been hurt, perhaps not as deeply as Glenn, but for the past few years I've been lonely and miserable. Glenn's still…hurting, but I've staked our future together on the conviction that time will heal those wounds."

"I'm pleased he told you about Angie." The look of relief relaxed Charlotte's strong face.

"Only a little. He loved her very much, didn't he?" Just saying the words hurt, but she successfully disguised a grimace.

"I won't deny it. Glenn did love her," Charlotte answered, then added to qualify her statement, "More than she deserved."

Maggie had guessed as much already. When Glenn committed himself to someone or something there would never be any doubts. He had loved her, but by his own words, he had no intention of pining away the rest of his life because she married another man. With their wedding vows, Glenn had pledged himself to Maggie. At moments like these and the one yesterday when she discovered the photos, this knowledge of his determination was the only thing that kept her from drowning in frustration.

"I think I always knew that Angie wasn't the right woman for Glenn. Something in my mother's heart told me things were wrong for them. However, it wasn't my place to intrude in his life. He seemed to love her so much."

This time Maggie was unable to hide the pain of Charlotte's words. She felt the blood drain from her face and lowered her eyes, not wanting her mother-in-law to know how tender her heart was.

"Oh dear, I've said the wrong thing again. Forgive me." Shaking her head as if silently scolding herself, Mrs. Lambert added, "That came out all wrong. He was happy, yes, but that happiness wouldn't have lasted and I suspect that even Glenn knew that." Charlotte stood and brought the quiche to the table along with two place settings.

"No, please continue," Maggie urged, needing to know everything about the situation she had married into.

Seeming to understand Maggie's curiosity, Charlotte rejoined her at the kitchen table. "Glenn cared enough for Angie to wait a year for her to decide she'd marry him. I've never seen Glenn so happy as the night she agreed to be his wife. We'd met Angie, of course, several times.

She has the roundest, darkest eyes I've ever seen. She's an intense girl, quiet, a little withdrawn, exceptionally loyal, and although she's hurt Glenn terribly, I'm afraid I can't be angry with her. Ultimately she made the right decision. It would have been wrong for her to have married Glenn when she was in love with another man."

The irony of the situation was more than Maggie could stand. It was wrong for Angie to have married Glenn in those circumstances, yet he had done exactly that when he married her. Apparently, Charlotte didn't see it that way. For that matter, Maggie was convinced that had she known beforehand, she probably would have married him anyway.

"And she never did take the ring," Charlotte finished.

"The ring?"

"My mother's," the older woman explained. "She willed it to me as part of my inheritance, and when Glenn graduated from college I opted to make it his. It's a lovely thing, antique with several small diamonds, but of course, you've seen it."

Maggie thrust an expectant look at her mother-in-law. "No… I haven't. Glenn's never mentioned any ring."

Charlotte dismissed the information with a light shrug. "I wouldn't worry about it, you'll receive it soon enough. As I recall, Glenn had it sized and cleaned when he and Angie decided…" Realizing her mistake, Charlotte lowered her gaze and fidgeted with her coffee cup. "He's probably having it resized and is keeping it as a surprise for Christmas. As it is I've probably ruined that. I apologize, Maggie."

The racket slammed against the tennis ball with a vengeance and Maggie returned it to Glenn's side of the court with astonishing accuracy. So he had his grandmother's antique ring that was to go to his wife. She was his wife. Where exactly was the ring? *Slam.* She returned the tennis ball a second time, stretching as far as she could reach to make the volley. Not expecting her return, Glenn lost the point.

Maggie's serve. She aced the first shot, making his return impossible. Fueled by her anger, she had never played a better match. The first two games were hers, and Glenn's jaw sagged open as he went into mild shock. He rallied in the third, and their fourth and fifth games were heated contests.

"I don't recall you ever being this good," he shouted from the other side of the court.

She tossed the ball into the air, and fully extending her body, wielded the racket forward, bending her upper torso in half.

"There are a lot of things you don't know about me, Lambert," she shouted back, dashing to the far end of the court to return the volley. She felt like a pogo stick hopping from one end of the clay surface to the other with a quickness she didn't know she possessed. At the end of the first set, Maggie was so exhausted that she was shaking. Good grief, she thought, she had a tennis court at the beach house that she never used. This match was a misrepresentation of her skill.

Wiping the perspiration from her face with a thick white towel, Maggie sagged onto the bench. Glenn joined her, taking a seat beside her. "You should have told me you were this good. I've never had to work this hard to win."

Her breath came in deep gasps. "That was quite a workout." She hoped he didn't suggest another one soon. A repeat performance of this magnitude was unlikely. The match had helped her vent her frustrations over the issue of his grandmother's ring—her normal game was far less aggressive.

Taking his mother's words at face value, Maggie decided the best thing she could do was patiently wait. Glenn had originally intended the ring would go to Angie, but he'd married Maggie. When he felt comfortable with the idea he'd present her with the ring, not before. Christmas was less than seven weeks away, and Charlotte was probably right. He'd give it to her then.

Maybe.

Regaining his breath, Glenn leaned forward and placed his elbows on his knees. "What did you and my mother have to talk about?" The question wasn't an idle one. His brows were drawn into a single tense line. All afternoon he had worried about that luncheon date. Maggie had a right to know everything, but he didn't want the information coming from his mother. If anyone was going to tell her, it would come best from him. He had thought to call and talk to his mother, and discreetly explain as much, but the morning had been hectic and by the time he was out of the board meeting, it had been too late.

Wickedly, Maggie fluttered her thick, dark lashes. "I imagine you'd love to know what tales she carried, but I'm not breaking any confidences."

"Did she give you her recipe for my favorite dinner?"

"What makes you think we discussed you?" Maggie tilted her flushed face to one side and grinned up at him, her smile growing broader.

"It only seems natural that the two women in my life would talk of little else." He placed his arm around her shoulder and helped her stand, carrying her tennis racket for her.

Maggie placed her arm around his waist, pleased with

the way he linked her with his mother. "If your favorite meal is beef Stroganoff, then you're in luck."

"The luckiest day of my life was when you agreed to be my wife," Glenn murmured as he looked down on her with a haunting look so intense that Maggie's heart throbbed painfully. Her visit with his mother hadn't been easy for him, she realized. He had probably spent the entire day worrying about what she'd say afterwards.

Her voice grew husky with emotion. "What an amazing coincidence, that's my favorite day, too."

The longing in his eyes grew all the more poignant as Glenn weighed her words. If they'd been anyplace else, Maggie was convinced he would have tossed their tennis rackets aside and pulled her into his arms.

"Come on," she chided lovingly. "If you're going to beat me when I've played the best game of my life, then the least you can do is feed me."

Laughing, Glenn kissed the top of her head and led her toward the changing room and then to the restaurant.

His good mood continued when they reached the condominium. Maggie was bushed, and although she had taken a quick shower at Glenn's club, she couldn't resist a leisurely soak in a hot tub to soothe the aching cries of unused muscles. This day had been their best yet. The tension eased from her sore muscles and her heart. The matter with the ring no longer bothered her. When Glenn decided to give it to her, she'd know that it came from his heart and she need never doubt again.

With her hair pinned up, and a terry-cloth bathrobe wrapped around her, Maggie walked into the living room, looking for her husband.

"Glenn."

"In here." His voice came from the den.

Remembering the photographs inside, Maggie paused in the doorway. Tension shot through her, although she struggled to appear outwardly composed. With monumental effort she kept her gaze from the large garbage can beside his desk.

"What are you doing?" She was exhausted and it was late. She'd have thought that after a workout on the courts he'd be ready for bed.

"I've got a few odds and ends to finish up here. I'll only be a few minutes," he answered without looking up, scribbling across the top of a computer sheet. When he did glance up he was surprised to find Maggie standing in the doorway as if she were afraid to come into the room. "I'd appreciate a cup of coffee."

Maggie shrugged. "Sure."

"Maggie." Glenn stopped her. "Is anything wrong?"

"Wrong?" she echoed. "What could possibly be wrong?" *Just that I'm such a coward I can't bear to look and see if those snapshots are still there,* she chastised herself, turning toward the kitchen.

"I don't know." Glenn's puzzled voice followed her.

The coffee only took a minute to make. Maggie stood in the kitchen, waiting for the liquid to drain into the cup and told herself she was behaving like an idiot.

She pasted a smile on her lips as she carried the mug into his den and set it on the edge of the desk. "Here you go."

"Thanks," Glenn murmured, busily working.

Maggie straightened and took a step backward. As she did, her gaze fell to the empty garbage can. Relief washed over her. He had gotten rid of them. She wanted to dance around the room and sing.

"Glenn." She moved behind his chair and slid her arms around his neck.

"Hmm…"

"How late did you say you'd be?" She dipped her head and nuzzled the side of his neck, darting her tongue in and out of his ear.

Glenn could feel the hot blood stirring within him. "Not long, why?"

"Why?" she shot back, giggling. "You need me to tell you why?"

Scooting the chair around, Glenn gripped her by the waist and pulled her into his lap. A brilliant smile came over her as she slid her arms around his neck.

Glenn's mouth twisted wryly as he studied her. He didn't know what had gotten into Maggie today. First she had surprised him on the tennis court. Then she had behaved like a shy virgin outside his door, looking in as if his office was a den of iniquity. And now she was a bewitching temptress who came to him with eyes that were filled with passion. Not that he was complaining, he'd never get enough of this woman.

Maggie's fingers fumbled with the buttons of his shirt so that she had the freedom to run her hands over his chest. She reveled in simply touching him, and pulled the shirt free of his shoulders. His muscles rippled as she slowly slid her hands upward to either side of his neck. Unhurried, she branded him with a kiss so hot it stole his breath.

"Maggie," he whispered hoarsely, intimately sliding his hands between her legs and stroking her bare thigh. "Maybe I haven't got so much paperwork to do after all."

Smiling dreamily, Maggie directed his mouth back to hers. "Good."

Eight

Two weeks passed and Maggie grew more at ease with her marriage. She realized that a silent observer to their world would have assumed that they had been married for several years. Externally, there was nothing to show that their marriage wasn't the product of a long, satisfying courtship. It didn't seem to matter that Glenn hadn't declared his love. He respected her, enjoyed her wit, encouraged her talent. They were happy…and it showed.

Maggie greeted each day with enthusiasm, eager to discover what lay in store for her. She purchased several cookbooks and experimented, putting her creativity to work in the kitchen. Glenn praised her efforts and accepted her failures, often helping her laugh when it would have been easy to lose patience. In the early afternoons, if there was time, Maggie explored Charleston with Glenn's mother and came to appreciate anew what a wonderful woman Charlotte Lambert was. They never spoke of Angie again.

South Carolina was everything Maggie had known it would be, and more than she'd ever expected. She was thrilled by the eighteenth- and nineteenth-century paintings that displayed regional history in the Gibbes Art Gallery and explored the Calhoun Mansion and the Confederate Museum, examining for the first time the Civil War from the Confederate point of view. One hundred and fifty years after the last battles of the war had been waged, Maggie felt the anguish of the South and tasted its defeat.

Her fingers longed to hold a paintbrush, but she satisfied her urgings with a pen and pad, sketching the ideas that came to her. Charlotte was amazed at her daughter-in-law's talent, and Maggie often gave Glenn's mother her pencil sketches. At Sunday dinner with his family, Maggie was embarrassed to find those careless drawings framed and hanging on the living room wall. Proudly, Glenn's eyes had met hers. They didn't often speak of her art, and Maggie basked in the warm glow of his approval.

For his part, Glenn was happy, happier than he ever imagined he'd be. In the afternoons he rushed home from the office, knowing Maggie would be there waiting for him. Maybe he hadn't married her for the right reasons, maybe what they had done was half-crazy, but, he thought tenderly, he wouldn't have it any different now, and he thanked God every single day that he'd acted on the impulse. Maggie gave his life purpose. In the afternoons she would be there waiting. And the minute he walked in the door, she'd smile. Not an ordinary smile, but a soft feminine one that lit up her dark eyes and curved the edges of her mouth in a sultry way that sent hot need coursing through him. In his lifetime, Glenn never hoped to see another woman smile the way Maggie did. Often he barely made it inside the door before he knew he had to kiss her. He would have preferred to react casually to his desire for her, but discovered that was impossible. Some days he couldn't get home fast enough, using every ounce of self-control he possessed not to burst in the door, wrap his arms around her and carry her into their bedroom. He couldn't touch, or taste, or hold her enough. Glenn felt he'd choose death rather than a life without her. Angie might have possessed his heart, but Maggie had laid claim to his soul.

He wondered sometimes if she had even an inkling of what she did to him physically. He doubted it. If she wasn't pregnant soon, he mused, it would be a miracle. The thought of Maggie heavy with his child, her breasts swollen, her stomach protruding, produced such a shocking desire within him that it was almost painful. The feeling left him weak with wonder and pride. They'd have exceptionally beautiful children.

For the first time, Glenn understood his brothers' pride in and awe of their children. At thirty, Glenn hadn't given much thought to a family. Someday, he had always thought, he'd want children, but he hadn't put faces or names to those who would fill his life. With Maggie he envisioned a tall son and a beautiful daughter. Every man wanted an heir, and now he yearned for a son until some nights he couldn't sleep thinking about the children Maggie would give him. On those evenings, late, when his world was at peace, Glenn would press his hand over her satiny smooth stomach, praying her body was nurturing his seed. A child would cement Maggie and him so firmly together that only death would ever separate them.

Their evenings were filled with contentment. Only rarely did he bring work home, lingering instead in front of the television, using that as an excuse to have Maggie at his side, to watch her. If he did need to deal with some paperwork, she sat quietly in his den, curled up in a chair reading. It was as though they couldn't be separated any longer than necessary and every moment apart was painful.

Maggie enjoyed watching Glenn in his home office more than any other place. He sat with simple authority at his desk while she pretended absorption in a novel, when actually she was studying him. Now and then he would look up and they'd exchange warm, lingering glances that left her wondering how long it would be until they could go to bed.

When they did head toward the bedroom, it was ridiculously early. The instant the light went off Glenn reached for her with such passion that she wondered if he would ever get his fill of her—then promptly prayed he wouldn't. Their nights became a celebration for all the words stored in their hearts that had yet to be spoken. Never shy nor embarrassed, Maggie came to him without reserve, holding nothing back. She was his temptress and mistress. Bewitching and bewitched. Seduced and seducer.

Maggie had assumed that the fiery storm of physical satisfaction their bodies gave each other would fade with time, not increase. But as the days passed, she was pleased that Glenn's constant need equaled her desire for him. Each time they made love, Maggie would lie in his arms thinking that their appetite for each other would surely diminish, and knew immediately that it wouldn't.

In the mornings when she woke to the clock radio, Maggie was securely wrapped in Glenn's arms. He held her close and so tight she wondered how she had managed to sleep. Some mornings Maggie felt the tension leave Glenn as he emerged from the last dregs of slumber and realized she remained with him. It was as though he feared she would be gone. Once assured she was at his side, Glenn would relax. As far as Maggie could tell, this insecurity was the only part of his relationship with Angie that continued to haunt him. One hundred times each day, in everything she did, every place she went, Maggie set out to prove she would never willingly leave him.

Life fell into a comfortable pattern and the third full week after Maggie arrived in Charleston, the condominium sold. Maggie met Glenn at the door with the news.

"The Realtor was by with an offer," she said, draping her arms around his neck and pressing her body to his.

Glenn held her hips and placed his large hands on her hips, as he kissed her. "As far as I can see we should be able to make the move within a week, two at the most," he commented a few minutes later, as he curled an arm around her shoulder and deposited his briefcase in the den.

"A week?" Now that she was here, Maggie would have welcomed the opportunity to settle in South Carolina. California, Denny, the beach house seemed a million miles away, light-years from the life she shared with Glenn here.

"You sound like you don't want to move." He leaned against the edge of his desk, crossing his long legs at the ankles.

"South Carolina is lovely."

"So is California," Glenn countered. "You don't mind the change, do you?"

In some ways she did. Their time in Charleston was like a romantic interlude—the honeymoon they'd never gotten. They were protected from the outside world. No one knew who Maggie was, or cared. For the first time in several years she was a regular person and she loved it. In Charleston she had blossomed into a woman who boldly met a passerby's glance. She explored the art galleries without fear that someone would recognize her. No one came to her with "get rich quick" schemes, seeking naive investors. No one rushed to wait on her or gain her attention or her gratitude. However, Maggie was wise enough to know that those things would follow in time.

"No," she told Glenn soberly. "I don't mind the move."

He turned, sorting through the stack of mail she had set on the desktop, smiling wryly. Maggie wanted to stay in Charleston for the same reasons he wanted to move to San Francisco. They were each looking for an escape to problems they would need to face sooner or later. For his part, Glenn chose the West Coast more for nostalgia than any need to escape. San Francisco felt right and Charleston held too many painful memories.

"Will you want to live at the beach house?" Maggie's one concern was that Glenn might not like her home. Her own feelings toward the house were ambivalent. On some days, it was her sanctuary and on others, her prison. She liked the house; she was comfortable there, but she didn't know that Glenn would be.

"Sure. Is there any reason you'd want to move?"

"No, it's just that…" The telephone rang and Maggie paused as Glenn lifted the receiver.

After a moment he handed it to her. "It's for you."

"Me?" She felt her heart rate accelerate. She'd given specific instructions that she wasn't to be contacted except for her brother. And Denny would only call if he was in financial trouble.

"Hello." Her voice was wispy with apprehension.

"Who was that?"

"Denny, are you all right?"

"I asked you a question first. It's not often I call my sister and a man answers the phone. Something's going on. Who is it, Maggie?"

"I'm with Glenn Lambert."

A low chuckle followed, but Maggie couldn't tell if her brother was pleased or abashed. "So you and Glenn are together. Be careful, Maggie, I don't want to see you hurt again." He hesitated, as though he didn't want to continue. "Are you living with him?"

"Denny," Maggie had been foolish not to have told her family sooner, "Glenn and I are married."

"Married," he echoed in shock. "When did this happen?"

"Several weeks ago."

A short, stunned silence followed. "That's sudden, isn't it? Linda and I would have liked to have attended the wedding."

"We eloped."

"That's not like you."

"It wasn't like either of us. I'm happy, Denny, really happy. You know what it's been like the past few years. Now don't worry about me. I'm a big girl. I know what I'm doing."

"I just don't want to see you get hurt."

"I won't," she assured him.

"Do Mom and Dad know?"

Denny had her there. "Not yet. We're planning to tell them once we're back in San Francisco."

"And when will that be?" His words were slow as if he were still thinking.

"A couple of weeks."

He didn't respond and the silence seemed to pound over the great echoing canyon of the telephone wire. Denny hadn't done a good job of disguising his reservations. Once he saw how good this marriage was for her, she was sure, he'd share her happiness. Her brother had been her anchor when she broke up with Dirk. He had seen firsthand the effects of one painful relationship and sought to protect her from another. Only Glenn wasn't Dirk, and when they arrived back in San Francisco Denny would see that.

"Is there a reason you phoned, Denny?"

"Oh, yeah." His voice softened. "Listen, I hate to trouble you but there's been some minor complications and the lawyer has to charge me extra fees. Also, Linda's been sick and the kids aren't feeling that well, either...."

"How much do you need?"

"I hate having to come to my sister like a pauper. But I swear as soon as everything's straightened out I'll repay every penny."

"Denny, don't worry about it. You're my brother, I'm happy to give you whatever you need. You know that." She couldn't refuse her own brother no matter what the reason.

"I know and appreciate it, Sis. I really do."

"You wouldn't ask if it wasn't necessary." She had hoped to make this difficult time in Denny's life smoother but sometimes wondered if she contributed more to the problem. Yet she couldn't say no. "I'll have Shirley write you a check."

Once he had gotten what he wanted the conversation ended quickly. Maggie replaced the receiver and forced a smile to her lips. "That was my brother," she announced, turning back to Glenn.

"Who's Shirley?" he asked starkly.

"My money manager." She lowered her gaze to the lush carpet, feeling her husband's censure. Glenn didn't understand the circumstances that had led to Denny's problems. They had both received a large inheritance. Maggie had received half of her great-aunt's fortune; her parents and Denny had split the other half. Everything had gone smoothly until Denny had invested in a business that had quickly gone defunct. Now his money—or what was left of it—was tied up in litigation.

"Does Denny need her name often?"

"Not really," she lied. "He's been having some cash flow problems lately." As in not having any, her mind added. "We were talking about the move to California when the phone buzzed, weren't we?"

"You don't want to discuss Denny, is that it?"

"That's it." Glenn couldn't tell her anything she didn't already know. She was in a no-win situation with her brother. She couldn't abandon him, nor could she continue to feed his dependence on her.

"Okay, if that's the way you want it." His eyes and voice silently accused her as he turned back and sorted through the mail.

"California will be good for us," Maggie said, hoping to lighten the atmosphere.

"Yes, it will," Glenn agreed almost absently, without looking up. "Before I forget, the office is having a farewell party for me Friday night. We don't have any plans, do we?"

Maggie had met Glenn's staff and seen for herself the respect his management had earned him. One afternoon when she had met him for lunch, Maggie had witnessed anew the quiet authority in his voice as he spoke to his associates. He was decisive and sure, calm and reassuring, and the office had thrived under his care. It went without saying that he was a popular manager and would be sorely missed.

Friday night Maggie dressed carefully, choosing a flattering cream-colored creation and pale blue designer nylons. She had never been one to enjoy parties, especially when they involved people she barely knew. This one shouldn't be so bad though, she reasoned. The focus would be on Glenn, not her.

"Am I underdressed?" she asked him, slowly rotating for his inspection. Not having attended this kind of function previously put her at a disadvantage. She didn't know how the other wives would dress and had chosen something conservative.

Glenn stood, straightening his dark blue silk tie. His warm chuckle filled their bedroom as he examined his wife. "As far as I'm concerned you're overdressed. But I'll take care of that later myself." His eyes met hers in the mirror and filled with sweet promise.

After inserting dangly gold earrings into her earlobes, Maggie joined Glenn in the living room. He was pouring them a drink and Maggie watched her husband with renewed respect. He was tall, athletic and unbearably handsome. Her heart swelled with the surge of love that raced through her. She hadn't been looking forward to the party; in fact, she had been dreading it from the moment Glenn had mentioned it. Early on, she had reconciled herself to being a good stockbroker's wife, and that meant that she'd be attending plenty of functions over the years. It would be to her advantage to adapt to them now. Although he hadn't said anything, Maggie was confident Glenn knew she was determined to make the best of this evening.

They arrived precisely at eight at the home of Glenn's regional manager, Gary Weir. Already the living room was filled with smoke, and from the look of things the drinks had been flowing freely. As Glenn and Maggie walked in the front door, spirited cheers of welcome greeted them. Maggie painted a bright smile on her lips as they moved around the room, mingling with the guests. Everyone, it seemed, was in a good mood. Everyone, that is, except Maggie.

She didn't know how to explain her uneasiness. There wasn't anything she could put a name to and she mentally chastised herself. Glenn's friends and associates appeared to be going out of their way to make her feel welcome. Her hostess, Pamela Weir, Gary's wife, was warm and gracious, if a bit reserved. Yet a cold persistence nagged at Maggie that something wasn't right. Glenn stayed at her side, smiling down on her now and then. Once her eyes fell upon two women whispering with their heads close together. They sat on the far side of the room and there wasn't any possibility that Maggie could hear their whispered conversation, but something inside told Maggie they were talking about her. A chill went up her spine and she gripped Glenn's elbow, feeling ridiculous and calling herself every kind of idiot. Lightly, she shook her head, hoping to toss aside those crazy insecurities.

A few minutes later Glenn was pulled into a conversation with some of the men and Maggie was left to her own devices. Seeing Maggie alone, Pamela Weir strolled over.

"It was such a pleasant surprise when Glenn announced he had married," Pamela said.

Maggie took a sip of her wine. Glenn was involved with his friends and moved to another section of the crowded room. "Yes, I imagine it was. But we've known each other nearly all our lives."

"That was what Glenn was saying." Pamela gave her a funny look and then smiled quickly. "For a long time Gary was worried that Glenn wanted the transfer because of a problem at the office."

Maggie forced a smile. "We decided when we married

that we'd live in San Francisco," she explained to the tall, elegant woman at her side. "We were both raised there."

"Yes, Glenn explained that too."

Maggie's throat constricted and she made an effort to ease the strange tension she felt. "Although I've only been in Charleston a few weeks, I'm impressed with your city. It's lovely."

Pamela's eyes revealed her pride in Charleston. "We do love it."

"I know Glenn will miss it."

"We'll miss him."

Silence. Maggie could think of nothing more to comment upon. "You have a lovely home," she said and faltered slightly. "Glenn and I both appreciate the trouble you've gone to for this evening."

"It's no bother. Glenn has always been special to the firm. We're just sick to lose him." The delicate hands rotated the stem of the crystal wineglass. "I don't mind telling you that Glenn is the best manager Gary has. In fact—" she paused and gave Maggie a falsely cheerful smile "—Gary had been hoping to move Glenn higher into management. Of course that won't be possible now."

As with his parents, Maggie was again put on the defensive. Leaving Charleston hadn't been her idea and she didn't like being made the scapegoat. Swallowing back a retort, Maggie lowered her gaze and said, "I'm sure Glenn will do just as well in San Francisco."

"We all hope he does," Pamela said with a note of censure.

Glenn's gaze found Maggie several moments later. She stood stiff and uneasy on the other side of the room, holding her drink and talking to Pamela Weir. Even from the other side of the room, he could see that Maggie was upset and he couldn't understand why. He had known from the beginning that she hadn't been looking forward to this party. He wasn't all that fond of this sort of affair himself. But since the party had been given in his honor, he couldn't refuse the invitation. Maggie's attitude troubled him. Earlier in the evening, he'd stayed at her side, but eventually he'd been drawn away for one reason or another. Good grief, he thought, he shouldn't have to babysit her. The longer he watched her actions with Pamela, the more concerned he became. He noticed Maggie wasn't making eye contact with Pamela and when his supervisor's wife moved away, Glenn crossed the room to Maggie's side.

She lifted her gaze to his and Glenn was shocked at the look of anger she sent him.

"What's wrong?" he asked.

She met his gaze with a determined lift to her chin. She was upset, more upset than she'd been since the first morning of their marriage. Glenn had let her walk into the party, knowing the resentment his co-workers felt toward her because he was leaving. "When we arrived tonight I kept feeling these weird vibes that people didn't like me. Now I know why...."

"You're being ridiculous," Glenn muttered, his hand tightening around his drink. "These are my friends and they accept you as my wife."

Glenn was on the defensive and didn't appear willing to listen to her. "You're wrong, Glenn," she murmured, "they don't like me and with good reason. We'll talk about it later."

Glenn said nothing. The sound of someone banging a teaspoon against the side of a glass interrupted their discussion.

"Attention everyone," Gary Weir called as he came to

stand beside Glenn and Maggie. With dull blue eyes that revealed several drinks too many, Gary motioned with his arms that he wanted everyone to gather around.

Maggie felt like a statue with a frozen smile curving her mouth as she watched the party crowding around them. Glenn placed an arm at her neck, but his touch felt cold and impersonal.

Ceremoniously clearing his throat, Gary continued. "As you're all aware, tonight's party is being given in honor of Glenn and his—" he faltered momentarily, and seemed to have forgotten Maggie's name "—bride." A red blush attacked the cheeks of the supervisor and he reached for his drink and took a large swallow.

"As we know," he said, glancing over his shoulder to Glenn and Maggie, "Glenn has recently announced that he's transferring to California." Gary was interrupted with several low boos until he sliced the air, cutting off his associates. "Needless to say, everyone is going to miss him. Glenn has been a positive force within our company. We've all come to appreciate him and it goes without saying that he'll be missed. But being good sports, we want to wish him the best in San Francisco." A polite round of applause followed.

"In addition," Gary went on, his voice gaining volume with each word, "Glenn has taken a wife." He turned and beamed a proud smile at the two of them. "All of us felt that we couldn't send you away without a wedding gift. So we took up a collection and got you this." He turned around and lifted a gaily wrapped gift from behind a chair, holding it out to Glenn and Maggie.

Clearing his throat, Gary finished by saying, "This gift is a token of our appreciation and well wishes. We'd all like to wish Glenn and Angie many years of happiness."

Maggie's eyes widened and she swallowed hard at the unexpectedness of it. An embarrassed hush fell over the room and Maggie felt Glenn stiffen. Not realizing his mistake, Gary flashed a troubled look to his wife who was mouthing Maggie's name.

To cover the awkward moment, Maggie stepped forward and took the gift from Gary's hand. He gave her an apologetic look and fumbled, obviously flustered and embarrassed.

"Glenn and I would like to thank you, Larry."

"Gary," he corrected instantly, some color seeping back into his pale face.

A slow smile grew across Maggie's tight features. "We both seem to be having problems with names tonight, don't we?"

The party loved it, laughing spontaneously at the way she had aptly turned the tables on their superior. Laughing himself, Gary briefly hugged her and pumped Glenn's hand.

Not until they were on their way home did Glenn comment on the mishap. "Thank you," he said as they headed toward the freeway.

"For what?"

"For the way you handled that." He didn't need to explain what "that" was. Maggie knew. Rarely in his life had Glenn felt such anger. He had wanted to throw Gary against the wall and demand that he apologize to Maggie for embarrassing her that way. Of course, the slip hadn't been intentional, but it hadn't seemed to matter.

Several times in the past few weeks, Glenn had questioned whether he was making the right decision leaving Charleston. Maggie had blossomed here and seemed to genuinely love the city. Now he knew beyond a shadow of a doubt that leaving was best. Angie would haunt their marriage in Charleston. He had been a fool not to realize why Maggie had been so miserable at the party. The thought that his co-workers would confuse her with Angie hadn't crossed his mind. It seemed impossible that only a few months back he had been planning to marry someone else. These days he had trouble picturing Angie and seldom tried. Angie would always hold a special place in his heart. He wished her a long and happy life with Simon. But he had Maggie now, and thanked God for the woman beside him. He might not have courted her the way he should have, the way she deserved, but he desperately needed her in his life.

He loved her. Simply. Profoundly. Utterly. He'd tell her soon. Not tonight though, he thought or she'd think the mistake at the party had prompted the admission. Glenn wanted to choose the time carefully. For several weeks now, he had realized she loved him. Yet she hadn't said anything. He couldn't blame her. Things would straighten themselves out once they were in San Francisco. The sooner they left Charleston the better. In California, Maggie need never worry that someone would bring up Angie's name again.

"Gary's mistake was an honest one. He didn't mean to embarrass anyone." Without a problem, Maggie excused Glenn's friend.

"I know," Glenn murmured, concentrating on his driving.

They didn't talk again until they were home and then only in polite phrases. They undressed in silence and when they lifted the covers and climbed into bed, Glenn gathered her close in his arms, kissing her softly. He was asleep long before she was and rolled away from her. Maggie lay staring at the ceiling, unable to shake what had happened earlier from her mind. The flickering moon shadows seemed to taunt her. All they had been doing for the past few weeks was pretending. The two of them had been so intent on making believe that there had never been another woman in Glenn's life that the incident tonight had nearly devastated them. That was the problem with fantasies—they were so easily shattered. Maggie didn't need to be told that Glenn had been equally disturbed. Angie was present in their lives; she loomed between them like an uninvited guest.

With a heavy heart, Maggie rolled over and tried to sleep, but she couldn't. Not until Glenn's arms found her and he pulled her into the circle of his embrace. But he had been asleep, and for all she knew, Maggie thought bitterly, he could have been dreaming it was "her" he was holding.

Monday morning after Glenn left for work, Maggie sat lingering over a cup of coffee, working the crossword puzzle. The first thing she should do was get dressed, but she had trouble shaking off a feeling of melancholy. No matter how hard she tried, she hadn't been able to forget what had happened Friday night. They hadn't spoken about it again, choosing to ignore it. For now the puzzle filled her time. Her pen ran out of ink and after giving it several hard shakes, she tossed it in the garbage. Glenn kept a dozen or more in his desk.

Standing, Maggie headed toward his office. One thing they had decided over the weekend was that Maggie would fly ahead of Glenn to California. Like a fool Maggie had suggested it on the pretense that she had several items that required her attention waiting for her. She had hoped that Glenn would tell her he wanted them to arrive together.

But he had agreed all too readily and she'd been miserable for the remainder of the day.

Pulling open Glenn's drawer, she found what she needed and started to close the desk drawer. As she did it made a light, scraping sound. Her first inclination was to shove it closed. Instead, she carefully pulled the drawer free and discovered an envelope tucked away in the back that had been forced upward when she'd gotten the pen.

It wasn't the normal place for Glenn to keep his mail, and she examined the envelope curiously. The even, smooth flowing strokes of the handwriting attracted her artist's eye. This was a woman's handwriting—Angie's handwriting. Maggie felt the room sway as she sank onto the corner of the swivel chair, her knees giving out. The postmark revealed that the letter had been mailed a week before Steve and Janelle's wedding.

Perspiration broke out across Maggie's upper lip and she placed a hand over her mouth. Her heart hammered so loudly she was sure it rocked the room. The letter must have meant a great deal to Glenn for him to have saved it. Although she hadn't searched through the condominium, she had felt confident that he'd destroyed everything that would remind him of the other woman. Yet the letter remained.

Half of her wanted to stuff it back inside the drawer and pretend she'd never found it. The other half knew that if she didn't know the contents of the letter she would always wonder. Glenn had told her so little. She was his wife. She had a right to know. He should have explained the entire situation long ago and he hadn't, choosing instead to leave her curious and wondering. If she looked, it would be his own fault, she argued with herself. He had driven her to it.

It was wrong; Maggie knew it was wrong, but she couldn't help herself. Slowly, each inch pounding in nails of guilt, she withdrew the scented paper from the envelope.

Nine

Carefully Maggie unfolded the letter and was again struck by the smoothly flowing lines of the even handwriting. Angie's soulful dark eyes flashed in Maggie's memory from the time she'd seen the other woman's photograph. The handwriting matched the woman.

Dear Glenn,

I hope that I am doing the right thing by mailing you this letter. I've hurt you so terribly, and yet I owe you so much. I'm asking that you find it in your heart to forgive me, Glenn. I realize the pain I've caused you must run deep. Knowing that I've hurt you is my only regret.

Glenn, I don't believe that I'll ever be able to adequately thank you for your love. It changed my life and gave Simon back to me. Simon and I were destined to be man and wife. I can find no other way to explain it. I love him, Glenn, and would have always loved him. You and I were foolish to believe I could have forgotten Simon.

My hope is that someday you'll find a woman who

will love you as much as I love Simon. You deserve happiness. Simon and I will never forget you. We both want to thank you for the sacrifice you made for us. Be happy, dear Glenn. Be very happy.
With a heart full of gratitude,
Angie

With trembling hands, Maggie refolded the letter and placed it back inside Glenn's drawer. If she had hoped to satisfy her curiosity regarding Angie, the letter only raised more questions. Angie had mentioned a sacrifice Glenn had made on her behalf. But what? He was like that, noble and sensitive, even self-sacrificing. Angie's marrying Simon clearly had devastated him.

All day the letter troubled Maggie, until she decided that if she were to help Glenn bury the past, she had to understand it. That night she would do the very thing she had promised she wouldn't: she would ask Glenn to tell her about Angie.

No day had ever seemed so long. She didn't leave the house, didn't comb her hair until the afternoon, and when she did, her mirrored reflection revealed troubled, weary eyes and tight, compressed lips. If Glenn could talk this out with her, their chances of happiness would be greatly increased. He had saved the letter, risked her finding it. Although he might not be willing to admit it, he was holding on to Angie, hugging the memory. The time had come to let go.

With her arms cradling her middle, Maggie paced the living room carpet, waiting for Glenn to come home from work. The questions were outlined in her mind. She had no desire to hurt or embarrass him. She wanted him to tell her honestly and freely what had happened with Angie and why he had stepped aside for Angie to marry Simon.

Yet for all her preparedness, when Glenn walked in the door Maggie turned abruptly toward him with wide, apprehensive eyes, her brain numb.

"Hello, Glenn." She managed to greet him calmly and walked across the room to give him a perfunctory kiss. She felt comfortable, but her cheeks and hands were cold. Earlier she had decided not to mention finding the letter, not wanting Glenn to know she had stooped so low as to read it. However, if he asked, she couldn't...wouldn't lie.

His hands found her waist and he paused to study her. "Maggie, what's wrong, you're as cold as an iceberg."

She felt ridiculously close to tears and nibbled at her lower lip before answering. This was far more difficult than she'd thought it would be. "Glenn, we need to talk."

"I can see that. Do you have another rule for our marriage?"

Absently, she rubbed the palms of her hands together. "No."

He followed her into the living room and took a seat while she poured him a glass of wine. "Do you think I'm going to need that?" He didn't know what was troubling Maggie, but he had never seen her quite like this. She looked almost as if she were afraid, which was ludicrous. There was nothing she had to fear from him. He was her husband, and she should always feel comfortable coming to him.

Maybe she was pregnant. His pulse leaped eagerly at the thought. A baby would be wonderful, exciting news. A feeling of tenderness overcame him. Maggie was carrying his child.

"Maggie," he asked gently, "are you pregnant?"

She whirled around, sloshing some of the wine over the side of the glass, her eyes wide with astonishment. "No, what makes you ask?"

Disappointed, Glenn slowly shook his head. "No reason. Won't you tell me what's troubling you?"

She handed him the drink, but didn't take a seat, knowing she would never be able to sit comfortably in one position. She was too nervous. Hands poised, her body tense, she stood by the window and looked down at the street far below. "I've been waiting to talk to you all day."

He wished she'd get to the point instead of leaving him to speculate what troubled her. He had never seen her this edgy. She resembled a child who had come to her parent to admit a great fault. "If it was so important, why didn't you phone me at the office?"

"I...couldn't. This was something that had to be done in person, Glenn," she said, then swallowed, clenching and unclenching her fists as she ignored the impatience in his eyes. "This isn't easy." She resisted the urge to dry her clammy palms on the pockets of her navy-blue slacks.

"I can see that," he said gently. Whatever it was had clearly caused her a lot of anxiety. Rushing her would do no good, and so he forced himself to relax as much as possible. He crossed his legs and leaned back against the thick cushions of the chair.

"I thought for a long time I'd wait until you were comfortable about this...this subject. Now I feel like a fool, forcing it all out in the open. I wish I were a stronger person, but I'm not. I'm weak." Slowly she turned and hesitantly raised her eyes to his. "Glenn, I'm your wife. Getting married the way we did may have been unconventional, but I have no regrets. None. I'm happy being married to you. But as your wife, I'm asking you to tell me about Angie."

Maggie watched as surprise mingled with frustration and grew across his face.

"Why now?" Angie was the last subject he had expected Maggie to force upon him. As far as he was concerned, his relationship with the other woman was over. He wouldn't deny that he had been hurt, but he had no wish to rip open the wounds of his pride. And that was what had suffered most. Even when he'd known he'd lost her, he had continued to make excuses to see and be with Angie. Something perverse within himself had forced him to go back again and again even when he had recognized that there wasn't any possibility of her marrying him. For weeks he had refused to let go of her even though he'd known he'd lost her and she would never be his.

Now was the opportunity to explain that she'd found the letter, Maggie thought. But she couldn't admit that she'd stooped so low as to read the extremely personal letter. "I...wanted to know.... It's just that..."

"Is it because of what happened the other night?"

Glenn offered her an excuse that Maggie readily accepted. "Yes."

Glenn's mouth tightened, not with impatience, but confused frustration. Maggie should have put it out of her mind, long ago. No good would come from dredging up the past. "Whatever there was between us is over. Angie has nothing to do with you and me."

"But ultimately she does," Maggie countered. "You wouldn't have married me if your engagement hadn't been broken."

"Now you're being ridiculous. We wouldn't have married if I hadn't attended Steve and Janelle's wedding, either."

"You know what I mean."

"Maggie, trust me. There's nothing to discuss." The words were sharp.

Previously when Glenn was angry, Maggie had marveled at his control. He rarely raised his voice, and never at her. Until now. The only evidence she had ever had of his fury was a telltale leap of muscle in his jaw. He moved from his chair to the far side of the room.

"Glenn," she ventured. "I don't understand why you're so reluctant to discuss her. Is it because I've never told you about Dirk? I would have gladly, but you see, you've never asked. If there's anything you want to know, I'll be happy to explain."

"No, I don't care to hear the sorry details of your relationship with another man, and in return I expect the same courtesy."

Her hand on the back of the sofa steadied her. All these weeks, she'd been kidding herself, living in a dreamer's world. As Glenn's wife, she would fill the void left when Angie married Simon, but now she knew she would never be anything more than a substitute. These glorious days in Charleston had been an illusion. She had thought they'd traveled so far and yet they'd only been walking in place, stirring up the roadway dust so that it clouded their vision and their perspective. Oh, she would cook his meals, keep his house and bear his children, and love him until her heart would break. But she would never be anything more than second best.

"All right, Glenn," she murmured, casting her eyes to the carpet. "I'll never mention her name again."

His eyes narrowed as if he didn't believe her. But he had asked her not to, and she wouldn't. She had swallowed her pride, and come to him when he must have known how difficult it had been for her. That meant nothing to him, she realized. It didn't matter what she said or did; Glenn wasn't going to tell her anything.

Purposefully, Maggie moved into the kitchen and started to prepare their evening meal. She was hurt and disillusioned. She realized that Glenn hadn't been angry, not really. The displeasure he had shown had been a re-action to the fact that he'd been unable to deal with his feelings for Angie. But he must, and she prayed he real-ized it soon. Only when he acknowledged his feelings and sorted it out in his troubled mind would he be truly free to love her.

It took Glenn several minutes to analyze his indigna-tion. Of all the subjects in the world, the last thing he wanted to discuss was the past. He had handled it badly. Maggie was upset, and he regretted that, but it was neces-sary. The farewell party was responsible for this sudden curiosity; Maggie had said so herself. He should have re-alized earlier the repercussions. Glenn made his way to the kitchen and pretended to read the evening paper, all the while studying Maggie as she worked, tearing lettuce leaves for a salad. *Someday soon he'd make it up to her and she'd know how important she was in his life...how much he loved her and needed her.*

In bed that night, the entire Alaska tundra might as well have lain between them. Glenn was on his side of the bed, his eyes closed, trying to sleep. He had wanted to make love and reassure Maggie, but she had begged off. He did his best to disguise his disappointment. Other than polite conversation, Maggie hadn't said a word to him all eve-ning. She cooked their dinner, but didn't bother to eat any of it. For his part, he could hardly stomach the fresh crab salad, although generally Maggie was a good cook and he enjoyed their meals together. Cleaning the kitchen afterward seemed to take her hours, and when she returned to the living room he had guiltily searched her face for evidence of what she was thinking. For a full ten minutes Glenn was tempted to wake Maggie and tell her he would answer any questions she had. Maggie was right. She did deserve to know and it was only his pride that prevented him from explaining everything. But she was asleep by then and he decided to see how things went in the morning. If Maggie was still troubled, then he'd do as she had asked. But deep down, Glenn hoped that Maggie would put the subject out of her mind so they could go on with their lives.

Maggie lay stiffly on her side of the bed, unable to sleep. That stupid comment about having a headache had been just that—stupid. Now she longed for the comfort of Glenn's body and the warmth of his embrace. He had hurt her, and refusing to make love had been her way of getting back. But she was the one who suffered with disappointment. She needed her husband's love more than ever. Her heart felt as if a block of concrete were weighing it down.

The more she thought about their conversation, the more angry she got. She was his wife and yet he withheld from her an important aspect of his life. Glenn was denying her his trust. Their marriage was only a thin shell of what it was meant to be. If Glenn wouldn't tell her about his relationship with Angie, then he left her no option. Maggie decided she would find Angie and ask her what had happened. From the pieces of information she'd gathered, locating the other woman wouldn't be difficult.

In the long, sleepless hours of the night, Maggie mentally debated the pros and cons of such an action. What she might discover could ruin her marriage. Yet what she didn't know was, in essence, doing the same thing. The thought of Glenn making love with the other woman caused such an intense physical pain that it felt as if something were cutting into her heart. Unable to bear it, she tried to blot the picture from her mind, but no matter how she tried, the fuzzy image stayed with her, taunting her.

By the early hours of the morning, Maggie had devised her plan. It worked with surprising ease.

Two days later Charlotte Lambert dropped Maggie off at the airport for a flight scheduled for San Francisco. As Glenn had agreed earlier, Maggie was going to fly ahead and take care of necessary business that awaited her. From the wistful look Glenn gave her that morning when she brought out her suitcases, she realized that he regretted having consented that she return before him. Some of the tension between them had lessened in the two days before the flight. With Maggie's plan had come a release. Glenn wouldn't tell her what she wanted to know, but she'd soon learn on her own.

The Delta 747 left Charleston for San Francisco on time, but Maggie wasn't on the flight. Instead, she boarded a small commuter plane that was scheduled to land in Groves Point. The same afternoon she would take another commuter plane and connect with a flight to Atlanta. If everything went according to schedule, Maggie would arrive in California only four hours later than her original flight.

Groves Point was a charming community. The man at the rental car agency gave her directions into town, and Maggie paused at the city park and looked at the statues of the Civil War heroes. She gazed at the drawn sword of the man standing beside the cannon and knew that if Glenn ever found out what she was doing then her fate would be as sure as the South's was to the North.

The man at the corner service station, wearing greasy

coveralls and a friendly smile, gave her directions to Simon Canfield's home. Maggie drove onto the highway past the truck stop, as instructed. She would have missed the turn-off from the highway if she hadn't been watching for it. The tires kicked up gravel as the car wound its way along the curved driveway, and she slowed to a crawl, studying the long, rambling house. Somehow, having Angie live in an ordinary house was incongruous with the mental image Maggie had conjured up. Angie should live in a castle with knights fighting to protect and serve her.

A sleek black dog was alert and barking from the front step and Maggie hesitated before getting out of the car. She wasn't fond of angry dogs, but she'd come too far to be put off by a loud bark. Cautiously she opened the car door and stepped out, pressing her back against the side of the compact vehicle as she inched forward.

"Prince. Quiet." The dark-haired woman wearing a maternity top opened the back door and stepped onto the porch.

Instantly the dog went silent and Maggie's gaze riveted to the woman. Maggie stood, stunned. The photos hadn't done Angie's beauty justice. No woman had the right to look that radiant, lovely and serene. Angie was everything Glenn's silence had implied—and more. Her face glowed with her happiness, although she wasn't smiling now, but was regarding Maggie curiously. Maggie had been prepared to feel antagonistic toward her, and was shocked to realize that disliking the woman would be impossible.

"Can I help you?" Angie called from the top step, holding the dog by the collar.

All Maggie's energy went toward moving her head in a simple nod. Angie's voice was soft and lilting with an engaging Southern drawl.

"Bob phoned and said a woman had stopped in and asked directions to the house."

Apparently Bob was the man at the gas station. Putting on a plastic smile, Maggie took a step forward. "I'm Maggie Lambert."

"Are you related to Glenn?"

Again it was all Maggie could do to nod.

"I didn't know Glenn had any sisters."

Forcing herself to maintain an air of calm, Maggie met the gentle gaze of the woman whom Glenn had loved so fiercely. "He doesn't. I'm his wife."

If Angie was surprised she did an admirable job of not showing it. "Please, won't you come inside."

After traveling so far, devising the plan behind her husband's back and, worse, following through with it—Maggie stood cemented to the spot. After all that, without allowing anything to dissuade her from her idea, she was suddenly amazed at the audacity of her actions. Wild uncertainty, fear and unhappiness all collided into each other in her bemused mind until she was unable to move, struck by one thought: *it was wrong for her to have come here.*

"Maggie?" Angie moved down the steps with the dog loyally traipsing behind. "Are you all right?"

Maggie tasted regret at the gentleness in Angie's eyes. No wonder Glenn loved her so much, she thought. This wasn't a mere woman. Maggie hadn't known what to expect, but it hadn't been this. Angie was the type of woman a man yearned to love and protect. More disturbing to Maggie was the innate knowledge that Angie's inner beauty far surpassed any outer loveliness. And she was gorgeous. Not in the way the fashion models portrayed beauty, with sleek bodies and gaudy cosmetics. Angie was soft and gentle and sweet—a madonna. All of this flashed through Maggie's mind in the brief moment it took for Angie to reach her.

"Are you feeling ill?" Angie asked, placing a hand on Maggie's shoulder.

"I... I don't think so."

"Here," she said softly, leading her toward the house. "Come inside and I'll give you a glass of water. You look as if you're about to faint."

Maggie felt that a strong gust of wind would have blown her over. Mechanically, she allowed Angie to direct her through the back door and into the kitchen. Angie pulled out a chair at the table and Maggie sank into it, feeling more wretched than she had ever felt in her life. Tears were perilously close and she shut her eyes in an effort to forestall them. Maggie could hear Angie scurrying around for a glass of water.

She brought it to the table and sat across from Maggie. "Should I call the doctor? You're so pale."

"No, I... I'm fine. I apologize for putting you to all this trouble." Her wavering voice gained stability as she opened her dry eyes.

A few awkward seconds passed before Angie spoke. "I'm pleased that Glenn married. He's a good man."

Maggie nodded. Everything she had wanted to say had been set in her mind, but all her well-thought-out questions had vanished.

"How long have you been married?" Angie broached the subject carefully.

"Five weeks." Holding the water glass gave Maggie something to do with her hands.

"Glenn must have told you about me?"

"No," Maggie took a sip of water. The cool liquid helped relieve the parched feeling in her throat. "He won't talk about you. He's married to me, but he's still in love with you."

A sad smile touched the expressive dark eyes as Angie straightened in the chair. "How well do you know Glenn?"

"We grew up together," Maggie said. "I… I thought I knew him, but I realize now that I don't."

"Do you love him?" Angie asked, then offered Maggie a faint smile of apology. "Forgive me for even asking. You must. Otherwise you wouldn't be here."

"Yes, I love him." Words felt inadequate to express t her feelings for her husband. "But that love is hurting me because I don't know how to help him forget you. He won't talk about what happened."

"Of course he wouldn't," Angie said with a sweet, melodic laugh. "His pride's at stake and as I recall, Glenn is a proud man."

"Very."

The dark eyes twinkled with encouragement. "First, let me assure you that Glenn isn't in love with me."

Maggie opened her mouth to contradict her, but Angie cut her off by shaking her head.

"He isn't, not really," Angie continued. "Oh, he may think he is, but I sincerely doubt that. For one thing, Glenn would never marry a woman without loving her. He holds his vows too sacred. He could have married me a hundred times after I first saw Simon again, but he wouldn't. Glenn was wise enough to recognize that if we did marry I would always wonder about Simon. Glenn's a gambler, and he gambled on my love. At the time I don't think I realized what it must have cost him to give me the freedom to choose between the two of them."

"You mean you would have married Glenn?"

"At the drop of a hat," Angie assured her. "Glenn Lambert was the best thing to come into my life for twelve years and I knew it. I cared deeply for him, too, but that wasn't good enough for Glenn. He wanted me to settle my past, and heal all the old wounds before we made a life together. It was Glenn who led me by the hand back to the most difficult days of my life. Glenn's love gave me back Simon and I'll always be grateful to him for that. Both Simon and I will. We realize how dearly it cost Glenn to step aside so I could marry Simon."

Maggie grimaced at Angie's affirmation of love for Glenn and briefly closed her eyes to the pain. So this was the sacrifice Angie had mentioned in the letter.

"Knowing this, Maggie, you couldn't possibly believe that Glenn would take his vows lightly."

She made it all sound so reasonable and sure, Maggie thought uncertainly. "But...but if he was so strongly convinced that you should settle your past, then why is he leaving his own open like a festering wound?"

"Pride." There wasn't even a trace of hesitation in Angie's voice. "I doubt that Glenn continues to have any deep feelings for me. What happened between us is a painful time in his life he'd prefer to forget. Be patient with him."

Maggie realized that she had rammed heads with Glenn's pride when she'd asked him to tell her about Angie. His indomitable spirit had been challenged, and admitting any part of his pain to her went against the grain of his personality. Logically, knowing Glenn, it made sense.

"Glenn deserves a woman who will give him all the love he craves," Angie continued. "I could never have loved him like that. But he's found what he needs in you. Be good to him, Maggie, he needs you."

They talked nonstop for two hours, sometimes laughing, other times crying. Angie told Maggie of her own love story with Simon and their hopes and dreams for the child she carried. When it came time for Maggie to leave, Angie followed her to the airport and hugged her before she boarded her flight.

"You're a special lady, Maggie Lambert," Angie stated with conviction. "I'm confident Glenn realizes that. If he doesn't, then he's not the same man I remember."

Impulsively Maggie hugged Angie back. "I'll write once we've settled. Let me know when you have the baby."

"I will. Take care now, you hear?"

"Thank you, Angie, thank you so much. For everything."

Maggie's throat filled with emotion. There were so many things she wanted to say. Glenn had given Angie her Simon, and in return Maggie now had Glenn. She could leave now and there would no longer be any doubts to plague her. Angie would always be someone special in Glenn's life, and Maggie wouldn't begrudge him that. She would leave him with his memories intact, and never mention her name. Angie was no longer a threat to their happiness. Maggie understood the past and was content to leave it undisturbed.

The flight from Groves Point to Atlanta and the connection from Atlanta to San Francisco went surprisingly well. Although before Maggie would have worried that each mile took her farther from Glenn, she didn't view the trip in those terms anymore. She was in love with her husband and the minute she touched down in San Francisco she planned to let him know her feelings.

A smile beamed from her contented face when she landed in the city of her birth. She took a taxi directly to the beach house, set her bags in the entryway and headed for the kitchen and the phone. She had to talk to Glenn; she burned with the need to tell him of her love. In some ways she was concerned. There was a better time and place, but she couldn't wait a second more.

His phone rang and she glanced at the clock. With the time difference between the East and the West Coast it was well after midnight in Charleston. Discouraged, she fingered the opening of her silk blouse, wondering if she should hang it up and wait until morning.

Glenn answered on the second ring. "Maggie?" The anger in his voice was like a bucket of cold water dumped over her head, sobering her instantly. Somehow, he had found out that she'd gone to Groves Point and talked to Angie.

"Yes," she returned meekly.

"Where the hell have you been? I've been half out of my mind worrying about you. Your flight landed four hours ago. Why did you have to wait so long to call me? You must have known I was waiting to hear from you." The anger in his voice had lessened, diluted with relief from his worries.

Maggie sagged with relief onto the bar stool positioned by the phone. He didn't know. "To be honest, I wasn't sure if you wanted me to phone or not."

"Not phone?" He sounded shocked. "All I can say is that it's a good thing you did." His voice grew loud and slightly husky. "It's like a tomb around here without you."

Maggie tried to suppress the happiness that made her want to laugh. *He missed her.* He was miserable without her and she hadn't even been away twenty-four hours.

"Whose idea was it for you to leave early anyway?"

"Mine," she admitted ruefully. "But who agreed, and said I should?"

"A fool, that's who. Believe me, it won't happen again.

We belong together, Maggie." He made the concession willingly.

From the moment she had left that morning, he'd been filled with regrets. He should never have let her go, he had realized. He'd tried phoning an hour after her plane touched ground in California. At first it didn't bother him that she didn't answer her cell and when he tried the house, she didn't pick up ther either. He figured she'd probably gone to Denny's, Glenn assured himself earlier. Later, when he hadn't been able to get hold of her, Glenn assumed she had unplugged the phone and taken a nap. After a time his worry had grown to alarm, and from alarm to near panic. If she hadn't called him when she did—he hadn't been teasing—he would well have gone stir crazy. His feelings were unreasonable, Glenn knew that. His reaction was probably part of his lingering fear that he'd lose Maggie, he rationalized. But there was no denying it: the past few hours had been miserable.

Glenn said they belonged together with such meaning that it took a moment before Maggie could speak. "Glenn," she finally whispered, surprised at how low her voice dropped. "There's something you should know, something I should have told you long before now."

"Yes?" His voice didn't sound any more confident than her own.

"I love you, Glenn. I don't know when it happened, I can't put a time to it. But it's true. It probably embarrasses you to have me tell you like this, there are better times and places—"

"Maggie." He interrupted her with a gentle laugh. "You don't need to tell me that, I already know."

"You know?" All these weeks she'd kept her emotions

bottled up inside, afraid to reveal how she felt—and he'd known!

"Maggie, it was all too obvious. You're an artist, remember? You don't do a good job of hiding your emotions."

"I see." She swallowed down the bitter disappointment. Although eager to tell him of her feelings, she had wondered how he'd react. In her mind she had pictured a wildly romantic scene in which he'd tenderly admit his own feelings. Instead, Glenn acted as if she were discussing the weather.

"Well, listen, it's late here, I think I'll go to bed." She tried to make her voice light and airy, but a soft sob escaped and she bit into her lower lip to hold back another.

"Maggie, what's wrong?"

"Nothing. I'll talk to you tomorrow. Maybe. There's lots to do and—"

"Maggie, stop. You're crying. You never cry. I want to know why. What did I say?"

The insensitive boor, she silently fumed, if he couldn't figure it out, she wasn't going to tell him. "Nothing," she choked out in reply. "It doesn't matter. Okay?"

"No, it's not all right. Tell me what's wrong."

Maggie pretended she didn't hear. "I'll phone tomorrow night."

"Maggie," he said. "Either you tell me what's wrong or I'm going to be upset."

"Nothing's wrong." Her heart was breaking. She'd just told her husband she loved him for the first time, and he'd practically yawned in her face.

"Listen, we're both tired. I'll talk to you tomorrow," she finished. Before he could argue, she gently replaced the receiver. The phone rang again almost immediately and Maggie simply unplugged it, refusing to talk to Glenn again that night. For a full five minutes she didn't move. She had left Atlanta with such high expectations, confident that she could create a wonderful life with Glenn. There was enough love in her heart to build any bridge necessary in their marriage. A half hour after landing in San Francisco, she was miserable and in tears. Maggie slept late, waking around eleven the next morning. She felt restless and desolate. Early that afternoon, she forced herself to dress and deal with her mail. By evening her desk was cleared and she phoned Denny. She was half-tempted to paint, but realized it would be useless with her mind in turmoil. Glenn would be furious with her for disconnecting the phone, and she had yet to deal with him. He might not have appreciated her actions, but it was better than saying things she was sure to regret later.

By early evening she had worked up her courage enough to dial his number. When he didn't answer she wasn't concerned. He was probably at the health club, she thought. An hour later she tried phoning again. By ten, Pacific Coast time, she was feeling discouraged. Where was he? She toyed with the idea of phoning his family and casually inquiring, but she didn't want to alarm them.

A noise in the front of the house alerted her to the fact that someone was at the door. She left her office and was halfway into the living room when she discovered Glenn standing in the entryway, setting his suitcases on the floor.

He straightened just in time to see her. Time went still as he covered the short space between them and reached for her, crushing her in his arms. "You crazy fool. If you'd given me half a chance I would have told you how much I love you."

"You love me?"

"Yes," he whispered into her hair.

With a smothered moan of delight, Maggie twined her arms around his neck and was lifted off the floor as his mouth came down hungrily on hers.

Ten

"Why didn't you say something earlier?" Maggie cried and covered Glenn's face with eager kisses, locking her arms around his neck.

"Why didn't you?" She was lifted half off the ground so that their gazes were level, his arms wrapped around her waist.

Maggie could hardly believe he was with her and stared at him in silent wonder, still afraid it could all be part of some fanciful dream. She couldn't very well admit that it had been her conversation with Angie that had convinced her that Glenn needed to know what was in her heart. The time had come to quit playing games with each other. The shock had come when he'd already known how she felt. Well, what did she expect? She'd never been good at disguising her feelings and something as important as love shouldn't be concealed.

"I take it you're pleased to see me?"

Happiness sparkled from her eyes as she raised her hands and lovingly traced the contours of his face. "Very."

His hold on her tightened. He hadn't slept in thirty hours. The first ten of those hours had been spent in complete frustration. He had tried countless times to get her to answer her cell until he realized she must have turned it off. The only thing that made sense was that she'd turned it off for the flight and then forgot to turn it back on, which was why he'd tried the house countless times. He needed to talk to her; to explain his reaction to her confession of loving him. It wasn't a surprise. He'd known almost from the first even if she hadn't verbalized her feelings. He'd been at a total loss to understand why she'd resorted to tears. He relived every word of their conversation and as far as he could see she was behaving like a lunatic. She announced she loved him and immediately shocked him by breaking into sobs. Maggie wasn't a crier. Several times in the first weeks of their marriage he would have expected a lot more than tears from her. He'd certainly given her enough reason. But Maggie had proudly held up her head unwilling to relinquish a whit of her pride. With startling clarity it had come to him in the early-morning hours. Maggie had expected him to declare his own love. What an idiot he'd been. Of course he loved her. He didn't know why she could ever question it. He had realized he felt something profound for Maggie the minute she had walked down the aisle at Steve and Janelle's wedding. She'd been vulnerable, proud and so lovely that Glenn went weak with the memory. He had originally assumed that his friends' wedding followed the lowest point of his life, but one look at Maggie and he'd nearly been blown over. She'd lived next door to him for most of his life and he'd blithely gone on his way not recognizing what was before his own eyes. Maggie shared his name and his devotion and, God willing, later she would bear his children. How could she possibly think he didn't love her? Just as amazing was the knowledge that he'd never told her. Glenn was astonished at his own stupidity. He would phone her as soon as she would talk to him, he had decided, and never again in her life would he give her reason to doubt.

In theory, Glenn felt, his plan sounded reasonable, but as the hours fled, and a rosy dawn dappled the horizon, he began to worry. In her frame of mind, Maggie might consider doing something stupid.

The first thing the following morning, Glenn decided not to jeopardize his marriage more than he had already. He would fly to Maggie on the first plane he could catch. When he tried phoning several times, and there wasn't any answer, he fretted all the more. For caring as much as he did he'd done a good job of messing things up.

Now that he was looking at her face flushed with a brilliant happiness, Glenn realized he'd done the right thing.

"Do you have to go back?"

"I probably should, but I won't." Her smile was solidly in place, he noticed. He adored that smile. "I don't deserve you, Maggie."

"I know."

Tipping back her head, she laughed and his heart was warmed by the sound. Maggie made his heart sing. Being around her was like lying on the sunny beach on a glorious day and soaking up energy. She was all warmth and vitality, both springtime and Christmas, and he couldn't imagine his life without her. Twisting her around in his embrace, he supported her with an arm under her legs and carried her down the long hall that led to the master bedroom.

"My dear Mr. Lambert, just where are you taking me?"

"Can't you guess?"

"Oh, yes," she said and her lips brushed his, enjoying

the instant reaction she felt from him when her tongue made lazy, wet circles outlining his mouth.

"Maggie," he groaned. "You're going to pay for that."

"I'm looking forward to it. Very forward."

She couldn't undress fast enough. When Maggie's fingers fumbled with the buttons of her blouse in her eagerness, Glenn stopped her, placing her hand aside. Slowly, provocatively, he unfastened each one. As the new area of her skin was exposed, Glenn's finger lovingly trailed the perfection until he finally slipped the smooth material of her blouse from her shoulders and down her arms, letting it fall to the carpet. Maggie felt an exhilarating sense of power at the awe reflected in her husband's eyes. Impatience played no role in their lovemaking. Glenn had taught her the importance of self-control. The excruciating wait seemed only to enhance their pleasure; the disciplined pauses heightened their eagerness. Maggie was a willing pupil.

As if he couldn't deny himself a second longer, Glenn wrapped her in his arms and in one sweeping motion buried his mouth over hers.

What had begun with impatient eagerness slowed to a breathless anticipation. When they moved, it was with one accord. They broke apart and finished undressing, then lay together on the thick, soft quilt.

"I love you," she whispered, raising her arms up to bring him to herself. "Please love me," she cried, surprised to hear her own voice.

"I do," Glenn breathed. "Always."

Afterwards, blissfully content, Maggie spread eager kisses over his face. Briefly she wondered if this exhilaration, this heartfelt elation would always stay with them.

She wondered if twenty years from now she would still experience a thrill when Glenn made love to her. Somehow, Maggie doubted that this aspect of their marriage would ever change.

Glenn shifted positions so that Maggie was lovingly cradled in his arms and his fingers lightly stroked the length of her arm. Her fingers played at his chest, curling the fine dark hairs that were abundant there. A feeling of overpowering tenderness rocked him. He reveled in the emotion of loving and being loved, and knew what they shared would last forever. He was tired, more than tired—exhausted. He looked down and discovered Maggie asleep in his arms. Everything was going to work out, he thought sleepily. He wasn't going to lose her.... Slowly, his eyes drifted closed....

Maggie was his.

The following morning Maggie woke and studied her husband as he slept. A trace of a smile curved his mouth and her heart thrilled with the knowledge that she had placed it there. He must have been worried, terribly worried, she thought, to have dropped everything and flown to her. Surely, he couldn't believe that she'd ever leave him. A woman didn't love as strongly as she did and surrender without doing battle. Glenn's arrival had proved that Angie was right.... Glenn took his vows far too seriously to have married her or anyone when he was in love with another woman. Maggie didn't know what Glenn felt for the other woman anymore, but it wasn't love. Utterly content, she silently slipped from the bed and dressed, eager for the new day.

Glenn woke with a smile as Maggie's lips brushed his

in a feather-light kiss. "Morning," he whispered, reaching up to wrap his arms around her waist.

"Morning," she returned brightly. "I wondered how long it'd take for you to join the living."

Glenn eased upright, using his elbow for support. "What time is it?"

"Noon."

"Noon!" he cried, rubbing the sleep from his face as he came fully upright. "Good grief, why didn't you wake me?"

Giggling, Maggie sat on the edge of the mattress and looped her arms around his strong neck. "I just did."

"You've been painting," he said, noticing that Maggie was in her smock.

"It felt good to get back to it. Charleston was wonderful, but it's great to be home and back into my regular schedule."

A light knock against the bedroom door attracted Maggie's attention. "Phone for you, Maggie," Rosa, the older Hispanic woman who was Maggie's housekeeper and cook, announced from the other side. "It's your brother."

"Tell him I'll be right there," Maggie said, and planted a tender kiss on Glenn's forehead. "Unfortunately, duty calls."

"Maggie." Glenn's hand reached for her wrist, stopping her. His eyes were questioning her as though he didn't like the idea of releasing her even to her own brother. "Never mind."

"I shouldn't be more than a few minutes. Do you want to wait for me here?"

He shook his head, already tossing aside the blankets as he climbed from the bed. "I'll be out of the shower by the time you've finished."

True to his word, Glenn leaned his hip against the

kitchen counter, sipping coffee and chatting easily to Rosa when Maggie reappeared.

"I see that you two have introduced yourselves," Maggie said, sliding her arms around Glenn's waist.

"Sí," Rosa said with a nod, her dark eyes gleaming. "You marry good man. You have lots of healthy *muchachos.*"

Maggie agreed with a broad grin, turning her eyes to her husband. "Rosa is going to teach me to cook, isn't that right?"

"Sí. Every wife needs to know how to make her man happy," Rosa insisted as she went about cleaning the kitchen. "I teach Maggie everything about cooking."

"Not quite everything," Glenn whispered near Maggie's ear, mussing the tiny curls that grew at her temple. "In fact you wouldn't even need to go near a kitchen to keep me happy."

"Glenn," she whispered, hiding a giggle. "Quiet, or Rosa will wonder."

"Let her." His hold tightened as the housekeeper proceeded to chatter happily in a mixture of Spanish and English, scrubbing down already spotless counters as she spoke.

The lazy November day was marvelous. They took a dip in the heated pool and splashed and dunked each other like feisty teenagers at a beach party. Later, as they dried out in the sauna, Glenn carefully broached the subject of Maggie's brother.

"Was that Denny this morning?"

"Yes. He and Linda have invited us to Thanksgiving dinner. I didn't think you'd mind if I accepted."

"That'll be fine. How's Denny doing?"

Maggie wiped a thick layer of perspiration from her cheeks using both hands, biding time while she formed her thoughts. "Fine. What makes you ask?"

"He seems to call often enough. Didn't you get a couple of calls from him when we were in Charleston?"

"Yes. He's been through some rough times lately."

"How rough?"

Wrapping the towel around her neck, Maggie stood and paced the small enclosure while the heavy heat pounded in around her. "As you probably know, Denny and my parents inherited a portion of Great-aunt Margaret's money. Denny made some bad investment choices."

"What happened?" As a stockbroker, Glenn felt his curiosity piqued.

"It's a long, involved story not worth repeating. Simply put, Denny invested heavily in what he felt would be a good investment, trusting friends he shouldn't have trusted and lost everything. The case is being decided in the courts now, but it looks like he'll only get a dime back on every dollar invested."

"So you're bailing him out?" The statement was loaded with censure.

Maggie had to bite her tongue to keep from lashing out at Glenn for being so insensitive. He should know that litigation and lawyers were expensive. She was only doing what any sister would do in similar circumstances. "Listen, what's between my brother and me is private. You don't want to talk about certain things in your life, and I don't, either. We're both entitled to that."

"Don't you think you're being overly defensive?"

Maggie looked at him sharply. "So what? Denny's my brother. I'll give him money any time I please."

Glenn was taken back by her bluntness. "Fine." He wouldn't bring up the subject again…at least not for a while.

Thanksgiving arrived and Maggie's parents flew out from Florida. The elder Kingsburys had reacted with the same pleased surprise as Glenn's family had when Maggie phoned to announce that she and Glenn had married. The gathering at Denny and Linda's was a spirited but happy one. Neither of Maggie's parents mentioned how brief her and Glenn's courtship had been, nor that they were shocked at the suddenness of the ceremony. The questions were in their eyes, but Maggie was so radiantly happy that no one voiced any doubts.

The traditional turkey was placed in the oven to be ready to serve at the end of the San Francisco 49ers football game. They ate until they were stuffed, played cards, ate again and watched an old movie on television until Maggie yawned and Glenn suggested they head home. The day had been wonderful and Maggie looked forward to Christmas for the first time since moving to the beach house.

Glenn's days were filled. He started work at Lindsey & McNaught Brokerage the Monday after his arrival in San Francisco, and continued to work long hours to build up his clientele. More often than not, it was well past seven before he arrived home. Maggie didn't mind the hours Glenn put in away from home. She understood his need to secure his position with the company branch. The competition was stiff and as a new boy on the block, the odds were against him.

"How are things going at the office?" she asked him one evening the first week of December.

"Fine," he responded absently as he sorted through the

mail. "How about a game of tennis? I need to work out some of my frustrations."

"Everything's fine at the office, but you want to use me as a whipping boy?" she joked lovingly.

Glenn raised his gaze to hers and met the teasing glimmer mingled with truth in her eyes.

"Are you sorry we're here?" she asked on a tentative note. In Charleston, Glenn had held more than a hundred million dollars in assets for his firm, a figure that was impressive enough for him to have quickly worked his way into a managerial position. In San Francisco, he was struggling to get his name out and establish himself with new clients. Some of his previous ones had opted to stay with him but others had decided to remain with the same brokerage. From the hours he was putting in during the day and several long evenings, the task must be a formidable one.

"I'm not the least bit sorry we're living in San Francisco," he said. "Where you and I are concerned, I have no regrets. Now," he added, releasing a slow breath, "are we going to play tennis or stand here and chat?"

Just as he finished speaking the telephone rang. "Saved by the bell," Maggie mumbled as she moved across the room to answer it. "Hello."

"Hi, Maggie," Denny said in the low, almost whiny voice she had come to know well.

"Hi. What's up?" She didn't want to encourage Denny to drag out the conversation when Glenn was in the room. Denny was a subject they avoided. She knew her husband disapproved of her handing over large sums of money to her brother, but she didn't know what else she could do—Denny needed her. The money wasn't doing her any good, and if she could help her only brother, then why not?

The argument was one Maggie had waged with herself countless times. As long as she was available to lean upon, the opposing argument went, then Denny would be content to do exactly that. He hadn't accomplished anything worthwhile in months. From conversations with her sister-in-law, Linda, Maggie had learned that Denny did little except decry his misfortune and plot ways of regaining his losses. Maggie could understand his circumstances well enough to realize he was in an impossible position. He didn't like it, she didn't like it, but there was nothing that either of them could do until the court case was settled.

"I just wanted you to know that I'll be meeting with the lawyers tomorrow afternoon."

"Good luck," she murmured.

A silence followed. "What's the matter? Can't you talk now?"

"That about sizes up the situation." Glenn was studying her and Maggie realized her stalling tactics weren't fooling him. He knew exactly whom she was talking to and did nothing to make the conversation any easier by leaving the room.

"Maybe I should phone you tomorrow," Denny suggested.

"That would be better." Maggie forced a carefree note into her tone. "I'll talk to you tomorrow then."

"Okay." Denny sounded disappointed, but there wasn't anything Maggie could do. She wanted to avoid another confrontation with Glenn regarding her brother.

Replacing the receiver, she met her husband's gaze. "You said something about tennis?" Her voice was remarkably steady for all the turmoil going on inside her.

"You're not helping him, you know," Glenn said calmly.

"All you've done to this point is teach him to come to you to solve his financial problems."

It was on the tip of her tongue to tell him that she was aware of that. She had seen it all herself, but she was caught in a vicious trap where her brother was concerned. "He needs me," she countered.

"He needs a job and some self-worth."

"I thought you were a stockbroker, not a psychologist."

Maggie could tell by the tightness in his jaw that she had angered Glenn. "Look, I'm sorry, I didn't mean to snap at you. Denny's in trouble. I can't let him down when he needs me the most. If you recall, I did ask you to stay out of it."

"Have it your way," he mumbled and handed her a tennis racket.

Their game wasn't much of a contest. Glenn overpowered her easily in straight sets, making her work harder than ever. Maggie didn't know if he was venting his frustrations from the office or if he was angry because of Denny. It didn't matter; she was exhausted. By the time he'd finished showering, she was in bed half-asleep. Glenn's pulling the covers over her shoulders and gently kissing the top of her head were the last things Maggie remembered.

With the approach of the Christmas holidays, Maggie felt a renewed sense of rightness. She was in love with her husband, they were together and her world seemed in perfect balance. Glenn worked hard and so did she, spending hours in her studio doing what she enjoyed most—painting. With her marriage, Maggie had discovered that there was a new depth to her art. She had once told Glenn that color was mood and brushwork emotion. Now with Glenn's love, her brush painted bold strokes that revealed a maturity in her scenes that had been missing before their wedding. She was happy, truly happy, and it showed in ways she'd never expected.

Maggie didn't mention Glenn's grandmother's antique ring, confident that he'd gift her with it on Christmas morning. And she would react with the proper amount of surprised pleasure.

She wore her wedding ring continually now, even when she worked. Glenn glanced at her hand occasionally to be sure it was there. It was an odd quirk of his, but she didn't really mind. The ring meant as much to her as their marriage vows and that was all he wanted. They had come a long way from the night she'd arrived in Charleston.

For their first Christmas, Maggie wanted to buy Glenn a special gift, something that would show the depth of her love and appreciation for the good life they shared. But what? For days she mulled over the problem. She could give him one of her paintings for his office, but he had already asked her for one. She couldn't refuse him by telling him that that was what she planned to give him for Christmas. He took one of her seascapes and she was left without an idea. And she so wanted their first Christmas together to be special.

For the first time in years Maggie went Christmas shopping in stores. Usually she ordered through the mail or over the Internet, but she feared missing the perfect gift that would please Glenn most. Janelle joined her one day, surprised at the changes in Maggie.

"What changes?"

"You're so happy," Janelle claimed.

"I really am, you know."

"I can tell. You positively glow with it."

The remark pleased Maggie so much she repeated it for Glenn later that evening.

"So you were out Christmas shopping. Did you buy me anything?"

How she wished. Nothing seemed special enough. She had viewed a hundred jewelry display cases, visited the most elite men's stores and even gone to obscure bookstores, seeking rare volumes of Glenn's favorite novels. A sense of panic was beginning to fill her.

"You'll have to wait until Christmas morning to find out," she told him, coyly batting her long lashes.

With so many relatives on their list, Glenn and Maggie were in and out of more department stores the following Saturday than Maggie cared to count. Soft music filled the stores and bells chimed on the street corners, reminding them to be generous to those less fortunate. The crowds were heavy, but everyone seemed to expect that and took the long waits at the cash registers in stride.

While Maggie stood in line buying a toy farm set for Glenn's nephew, Glenn wandered over to the furniture department. Lovingly, Maggie's gaze followed him as he looked over cherry wood bookcases in a rich, deep-red color. Bookcases? Glenn wanted something as simple as bookcases? Maggie couldn't believe it. After days of looking at the latest gadgets and solid-gold toys, she stared in disbelief that he could be interested in something as simple as this. When the salesman approached, Glenn asked several questions and ran his hand over the polished surface.

"Did you see something?" she asked conversationally when he returned to her side. He wanted those bookcases, but she doubted that he'd mention it to her.

"Not really," he replied, but Maggie noted the way his gaze returned and lingered over the cases.

Maggie's heartbeat raced with excitement. At the first opportunity she'd return and buy Glenn those bookcases.

"You're looking pleased about something," Glenn commented over dinner Wednesday evening.

His comment caught her off guard and she lightly shook her head. "Sorry, I was deep in thought. What did you say?"

"I could tell," he chided, chuckling. Standing, he carried his clean plate to the sink. "Do you want to talk about it, or is this some deep dark secret you're hiding from your husband?"

"Some deep dark secret."

"What did you do today?" he asked, appreciating anew how beautiful his wife had become. She was a different woman from the one who'd met him at the airport months ago. He liked to think the changes in her were due to their marriage. He was different too and credited Maggie with his renewed sense of happiness.

"What did I do today?" Maggie repeated, her dark eyes rounding with shock. Swallowing back her unease, she cast her gaze to her plate. "Christmas cards." The truth nearly stuck in her throat. She had written Christmas cards, but in addition she had penned a long letter to Angie, thanking her for everything the other woman had shared the day of their brief visit. In the letter, Maggie told Angie how improved her marriage was now that she'd told Glenn how much she loved him, and was confident that he loved her in return.

As impractical as it sounded, Maggie would have liked to continue the friendship with Angie. Rarely had Maggie experienced such an immediate kinship with another woman. Impractical and illogical. Of all the people in the world, Maggie would have thought she'd despise Angie

Canfield. But she didn't. Now, weeks later, Maggie felt the need to write the other woman and extend her appreciation for their afternoon together and to wish her and Simon the warmest of holiday greetings. The letter had been interrupted by Glenn's homecoming and she had safely tucked it away from the other cards she kept on top of her desk.

"I still have several things that need to be done before Christmas," she said in order to hide her discomfort.

Glenn was silent for a moment. "You look guilty about something. I bet you went out shopping today and couldn't resist buying yourself something."

"I didn't!" she declared with a cheery laugh.

Later, in the den, when Glenn was looking over some figures, Maggie joined him. She sat in the chair opposite his desk. When Maggie glanced up she found her husband regarding her lazily with a masked expression, and she wondered at his thoughts.

On the other side of the desk, Glenn studied his wife, thinking that she was more beautiful that night than he ever remembered. Her eyes shone with a translucent happiness and a familiar sensation tugged at his heart. Something was troubling her tonight…no, troubling was too strong a word. She was hiding something from him. Which was natural, he supposed. It was Christmastime and she had probably cooked up some scheme for his gift, yet Glenn had the feeling this had nothing to do with Christmas.

Convinced he shouldn't go looking for trouble, he shook his mind free of the brooding sensation. Whatever it was probably involved Denny, and it was just as well that he didn't know. It would only anger him.

Glenn pushed back his chair and stood. "I'll be right back. I'm going to need a cup of coffee to keep these figures straight. Do you want one?"

Maggie glanced up from the book she was reading and shook her head. The caffeine would keep her awake. "No, thanks," she said as he left the room.

The phone rang and Glenn called out that he'd answer it. The information didn't faze Maggie until she realized that he had probably gone into her office since the phone was closer there.

He returned a minute later, strolling into the room with deceptive casualness. "It's your leeching brother," he told her.

Eleven

"Glenn, what a nasty thing to say." Maggie couldn't help knowing that Glenn disapproved of the way she gave Denny money, but she hadn't expected him to be so blunt or openly rude. "I hope Denny didn't hear you," she murmured, coming to her feet. "He feels terrible about the way things have turned out."

"If he honestly felt that, he wouldn't continue to come running to you at every opportunity."

Straightening her shoulders to a military stiffness, Maggie marched from the room and picked up the telephone. "Hello, Denny."

A short silence followed. "Hi. I take it I should call back another time."

"No," she contradicted firmly. She wasn't going to let Glenn intimidate her out of speaking to her own brother. "I can talk now."

"I just wanted to tell you that my lawyer didn't have anything new to tell me regarding our case. It looks like this thing could be tied up in the courts for years. I'm telling you, Maggie, this whole mess is really getting me down."

"But you don't need to worry, I'm here to help you," she offered sympathetically.

"But Glenn..."

"What I do with my money is none of his concern." In her heart Maggie knew that Glenn was right, but Glenn was a naturally strong person, and her brother wasn't to be blamed if he was weak. They had to make allowances for Denny, help him.

"You honestly mean that about helping, don't you?" Denny murmured, relief and appreciation brightening his voice.

"You know I do."

Ten minutes later Maggie rejoined her husband. All kinds of different emotions were coming at her. She was angry with Glenn for being so unsympathetic to her brother's troubles, infuriated with Denny because he pushed all the right buttons with her, and filled with self-derision because she gave in to Denny without so much as a thoughtful pause. Denny had only to give his now familiar whine and she handed him a signed check.

"Well?" Glenn glanced up at her.

"Well what?"

"He asked for money, didn't he?"

"Yes," she snapped.

"And you're giving it to him?"

"I don't have much choice. Denny is my brother."

"But you're not helping him, Maggie, don't you see that?"

"No," she cried, and to her horror tears welled in her eyes. It was so unlike her to cry over something so trivial that Maggie had trouble finding her breath, which caused her to weep all the louder.

Glenn stood and gently pulled her into his arms. "Maggie, what is it?"

"You... Denny...me," she sobbed and dramatically shook her hands. "This court case might take years to decide. He needs money. You don't want me to lend him any, and I'm caught right in the middle."

"Honey, listen." Glenn stood and gently placed his arms around her. "Will you do something for me?"

"Of course," she responded on a hiccupping sob. "What?"

"Call Denny back and tell him he can't have the money...."

"I can't do that," she objected, shaking his arms free. She hugged her waist and moved into the living room where a small blaze burned in the fireplace. The warmth of the fire chased the chill from her arms.

"Hear me out," Glenn said, following her. "Have Denny give me a call at the office in the morning. If he needs money, I'll loan it to him."

Maggie was skeptical. "But why...?"

"I don't want him troubling you anymore. I don't like what he's doing to you, and worse, what he's doing to himself." He paused, letting her take in his offer. "Agreed?"

She offered him a watery smile and nodded.

With Glenn standing at her side, Maggie phoned Denny back and gave the phone over to her husband a few minutes later. Naturally, Denny didn't seem overly pleased with the prospect of having to go through Glenn, but he had no choice. Maggie should have been relieved that Glenn was handling the difficult situation, but she wasn't.

In the morning, Maggie woke feeling slightly sick to her stomach. She lay in bed long after Glenn had left for the office, wondering if she could be pregnant. The tears the evening before had been uncharacteristic and she'd had a terrible craving for Chinese food lately that was driving her crazy. For three days in a row she had eaten lunch in Chinatown. None of the symptoms on their own was enough for her to make the connection until this morning.

A smile formed as Maggie placed a hand on her flat stomach and slowly closed her eyes. A baby. Glenn would be so pleased. He'd be a wonderful father. She'd watched him with Denny's girls on Thanksgiving and had been astonished at his patience and gentleness. The ironic part was all these weeks she'd been frantically searching for just the right Christmas gift for Glenn, and all along she'd been nurturing his child in her womb. They both wanted children. Oh, she'd get him the bookcases he had admired, but she'd keep the gift he'd prize most a secret until Christmas morning.

Not wanting to be overconfident without a doctor's confirmation, Maggie made an appointment for that afternoon, and her condition was confirmed in a matter of minutes. Afterward she was bursting with excitement. Her greatest problem would be keeping it from Glenn when she wanted to sing and dance with the knowledge.

When Maggie returned to the beach house Rosa had left a message that Denny had phoned. Maggie returned his call immediately.

"How did everything go with Glenn?" she asked him brightly. Nothing would dim the brilliance of her good news, not even Denny's sullen voice.

"Fine, I guess."

"There isn't any problem with the money, is there?" Glenn wouldn't be so cruel to refuse to make the loan when he'd assured her he'd help her brother. Maggie was confident he wouldn't do anything like that. Glenn understood the situation.

"Yes and no."

Her hand tightened around the receiver. "How do you mean? He's giving you the money, isn't he?"

"He's lending me the money, but he's got a bunch of papers he wants me to sign and in addition he's set up a job interview for me. He actually wants me to go to work."

By the time Denny finished with his sorry tale, Maggie was so furious she could barely speak. Lending him the money—making him sign for it—a job interview. Glenn had told her he was going to help her brother. Instead he was stripping Denny of what little pride he had left.

By the time Glenn arrived home that evening, he found Maggie pacing the floor. Sparks of anger flashed from her dark eyes as she spun around to face him.

"What's wrong? You're looking at me like I was Jack the Ripper."

"Did you honestly tell Denny that he couldn't borrow the money unless he got a job?" she said in accusation. Her hands were placed defiantly on her hips, challenging Glenn to contradict her.

Unhurriedly, Glenn removed his raincoat one arm at a time and hung it in the hall closet. "Is there something wrong with an honest day's toil?"

"It's humiliating to Denny. He's…accustomed to a certain lifestyle now…. He can't lower himself to take a job like everyone else and…"

Maggie could tell by the way Glenn's eyes narrowed that he was struggling to maintain his own irritation. "I live in a fancy beach house with you and somehow manage to suffer the humiliation."

"Glenn," she cried. "It's different with Denny."

"How's that?"

Unable to remain still, Maggie continued to stalk the tiled entryway like a circus lion confined to a cage. "Don't you understand how degrading that would be to him?"

"No," Glenn returned starkly. "I can't. Denny made a mistake. Any fool knows better than to place the majority of his funds in one investment no matter how secure it appears. The time has come for your brother to own up to the fact he made a serious mistake, and pay the consequences of his actions. I can't and won't allow him to sponge off you any longer, Maggie."

The tears sprang readily to the surface. Oh how she hated to cry. Hopefully she wouldn't be like this the entire pregnancy. "But don't you understand?" she blubbered, her words barely intelligible. "I inherited twice the money Denny did."

"And he's made you feel guilty about that."

"No," she shouted. "He's never said a word."

"He hasn't had to. You feel guilty enough about it, but my love, trust me. Denny will feel better about you, about himself, about life in general. You can't give him the self-worth he needs by handing him a check every time he asks for it."

"You don't understand my brother," Maggie cried. "I can't let you do this to him. I... I told you once that I wanted you to stay out of this."

"Maggie—"

"No, you listen to me. I'm giving Denny the money he wants. I told him that he didn't need to sign anything, and he doesn't need to get a job. He's my brother and I'm not going to turn my back on him. Understand?"

Silence crackled in the room like the deadly calm before an electrical storm. A muscle leaped in Glenn's jaw, twisting convulsively.

"If that's the way you want it." His voice was both tight and angry.

"It is," she whispered.

What Maggie didn't want was the silent treatment that followed. Glenn barely spoke to her the remainder of the evening, and when he did his tone was barely civil. It was clear that Glenn considered her actions a personal affront. Maybe it looked that way to him, she reasoned, but she'd explained long ago that she preferred to handle her brother herself. Glenn had interfered and now they were both miserable.

When morning arrived to lighten the dismal winter sky, Maggie rolled onto her back and stared at the ceiling, realizing she was alone. The oppressive gray light of those early hours invaded the bedroom and a heaviness settled onto Maggie's heart. She climbed from the bed and felt sick and dizzy once again, but her symptoms were more pronounced this morning. Her mouth felt like dry, scratchy cotton.

Glenn had already left for the office and the only evidence of his presence was an empty coffee cup in the kitchen sink. Even Rosa looked at Maggie accusingly and for one crazy instant Maggie wondered how the housekeeper knew that she and Glenn had argued. That was the crazy part—they hadn't really fought. Maybe if they had, the air would have been cleared.

The crossword puzzle didn't help occupy her mind and Maggie sat at the kitchen table for an hour, drinking cup after cup of watered-down apple juice while sorting through her thoughts. With a hand rubbing her throbbing temple, Maggie tried to recall how Glenn had been as a youth when he was angry with someone. She couldn't remember that he had ever held a grudge or been furious with anyone for long. That was a good sign.

Tonight she'd talk to him, she decided, try to make him understand why she had to do this for Denny. If the situation was reversed and it was either of his brothers, Glenn would do exactly the same thing. Maggie was sure of it.

Because of the Christmas holidays, the stock market was traditionally slow, and Glenn had been home before six every night for the past week. He wasn't that night. Nor was he home at seven, or eight. He must be unbelievably angry, she thought, and a part of Maggie wondered if he'd ever be able to completely understand her actions. Apparently, he found it easier to blame her than to realize that he'd forced her into the situation. Maggie spent a miserable hour watching a television program she normally disliked.

The front door clicked open and Maggie pivoted sharply in her chair, hoping Glenn's gaze would tell her that they'd talk and clear up the air between them.

Glenn shrugged off his coat and hung it in the hall closet. Without a word he moved into his den and closed the door, leaving Maggie standing alone and miserable.

Desolate, she sat in the darkened living room and waited. She hadn't eaten, couldn't sleep. Leaving the house was impossible, looking and feeling the way she did. Her only companion was constant anxiety and doubt. There wasn't anything she could do until Glenn was ready to talk.

When he reappeared, Maggie slowly came to her feet. Her throat felt thick and uncooperative. Her hands were clenched so tightly together that the blood flow to her fingers was restricted. "Would you like some dinner?" The question was inane when she wanted to tell him they were both being silly. Arguing over Denny was the last thing she wanted to do.

"I'm not hungry," he answered starkly without looking at her. His features tightened.

Undaunted, Maggie asked again. "Can we at least talk about this? I don't want to fight."

He ignored her and turned toward the hallway. "You said everything I needed to hear last night."

"Come on, Glenn, be reasonable," she shouted after him. "What do you want from me? Are you so insensitive that you can't see what an intolerable situation you placed me in?"

"I asked you to trust me with Denny."

"You were stripping him of his pride."

"I was trying to give it back to him," he flared back. "And speaking of intolerable positions, do you realize that's exactly what you've done to me?"

"You… How…?"

"You've asked me to sit by and turn a blind eye while your brother bleeds you half to death. I'm your husband. It's my duty to protect you, but I can't do that when you won't let me, when you resent, contradict and question my intention."

"Glenn, please," she pleaded softly. "I love you. I don't want to fight. Not over Denny—not over anything. It's Christmas, a time of peace and goodwill. Can't we please put this behind us?"

Glenn looked as weary as she felt. "It's a matter of trust too, Maggie."

"I trust you completely."

"You don't," Glenn announced and turned away from her, which only served to fuel Maggie's anger.

Maggie slept in the guest bedroom that night, praying

Glenn would insist she share his bed. She didn't know what she had thought sleeping apart would accomplish. It took everything within Maggie not to swallow her considerable pride and return to the master bedroom. A part of her was dying a slow and painful death.

Maggie couldn't understand why Glenn was behaving like he was. Only once had he even raised his voice to her in all the weeks they'd been married. But now the tension stretched between the two bedrooms was so thick Maggie could have sliced it with a dull knife. Glenn was so disillusioned with her that even talking to her was more than he could tolerate. He wasn't punishing her with the silent treatment, Maggie realized. He was protecting her. If he spoke it would be to vent his frustration and say things he'd later regret.

Instead of dwelling on the negative, Maggie recalled the wonderful love-filled nights when they had lain side by side and been unable to stay out of each other's arms. The instant the light was out, Glenn would reach for her with the urgency of a condemned man offered a last chance at life. And when he'd kissed her and loved her, Maggie felt as though she was the most precious being in the world. Glenn's world. He was a magnificent lover. She closed her eyes to the compelling images that crowded her mind, feeling sick at heart and thoroughly miserable.

In the other room Glenn lay on his back staring at the ceiling. The dark void of night surrounded him. The sharp edges of his anger had dulled, but the bitterness that had consumed him earlier had yet to fade. In all his life he had never been more disappointed and more hurt—yes, hurt, that his wife couldn't trust him to handle a delicate situation and protect her. He wasn't out to get Denny; he sincerely wanted to help the man.

Morning arrived and Maggie couldn't remember sleeping although she must have closed her eyes sometime during the long, tedious night. The alarm rang and she heard Glenn stirring in the other room.

While he dressed, Maggie moved into the kitchen and put on coffee. Ten minutes later, he joined her in the spacious room and hesitated, his gaze falling to her wide, sad eyes. Purposely he looked away. There was no getting around it. He had missed sleeping with his wife. A hundred times he had had to stop himself from going into the bedroom and bringing her back to his bed where she belonged. Now she stood not three feet from him in a sexy gown and his senses were filled with her. He should be aware of the freshly brewed coffee, but he discovered the elusive perfumed scent of Maggie instead. Silently he poured himself a cup of coffee and pulled out a kitchen chair. He tried to concentrate on something other than his wife. He reached for the newspaper and focused his attention on that. But mentally his thoughts were involved in this no-win situation between him and her blood sucking brother. When he'd learned exactly how much money Denny had borrowed he'd been insensed. This madness had to stop and soon or he'd bleed Maggie dry.

Sensing Glenn's thoughts, Maggie moved closer, wanting to resolve this issue, yet unsure how best to approach a subject that felt like a ticking time bomb.

Propping up the newspaper against the napkin holder, Glenn hid behind the front page, not wanting to look at Maggie yet he struggled to keep his eyes trained on the front page headlines. "Will you be home for dinner?" Maggie forced the question out. Leaning against the kitchen counter, her fingers bit into the tiled surface as she waited for his answer.

"I've been home for dinner every night since we've been married. Why should tonight be different?"

Maggie had only been trying to make idle conversation and break down the ice shield that positioned between them. "No reason," she murmured and turned back to the stove.

A few minutes later Glenn left for the office with little more than a casual farewell.

By noon Maggie was convinced she couldn't spend another day locked inside the confines of the beach house. Even the studio that had been her pride now became her torture chamber. One more hour dealing with this madness and she'd go stir-crazy.

Aimlessly, she wandered from room to room, seeking confirmation that she had done the right thing by Denny and finding none. She took a long, uninterrupted walk along the beach where gusts of ocean air carelessly whipped her hair across her face and lightened her mood perceptibly. Christmas was only a week away, and there were a hundred things she should be doing. But Maggie hadn't the heart for even one.

Recently she had been filled with such high expectations for this marriage. Now she realized how naive she'd been. She had always thought that love conquered all. What a farce that was. She had been unhappy before marrying Glenn; now she was in love, pregnant, and utterly miserable. And why? Because she'd stood by her brother when he needed her. It hardly seemed fair.

A light drizzle began to fall and she walked until her face felt numb with cold. She trekked up to the house, fixed herself something hot to drink and decided to go for a drive.

The ride into the city was sluggish due to heavy traffic. She parked on the outskirts of Fisherman's Wharf and took a stroll. A multitude of shops and touristy places had sprung up since her last visit—but that had been years ago, she realized. She dropped into a few places and shopped around, finding nothing to buy. An art gallery caught her eye and she paused to look in the window at the painting on display. A card tucked in the ornate frame revealed the name of the painting was *The Small Woman*. The artist had used a black line to outline the painting, like lead surrounding the panes in a stained-glass window. The colors were bold, the setting elaborate. The simple woman, however, was strangely frail and pathetic, detached from the setting as though she were a sacrifice to be offered to the gods in some primitive culture. Examining the painting, Maggie saw herself in the tired woman and didn't like the reflection.

A blast of chilling wind whipped her coat around her legs, and to escape the unexpected cold, Maggie opened the glass door and entered the gallery. The room was deceptively large, with a wide variety of oil paintings, some watercolors, small sculptures and other artworks in opulent display.

"Can I help you?"

Maggie turned toward the voice to find a tall, slender woman dressed in a plaid wool skirt and creamy white silk blouse. She appeared to be studying Maggie closely, causing Maggie to wonder at her appearance. The wind had played havoc with her hair and…

"Maggie?"

Maggie blinked twice. She didn't recognize the woman. "Pardon?"

"Are you Maggie Kingsbury?"

"Yes…my married name is Lambert. Do I know you?"

The woman's laugh was light and sweetly musical. "I'm Jan Baker Hammersmith. Don't you remember we attended…"

The name clicked instantly. "Jan Baker." The two had been casual friends when Maggie was attending art school. "I haven't seen you in years. The last I heard, you were married."

"I'm divorced now."

Maggie dropped her gaze, desperately afraid that she would be adding that identical phrase someday when meeting old friends. "I'm sorry to hear that."

"I am, too," Jan said with a heavy sadness. "But it was for the best. Tell me, are you still painting?" Maggie noted how Jan quickly diverted the subject away from herself.

"Occasionally. Not as much since I married."

Jan strolled around the gallery with proud comfort. "I can still remember one of your paintings—a beach scene. The detail you'd put into it was marvelous. Whatever happened to that?"

"It's hanging in our living room."

"I can understand why you'd never want to sell that." Jan's eyes were sincere. "Rarely have I seen a painting with such vivid clarity and color."

"It would sell?" Maggie was surprised. Ridiculous as it seemed, she'd never tried to sell any of her paintings. There hadn't been any reason to try. She gave them away as gifts and to charities for auctions but she didn't have any reason to sell them. She didn't need the money and inwardly she feared they might not sell. Her artwork was for her own pleasure. The scenes painted by her brush had been the panacea for an empty life within the gilded cage.

"It'd sell in a minute," Jan stated confidently. "Do you think you'd consider letting the gallery represent you?"

Maggie hedged, uncertain. "Let me think about it."

"Do, Maggie, and get back to me. I have a customer I know who'd be interested in a painting similar to the beachscape, if you have one. Take my card." They spoke for several minutes more and Maggie described some of her other works. Again Jan encouraged her to bring in a few of her canvases. Maggie noted that Jan didn't make any promises, which was reasonable.

Sometime later, Maggie returned to her car. Meeting Jan had been just the uplift she'd needed. Already her mind was buzzing with possibilities. There wasn't any reason she shouldn't sell her work. Glenn's car was in the driveway when she returned and she pulled to a stop in front of the house and parked there. A glance at her watch told her that it was later than she suspected. Her spirits were lighter than at any time during the past two days, but she didn't hurry toward the house.

"Where have you been?" Glenn asked the minute she walked in the door. Not granting her the opportunity to respond, he continued. "You made an issue of asking me if I was going to be home for dinner and then you're gone."

Carelessly, Maggie tossed her coat over an armchair. "I lost track of the time," she explained on her way into the kitchen. Glenn was only a step behind. From the grim set of his mouth, Maggie recognized that once again she'd displeased him. Everything she'd done the past few days seemed to fuel his indignation.

He didn't say another word as she worked, dishing up the meal of baked pork chops and scalloped potatoes Rosa had prepared for them. Maggie could feel his gaze on her defeated shoulders, studying her. He looked for a moment as if he wanted to say something, but apparently changed his mind.

"I was in an art gallery today," she told him conversationally.

"Oh."

"I'm thinking of taking in some of my work."

"You should, Maggie."

Silence followed. This was the first time they'd had a decent conversation since she'd sided with her brother against him.

Their dinner was awkward, each trying to find a way to put their marriage back on track. Glenn sat across from her, cheerless and somber. Neither ate much.

"Did the mail come?" Maggie asked, setting the dinner dishes aside.

"It's in your office," Glenn answered without looking up. "Would you like me to bring it in to you?"

"Please. I'll finish up here in a minute." Well, at least they were speaking to each other, she thought. It was a start. Together they'd work things out. The situation with Denny was probably the first of many disagreements and misunderstandings they would face through the years. It might take time, she told herself, but they'd work it out. They loved each other too much to allow anything to wedge a space between them for long. They had both behaved badly over this issue with Denny, but if she'd bend a little, Glenn would, too.

When Glenn returned to the living room, he said her name with such fervor that her head came up. Unconsciously Maggie pressed farther back into the thick cushions of her chair, utterly stunned by the look that flashed from her husband's eyes. She could think of nothing that would cause him such anger.

"Explain this," he said and thrust her letter to Angie in front of Maggie's shocked face.

Twelve

Maggie's mind was in complete turmoil. She'd known it was a risk to write Angie, and later had regretted it. She hadn't mailed the card. Yet she'd left the letter on top of her desk for Glenn to find. Perhaps subconsciously she had wanted him to discover what she'd done.

Tension shot along her nerves as she struggled to appear outwardly calm. Lifting the chatty letter Glenn handed her, she examined it as if seeing it for the first time, amazed at her detachment. Whatever she wished, consciously or subconsciously, Glenn had found it and the timing couldn't be worse. They were just coming to terms with one major disagreement and were about to come to loggerheads over another. Only this issue was potentially far more dangerous to the security of their marriage. Going behind Glenn's back had never felt right. Maggie had regretted her deception a hundred times since. And yet it had been necessary. Long ago Maggie had admitted that Glenn had forced her into the decisive action. She had asked him about Angie and he'd refused to discuss the other woman. Maggie was his wife and she loved him; she had a right to know. But all the rationalization in the world wasn't going to help now.

"How do you explain this?" His voice went deep and low, as though he couldn't believe what he'd found. Maggie hadn't trusted him to help her brother, he thought, somewhat dazed, and now he'd learned that she had betrayed his trust in another situation as well.

Glenn knew he should be furious. Outraged. But he wasn't. His emotions were confused—he felt shocked, hurt and discouraged. Guilt was penned all over Maggie's pale face as she sat looking up at him, trying to explain. There couldn't possibly be a plausible one. Not one. Feeling sick with defeat, he turned away from her.

Maggie's heartbeat quickened at the pained look in Glenn's dark eyes. "I met Angie."

"When?" he asked, still hardly able to comprehend what she was saying. He paced the area in front of her in clipped military-like steps as if standing in one place were intolerable.

Maggie had never seen any man's features more troubled. "The…the day I flew to San Francisco… I took a flight to Groves Point first and then flew from there to Atlanta before heading home."

If possible Glenn went even more pale.

"I asked you to tell me about the two of you but—" Maggie attempted to explain and was quickly cut off.

"How did you know where she lived?"

Admitting everything she had done made it sound all the more sordid and deceitful. She hesitated.

"How did you know where she lived?" he repeated, his rising voice cold and deliberate. Maggie was pressed as far back against the chair cushion as possible as dread settled firmly over her.

"I found her letter to you…and read it." She wouldn't minimize her wrongdoing. The letter had been addressed to him and she had purposely taken it from the envelope and read each word. It was wrong. She knew it was wrong, but given the opportunity, she would do exactly the same thing again.

Shocked, all Glenn seemed capable of doing was to stare back at her. She yearned to explain that she hadn't purposely searched through his drawers or snooped into his private matters. But she could see that expounding on what had happened wouldn't do any good. Reasoning with Glenn just then would be impossible. She felt wretched and sick to her stomach. The ache in her throat was complicated by the tears stinging her eyes. With everything in her, she struggled not to cry.

"What else did you try to find?" he asked. "How many drawers did you have to search through before you found the letter? Did you take delight in reading another woman's words to me? Is there anything you don't know?"

"It wasn't like that," she whispered, her gaze frozen in misery.

"I'll bet!" He moved to the other side of the living room. His anger died as quickly as it came, replaced by a resentment so keen he could barely stand to look at Maggie. She couldn't seem to let up on the subject of Angie. For months he had loved Maggie so completely that he was amazed that she could believe that he could possibly care for another woman. Worse, she had hounded the subject of Angie to death. It was a matter of trust, and she'd violated that and wounded his pride again and again.

"Are you satisfied now? Did you learn everything you were so keen to find out?" His voice was heavy with defeat. "You don't trust me or my love, do you, Maggie? You couldn't, to have done something this underhanded."

"That's not true," she cried. Glenn wanted to wound her;

she understood that. She had hurt him when all she'd ever wanted to do was give him her love, bear his children and build a good life with him. But their marriage had been clouded with the presence of another woman who stood between them as prominently as the Cascade mountain range. Or so it appeared at the time.

With a clarity of thought Glenn didn't realize he possessed, he knew he had to get out of the room...out of the house. He needed to sit down and do some serious thinking. Something was basically wrong in a relationship where one partner didn't trust the other. He loved Maggie and had spent the past few months trying to prove how much. Obviously he'd failed. He crossed the living room and jerked his raincoat off the hanger.

"Where are you going?" Maggie asked in a pathetically weak voice.

He didn't even look at her. "Out."

Trapped in a nightmare, her actions made in slow motion, Maggie came to her feet. The Christmas card and letter were clenched in her hand. Glenn turned to look back at her and his gaze fell to the brightly colored card. His mouth twisted into a scowl as he opened the door and left Maggie standing alone and heartbroken.

Maggie didn't allow the tears to escape until she was inside their bedroom with the door securely closed. Only then did she vent her misery. She wept bitter tears until she didn't think she could stop. Her throat ached and her sobs were dry; her eyes burned and there were no more tears left to shed. She had hoped to build a firm foundation for this marriage and had ruined any chance. Glenn had every reason to be angry. She had deceived him, hurt him, invaded his privacy. The room was dark and the night half-spent when Glenn came to bed. His movements sounded heavy and vaguely out of order. The dresser drawer was jerked open, then almost immediately slammed shut. He stumbled over something and cursed impatiently under his breath as he staggered to the far side of the bedroom.

Remaining motionless, Maggie listened to his movements and was shocked to realize that he was drunk. Glenn had always been so sensible about alcohol. He rarely had more than one drink. Maggie bit into her lower lip as he jerked back the covers and fell onto the mattress. She braced herself, wondering what she'd do if he tried to make love to her. But either he was too drunk or he couldn't tolerate the thought of touching her.

She woke in the morning to the sounds of Glenn moving around the room. Her first thought was that she should pretend to be asleep until he'd left, but she couldn't bear to leave things unsettled any longer.

"Glenn," she spoke softly, rolling onto her back. At the sight of his suitcase she bolted upright. "Glenn," she said again, her voice shaking and urgent. "What are you doing?"

"Packing." His face devoid of expression, told her nothing.

He didn't look at her. With an economy of movement he emptied one drawer into a suitcase and returned to the dresser for another armload.

Maggie was shocked into speechlessness.

"You're leaving me?" she finally choked out. He wouldn't...couldn't. Hadn't they agreed about the sanctity of marriage? Hadn't Glenn told her that he felt divorce was wrong and people should work things out no matter what their problems?

Glenn didn't answer; apparently his actions were enough for her to realize exactly what he was doing.

"Glenn," she pleaded, her eyes pleading with him. "Please don't do this."

He paused mid-stride between the suitcase and the dresser. "Trust is vital in a relationship," he said and laid a fresh layer of clothes on top of the open suitcase.

Maggie threw back the covers and crawled to the end of the mattress. "Will you stop talking in riddles for heaven's sake. Of course trust is vital. This whole thing started because you didn't trust me enough to tell me about Angie."

"You knew everything you needed to know."

"I didn't," she cried. "I asked you to tell me about her and you refused."

"She had nothing to do with you and me."

"Oh, sure," Maggie shouted, her voice gaining volume with every word. "I wake up the morning after our wedding and you call me by her name. It isn't bad enough that you can't keep the two of us straight. Even…even your friends confuse our names. Then…then you leave her picture lying around for me to find. But that was nothing. The icing on the cake comes when I inadvertently find a letter tucked safely away in a drawer to cherish and keep forever. Never mind that you've got a wife. Oh, no. She's a simpleminded fool who's willing to overlook a few improprieties in married life."

Rising to her knees, Maggie waved her arms and continued. "And please note that word 'inadvertently,' because I assure you I did not go searching through your things. I found her letter by accident."

Glenn was confused. His head was pounding, his mouth felt like sandpaper and Maggie was shouting at him, waving her arms like a madwoman.

"I need to think," he murmured.

Maggie hopped off the bed and reached for her bathrobe. "Well, think then, but don't do something totally stupid like...like leave me. I love you, Glenn. For two days we've behaved like fools. I'm sick of it. I trusted you enough to marry you and obviously you felt the same way about me. The real question here is if we trust our love enough to see things through. If you want to run at the first hint of trouble then you're not the Glenn Lambert I know." She tied the sash to her robe and continued, keeping her voice level. "I'm going to make coffee. You have ten minutes alone to 'think.'"

By the time she entered the kitchen, Maggie's knees were shaking. If she told Glenn about the baby he wouldn't leave, but she refused to resort to that. If he wanted to stay, it would be because he loved her enough to work out their differences.

The kitchen phone rang and Maggie stared at it accusingly. The only person who would call her this time of the morning was Denny. If he asked her for another penny, she'd scream. It used to be that he'd call once or twice a month. Now it was every other day.

On the second ring, Maggie nearly ripped the phone off the hook. "Yes," she barked.

"Maggie, is that you?" Denny asked brightly. "Listen, I'm sorry to call so early, but I wanted to tell you something."

"What?" Her indignation cooled somewhat.

"I'm going to work Monday morning. Now don't argue, I know that you're against this. I'll admit that I was, too, when I first heard it. But I got to thinking about what Glenn said. And, Maggie, he's right. My attitude toward life, toward everything, has been rotten lately. The best thing in the world for me right now is to get back into the mainstream of life and do something worthwhile."

"But I thought…" Maggie couldn't believe what she was hearing.

"I know. I thought all the same things you did. But Linda and I had a long talk a few days ago and she helped me see that Glenn is right. I went to an interview, got the job and I feel terrific. Better than I have in years."

Maggie was dumbfounded. She lowered her lashes and squeezed her eyes at her own stupidity. Glenn had been right all along about Denny. Her brother had been trapped in the same mire as she had been. Maggie should have recognized it before, but she'd been so defensive, wanting to shield her brother from any unpleasantness that she had refused to acknowledge what was right in front of her eyes. Denny needed the same purpose that Glenn's love had given her life.

The urge to go back to their bedroom and ask Glenn to forgive her was strong, but she resisted. Denny was only one problem they needed to make right.

Glenn arrived in the kitchen dressed for the office. Silently he poured himself a cup of coffee. Maggie wondered if she should remind Glenn that it was Saturday and he didn't need to go to work. No, she'd let him talk first, she decided.

He took a sip of the hot, black coffee and grimaced. His head was killing him. It felt as if someone was hammering at his temple every time his heart beat. Furthermore he had to collect his car. He'd taken a taxi cab back to the house, far too drunk to get behind a wheel.

"Who was on the phone?" he asked. The question was not one of his most brilliant ones. Obviously it had been Denny, but he hoped to get some conversation going. Anything.

"Denny."

Glenn cocked a brow, swallowing back the argument that sprang readily to his lips. If she was going to write WELCOME across her back and lie down for Denny to walk all over her there wasn't anything he could do. Heaven knew he'd tried.

"He...he called because..."

"I know why he phoned," Glenn tossed out sarcastically.

"You do?"

"Of course. Denny only phones for one reason."

"Not this time." Her pride was much easier to swallow after hearing the excitement and enthusiasm in her brother's voice. "He's got a job."

Glenn choked on a swallow of coffee. "Denny? What happened?"

"Apparently you and Linda got through that thick skull of his and he decided to give it a try. He feels wonderful."

"It might not last."

"I know," Maggie agreed. "But it's a start and one he should have made a long time ago."

Her announcement was met with silence. "Are you telling me I was right?"

"Yes." It wasn't so difficult to admit, after all. Her hands hugged the milk-laced herbal tea and lent her the courage to continue. "It was wrong to take matters into my own hands and visit Angie. I can even understand why you loved her. She's a wonderful person."

"But she isn't you. She doesn't have your beauty, your artistic talent or your special smile. Angie never made up crazy rules or beat me in a game of tennis. You're two entirely different people."

"I'll never be like her," Maggie murmured, staring into the creamy liquid she was holding.

"That's a good thing, because I'm in love with you. I married you, Maggie, I don't want anyone else but you."

Maggie's head jerked upright. "Are you saying…? Do you mean that you're willing to forgive me for taking matters into my own hands? I know what I did wasn't right."

"I'm not condoning it, but I understand why you felt you had to meet her."

If he didn't take her in his arms soon, Maggie thought, she'd start crying again and then Glenn would know her Christmas secret for sure.

He set the coffee cup aside and Maggie glanced up hopefully. But instead of reaching for her, he walked out of the kitchen and picked up the two suitcases that rested on the other side of the arched doorway.

Panic enveloped her. "Glenn," she whispered. "Are you leaving me?"

"No. I'm putting these back where they belong." He didn't know what he'd been thinking this morning. He could no more leave Maggie than he could stop breathing. After disappearing for a moment, he returned to the kitchen and stood not more than three feet from her.

Maggie's heart returned to normal again. "Are we through fighting now? I want to get to the making up part."

"We're just about there." The familiar lopsided grin slanted his mouth.

"Maybe you need a little incentive."

"You standing there in that see-through outfit of yours is giving me all the incentive I need." He wrapped his arms around her then and held her so close that Maggie could actually feel the sigh that shuddered through him.

She met his warm lips eagerly, twining her arms around his neck and tangling her fingers in the thick softness of his hair. Maggie luxuriated in the secure feel of his arms holding her tight. She smiled up at him dreamily. "There's an early Christmas gift I'd like to give you."

Unable to resist, Glenn brushed his lips over the top of her nose. "Don't you think I should wait?"

"Not for this gift. It's special."

"Are you going to expect to open one of yours in return?"

"No, but then, I already have a good idea of what you're getting me."

"You do?"

Maggie laughed outright at the way his eyes narrowed suspiciously. "It wasn't really fair because your mother let the cat out of the bag."

"My mother!"

"Yes, she told me about your grandmother's ring."

His forehead wrinkled into three lines. "Maggie, I'm not giving you a ring."

He couldn't have shocked her more if he'd dumped a bucket of ice water over her head. He wasn't giving her the ring! "Oh." She disentangled herself from his arms. "I...guess it was presumptuous of me to think that you would." Her eyes fell to his shirt buttons as she took a step backward.

"Just so there aren't any more misunderstandings, maybe I should explain myself."

"Maybe you should," she agreed, feeling the cold seep into her bones. It never failed. Just when she was beginning to feel loved and secure with their marriage, someone would throw a curve ball at her.

"After the hassle we went through with the wedding rings—"

"I love my rings," she interrupted indignantly. "I never take them off anymore. You asked me not to and I haven't."

She knew she was babbling like an idiot, but she wanted to cover how miserable and hurt she was. All those months she had put so much stock in his grandmother's ring and he wasn't even planning on giving it to her.

"Maggie, I had the ring reset into a necklace for you."

"A necklace?"

"This way you won't need to worry about putting it on or taking it off, or losing it, for that matter."

The idea was marvelous and Maggie was so thrilled that her eyes misted with happiness. "It sounds wonderful," she murmured on a lengthy sniffle and rubbed the tears from her face.

"What is the matter with you lately?" Glenn asked, his head cocked to one side. "I haven't seen you cry this much since you were six years old and Petie Phillips teased you and pulled your braids."

Maggie smiled blindly at him. "You mean you haven't figured it out?"

"Figured what out?"

Glenn's dark brown eyes widened as he searched her expression as if expecting to find the answer hidden on her face. His eyebrows snapped together. "Maggie," he whispered with such reverence one would assume he was in a church, "are you pregnant?"

A smile lit up her face, and blossomed from ear to ear. "Yes. Our baby is due the first part of August."

"Oh, Maggie." Glenn was so excited that he longed to haul her into his arms and twirl her around the room until they were both dizzy and giddy. Instead, he pulled out a chair and sat her down. "Are you ill?"

"Only a little in the mornings," she informed him with a small laugh. "The worst thing is that I seem to cry over the tiniest incident."

"You mean like me packing my bags and leaving you."

"Yes." She giggled. "Just the minor things."

"A baby." Glenn paced the area in front of her, repeatedly brushing the hair off his forehead. "We're going to have a baby."

"Glenn, honestly, it shouldn't be such a shock. I told you in the beginning I wasn't using any birth control."

"I'm not shocked…exactly."

"Happy?"

"Very!" He knelt in front of her and gently leaned forward to kiss her tummy.

Maggie wrapped her arms around his head and held him to her. "Merry Christmas, my love."

Glenn heard the steady beat of Maggie's heart and closed his eyes to the wealth of emotions that flooded his being. She was a warm, vital woman who had made him complete. Wife, friend, lover…the list seemed endless and he had only touched the surface.

"Merry Christmas," he whispered in return and pulled her mouth to his.

* * * * *

JURY OF HIS PEERS

For
Ted Macomber, our son,
the wonderful negotiator

One

There was something vaguely familiar about him. Caroline Lomax's gaze was repeatedly drawn across the crowded room where the prospective jury members had been told to wait. He sat reading, oblivious to the people surrounding him. Some were playing cards, others chatting. A few were reading just as he was. It couldn't be Theodore Thomasson, Caroline mused, shaking her head so that the soft auburn curls bounced. Not "Tedious Ted," the childhood name she had ruthlessly given him because of his apparent perfection. The last time she'd seen him had been the summer he was fifteen and she was fourteen, just before her father's job had taken them to San Francisco. It wasn't him; it couldn't be. First off, Theodore Thomasson wouldn't be living on the West Coast and, second, she would have broken out in a prickly rash if he were. Never in her entire life had she disliked anyone more.

Determined to ignore the man completely, Caroline picked up a magazine and idly flipped through the dog-eared pages. If that was Theodore, which it obviously couldn't be, then he'd changed. She would never openly admit that he was handsome back then. Attractive, maybe, in an eclectic way. But this man... If it was Theodore, then his eyes were the same intense blue of his youth, but his ears no longer had the tendency to stick out. The neatly trimmed dark hair was more stylish than prudent, and if Tedious Ted was anything, he was sensible, levelheaded and circumspect. And rational. Rational to the point of making her crazy. Admittedly, her own father was known to be rational, practical, discriminating and at times even parsimonious. As the president of Lomax, Inc., the fastest growing computer company in the world, he had to be.

The thought of her stern-faced father produced an involuntary smile. What a thin veneer his rationality was, at least where she and her mother were concerned. He loved his daughter enough to allow her to be herself. Caroline realized that it was difficult for him to accept her offbeat lifestyle and her choice to go to culinary school with the intent of becoming a chef, not to mention that she'd opted for a lower standard of living than what she was accustomed to. She knew he would rather see her in law school. Regardless, he supported her and loved her, and she adored him for it.

A glance at the round clock on the drab beige wall confirmed that within another fifteen minutes the prospective jurors would be free to go. Her first day of jury duty had been a complete waste of time. This certainly wasn't turning out as she'd expected. Her mind had conjured up an exciting murder trial or at least a dramatic drug bust. Instead she'd spent the day sitting in a room full of strangers, looking for a way to occupy herself until her name was called for a panel.

Fifteen minutes later, as they stood to file out of the room, Caroline toyed with the idea of saying something to the man who resembled Theodore, but rejected the idea.

If it was him, she decided, she didn't want to know. In addition, she needed to hurry to the Four Seasons Hotel. Her dad had a business meeting in Seattle with an export agency, and her mother had come along to visit Caroline, a plan that was derailed when fate decreed that Caroline would spend the day in a crowded, stuffy room being bored out of her mind. Tonight the three of them were going out to dinner. From the restaurant they would take a cab, and she would see her parents off on a return flight to San Francisco.

At precisely five, she walked down the steps of the King County Courthouse and glanced quickly at the street for the bus. She swung her backpack over her shoulder and hurriedly stepped onto the sidewalk. Thick, leaden-gray clouds obliterated the March sun, and she shook off a sensation of gloom and oppression. This feeling had been with her from the moment she'd walked into the jury room, and she suspected that it didn't have anything to do with the early spring weather.

A few minutes later she smiled at the doorman in the long red coat who held open the heavy glass doors of the posh hotel. Moments later she stepped off the elevator, knocked, and was let into her parents' suite.

Ruth Lomax glanced up from the knitting she was carrying, and her eyes brightened. Her bifocals were perched on the tip of her nose, so low that it was a wonder they didn't slip completely free. "How'd it go?" she asked as she sat back down.

"Boring," Caroline answered, taking the seat opposite her mother. "I sat around all day, waiting for someone to call my name."

A smile softened her mother's look of concentration. There was only a faint resemblance between mother and daughter, which could be attributed mostly to their identical hair color. Although Ruth's was the deep combination of brown and red that was sometimes classified as chestnut, Caroline's was a luxuriant shade of brilliant auburn. Other similarities were difficult to find. A thousand times in her twenty-four years, Caroline had prayed that God would see fit to grant her Ruth's gentle smile and generous personality. Instead, she had been pegged a rebel, a nonconformist, bad-mannered and unladylike—all by her first grade teacher. From there matters had grown worse. In her junior year she was expelled from boarding school for impersonating a nun. Her father had thrown up his hands at her shenanigans, while Ruth had smiled sweetly and staunchly defended her. Ruth seemed to believe that Caroline could have a vocation for the religious life and the family shouldn't discount her interest in this area. Caroline was wise enough to smother her giggles.

"You know who I thought I saw today?"

"Who, dear?" Folding her glasses, Ruth set them aside and gave her full attention to her daughter.

"Theodore Thomasson."

"Really? He was such a nice boy."

"Mom!" Caroline exclaimed. "He was boring."

"Boring?" Ruth Lomax looked absolutely shocked and smiled gently. "Caroline, I don't know what it is you have against that boy. You two never could seem to get along."

"Being with him was like standing in a room and listening to someone scrape their nails down a blackboard." Irritated, Caroline yanked the backpack off and tossed it carelessly aside. "I suppose you're going to want me to wear a dress tonight." Her usual jeans and T-shirt had been a constant source of aggravation to her father. However, tonight Caroline wanted to keep the peace and do her best to please him.

Ruth ignored the question, her look thoughtful as she set aside her knitting. "He was always so well-mannered. So polite."

"'Stuffy' is the word," Caroline interjected. "It's the only way to describe a fifteen-year-old boy who takes dancing lessons."

"Lots of people take dance lessons, dear."

Caroline opened her mouth to object, then closed it again, not wishing to argue. As a boy, Theodore had been so courteous, charming and full of decorum that she'd thought she would throw up.

"He was thoughtful and introspective. As I recall, you were dreadful to him that last summer."

Caroline shrugged. Her mother didn't know the half of it.

"Sending him all those mail-order acne medications was outrageous." She wasn't able to completely disguise a smile. "C.O.D. at that. How could you, Caroline?"

"I wanted him to know what it was like not to be perfect in every way."

"But his skin was flawless."

"That's just it. The guy didn't have the common decency to have so much as a pimple."

Slowly, her mother shook her head. "And you had pimples and freckles."

"Don't forget the braces."

"And he teased you?"

Caroline tossed her jacket over a chair without looking at her mother. "No, he wouldn't even do that. I'd have liked him better if he had."

"It sounds to me as if you were jealous."

"Oh, really, Mother, don't get philosophical on me. What's there to like about a kid whose favorite television program is *Meet the Press?* Believe me, there's nothing to envy."

Although her mother didn't comment, Caroline felt her frowning gaze as she busied herself, pulling out a skirt and sweater from the backpack. "What ever became of him, Mom, do you know?"

"The last I heard, he was working for the government."

"Probably the Internal Revenue Service," Caroline said with a mocking arch of her brow.

"You may be right."

That secret smile was back again, and Caroline wondered exactly what her mother was up to. "He's the type of guy who would relish auditing people's tax returns," Caroline mumbled under her breath, running a brush through her thick hair until it curled obediently at her shoulders.

"By the way, Caroline, your father and I are definitely getting you a bed for your birthday."

"Mom, I don't have room for one."

"It's ridiculous to pull that…thing down from the wall every night. Good grief, what would you do if it snapped back into place in the middle of the night?"

Caroline smiled. "Cry for help?" It wasn't that she didn't appreciate the offer, but her apartment was small enough as it was. Having a fold-up bed was the most economical use of the limited space. The apartment was cozy—all right, snug—but its location offered several advantages. It was close to the Pike Place Market and the heart of downtown Seattle. In addition, her school was within walking distance. As far as she was concerned, she couldn't ask for more.

"You need a decent bed," her mother argued. "How

do you expect to find a job if you don't get a good night's rest?"

"I sleep like a baby," Caroline returned, hiding a smile. "Now, about dinner tonight. Would you prefer to take a taxi to meet Dad, or are you brave enough to try the backseat of my scooter?" She only suggested this for shock value. The scooter was safely tucked away in the basement of her apartment building.

"Your scooter?" Ruth's voice rose half an octave as she turned startled eyes toward her daughter.

"Don't worry, I can see you'd prefer the taxi."

Since Charles Lomax was tied up later than expected in a meeting, Caroline and her mother took a taxi directly to La Mer, an elegant Seattle restaurant that overlooked the ship canal connecting Lake Union with Puget Sound. A large stone fireplace with a crackling fire greeted them. As they checked their coats, Caroline glanced around the expansive room, seeking her father's burly figure. When she caught sight of two men rising from a table in the middle of the room, her heart dropped. Next to her father was the same man she'd seen in the jury room, and something told her it really was Theodore Thomasson. So this was the reason for her mother's strange little smiles. Everything fit into place now. This business deal with the export outfit was somehow linked to Theodore.

"Ted, how nice to see you again." Ruth Lomax embraced him and stepped back to study him. "You've grown so tall and good looking."

"The years have only enhanced your beauty." He looked beyond Ruth to Caroline. "I wondered if that was you today."

So he had noticed her. Caroline's throat felt scratchy and dry. On closer inspection, she was forced to admit that

Theodore had indeed changed. The boyish good looks of fifteen had matured into strikingly handsome sculpted features that were the picture of both strength and character. Theodore Thomasson was attractive enough to cause more than a few heads to turn. And Caroline was no exception. Her bemused thoughts were interrupted by his deep male voice, which was as intriguing as his looks.

"Hello, Caroline." His eyes moved with warm appraisal from her mother to rest solidly on her. Then the friendliness drained from the brilliant blue gaze as they sought and met hers. "It's good to see you again, Hot Stuff."

Caroline fumed at the reference to that last summer and the incident she sincerely hoped her parents never connected with her. With an effort, she managed to shrug lightly and smile. "Touché, Tedious Ted."

With a hearty laugh, Charles Lomax pulled out a chair and seated his wife. Before Ted could offer her the same courtesy, Caroline seated herself.

"I see you're not intimidated by my daughter," her father told Ted with a smile.

Silently, Caroline gritted her teeth. Theodore Thomasson wasn't getting the best of her that easily. Her chance would come later.

Her gaze was drawn to the huge windows that provided an unobstructed view of the ship canal. Sailboats, their sails lowered, glided past, with the brilliant golden sun setting in the background.

Inside the restaurant, the tables, covered in dark red linen, were each graced with a single long-stemmed rose. La Mer was rated among the best restaurants in Seattle. She had never eaten here before, but the elegance of the room assured her that no matter what the food was like, this was going to be a special treat.

"I understand you work for the government. The Internal Revenue Service, is it?" Caroline asked Ted with mock-sweetness, then turned away to study the elaborate menu. She hoped the dig hit its mark.

"And exactly what is it that *you* do?" From beneath dark brows he observed her with frank interest. She noted that he hadn't answered her question. Although his eyes didn't spark with challenge, there was an uncompromising authority in the set of his jaw that wasn't the least bit to Caroline's liking.

Her mother spoke up quickly. "Caroline graduated cum laude from—"

"I'm training at the Natalie Dupont School," Caroline interrupted. Unsure that he would recognize the name of the nationally famous culinary school, she added, "I'm a chef—or I will be shortly. I've just completed a year's apprenticeship." Her father had had a difficult time accepting the fact that she'd chosen a career as menial as cooking. Ambition and hard work had driven Charles Lomax to the top of his profession. Caroline didn't doubt that she would have to work just as hard making a name for herself, but though he rarely argued the point with her, she knew her father didn't agree.

The aggressive vitality in Ted's eyes demanded that she look at him. "So you didn't grow up to be a fireman," he said with a smile.

Caroline felt a cold sweat break out across her upper lip. Her family knew nothing of the fireworks display she had rigged outside his bedroom the night of July third.

"No." She forced her voice to sound as innocent as possible, as if her memory had blotted out that unfortunate chain of events that had set the balcony on fire.

"Shame," he responded casually. "You displayed such a talent for pyrotechnics."

"What's this?" her father asked, his gaze swinging from Caroline to Ted.

"Nothing, Dad." She gave him her most engaging smile. "Something from when we were kids."

Ted's mouth quirked in a half smile.

Caroline tilted her chin and haughtily returned his gaze. "You were such an easy target," she whispered.

"Not anymore, I'm not."

Smoothing the starched linen napkin over her lap, Caroline gave him a cool look. "I never have been able to turn down a challenge."

"Am I missing something here?" her father demanded.

"Nothing, Dad," Caroline answered. "Tell me, Theodore, what brought you to Seattle? I always thought you'd think of Boston as home."

"Most people call me Ted."

"All right... Ted."

"Seattle's a beautiful city. It seemed a nice place to live."

"Are you always so vague?" Caroline's voice was sharp enough to cause her mother to eye her above the top of the menu. Unbelievable! She actually found Theodore—Ted—as irritating now as she had when they were teenagers. Worse, even.

"Only when I have to be," he taunted lightly, doing a poor job of disguising a smile.

Caroline itched to find a way to put him in his place and was surprised at the intensity of her feelings.

The meal was an uncomfortable experience. Countless times Caroline found her gaze drawn to Ted. In astonishment, she noticed the way his eyes would warm when they rested on her mother and immediately turn icy cool when they skimmed over her. He didn't like her, that much was obvious. But then, he had little reason to do anything but hate the sight of her.

Through the course of the conversation, Caroline learned that though Ted might have worked for the federal government at one time, he didn't now. From the sound of things, her guess had been right and he was employed by the export company that had brought her father to Seattle. She didn't want to ask for fear of sounding interested.

The meal was as delicious as she'd been led to believe it would be, so she focused on that and made only a few comments, spoke only when questioned and smiled demurely at all the appropriate times.

"So you two are both serving jury duty this week," her father said after an uncomfortable pause in the conversation. "What a coincidence."

Caroline's and Ted's eyes met from across the table.

"I call it bad luck," Caroline answered. She toyed with the last bit of baked potato as she dropped her gaze.

"And neither of you was aware that the other lived here?"

"No." Again it was Caroline who answered, then mumbled under her breath that moving to California was looking more appealing by the minute. If she expected a reaction from Ted, he didn't give her one. He'd heard her, though, and one corner of his mouth jerked upward briefly. Somehow she doubted that the movement was in any way related to a smile.

"Never served on a jury myself," her father continued. "Don't know that I ever will."

"It must have been twenty years ago when I was called. You remember the time, don't you, Charles?" Ruth chimed in, and detailed the account of the robbery trial on which she'd sat.

When Caroline did chance a casual look Ted's way, she was rewarded with a slightly narrowed gaze. Outwardly, he looked as if he hadn't a care in the world and was thoroughly enjoying himself. She couldn't imagine how. He couldn't help but feel her obvious dislike. Occasionally she would catch him studying her and flush angrily. His pleasant, amused expression never varied, which only served to aggravate her more. He should be the uncomfortable one. Instead, he exchanged pleasantries with her parents, then spoke affectionately of his own family. When the bill was presented, Ted insisted on paying, and in the same breath offered to drive her parents to the airport.

"But I thought I was taking you," Caroline objected.

"Your father and I can hardly ride on the back of your scooter," her mother said with a teasing glint in her eye.

"Scooter?" Ted repeated with a curious tilt of his head.

Caroline bristled, waiting for a cutting remark that didn't come.

"It's the most economical way of getting around," she supplied and granted him a saccharine smile.

"It's a shame my daughter has to be economical about anything," her father said with a rumbling chuckle. "She's taking this cooking business seriously. Living within her means. I give her credit for that."

Caroline had to bite her tongue to keep from reminding him that she was training to be a chef, not a short-order cook. A year of schooling, plus another year's apprenticeship, proved that this was serious business. In four years of college she hadn't worked as hard as she had in the last two years.

"It will work out fine to have you drop us off at the airport," her father continued.

"I'll take a taxi from here," Caroline said. The thought of getting stuck alone with Ted Thomasson on the return ride from the airport was more than she could tolerate.

"Nonsense. I'll see you home," Ted said smoothly, one dark brow rising arrogantly, daring her to refuse.

"Theodore, you were always so polite," Ruth said, smiling at her daughter as if to point out that Caroline had indeed misjudged him all these years.

Personally, Caroline doubted that. He might have matured into a devilishly handsome man, but looks weren't everything.

From the restaurant, the foursome returned to the Four Seasons Hotel so the Lomaxes could collect their luggage. The ride to the airport took an additional uneasy twenty minutes. Caroline buried her hands deep inside her pockets as she walked down the concourse at Sea-Tac International. She dreaded the time when she would have to face Ted without her parents present to buffer the conversation.

Her father and mother hugged her goodbye and Caroline promised to email more often. In addition, they promised to pass on her love to her older brother, Darryl, who lived in Sacramento with his wife and two young sons. All the while they were saying their farewells, Caroline could feel Ted's eyes studying her.

He didn't say anything until her parents had disappeared into the security line.

"The cafeteria's open."

She cast him a curious glance. "We just ate a fantastic meal. You couldn't possibly want another."

One brow arched briefly. "I'm suggesting coffee."

"No thanks."

"Fine." His long stride forced her to half walk, half run in order to keep up with him. By the time they were in the parking garage, she was straining to breathe evenly. Not for anything would she let him know she was winded.

The ride back into the city was completed in grating silence. It wasn't until they were near the downtown area that she relayed her address. Even then, she said it in a mechanical monotone. Ted glanced at her briefly and his fingers tightened around the steering wheel. This was even worse than she'd imagined.

When he pulled into a parking lot across from her apartment, turned off the engine and opened the car door, butterflies filled her stomach. "I didn't invite you inside," she said indignantly.

"No," he agreed. "But I'm coming in anyway." A thread of steel in his voice dared her to challenge him. In disbelief, she watched as his slow, satisfied smile deepened the laugh lines at his eyes. Too bad. Whatever he had in mind, she wasn't interested.

"Listen," she said, striving for a cool, objective tone. "If you want an apology for what happened that summer, then I'll give you one."

Ted acted as if she hadn't spoken. Agilely, he stepped out of the car and slammed the door closed. Caroline climbed out on her own before he could walk around to her side. Opening a lady's car door was something he would obviously do, given the kind of man he was.

She stopped and looked both ways before stepping off the curb. A hand at her elbow jerked her back onto the sidewalk. "What are you doing?" he demanded.

Caroline stared at him speechlessly. "Crossing the street," she managed after a long moment.

"The light's this way."

Ted hadn't changed, not a bit. Good grief, he didn't even jaywalk. She clenched her jaw, hating the thought of him invading her home.

"Did you hear what I said earlier?" she asked. "I owe you an apology. You've got one. What more do you want?"

His hand cupped her elbow as they stopped at the traffic light. She pulled her arm free, angrier with her body's warm response to his touch than the fact that he'd taken her arm.

The light changed, and they crossed the street. The brick apartment building was four stories high. Caroline's tiny apartment was on the third floor. All the way up the stairs, she tried to think of a way of getting rid of Ted. She realized that arguing with him wasn't going to do any good. She might as well listen to what he had to say and be done with it.

The key felt cool against her fingers as she inserted it into the lock. A flip of the light switch bathed the room in a gentle glow.

Standing just inside the apartment, Ted made a sweeping appraisal of the small room. Caroline couldn't read the look in his eyes. Hooking her backpack over the doorknob, she turned to him, hands on her hips. "All right," she said in a slow breath. "What is it you want?"

"Coffee."

Seething, she marched across the room to the compact kitchen. With anyone else she would have ground fresh-roasted beans. As it was, she brought down one earthenware mug, dumped a teaspoon of instant coffee inside and heated the water in the microwave.

"Satisfied?" she asked sarcastically as she handed him the steaming mug.

"Relatively so." His half smile was maddening.

Pulling out a chair, he sat and looked up at her standing stiffly on the other side of the narrow room. "Have a seat."

"No thanks. I prefer to stand."

He shrugged as if it made no difference to him and blew on the coffee before taking a tentative sip.

Stubbornly, Caroline crossed her arms in front of her and waited.

"I want to know why," he said at last.

"Why what?" she snapped.

"Why do you dislike me so much?"

"Have you got a year?"

"I have as much time as necessary."

"Where would you like me to begin?" Her voice was deceptively soft, but her feelings were clear. By the time she was finished, his ears would burn for a week.

"That last summer will do." He still refused to react to the antagonism in her voice.

"All right," she said evenly. "You were perfect in every way. Honest, sincere, forthright. What kind of kid is that? Darryl and I had stashed away fireworks for weeks, and you acted as if we'd robbed a bank."

"They were illegal. You're lucky you didn't blow your fool head off. As it was—"

"See." She pointed an accusing finger at him. "If you didn't want any part of it, that was your prerogative, but tattling to my dad was a spiteful thing to do. It's that goody-goody attitude I couldn't tolerate," she continued, warming to the subject.

Ted looked genuinely taken back. "What? I didn't say a word to your family."

Caroline's lungs expanded slowly. Ted Thomasson probably hadn't stretched the truth in his life. She couldn't do anything but believe him. "Then how did Dad find out I had them?"

"How am I supposed to know?" His eyes nearly sparked visible blue flame.

"At least he never found out how I got rid of them."

"What were my other crimes?"

Uneasy now, Caroline shrugged weakly.

"Well?" he demanded.

"You wouldn't go swimming with me." The one afternoon she'd made an effort to be nice, Ted had flatly rejected her offer of friendship.

A brief smile touched his eyes. "True, but did you ever ask yourself why?"

"I don't care to know. What was the matter? I was trying to be nice. Were you afraid I was going to drown you?"

"Knowing your past history, that was a distinct possibility."

"It wasn't my fault the brakes on that golf cart failed."

"Don't lie to me, Caroline. You never hid what you thought of me before."

Guilt colored her face a hot shade of red. "Okay, I'll admit it. I never liked you. And I never will." She crossed her arms again to indicate that the conversation was closed.

"Why didn't you like me?" he asked softly, setting his coffee aside. The chair slid back as he suddenly stood.

Caroline pinched her mouth tightly closed. When he moved so that he loomed over her, she clenched her jaw.

"Why?" he repeated.

"I...just didn't...that's all." She detested the way her voice shook.

"There's got to be a logical reason." His eyes cut through her.

"Your hair was always perfectly trimmed." Her gaze

locked with his in a fierce battle of wills. "It still is," she added accusingly.

"Yours is still the same fiery red." As if he couldn't resist, he reached out and wove a thick strand around his index finger. "I remember the first time I saw it and wondered if your hair color was the reason you were so hot-tempered."

"A lot you know." Her voice gained strength and volume. "My hair is auburn."

He laughed softly, as if he found her protestations amusing.

"You've probably never done anything daring in your life," she went on. "You were always afraid of one thing or another. You're the most boring person I ever met."

"And you're a hellion."

"But I've never bored anyone in my life," she snapped defensively.

"Neither have I. You simply didn't give me the chance to prove it to you." He released her hair to slide his fingers around her nape in a slow, easy caress.

Caroline drew in a sharp breath and tried to shrug his hand free. A crazy whirl of sensations caused her stomach muscles to tense.

"Take your hand off me." She grabbed his arm in an effort to free herself.

He ignored her protests. "Was there anything else?"

"You...took dancing lessons."

Nodding, he laughed softly. "That I did. Only I hated them more than you'll ever realize."

"You—never wanted to do anything fun." Desperately her mind sought valid reasons for her intense dislike of him and came up blank.

"I want to do things now," he drawled in a voice that was

barely perceptible. Ever so slowly, he lowered his mouth to hers.

Mesmerized, her heart pounding like the crashing waves upon a sandy shore in a storm, Caroline was powerless to stop him. When he fitted his mouth over hers, she made a weak effort by pushing against his chest. No kiss had ever been so sweet, so perfect, so wonderful. Soon her hands slid around his neck as she pressed her soft figure to his long length, clinging to him for support.

When they broke apart, she dropped her arms and took a staggering step backward. The staccato beat of her heart dropped to a sluggish drum roll at the wicked look twinkling in Ted's eyes. He'd wanted to humiliate her as she'd done to him all those years ago. And he'd succeeded.

"I bet you didn't think kissing 'Tedious Ted' could be so good, did you, Caroline?"

Two

Caroline woke with the first light of dawn that splashed through her beveled-glass window. The sky was cloudless, clear and languid. Her first thought was of Ted and her overwhelming response to his kiss. Silently, she seethed, detesting the very thought of him. To use sensory attraction against her was the lowest form of deceit. He'd wanted to humiliate her and had purposely kissed her as a means of punishment for the innocent crimes of her youth. And what really irritated her was that it had been the most sensual kiss of her life. Her cheeks burned with mortification, and she pressed cool palms to her face to blot out the embarrassment. Ted Thomasson was vile, completely without scruples, and that was only the tip of the iceberg as far as she was concerned.

The morning was chilly, but Caroline had her anger to keep her warm. If she'd disliked Ted Thomasson at fourteen, those feelings paled in comparison to the intensity of her feelings now. Yet she had to paint on a plastic smile and sit in the same room with him today, pretending she hadn't been the least bit affected by what had happened. If she were lucky, she would be called out early for a trial, but at the rate her luck was running, she would end up stuck sitting next to him for the next four days.

The brisk walk to the King County Courthouse helped cool her indignation. She bought a cup of coffee from a machine and carried it with her into the jury room. The bailiff checked off her name and gave her a smiling nod. Caroline didn't pause to look around, afraid Ted would see her and think that she was seeking him out. As far as she was concerned, if she saw him in another eighty years it would be a hundred years too soon.

The coffee was scalding, and she set it on a table to cool while she reached for a magazine—an outdated copy of *Time*. Flipping through the pages, she noted that the stories that had captured the headlines six months ago were still in the news today. Little had changed in the world. Except Ted—he'd changed. His aggressive virility had captured her attention from the minute they'd stepped into the restaurant. Forcibly, she shook her head to reject the thought of him. She detested the way he'd invaded her mind from the minute she'd climbed out of bed.

She caught a movement out of the corner of her eye and turned to see. Ted stood framed in the doorway of the large, open room. He wore an impeccable three-piece gray suit with leather shoes. Italian, no doubt. After spending a restless day lounging in the jury room, almost everyone else had dressed more casually today. She herself had slipped on dark cords and an olive-green pullover sweater. But not Mr. Propriety. Oh, no, his long legs had probably never known the feel of denim. Angrily she banished the image of Ted in a pair of tight-fitting jeans.

"Morning." He claimed the empty chair beside her. "I trust you slept well. I know I did."

Wordlessly, she took her cup of coffee and moved to a vacant seat three chairs down.

Without hesitating, Ted stood and followed her. "Is something wrong?"

Despite her anger, she managed to make her voice sound calm and reasonable. "If you insist on pestering me, then you leave me no option but to report you to the bailiff."

"Did I pester you last night, Caroline?" he asked in a seductive drawl that sent shivers racing down her spine.

"Yes." She felt like shouting but made an effort and kept her voice low.

"Funny, that wasn't the impression I got."

"You're so obtuse you wouldn't recognize a—"

"Your response to me was so hot it could have set off a forest fire."

She drew a rasping breath. She tried and failed to think of a comeback that would wipe that mocking grin off his face.

"From the time we were children, I've disliked you," she murmured, her gaze fixed on her coffee. "And nothing's changed."

His soft chuckle caught her off guard. She'd expected something scathing in retaliation, but certainly not laughter. In hindsight, she realized that Ted had probably never raised his voice to a woman.

"That's not the impression you gave me last night," he taunted.

Seething, Caroline closed her eyes. Her mind groped for a logical explanation of what had happened. She'd only had one glass of wine with the meal, so she couldn't blame her response on the influence of alcohol. Telling him that her biorhythms were out of sync would make her sound like an idiot. "Knowing that you've always been perfect in every way, I don't expect you to understand a momentary lapse of discretion on my part," she finally said.

"I don't believe that any more than you do," he said with cool calm.

Crossing her arms in front of her, she refused to look at him. "Fine. Believe what you want. I couldn't care less."

"You care very much," he returned flatly.

Pinching her mouth tightly closed, she refused to be drawn further into the conversation.

"You intrigue me, Caroline. You always have. I've never known anyone who could match your spirit. You were magnificent at fourteen. With that bright red hair and freckles dancing across your nose, I found you absolutely enchanting."

Slowly, she appraised him, searching each strongly defined feature for signs of sarcasm or derision. She was so taken aback by the gentle caress of his voice that any response died in her throat. "How can you say that?" she managed at last. "I was horrible to you."

"Yes," he chuckled, "I know."

"You should hate me," she said.

"I discovered I never could."

The bailiff began reading the names on the first panel of jurors, and Ted paused to listen, along with the hundred and fifty other people seated in the room. Periodically during the day, the court sent requests down to the jury room and names were drawn in a lottery system, and this same hush fell over the crowd every time.

Caroline's name was one of the first to be called. At last, she thought, she was going to see some of the action. A few seconds later she heard Ted's name. They were being called along with several others for the same trial.

They were led as a group into an upstairs courtroom

and seated outside the jury box. Caroline sat down on the polished mahogany pew, uncomfortably distracted by the knowledge that Ted was behind her. Their conversation lingered in her mind, and she wanted to free her thoughts for the task that lay before her. She looked up and noticed that several people were studying the potential jurors. The judge, in his long black robe, sat in the front of the courtroom, his look somber. The attorneys were at their respective tables, as was the defendant. She found her gaze drawn to the young man who stared at the group with a belligerent sneer.

Everything about him spoke of aggressive antagonism—his looks, his clothes, the way his eyes refused to meet anyone else's. His slouched posture, with arms folded defiantly across his chest, revealed a lack of respect for the court and the legal proceedings. The defense attorney leaned over to say something to him, but the defendant merely shrugged his shoulders, apparently indicating that he didn't care one way or the other. What an unpleasant man, Caroline thought, holding back her instant feelings of dislike. Above all, she wanted to be impartial and, if she were chosen for the jury, base her decision on the evidence, not the look of the defendant.

The judge spoke, announcing that the defendant, Nelson Bergstrom, was being tried for robbery and assault. Twelve of the panel members were led to the jurors' box. Caroline was the last to be seated in the first row. A series of general questions was addressed to the prospective jurors. No one answered out loud, instead raising their hands if their response was positive. No one on the jury knew the defendant personally. Several had heard of this case through the media, since there had been a string of similar late-night assaults against female clerks. No one had an arrest record of their own. Three members had been the victims of crime. After the general questions, each juror was interviewed individually.

The attorney who approached the box smiled at Caroline, who thought that Ted was dressed more like a lawyer than this lanky guy with an easy grace and charming grin. One by one, he asked the prospective jurors specific questions regarding friends, attitudes and feelings. When he was finished, his opposite number stepped up and had his own questions for them. Neither attorney challenged Caroline for cause, but she was surprised at the number of available jurors who were dismissed for a variety of reasons, none of which seemed important to her. The two lawyers went through the first twelve-member panel and called for another. In the end, she, Ted and eleven others were chosen. The thirteenth member was an alternate who would listen to all the testimony. However, he would be called into the deliberation only if one of the jurors couldn't continue for some reason, a procedure intended to prevent the need for a retrial.

The trial began immediately, and the opening statements made by each attorney filled in the basic details of the case. A twenty-three-year-old clerk, a woman, had been robbed at gunpoint at a minimarket late one night shortly before Thanksgiving. Terrified, the woman handed over the money from the till, as requested. The thief then proceeded to pistol whip her until her jaw was broken in two places. Although the details of the crime were relayed unemotionally, Caroline felt her throat grow dry. The defendant revealed none of his feelings while the statements were being made. His face was an unyielding mask of indifference and hostility, a combination she had never thought was possible. Again and again she found her gaze drawn to him. In her heart she realized that she fully believed Nelson Bergstrom was capable of such a hideous crime. As soon as she realized that she was already forming an opinion, she fought to cast it from her mind.

By the end of the first day, Caroline's thoughts were troubled as the jurors filed from the courtroom. Serving on a jury wasn't anything like what she'd anticipated. When she'd been contacted by mail with her dates of service, her emotions had been mixed. This was her first free week after completing her apprenticeship, and she'd hated the thought of spending it tied up in court. Now that she was sitting on a case, the reality of the crime genuinely distressed her. The victim was no doubt sitting in the courtroom. Caroline hadn't picked her out of the small crowd, but she knew she had to be there. Absently she wondered how the poor woman could endure the horror of that night.

"Are you all right?" Ted asked her once they hit the steps outside the courthouse.

"Of course," she said, struggling to sound offhand. It had been another stroke of bad luck to have Ted on the same trial. She hadn't seen him in ten years, and now, in a mere two days, he had become an irritating shadow she couldn't shake.

The jury had been warned against discussing any of the details of the case with each other. Caroline yearned to ask Ted what his impression of the proceedings had been but bit back the words. She felt strangely, unaccountably melancholy. Bemused, she frowned at the brooding sense of responsibility that weighed her down. This was only the beginning of the trial, and already she felt intimately involved with the victim *and* the defendant.

"Let's go have a drink," Ted said, taking her elbow. "We both need to relax."

She felt as if she'd been anesthetized and didn't argue—another clear sign of her confusion.

It wasn't until they entered the bar that Caroline realized she was acting as docile as a lamb being led to the slaughter.

"The Tropical Tradewinds?" She raised questioning eyes to Ted.

"You look like you're in the mood for something exotic."

She shook her head and released a slow sigh. Honestly, it was just like Ted to bring her somewhere like this. Oh, the Tropical Tradewinds had a wonderful reputation, but it certainly wasn't her style. She doubted that a place like this even carried something that didn't call for at least six ingredients. "What I'm in the mood for is a good ol' fashion beer."

"Fine, I'll order you one," he returned, pressing a hand to the small of her back as he directed her toward a vacant table. Politely, he held out a chair for her, and, struggling to hold her tongue, she took a seat. She never could understand why men found it necessary to seat women. They seemed to assume that the weaker sex was incapable of something as simple as sitting without assistance. Obviously Ted felt she needed his help, and this once she would let it pass; she simply wasn't in the mood to get into a fight with him.

The waitress arrived, and before Caroline could open her mouth, Ted placed their order. Unable to restrain her reaction, her blue eyes clashed with his as the waitress headed to the bar.

"What did I do wrong now?" he asked quietly, his gaze studying her.

"Does it look as if I've lost control of my tongue?"

"No, but I was hoping." His devilish grin served only to aggravate her further.

"Incidents like these irritate the hell out of me," she said, crossing her legs.

"Incidents like what?"

"Pulling out my chair, ordering my drink, opening a car door. Do I honestly look so helpless?"

"A gentleman always—"

"Can it, Thomasson. I'm not up to hearing a dissertation on the proper behavior of the refined adult male."

"Caroline," Ted replied curtly, "in this day and age a man is often placed in an unpleasant position. Half the time I don't know which a lady prefers. If I don't hold out her chair, I'm considered a creep, and if I do, I'm a chauvinist. It's a no-win situation."

"I suppose you'll pay for this with a gold-plated credit card, too."

"What's that got to do with anything?" His mouth hardened with displeasure, then softened into a faint smile as their waitress approached. She placed two thick paper coasters on the round tabletop, and set down Caroline's beer and Ted's scotch.

One look at his drink and Caroline rolled her eyes.

"Now what?" The acid in his voice was scathing.

"You're drinking scotch?"

"I would have thought that much was obvious when I ordered." He started to say more, then stopped, as if he couldn't trust himself to speak.

Remorse brought a flush of guilt to Caroline's cheeks. Ted was only trying to be nice, and her behavior was inexcusable. "Listen, Ted, I apologize for... I don't mean to be so rude. It's just that we're so different. We'll never be able to agree on anything."

Her casual apology didn't seem to please him either.

"If it's any consolation, you turned out about a thousand times better than I ever imagined," she continued. More than his good looks prompted the statement. He really wasn't the bore she would have expected. He was a little too concerned with propriety, but some women would appreciate that quality. Not her, but someone else.

His blue gaze frosted into an icy glare as he stared at her.

"See," she murmured triumphantly, catching his look. "You and I grate against each other. I prefer a beer out of a can."

"And I enjoy the finest scotch."

"Exactly." She supposed she should be pleased that he agreed with her so readily. "I'm a morning person." She looked at him questioningly.

"I do my best work at night."

"Baseball is my favorite sport." She leaned back in the chair and took a drink of the cold beer. It helped ease the dryness in her throat. "I suppose you enjoy polo."

"No." He shook his head and lowered his gaze to his glass. "Curling."

"Of course." She did her best to disguise a smile.

"I'm certain that if we looked hard enough we'd discover several common interests."

"Such as?" Her look was skeptical.

The beginning of a smile added attractive brackets to the corners of his mouth. "You're a chef, and I definitely enjoy eating."

"Well, you didn't deny working for the Internal Revenue Service at one time, but I don't enjoy paying taxes."

"Caroline," he muttered with obvious control, "I was employed for a brief time by the federal government, but that was years ago. I'm in exports now."

He regarded her steadily with sky-blue eyes. He really had wonderfully expressive eyes. The thick lashes were the same dark color as his hair. If she allowed it, she realized, she could watch him forever. She lowered her own eyes, fearing what he might read in them.

"We should concentrate on the interests we share."

"Good idea." She scooted closer to the table. "Do you play cards?"

"I'm a regular shark."

"Great." Perhaps the real problem between them was something as simple as her own attitude. They were bound to find several things to enjoy about each other if they looked hard enough.

"How about bridge?" he asked.

"Bridge?" Caroline spat out the word. "I hate it. It's the most boring game in the world. I like poker."

Ted stared at her in amazed disbelief. "Okay, we'll forget cards."

"What about music?" At the cynical arch of his brow, she added, "My tastes may surprise you."

"Everything about you surprises me."

"Ha!" She was beginning to enjoy this. "I already know your tastes. You appreciate Michael Bublé, I bet."

"Talented guy," Ted agreed.

"And," she paused to give some thought to his tastes, "I imagine you enjoy some of the early rock and roll stars like Buddy Holly. I'll throw in the Kingston Trio just to be on the safe side. In addition, I'm sure you're crazy about classical."

"Very good." His smile was devastating. "I'm impressed."

"All right." Gesturing with her hand, she offered him the opportunity to add his own speculations regarding *her* musical tastes. "Do your worst—or best, as the case may be."

He chuckled, and amusement flickered across his features. "I couldn't begin to venture a guess. You are a complete enigma to me and always have been. That's what makes you such an enchantress."

Caroline's smile was filled with confident amusement, sure she was about to surprise him. "I adore Mozart, Gene Autry and Billy Joel."

"Not Kermit the Frog?"

"Don't tease," she replied cheerfully. "I'm serious."

"So was I."

For the first time that evening, she felt completely at ease. She lounged back in the chair and tucked one foot under her. "Shall we dare venture into television?"

"Speaking of which, did you see the recent PBS special on fungus?"

For a moment she assumed he was teasing, but one look assured her that he was completely serious. All her energy was expended in an effort not to laugh outright. "No, I must have missed that. I was watching old reruns of *I Love Lucy.*"

"From the sounds of this, perhaps it would be best to move on to something else."

"What was the last book you read?"

He shifted uncomfortably and took a sip of his drink. "I think we should skip this one, too."

"Ted," she whispered saucily, "don't tell me you're into erotica."

"What? *No*," he responded emphatically, obviously uneasy. "If you must pursue this, I recently finished Homer's *Iliad*."

Caroline pushed the errant curls from her forehead. "In the original Greek?"

He nodded.

"I should have known," she muttered under her breath. Absolutely nothing about this man would surprise her anymore. He was brilliant. She wanted to resent that fact, but instead she found a grudging respect taking root.

"What about you?"

"I enjoy romances and science fiction and Dick Francis."

"Dick who?"

"He writes horse-racing mysteries. You have to read him to believe how good he is. I'll lend you some of his books if you'd like."

"I would."

Caroline offered him a bright, vivacious smile as she polished off her beer. "You realize we haven't found a single interest we share."

"Does it matter?" Just the way he said it sent a chord of sensual awareness singing through her, igniting an answering reprise within her heart. She couldn't believe that she was looking at Theodore Thomasson and hearing music. That was something reserved for novels. Romances. No, science fiction.

"Caroline…"

She shook her head to clear her thoughts. "Sorry, what were you saying? I wasn't listening."

"I was asking you to have dinner with me."

"Here?"

His look was one of tolerant amusement. "No, you choose."

"Great." Mentally she discarded her favorite Egyptian restaurant and asked, "Is Italian okay?"

"Anything's fine."

She sincerely doubted that but managed to hide her knowing grin. "There's a seafood place within walking distance if you'd rather."

"The choice is yours," he said.

"Don't be so accommodating," she said, raising her voice. "There's only so much of that I can take."

With a wide grin, Ted stood. She noted that he didn't offer her his hand as she got out of her chair, a small courtesy for which she was disproportionately grateful.

Dusk had settled over the city as they moved onto the sidewalk. Streetlights were beginning to flicker around them.

"Your dad said you went to college. What's your degree in?"

"Biochemistry." She watched the surprise work its way over his features and marveled at the control he exhibited.

"Biochemistry," he repeated in bewilderment. "And now you're in culinary school?"

"Yup. I felt that of all the majors I could have chosen, biochem would be the most value to me."

Confusion shone from his expressive eyes. "I don't think I care to follow your line of reasoning."

"It's not that difficult," she answered brightly. "You see, Dad never was thrilled with my ambitions in the kitchen. I am, after all, his daughter, and he didn't feel I was aiming high enough, if you catch my drift."

"I understand."

"So instead of constantly arguing, we made an agreement. I'd go to college and get my degree, and in exchange he'd continue to support me while I went to culinary school afterwards."

"That sounds like a fair compromise. Did you come up with it?"

"Who, me?" She pressed her palm to her breast. "Hardly. I was too involved in defending my individual rights as a human being to see any solution. Mom was the one who suggested that course of action."

"But why did you choose biochemistry?"

"Why not?" she tossed back. "I'd like to think of myself as a food scientist. There's a whole world out there that has only been touched on."

"I'm surprised your father didn't insist on sending you to Paris, if you were so sure that cooking was what you wanted to do."

"He offered." The frustration remained vivid in her memory. "Only the best for his little girl and all that rot. But I didn't want to go overseas. The Natalie Dupont School here in Seattle is one of the best, and it offers a focus on baking. I'd like to focus my efforts in the area of breads. The average person looks at a loaf and thinks of sandwiches or toast. I see lipids, leaveners, proteins and biological structures. Yeast absolutely fascinates me."

"Obviously I'm a less complicated soul. What fascinates me most is you."

The tender look in his eyes nearly stopped her heart. "Me?" She stared at him, hardly believing the pride and wonder in his gaze. His blue eyes were full of warmth, and he was smiling at her with gentle understanding in a way she never would have suspected.

"Have you noticed your sense of timing is several years off?"

"My what?" Caroline's look was bewildered. "How do you mean?"

"At a time when most women are happy to get out of the kitchen, you're battling your way in."

Smiling, she nodded and placed her hand in the crook of his arm. Within the span of one day, she felt as if Ted and she had always been the closest of friends. True, they didn't share a lot of common interests, but there was a bond between them that was beyond explanation. The knowledge stunned her, and she paused, wanting to speak, but not knowing what to say or how to say it.

Caroline knew when he lowered his head that he intended to kiss her, and her eyelids slowly fluttered closed with eager anticipation. When nothing happened, her eyes shot open to discover him staring down at her. Reluctantly, it seemed, he kissed the top of her head and took her hand as they continued to stroll down the street.

Mortified, she felt the embarrassment extend all the way to her hairline. Seconds earlier they'd experienced a spiritual communication that left her breathless with wonder, and now... The traffic light changed, and a long series of cars whizzed past. In a flash, Caroline understood that as much as he might want to, Ted wouldn't kiss her on a busy Seattle street. Not with the possibility of them being seen.

Their meal was wonderful. It could have been the wine, but she doubted it. In spite of their many differences, they found several subjects on which they shared similar opinions. They both enjoyed chess and Scrabble and, most surprisingly, shared the same political affiliation, though Ted's sense of humor was more subtle than her own. By the time they left the Italian restaurant, Caroline couldn't remember an evening she'd enjoyed more. She'd laughed until her stomach ached.

Ted's hand at the back of her neck warmed her spine as they lazily strolled toward her apartment.

"I had a good time," she said casually, reaching over and entwining her fingers with his.

"Don't sound so surprised." His chin nuzzled the crown of her head.

"I can't help it. Darryl would keel over if I told him I'd spent an enjoyable evening with you."

She basked in the warmth of his slow, easy smile.

"I never did understand how your parents could possibly have two such completely different children. Darryl's exactly like his father, and you…well, it's just hard to believe you're his sister."

Caroline pulled her hand free. Disappointment and anger burned through her. "I've already apologized for my childhood bad behavior. You're right, I treated you terribly. I tricked you. I lied about you. I nearly burned the house down in an effort to undermine you. But that was twelve years ago." Whirling, she marched away.

"Caroline?" Hurried footsteps sounded behind her. "What did I say?"

"You know exactly what you said." She tried to walk faster, her pace just short of an outright jog.

"I *don't* know," he countered. His hand on her shoulder stopped her. Turning her around, he held her shoulders while his bewildered gaze roamed her face. A frown drew his thick brows together. "I've hurt you."

"What you said about not knowing how…how I could possibly be Darryl's sister, when you know good and well that I'm not."

A stunned look drained the color from his face. "Are you saying you're adopted?"

Her narrowed, fiery glare answered the question for him. "That's impossible," he whispered.

Three

"Just what exactly do you mean by that remark?" Hands on her hips, Caroline stared into his face.

"You look—"

"Like my mom? No I don't."

"The hair—"

"That's the only thing, but otherwise we're nothing alike. Mom's gentle, patient, forgiving. Every day of my life I've wanted to be exactly like her. I've honestly tried, but I'm—"

"Stubborn, quick-tempered and often impertinent," Ted supplied for her.

She opened her mouth to argue, then thought better of it. "Yes," she admitted, then rammed her hands inside the pockets of her cords and began shuffling backwards. "Thank you for tonight, I'm sorry it has to end this way."

"Come on, Caroline. I can't be blamed for an innocent mistake. I didn't know."

"You do now."

"What difference does it make?"

"Think about it," she snapped. "You're a smart man. You'll figure it out."

"Since we're tallying your faults, you can add unreasonableness to your growing list. I've never met a more frustrating woman."

Turning, Caroline made her escape, running up the three flights of stairs that led to her apartment. She knew she was behaving badly, but she couldn't help it. From childhood, Ted had been Mr. Prim-and-Proper and she had ridiculed him for it. But that wasn't the real reason she'd disliked him so intensely. The truth was, he was everything she wanted so badly to be.

If she were even half as refined as Theodore Thomasson, her mother would have been so proud. If only she could have maintained high grades and managed to stay out of trouble, everything would have been so grand. But no matter how hard she tried or how many promises she made, she simply couldn't be something she wasn't. Her temper flared with the least provocation, her poise was as fragile as fine china, and her self-confidence was shattered by every grade school teacher who was unfortunate enough to have her in class. Perhaps she could have accepted herself more readily if her mother hadn't been so tolerant and forgiving. She'd wanted to cry and beg her mother's forgiveness for every minor blunder, but her mother would never allow that. She loved her daughter exactly the way she was. Often when Caroline was sent to her room without dinner by her father—the ultimate punishment—her mother would smuggle in fruit and cookies. More times than Caroline could count, her mother had calmly intervened between her and her father. Amazing as it was, she shared a strong relationship with her mother. There wasn't anything Caroline felt she couldn't share with her. No mother could have been more wonderful.

Each year, on Caroline's birthday, her mother told the

story of how she'd longed for a daughter. Darryl was her
son and she loved him dearly, but she wanted a daughter
and had prayed nightly that God would smile upon her a
second time and grant her another child—a girl. After five
years it became apparent that she wouldn't have more children, and they'd decided to adopt. On their first visit to
the caseworker, Ruth had seen a picture of a fiery-haired,
two-year-old toddler and known instantly that this was
just the little girl she wanted. At that point in the tale her
father always interrupted to add that the caseworker had
discouraged them from adopting the tiny hellion. But Ruth
had persisted until the caseworker relented and brought
the four of them together for the first time. Usually at this
point her brother, Darryl, would insert that the first time
he'd seen Caroline, she'd bitten him on the leg. He claimed
she'd marked him for life and had the scar to prove it. So
she had been adopted into this family who loved her in
spite of her rambunctious behavior. For their love, Caroline would be forever grateful, but in her heart she would
never really feel a part of them. Theodore Thomasson was
a constant reminder of exactly how different she was. Next
to him, her imperfections were magnified a hundred times.

An air of expectancy hung over the proceedings early
the following morning. The jury was seated in a closed
room adjacent to the courtroom, but Caroline arrived in
time to see the defendant being brought into the court and
seated. Again she noted his apparent lack of concern. It
was almost as if he didn't care what the jury or anyone else
thought. He was purposely making himself unlikable, and
she couldn't understand that.

She stepped into the room reserved for the jury and sat

beside a grandmotherly woman who paused in her knitting and said hello.

"I want to talk to you," Ted whispered.

Caroline smiled apologetically to the older woman, who had already gone back to her knitting. "I don't know that man. Would you kindly tell him that if he continues to pester me, I'll be forced to report him to the bailiff?"

"I can't understand what's the matter with these young men today." The metal needles clicked as they wove the fine strands of yarn in and out. She had been knitting through the entire proceedings the day before, and Caroline had dubbed her Madame La Farge.

Now Madame La Farge turned and gifted Ted with what Caroline was sure was a scathing look. "Kindly leave this young lady alone."

"Caroline..." Ted ground out her name, his voice ringing with frustration.

Ignoring him, she scanned the faces of her fellow jurors, thinking that they resembled a fair cross section of society. All the men were dressed casually, except Ted, who wore a pin-striped suit. There were an electrician, a real estate broker, an engineer and others whose occupations Caroline couldn't recall. The other four women on the jury were all middle-aged.

"All rise, this court is now in session," the bailiff announced, and a rustling sounded in the jury room as those in the courtroom rose to their feet.

Within minutes the door opened and the jury was led in and seated. The prosecutor stood to present his case, calling several witnesses. The defendant, Nelson Bergstrom, had been tried and found guilty of assault and robbery five years before, and had been on parole only six weeks at the time of the minimarket robbery. His parole officer testified that Nelson had been living within ten blocks of the market. Another witness testified that he had seen Nelson at the store the day before the robbery.

The arresting officer followed with his report.

The next witness, Joan MacIntosh, was called. Caroline saw a young woman slowly enter the courtroom. Obviously nervous and shaky, Joan cast a pleading glance to the large man who had walked in with her. He gave her an encouraging smile and squeezed her hand, then took a seat. From the fear in the woman's eyes, Caroline realized that Joan MacIntosh must be the woman who had been assaulted. She was petite, barely five feet, with a fragile, delicate look. If she weighed over a hundred pounds, it would have been a surprise. The woman was terrified, that much was obvious. She hesitated once and glanced back. The man who'd come in with her nodded reassuringly several times, and Joan squared her shoulders before continuing forward.

The scene was poignant. Whatever physical harm had been done her had apparently healed, but it was obvious that the psychological damage had been far greater. Caroline looked at Joan and was overcome with sympathy. They were close in age, and from the address, Caroline knew they didn't live more than three miles apart. It could have been her instead of Joan who had been treated so brutally.

After being sworn in, Joan took the witness stand. Following a series of perfunctory questions, the prosecutor leaned against the polished banister. "Joan, to the best of your ability, I'd like you to tell the court the events of the night of November twenty-third."

Joan's voice had been weak and wobbly, but as she began speaking, she gained confidence and volume. "I was working as a clerk for the market for.only two weeks.

There—really isn't much to tell. I was alone, but that didn't bother me, because there had been a steady stream of customers in and out most of the night."

The prosecutor gave her an encouraging smile. "Go on."

"Well…it must have been close to eleven, and things had slowed down. I noticed someone hanging around outside, but I didn't think much of it. A lot of kids hang around the store."

Caroline noticed that Joan's hands were tightly clenched, and that a tissue she was holding was shredded.

"Anyway—he…the man who had been outside, came into the store. He went to the back by the refrigerator unit. I assumed he was going to buy beer or something. But when he approached the register I noticed that he had a ski mask over his face. And he had a gun pointed at my heart." Joan's voice grew weak as she remembered the terror. Briefly, she closed her eyes.

"Go on, Joan."

"He…he didn't say anything to me, but he pointed the gun at the cash register. I wanted to tell him he could have everything, but I couldn't talk. I was…so scared." She blinked, and Caroline could see tears working their way down her face. "I would have done anything just so he wouldn't hurt me."

"What happened next?"

"I opened the till to give him the money." She hesitated and bit her trembling bottom lip. "He told me to put all the money in a sack. I did that—I even gave him the change. I was so frightened that I dropped the bag on the counter. All the time I was praying that someone would come. Anyone. I didn't want to die…. I told him that over and over again. I begged him not to hurt me." Her voice cracked, and she placed a hand over her mouth until she'd regained her composure. "Then he looked inside the sack and told me it wasn't enough."

"What did you tell him?"

"I said I'd given him all the money there was and that he could take anything else he wanted."

"How did he react to that?"

"He told me to give him my purse, which I did. But I only had a few dollars, and that made him even angrier. He started waving the gun at me. I begged him not to shoot me. He told me to get more money. He shouted at me over and over that he needed more money. Then he started hitting me with the gun. Again and again he hit my face, until I was sure I'd never live through it. The pain was so bad that I wanted to die just so it would stop hurting."

Caroline could barely make out the words, because Joan was sobbing now. The man who'd accompanied her stood and clenched his fists angrily at his sides. The bailiff pointed to him, indicating that he should sit down again. The man did, but Joan's testimony was obviously upsetting him.

Caroline doubted that anyone could remain unaffected by the details. Joan MacIntosh was a delicate young woman who had been brutally attacked and beaten for less than twenty dollars. Caroline felt that any man who could beat someone so much smaller and virtually defenseless—or anyone, for that matter—should rot in prison.

After a few more questions, the prosecutor stepped back and sat down, and the defense attorney came forward. Joan sat up and eyed him suspiciously.

"Can you describe to the court what the man who attacked and robbed you looked like?" he asked in a calm, cool voice.

"He...he was average height, about a hundred and sixty pounds, dark hair, dark eyes...."

"Did you ever get a clear view of his face?" the defense attorney pressed. "I noted in your testimony that you claim that the man who beat you had been hanging around outside the store."

"Well, I..."

"It seems to me that you would have had ample opportunity to clearly see his face," he pressed.

"Not entirely. He wore a ski mask."

"What about before, when he was outside the store? When he first came in?"

"He...he averted his... I only saw his profile."

"Before you answer the following question, Ms. MacIntosh, I want you to think very carefully about your answer. Is the man who attacked you in this courtroom today?"

Caroline's eyes flew from Joan to the defendant. Nelson Bergstrom was sneering at the young woman in the witness box, all but challenging her to name him.

"Is that man in the courtroom today?" the defender repeated.

"I...think so."

The attorney placed the palms of his hands on the bannister and leaned forward. "A man's entire future is at stake here, Ms. MacIntosh. We need something more definite than 'I think so.'"

"Objection." The prosecutor vaulted to his feet.

Caroline listened as the two men argued over a fine point of law that she didn't entirely understand, and then the defense attorney went back to questioning Joan. When the cross-examination was complete, the judge dismissed the court for a one-hour lunch break.

After the defendant was led away, the courtroom emptied into the hall. Ted was standing outside the large double doors waiting for Caroline. She paused, and their eyes met and held. Listening to the morning testimony had drained her emotionally and physically. She waited for the rising tide of resentment she'd so often experienced in his presence, but none came. After last night she realized that it would be best to keep their relationship strictly impersonal.

His look was long and penetrating, as if he were reading her thoughts. A full minute passed before he spoke. "Are you going to talk to me, or am I going to be forced to send you notes through your bodyguard with the knitting needles?" The quiet tenderness in his deep voice softened her struggling resolve to remain detached. He hadn't done anything to provoke her, not really. She could hardly blame *him* for the circumstances of her birth.

"We can talk," she said, and looped the long strap of her purse over her shoulder. "Really, I should be the one who does the talking."

Ted touched her elbow, guiding her in the direction of the elevator. As if forgetting himself, he quickly lowered his hand. Caroline managed to hide a secret smile. He was trying so hard to please her. She simply couldn't understand why he would want to go to that much trouble.

"Once again, I find myself in the position of having to apologize to you," she began as they paused on the outside steps. "I realize now that you didn't know I was adopted. In fact, I find it a compliment that you hadn't guessed years ago."

"Apology accepted," he said, smiling down at her. Together they walked down the long flight of stairs that led to the busy sidewalk. "I don't know what made you so angry, but then, I've given up trying to understand what makes you tick."

In spite of herself, Caroline laughed. "Dad said the same thing to me when I as ten."

"I'm a slow learner," Ted admitted and slipped an arm around her shoulder. "It took me until late last night to realize that I'll probably never understand you. With that same thought came the realization that you mattered enough to me to keep trying."

"Why would you even want to?" His reasoning was beyond Caroline. And he thought *she* was difficult to comprehend!

His expression softened, and he looked at her with an unbearable gentleness. He traced a finger along the delicate curve of her jaw and down her chin to linger at the pulse that hammered wildly at the base of her neck. The muscles of her throat constricted, and she swayed involuntarily toward him.

"I'm not exactly sure why," he admitted, slowly shaking his head. "Maybe it's as simple as the magnetic attraction between opposites."

"No one is more opposite than you and I."

"That is something we can definitely agree on," he said, and led her across the street.

"Where are we going?"

"There's an excellent French restaurant a couple of blocks from here." There was a guarded edge to his voice as he studied her. "You don't like French food." It was more statement than question.

"It's fine. It's just I'm not very hungry. I was thinking of walking down to the waterfront and ordering clam chowder from Ivar's."

"Listening to the testimony this morning bothered you, didn't it?"

They had been strictly warned against discussing any

of the details of the trial. Fearing that once she answered she would blurt out the opinions she was already forming, Caroline simply nodded. "I could feel that poor woman's terror."

"I don't think there was a person in the room who wasn't affected by it," he agreed.

She dragged her eyes from his, wanting to say more and knowing she didn't dare. "Jury duty is so different from what I thought it would be. Monday morning I was hoping I'd get on an exciting murder trial. Today I'm having difficulty dealing with the emotional impact of an assault and robbery. Can you imagine what it's like for the jury on something as horrible as a murder case?"

"I don't think I want to know," Ted murmured with feeling.

They strolled down to Seattle's busy waterfront. The smell of salt water and seaweed drifted toward them. A sea gull squawked as it soared in the cloudless blue sky and agilely landed on the long pier beside the take-out seafood stand.

Caroline insisted on paying for her own lunch, which consisted of a cup of thick clam chowder, a Diet Pepsi and an order of deep-fried mushrooms. Ted ordered the standard fish and chips.

They sat opposite each other at a picnic table. As much as she tried to direct her thoughts into other channels, her mind continued to replay the impassioned testimony she'd heard that morning.

"Are you seeing anyone?" Ted's question cut into her introspection.

"Pardon?"

"Are you involved with someone?"

Caroline stared at him and noted that his dark brows

had lifted over inscrutable blue eyes. That he didn't like asking this question was obvious.

But even if he didn't like asking it, ask it he had, and she wasn't all that pleased to be answering it. "Not this month," she said flippantly.

"Caroline," he said with a sigh. "I'm serious."

"So am I. Romance is a low priority right now. I'm more interested in finding a job."

He didn't even make a pretense of believing her. "Who was he?" he asked softly.

"Who?"

"The man who hurt you."

She laughed lightly. "And people say *I* have a wild imagination."

"I'm not imagining things. The minute I asked you about a man, a funny, hurt look came over you."

Still? Caroline expelled her breath in a slow, even sigh. Clay had broken up with her over two months ago, but the memory of him was still as painful as it had been the night they'd finally split. She opened her mouth to deny everything, then realized she couldn't. The only person who knew the whole story was her mother. Caroline had enjoyed being with Ted the last couple of days, but that didn't mean she was up to sharing the most devastating experience of her life with him. And yet she couldn't stop herself from speaking.

"His name was Clay," she began awkwardly, repeatedly running her index finger along the rim of her cup. "There's not much to say, really. We dated for a while, decided we weren't suited and went our separate ways."

Ted's smile was sympathetic but firm. "You're not telling me the half of it."

"You're right, I'm not," she confirmed hotly. "Who said

you had the right to butt into my personal life? What makes you think I'd share a painful part of my past with you? Good grief, I'm not even sure I like you. At any minute you're likely to turn back into 'Tedious Ted.'" Tension and regret were building within her at a rapid rate. She regarded him with cool disdain. How dare he put her in this position? "What would you know about love? In your orderly existence, I doubt that you've..." She stopped before she said something she would regret. "I didn't mean that," she finished, feeling wretched.

He took her hand, his fingers folding around hers. "I'm sorry I asked."

She refused to lower her gaze, although it demanded every ounce of her willpower. "It was over several weeks ago.... I don't know why I reacted like that."

"Are you still in love with him?" he asked meaningfully.

Caroline pasted a smile on her mouth and glanced his way with a false look of certainty. "No, of course not." Not if she could respond to Ted's kiss the way she had. Her overwhelming reaction to him had been a complete shock. His mouth had claimed hers and it was as if Clay had never existed. However, that night, that kiss, had been a fluke. It had been so long since a man had kissed her with such passion that it was little wonder that she'd responded.

An uneasy silence stretched between them, until Ted slid off the bench and stood. "We should think about getting back."

"Yes, I suppose we should," she replied stiffly. She rose. Pausing, she turned her eyes toward the long row of high-rise structures, her gaze seeking the courthouse. A sinking sensation landed in the pit of her stomach. "I have the funniest feeling about this case," she murmured, and stopped, surprised that she'd spoken out loud.

Ted was giving her a look that said he was experiencing the same mixed feelings. "Come on, let's get this afternoon over with." He reached for her hand, and Caroline had no objection.

The jury entered the courtroom using the same procedure as they had that morning and sat down to hear testimony.

The defending attorney presented his defense by recalling two of the morning's witnesses for an additional series of questions.

Caroline kept expecting Nelson Bergstrom to take the stand in his own defense, but it soon became obvious that he wasn't going to be called. It didn't take much to understand why. With his attitude, he would only hurt his own chances.

The closing arguments were completed by three o'clock, and the jury entered into deliberation at three-fifteen. By the time they were seated at the long jury table, Caroline's thoughts were muddled. She didn't know what to think.

The first order of business was electing a foreman. The first choice was Ted, which surprised her. She decided to attribute it to his crisp business suit, which made him look the part. He declined, and the engineer was elected.

A short discussion followed, in which points of law were discussed, and then they went on to the evidence. This was the first time any of the jury members had been given the opportunity to discuss the trial and voice their opinion.

"If looks count for anything, that young man is as guilty as sin," Madame La Farge said, her knitting needles clicking as her fingers moved with an amazing dexterity.

"They don't," Ted said in a flat, hard voice.

"Everything that was said today, every piece of evidence, was circumstantial." Caroline felt obliged to state her feelings early. From the looks of those around her, everyone else had already made up their minds.

"As far as I see it," the real estate agent inserted, "it's an open-and-shut case. That man repeatedly hit that poor girl, and nobody's going to convince me otherwise."

"None of the money was recovered."

"Of course not," Madame La Farge inserted, planting her needlework on the tabletop. "That boy was desperate. Obviously he spent it as fast as he could on drugs. Crack, no doubt. One look at that man and anyone can tell he's an addict. No one in his right mind would act the way he did otherwise."

"He was wearing the same jacket as the assailant. What more evidence do we need?" someone else piped in.

"He was wearing a Levi's jacket, which is probably the most popular men's jacket in America. We can't convict a man because of a jacket," Caroline added heatedly.

"He lived in the neighborhood, and he had been seen there the day before."

"I know," Caroline agreed, backing down. She looked at the faces studying her and realized that she could well be standing alone on this. "I am as appalled by what happened to Joan MacIntosh as anyone here. I would like to see the man who did this to her rot behind bars. But even stronger than my sense of righteousness is the fact I want to be certain we don't punish the wrong man."

"That's everyone's concern," the foreman told her.

"The evidence is overwhelming."

"What evidence do we really have?" Ted asked.

"She identified him," Madame La Farge commented as if she were discussing the weather, pausing to cover her mouth when she yawned. "I really would like to be home

before five today. Do you think we could have a vote?"
She directed her question to the foreman.

"I'm not ready," Caroline insisted. "And she *didn't* iden-
tify him," she added, contradicting the older woman's
statement. "Joan MacIntosh said that she *thought* it was
him. In her mind there was a reasonable doubt. There's
one in mine, too."

Half the room eyed her balefully. An hour later Caroline
was convinced they would never reach a unanimous decision. Caroline felt taxed to the limit of her endurance. The
only other person in the room who had voiced the same
doubts as she was Ted.

"I have misgivings, as well," he said now.

"Maybe these two are right," one woman said softly.
Groans went up around the room.

"Are we going to let that...that beast walk out of here
after what he did?" The real estate agent rolled his pencil
across the table in disgust. "Come on, folks. The sooner
we agree, the sooner we can go home."

"Listen, everyone," Ted said, squaring his shoulders as
he sat straighter. "I'm as anxious to get home as the next
person, but we can't rush these proceedings."

A half hour later the judge sent in a note, asking if they
were anywhere close to reaching a verdict.

"See?" the real estate agent fumed. "Even the judge is
shocked at how long this is taking. We should have been
out of here an hour ago."

The foreman wrote out a reply and sent it back to the
judge. Within fifteen minutes they were dismissed and
told to return in the morning.

This time it was Caroline who was waiting in the hallway for Ted. Her hands were clenched at her sides as waves
of intense anger washed over her. He paused and grinned

at her, but she waited until they were alone to speak, then struggled to make her voice sound normal. "Just what do you think you're doing?"

"Doing?" he asked in confusion.

"Listen, I don't need anyone to defend me, so step off your shining white horse and form your own opinions. I don't appreciate what you're doing." She caught his startled look and ignored it.

"What are you talking about?"

"This case. Don't you think I know what you're doing? It's that chauvinistic attitude of yours. The fanatical gentleman in you who refuses to let me stand alone against the others."

A look of sorely tried patience crossed his face. "Believe what you will, but I happen to share your sentiments regarding the case."

"Ha!" she snapped.

The controlled fury in his eyes was enough to knock the breath from her lungs. She noted the red tinge that was working its way up his neck and the tight, pinched look of his mouth. "I can assure you, Miss Lomax, that I consider it a miracle that we share any opinion. I would appreciate it, however, if you'd afford me the intelligence to decide for myself how I feel about this case without making unwarranted assumptions."

Suddenly drowning in resentful embarrassment, she murmured, "If I've misjudged your actions, then I apologize."

"From the time you were a girl your mouth has continued to outrun your brain," he said with deadly calm. "I have endured your anger, your lack of manners, even your temper. But I have no intention of being further subjected to your stupidity."

Hot color invaded her cheeks, and Caroline experienced an unwanted pang of misgiving. "Maybe I spoke out of turn."

The look he gave her would have frozen rainwater. Without a word, he pivoted sharply and left her standing alone in the wide hall. She pushed the curls from her face and forcefully expelled her breath. Tendrils of guilt wrapped themselves around her heart. She'd done it again. And this time she'd messed it up good. Ted wouldn't have anything to do with her now. She should be glad, but instead she discovered a sense of regret dominating her thoughts. Maybe they could settle things after the trial. Maybe, but from his look, she doubted it.

Four

"Has the jury reached a verdict?" the stern-faced judge asked the foreman. The engineer rose awkwardly to his feet. The courtroom was filled with tense silence. Every face in the crowded room turned to stare expectantly at the twelve men and women sitting in the jury box.

The foreman shifted uneasily, casting his gaze to his nervously clenched hands. "No, we haven't, Your Honor."

Low hissing whispers filled the room. Caroline lifted her gaze to the young victim and watched angry defeat dull her eyes as she cupped her trembling chin. Joan MacIntosh gave a small cry before burying her face in the shoulder of the man Caroline suspected was her husband.

After long, tedious hours of holding her ground, repeating the same arguments over and over until she longed to weep with frustration, Caroline was unsure about the evidence and how she should vote. As much as anyone, she wanted the man who had so brutally attacked Joan MacIntosh punished. But as much as she yearned for justice, she also needed to feel sure that she was sending the right man to prison.

Holding her ground hadn't been easy. Neither she nor

Ted had wavered from their earlier stand, although others had made some persuasive—and heated—arguments. Still, Caroline couldn't change what she believed simply because someone else saw things differently. A mistrial was the worst possible outcome, as far as the courts were concerned. The jury members had been warned earlier that if it were possible to make a decision, one should be made. But since they couldn't agree unanimously, there had been no choice but to return to the courtroom and the judge.

"What was the vote?' The deepening frown in the judge's weathered face revealed his displeasure.

"Ten to two," the foreman returned, pausing to clear his throat. "Ten of us felt the defendant was guilty, the other two," he hesitated and swallowed, "didn't."

The judge studied the twelve jury members, then called for a jury poll.

When her turn came, Caroline slowly, reluctantly, said, "Not guilty." Unable to meet the judge's penetrating glare, she lowered her eyes. Unexpectedly her gaze clashed with the surly defendant's. A ghost of a grin hovered around his mouth, as if he were silently laughing at everything that was going on around him. Caroline was reminded again that Nelson Bergstrom had already been proven capable of such a hideous crime.

"You leave me with no option but to declare a mistrial." The judge spoke in a solemn voice, and it seemed to Caroline that his tone was sharp and angry. "The defendant is free on ten thousand dollars bond. A new court date will be set at the end of the week. The jurors will return tomorrow to fulfill the rest of their obligation to serve."

Joan MacIntosh burst into tears, her sobs reverberating against the hallowed walls. A dark shroud of uncertainty wrapped around Caroline's tender heart. She felt tears prickle the corners of her eyes, and she pinched her lips tightly together as the gavel banged down and the jurors were dismissed.

It seemed as if everyone in the room was accusing her with their eyes. She wanted to stand by Ted, lean on him for support, but since their last argument, he had barely spoken to her. Even her greetings had been met with clipped, disinterested replies. Ted wasn't the sort to get angry easily, and to his credit, he'd put up with a lot from her over the years. But when she'd questioned his integrity, she had committed the unforgivable. A hundred times since, she'd wished she could have pulled back the thoughtless words, but the truth was, defending her decision was just the kind of thing Ted would think chivalrous. If anything, she was pleased they shared the same opinion. If ever she needed a friend, it had been today, standing against her the fellow members of the jury. Yet even when their decisions concurred, they were treating each other as enemies.

The line of accusing faces didn't fade when Caroline and Ted entered the wide hallway outside the courtroom. The man who had sat with Joan MacIntosh was waiting for them, as were photographers from the local newspapers.

The moment Caroline appeared, the presumed Mr. MacIntosh started spewing a long list of obscenities at her with the venom of a man driven past his endurance. At first she was stunned, too shocked to react, and then she couldn't believe anyone would talk to her that way. She had been called some rotten things in her life, but nothing even close to this.

"I didn't mean to upset you," she pleaded, yearning desperately to explain. "I'm so sorry," she went on, "but if you only understood why I voted the way I did—"

She wasn't allowed to finish, as another tirade of harsh,

angry words broke across her explanation. Bright lights flashed as the press took in the bitter scene.

"Caroline," Ted said sharply, coming to her side. "It won't do any good to reason with him. Let's get out of here."

"But he needs to understand. Everyone does," she insisted, turning toward the reporters. "Ted and I agonized over the decision."

"Ted?" one reporter tossed back at her.

"Ted Thomasson," she clarified.

"And you are?" the reporter pressed.

"Caroline Lomax."

"Caroline," Ted snapped angrily, "don't give them our names."

"Oh." She swallowed quickly. "I didn't mean… Oh dear." She felt utterly and completely confused.

Without allowing her to speak further, Ted took her hand and led her away. Even as they briskly walked down the wide corridor, they were followed by the reporters, who hounded them with a series of rapid-fire questions.

To every one, Ted responded in a crisp voice, "No comment."

"What about you, Miss?"

Still reeling from the shock of the encounter outside the courtroom, she opened and closed her mouth, unsure what to say. A fiery glare from Ted convinced her to follow his lead. "No comment."

Because his stride was so much longer than her own, she was forced to trot to keep even with him. "Where are we going?" she asked breathlessly as they raced down the steps and sped toward the parking lot.

"I'm taking you home."

"Home," she echoed, disappointed. Tonight she would have enjoyed a leisurely drink or a peaceful dinner out.

He stopped in front of his car, took out his key and pressed the button to unlock the doors. Before he had a chance to open the passenger door for her, Caroline climbed inside. Ted stared at her for a long moment, then opened his own door and slid in. He braced his hands against the steering wheel and exhaled sharply. She understood his feelings. She had never been so glad to be out of a place in her life. Not even when she'd been caught raising prissy Jenny Wilson's gym shorts up the flagpole had she felt more glad to escape a situation. The leather-upholstered seat felt wonderful, almost comforting. The tension eased from her stiff limbs, and she slowly expelled a long sigh of relief as she leaned her head back. It felt like heaven to close her eyes.

Wordlessly, Ted started the engine and pulled out of the narrow space.

The silence was already grating on her as they pulled onto the busy Seattle street, which was snarled with rush-hour traffic. She searched her mind for something casual to say and came up blank. When she couldn't stand it any longer, she gave in and asked the question that had been paramount in her mind.

"Are you still angry with me?" she asked tentatively, surprised by how much the answer mattered to her.

"No."

"Good." For the life of her, she couldn't come up with something more clever to say. She was too drained emotionally to be original and come up with some witty remark that would restore the balance to their relationship. The funny part was that though she wasn't entirely sure they were capable of being friends, a whole day of hostility had left her decidedly upset. Previously, she'd delighted in tormenting him, had taken pride in coming up with ways to needle "Tedious Ted." Lately, though, she'd been hard-pressed to know who was tormenting whom.

Instead of pulling into the parking lot across the street from her apartment building, Ted eased to a stop at her curb.

"You aren't coming in?"

"No."

"Why not?" He made no move to turn and look at her, which only served to upset her further.

"It's been a long day."

"It's barely four-thirty," she countered. In her mind she'd pictured spending a quiet evening together. She'd even thought of cooking a meal for him, so she could impress him with her considerable culinary skills. After a day like theirs, they needed to talk and unwind.

"Another time, maybe."

Just the nonchalant way he said it grated on Caroline's nerves. She knew a brush-off when she heard one. What did she care if he came inside or not? She wasn't desperate for a man's companionship. She didn't even like Theodore Thomasson, so it wasn't any skin off her nose if he preferred his own company. At least that was what she told herself as she swallowed back the unpleasant taste of disappointment.

"All right. I'll see you tomorrow, then," she said, tightening her hand around the door handle. Still she hesitated, not wanting to part. "Thanks for the ride."

"You're welcome."

If he didn't stop being so polite, she was going to scream. Finally she got out, and when she was safely on the sidewalk and had closed the car door, he pulled away. He didn't even have the common decency to speed. She would have liked him better if he had. For a long moment she didn't move. He might claim that he'd forgiven her, but she knew he hadn't. His sleek Chevrolet was long out of sight when she finally sighed with defeat and entered her apartment building.

As it turned out, she didn't even bother cooking a meal. After years of schooling to be a cordon bleu chef and countless arguments with her father over her chosen vocation, she ate a bowl of corn flakes in front of the television. The mistrial was barely given a mention on the local news, leaving her relieved. She felt as if she were wearing a scarlet letter as it was.

Tucking her bare feet beneath her, she leaned her head back and closed her eyes as a talk show came on after the national news. The next thing she knew, the sound of shrill ringing assaulted her ears, jolting her into full awareness. Straightening, she searched around her for the source. The phone pealed again, and she reached for it.

"Hello."

Hollow silence was followed by an irritating click.

Angrily, she stared at the receiver, silently accusing it of rousing her from a sound nap. A deep yawn shuddered through her, and she wrapped her sweater more tightly around her. She supposed she was glad Ted hadn't come inside after all. As sleepy as she was, she wouldn't have been much of a hostess. She told herself he had probably recognized how much the day had drained her, that he was only being thoughtful when he refused her invitation. She told herself that, but deep down she knew it wasn't true.

Although she'd had a long nap, she slept well that night and woke refreshed early the next morning. She dreaded another day at the courthouse. There was a possibility she could be called to sit on another trial. The thought filled her with apprehension.

As she was grabbing her raincoat, the phone rang. She answered it on the second ring, and once again the caller immediately disconnected. Slowly Caroline replaced the receiver, perplexed.

Ted was already seated in the jury room when she arrived. She felt a sense of relief at seeing him and took the vacant chair next to him. He glanced up from his crossword puzzle but didn't greet her.

"Did you try to phone me last night?" she asked, sipping coffee from the steaming cup she'd picked up on her way in. It burned her mouth, and she grimaced.

"No." He gave her a look of condescension, as if to say she ought to know enough to let her coffee cool before trying to drink it. But that was the sensible thing to do, and she had never been sensible.

"What about this morning?" she asked.

"I didn't phone you this morning, either."

He didn't need to sound so pleased with himself. So he hadn't phoned. Deep down, she'd hoped it had been him.

"The reason I asked," she hurried to explain, "is that twice now someone has phoned and hung up when I answered. Caller ID just said private caller."

"Surely you don't think I—"

"No," she interrupted. "Listen, I'm sorry I asked. It was a mistake. Okay?" Irritated, she crossed her legs and studied his crossword puzzle, amazed that it was nearly complete. She hated the ones that gave the average solution time. It took her twenty minutes just to sharpen her pencil, find a comfortable position and figure out one-across. Since she was lousy at them, it naturally meant that Ted was a whiz at crossword puzzles. If the one he set aside now was any indication, he could win competitions.

The morning passed slowly. Several panels were called

out for jury selection, but her name was not among them. That was more than fine with her.

At lunchtime Ted left the building without suggesting they eat together. She'd expected that, although she couldn't help feeling a twinge of regret. Without meaning to follow him, she discovered that they'd chosen the same place along the waterfront where they'd eaten a few days earlier. As usual, the outdoor restaurant was crowded, and once her order had been filled, there wasn't a place to sit. She could ask some strangers if they would mind sharing a table with her, but no one looked that interesting.

"Do you mind if I sit down?" she finally asked, standing directly in front of Ted.

"Go ahead." He didn't sound welcoming, but at least he didn't sound unwelcoming, either.

"I didn't follow you here," she announced, pulling out the bench opposite him. Vigorously she stirred her thick clam chowder.

"I didn't think for a minute that you had." He avoided her eyes and sat looking out over the greenish waters of Puget Sound.

"Are you always like this?"

"How do you mean?" He turned his gaze to her for an instant, then looked back to the choppy waters, seeming to prefer the view of the busy waterway to her.

"Are you always sullen and uncommunicative when you're angry with someone?" She considered it her greatest weakness that she really was miserable when someone was upset with her. In the past, this personality quirk had only applied to people she cared about, which meant that her current uneasiness over Ted was troubling her more every minute.

"Usually," he agreed.

"How long does it last?"

"That depends," he said, nibbling on a French fry.

"On what?"

"On how offended I am."

"How much have I offended you?"

"On a scale of one to ten," he stated casually, "I'd say a solid nine."

A thick lump worked its way down Caroline's dry throat. She had done some regrettable things in her life, and pulled enough shenanigans to cause her father a headful of gray hair. But there hadn't been a time when she regretted any words more than she regretted the ones she'd spoken to Ted. She'd felt recently that they had been on the brink of something special. She didn't know how to explain it. She wasn't even sure she liked him, but she felt a strange and powerful attraction to him. "I can't do anything more than apologize."

"I know." A sad smile touched the edges of his mouth. He didn't say anything when she slid off the bench and stood. She wanted to ask him how long he planned to be this way but didn't. They only had one more day of jury duty, and from the looks of things it would take far more time than that.

If the morning was dull, the afternoon was doubly so. Caroline intentionally sat as far away from Ted as possible, doing her best to ignore him. Yet again and again, as if by a force more potent than her own will, her gaze was drawn to him. He was by far the most attractive man in the room. There was a quiet authority about him that commanded the respect of others. The masterful thread in his voice hadn't gone unnoticed, either. From her experience being on the jury with him, she knew that he was quick, sure and decisive. If it hadn't been for his strength against the others, she sincerely doubted that she would have been able to withstand the concerted pressure to change her vote.

Later that afternoon she returned to her apartment, which didn't feel as welcoming as it usually did. Sluggishly she removed her backpack and looped it over the closest doorknob. She was physically drained and mentally exhausted, and thoroughly disgusted with life. Once again her sense of timing had been off-kilter. She didn't know how to explain her life in better terms. It was as if everyone else was marching "left, right, left, right," and she was loping along her merry way—"right, left, right, left." Another woman would have looked at Ted Thomasson and immediately recognized what a devastatingly attractive man he was. She saw it, didn't trust it and chose to insult him. Only when it was too late did she recognize his appeal. At least after tomorrow their forced proximity would be over and she could go about her life, forgetting that she'd ever had anything to do with Tedious Ted Thomasson.

The phone started ringing at six that evening. The first time she was scrambling eggs for dinner and reached for it automatically. The pattern was the same. She picked up the phone, heard some distant breathing and then the caller disconnected. Obviously some weirdo had gotten her number and was determined to play games with her. Fifteen minutes later it happened again. After the third time, she unplugged her phone.

Refusing to give in to fear, she told herself that calls like these were normally harmless. What she needed to stir her blood was a little exercise. She changed into her jogging outfit and ran in place. She stopped only when the tenants below her began pounding on their ceiling. Panting, she turned off the record and slumped onto the sofa, panting.

Feeling invigorated and secure, she plugged her phone back in. It rang immediately. She practically jerked the receiver up to her ear. "If you don't stop bothering me, I'm calling the cops." That should frighten the jerk who was playing these games.

A moment of stunned silence followed. "Caroline, is that you?"

It was her mother.

"Oh, hi, Mom." She laughed in relief and briefly explained what had happened as she slumped against the thick sofa cushions. "I thought you were my prank caller."

"I'm so relieved," her mother said, and laughed softly. "You know how I live in fear of the police." Then she said, excitement brimming in her voice, "I have news. Your father and I are taking off for a little while." She paused, then added, "To China."

"China!"

"We leave tomorrow, and we're both very pleased. You know this is just the market he's been wanting to reach."

"How long will you be gone?"

"Two weeks. It's going to be a wonderful trip."

"It sounds like it." Caroline would miss her mother. Although they lived several hundred miles apart, they talked at least twice a week.

"Have you seen Theodore again?" The question had been asked casually, but she knew her mother well enough to sense the interest she was struggling to disguise.

"I see him every day in the jury room."

"He's grown up into someone pretty impressive, don't you think?"

"Yes, Mom, I do."

"You do?" Her mother was clearly having trouble disguising her surprise, and the line went silent for a moment. "You like him, don't you?"

"I insulted him. I didn't mean to, but it just slipped out, and now I doubt that we're capable of anything more than a polite greeting."

"He'll get over it," her mother said knowingly.

"Sure, just as soon as the moon turns blue."

"Caroline, I saw the way he looked at you. He'll come around, don't worry."

Caroline wished she had as much confidence as her mother, but she didn't.

The next morning it was Caroline who arrived at the federal courthouse first. She'd brought along a book to occupy her time—a best-seller that was said to be irresistibly absorbing. She certainly hoped so.

When Ted entered the room, she pretended to be immersed in the thrilling plot of the book, though she couldn't even remember its title, let alone the characters or the story.

He took the seat beside her. "Morning." The greeting was clipped.

"Hello." She continued reading, proud that she'd resisted the urge to turn and smile at him, then cursed her heart for pounding because she was so glad he'd chosen to sit beside her.

"Did you try to phone me last night?" he questioned dryly.

So that was it. "No."

He leaned back in his chair and rubbed a hand over his face. "Someone was playing tricks on me half the night. Phoning, then hanging up."

"Surely you don't think I would do something like

that?" She snapped her book closed and stiffened. "I'll have you know—"

"Caroline," he said, and gently placed a hand over hers to stop her. "Weren't you telling me the same thing was happening to you?"

"Yes," she said, still angry that he would think she'd done something so childish and trying not to remember that she'd all but accused him of the same thing just yesterday.

"Did it happen again last night?"

"Yes." She turned frightened eyes to him as she felt her facial muscles tense. "I thought it was a prankster...a joker, but now it's happening to you, too?"

"I don't think it's anything to worry about."

"Probably not," she agreed, but in truth she was frightened out of her wits. "But I think there has to be some connection between the phone calls and the trial."

"Still...a friend of mine is a detective. It might be a good idea if we have a chat with him."

"Do you think it's necessary?"

"I don't know, but I'd feel better if we knew where we stood."

"We're not standing anywhere. We're sitting ducks."

"Caroline, we're not. Whoever is doing this is angry because of the mistrial, but it will blow over in a day or two." His face revealed none of his thoughts.

"Right," she said, crossing her legs and starting to nibble on her bottom lip. She wished he hadn't said anything about the calls he'd gotten. Ignorance really was bliss.

"Listen," he announced a minute later. "I'm sure I'm just overreacting. We've both gotten a few harmless phone calls, but there's no need to contact the police."

She wasn't nearly as convinced, but she let the subject drop.

They sat together for the rest of the day, though they barely spoke. At lunchtime they bought sandwiches and ate in the cafeteria.

"I'll drive you home," Ted announced at the end of the day.

Caroline didn't argue. Silently they walked toward the parking lot. Her hands were tucked deep within the pockets of her light jacket. She had a sinking feeling that something was about to happen, which caused chills to run up and down her spine. She would never lay claim to possessing any supernatural insight, not in the least, but her imagination had flipped into overdrive.

Ted stopped abruptly and released a mumbled curse.

"What's wrong?"

He pointed to his car, which had been smeared with raw eggs.

Caroline's earlier chill became so intense that she feared frostbite. "The person who did this has to be the same one who's making the phone calls," she murmured, struggling to disguise her alarm. If he was doing this to Ted, then something was bound to happen to her, as well.

"We don't have any proof of that."

He sounded so calm and reasonable that she wanted to shake him. "What are we going to do?"

"For starters, we'll head for a car wash."

"And then?"

"And then my friend's office."

"Okay." She was more than ready to agree.

Detective Charles Randolph was a brown-haired, clean-shaven man whose mouth widened with a ready smile when

Ted walked into his office. Caroline followed closely on his heels and nodded politely when introduced. She resisted shaking hands, since hers were clammy with fear.

Ted briefly explained the reason for their visit. Detective Randolph sympathized, but he told them that chances were good their tormentor would stop his games in a day or so, and then he added that there was little he could do. He did offer some helpful suggestions, and assured them that the minute they could pinpoint a suspect or prove anything, he would do everything within the limits of the law to put an end to the problem.

Afterward Ted escorted Caroline to her apartment, and this time he accepted her invitation to go up for a cup of coffee. This time she ground the beans and went through elaborate steps to prolong the process to keep him with her as long as possible.

"You're not frightened, are you, Caroline?" he asked, his eyes dark and serious as he studied her.

"Who, me?" She laughed bravely and claimed the overstuffed chair across from him, her hands cupping her steaming mug.

"I agree with Randolph. Whoever is doing this is unlikely to hurt either one of us."

"Right." *Wrong*, her mind countered.

Ted didn't take more than a few sips of his coffee before he stood. Caroline sent him a pleading glance, but she wasn't about to ask him to stay if he was intent on leaving. She might be frightened half to death, but she still had her pride.

"Don't let any strangers into your apartment," he cautioned.

Was he kidding? Her own brother would have to break down the door.

"Call me if anything happens. Okay?" he went on.

Wonderful. She had to wait until her life was in danger before contacting him. "Define 'happens.'" Her eyes were begging him to stay, to move in if necessary, at least until this craziness passed.

Ted appeared to be weighing her question. "You'll know."

"That's what I'm afraid of."

He hesitated in the open doorway. "You're sure you'll be all right?"

"I'll be fine." She was shocked that she could lie with such ease, but if he was determined to leave her to an unknown fate, then she would let him. No wonder she'd disliked him so much all these years. Maybe this was how he'd chosen to take his revenge.

He waited on the other side of the apartment door until she turned the lock and it clicked into place.

After he left, she managed to push the crank caller to the back of her mind by keeping busy. She baked bran muffins and ate one with a slice of bologna and cheese for dinner. Everything on television bored her, so she picked up the book she'd tried to read earlier that day with no success. By ten-thirty her eyelids were drooping. Chastising herself for being afraid to go to sleep, she slipped into her nightgown and started humming the national anthem. Her duty as a patriotic citizen had gotten her into this mess.

She crossed the room to pull the drapes closed when she noticed a burly figure of a man standing on the sidewalk below. He looked like the same man who had accompanied Joan MacIntosh. The resemblance was enough to cause her heart to flutter wildly and panic to fill her.

Ted had told her to wait until something happened. But

she wasn't waiting until the commando below decided to break into her apartment.

Her fingers were shaking so badly that she could barely punch out Ted's telephone number.

He answered on the first ring.

"Ted." She heard the nervous tremor in her voice and tried unsuccessfully to calm herself.

"What is it?" He was instantly alert.

"A man… The man from the trial…he's here."

"In your apartment?"

"Not yet. He's standing outside my building. I…went to close the drapes, and I saw him staring up at my window."

"Did he see you?"

"I don't know," she said sarcastically. "Do you want me to stick my head out the window and ask him?"

"Are you sure it's him? Nelson Bergstrom?"

"Not Nelson, Joan MacIntosh's husband. At least I think it's him. He was standing in the shadows, but it looked like it was him, and…"

"Caroline," he said her name so gently that she wanted to cry. "You're worrying too much. It's probably nothing."

"Nothing?" she echoed, hurt and angry. "I'm locked in an apartment with a man seeking revenge outside my door. In the meantime you're probably sitting there in front of a cozy fireplace, smoking your pipe and…and you have the nerve to tell me I'm overreacting."

"Caroline—"

A loud knock sounded against her door and echoed like a taunt around the room.

"What was that?" Ted asked.

"He's here," she whispered, so frightened she thought she was going to faint.

Five

"Caroline!" Her name was followed by frantic pounding on her front door. "Caroline! Are you all right?"

"Ted?" His name was wrenched from the stranglehold of shock and fear that gripped her throat. Her hands were trembling so hard that she could barely unlatch the door and open it. A shock wave shuddered through her bones at the sight of him. His eyes were narrowed and hard, and flickered possessively over her like tongues of fire, checking to see that she was unharmed. She had never seen a more intense expression. At that moment, she didn't doubt that he would have seriously hurt anyone who'd hurt her.

"Thank God." He closed the door and swept her into his arms, crushing her slender frame to his with such force that the oxygen was knocked from her lungs. She didn't care how hard he held her. He was here, and she was safe. She wanted to tell him everything that had happened, but the only sounds that escaped her fear-tightened throat were gibberish.

The unexpected strength of his kiss forced her head back so that she was pressed against the apartment wall. He moved his hands to cup her face, and his mouth pillaged hers with such hunger that her knees gave way. Her grip on his shoulders was the only thing that kept her upright. Consuming fear gave way to delicious excitement as she opened her mouth to him and met his lips with burning eagerness. His touch chased away the freezing cold of stark fear, and she nestled closer to his warmth, trembling violently. When his mouth trailed down her throat to explore her neck, Caroline fought her way through the haze of engulfing sensations. For days she'd wanted Ted to kiss her. She'd planned to treat him as he'd done her and make fun of him with some cutting remark. But one kiss and she'd melted into his arms. Her resistance amounted to little more than wafer-thin walls. Of course, the circumstances undoubtedly had something to do with the strength of her response. And now, instead of rejecting him, she held him as if she wasn't sure she could survive if he let her go.

"He didn't hurt you?"

"No." Her voice wavered, betraying the havoc he was causing to her self-control.

"When I saw the blood, I think I went a little crazy."

"Blood?" He wasn't making any sense. She hadn't answered the knock, and whoever wanted in had been content to make a few strange noises outside her door before leaving.

"The door," Ted muttered. His hands roved gently up and down her spine, molding her closer to him, as though he couldn't let her go.

"I didn't let him in." She still wasn't sure what he was talking about, but it didn't seem to matter when he was touching her with such tenderness.

"Caroline." He lifted his head long enough for the intimate look in his sapphire eyes to hold her captive.

"Yes?"

He shook his head from side to side, as if he couldn't bring himself to speak. Ever so slowly he lowered his mouth to hers again. She breathed deeply to control the excitement that tightened her stomach. If his first kiss had shocked her into melting bonelessly, this kiss completely and utterly devastated her.

Her hands strained against his shirt, clenching and bunching the material, but she didn't know if she meant to push him away or pull him closer. After a moment she didn't care.

"I would have hurt him—a lot—if he'd touched you," Ted growled against her lips.

Remembering the feral light in his eyes earlier, she didn't doubt his words.

His breath filled her lungs. It felt warm and drugging, muddling her already-confused thoughts. "But he didn't, and I'm fine." Or she would be once her blood pressure dropped, but she didn't know who to blame for that—the lunatic or Ted.

Relaxing his hold, Ted slid his arm around her waist and securely locked the front door. "All right, my heart's back where it belongs. Tell me what happened."

His heart might have been fine, but hers wasn't. She felt as if she was standing on a dangerous precipice where the view was heavenly and heady, and stepping off looked like a distinct possibility. But she had only to look down the deep abyss below to realize what dangerous ground she was standing on. Mentally she took a step in retreat.

"Caroline," he coaxed, tenderly guiding her to the cushioned chair and sitting her down. He knelt in front of her, his hands clasping hers. "Tell me what happened. Tell me everything."

"Nothing happened, really. He—or whoever it was—

knocked a few times. I... I didn't answer, and after a little while and a few weird noises, he went away." She didn't add that she'd stood stock-still, deathly afraid that whoever was doing this would come back. Not knowing if she should run from the apartment or stay put, she had waited, praying that Ted would arrive before her tormentor decided to return.

Ted expelled his breath. "I think I broke the land speed record getting here. If anything had happened to you, I never would have forgiven myself."

"I wouldn't have forgiven you, either," she said, rallying slightly, remembering how he'd abandoned her to an unknown fate earlier. "Why didn't you stay with me before? I was frightened and you knew it, yet you chose to leave."

"I couldn't stay." He raised his head, but he refused to meet her gaze. "I had another commitment."

"Another commitment." She spoke the words with all the venom of a woman scorned. So Theodore Thomasson had some hot date that was more important to him than her welfare. How incredibly stupid she'd been not to have guessed it sooner. No wonder he hadn't been able to get out of her apartment fast enough.

Raging to her feet, she stalked to the other side of the room as two bright spots of color blossomed in her cheeks. He'd left the arms of another woman to rescue her, then had the nerve to kiss her like that. She felt as if she was going to be sick. The worst part was that she'd kissed him back, encouraged him, and, yes, wanted him. Her throat ached as she battled back stinging tears.

"Well, as you can see, I'm unscathed." She did her best to sound normal. "Now that you've assured yourself of that, you'll want to go back to the ready arms of your calendar girl. I apologize if I inconvenienced your plans in any way."

"My calendar girl? What are you talking about?" he asked in confusion. "Have you taken leave of your senses?"

"Yes," she said. She had indeed abandoned sanity the minute he'd pulled her into his arms. "And don't you ever... ever—" She whirled on him, pointing her index finger at him like a weapon. "Don't you ever touch me again."

A weary glitter shone in his eyes, as if he were attempting to make sense of her words. "From the impression you gave me, I'd say you were enjoying my kiss."

"I was in shock," she countered, her expression schooled and brittle. "I didn't know what I was doing."

He ran his fingers through his hair, mussing it all the more. "All right, all right, we both didn't know what we were doing. Chalk it up to the unpleasant events of the last week. I'll admit kissing you was a mistake."

"I don't want it to happen again."

His frown deepened into a dark scowl. "It won't. Does that soothe your outrage?"

She swallowed past the lump that was choking her throat. Her answer was little more than a curt nod. "You can go now," she finally managed. She shivered, then wrapped her arms around herself to ward off the sudden chill. Ted opened her closet and took out a bulky-knit cardigan. It cost her more pride than he knew to let him drape it around her shoulders.

"Where's a bucket?" he asked, taking off his coat and rolling up his shirt sleeves.

"A bucket?"

"A couple of rags, too, if you have them?"

"Why?"

"Why?" he repeated, glancing at her as though she'd lost her mind. "Because of the blood."

Her face went sickly pale as she suddenly remembered what he'd said earlier. "What blood?"

"You didn't see your door?"

"No. What's wrong with it?" She marched across the room, but Ted stopped her before she made it halfway to the door. Their eyes locked in a battle of wills. "Ted?"

"There are a few unsavory words painted on it. I'm sure you've read them before."

"He—he wrote something on my door...in blood?"

"It's probably spray paint, but I thought...never mind what I was thinking."

"But..."

"Just get me a bucket, Caroline."

Numbly, she complied, leading the way into her kitchen and taking out a yellow plastic pail from beneath her sink. "Why would he knock if all he wanted to do was write some ugly words on my door? That doesn't make any sense."

"After spending this week in your company, there's little left in this world that does. How do I know what he was thinking? Maybe he wanted to know if you were home before he defaced your property," he said, and his mouth thinned with irritation. He took the plastic pail from her hands and filled it with soapy water. "And for that matter, who knows what he would have done if you *had* opened the door."

"There was no chance of my doing that. Maybe he would have gotten scared if I answered and gone away."

"There's no way of knowing that." Preoccupied, he pulled open a kitchen drawer and withdrew a couple of clean dishrags.

"There's no need for you to clean up. I'm perfectly capable of washing my own front door. Besides, you probably want to get back to your hot date."

"My hot date?"

"Would you stop repeating everything I say?"

His gaze seized hers in a hold that felt as physical and punishing as if he'd grabbed her arm. Pride demanded that she meet his eyes, but it wasn't easy. Never had Caroline seen anyone look so angry. His dark blue eyes were snapping with fire. "You certainly have a low opinion of me."

"I— You were the one who said you had an earlier commitment."

"And you assumed it was with a woman."

"Well…yes." She wished her voice would stop wavering. "You mean it wasn't?" Each word dropped in volume until they emerged in little more than a low whisper.

He didn't answer her. "Why don't you change your clothes while I wipe down your door?"

"Change my clothes?" For the first time she realized that she was wearing a five-year-old flannel nightgown that had faded from a bright purple to a sick blue from years of washing. As if that wasn't bad enough, the hem had ripped out and was dragging against the floor. Complementing her outfit was a pair of glorious, scarlet knee-high socks.

"For once in your life, don't argue with me," he said in a voice that told her his patience was gone.

"I wasn't going to."

Ted's expression revealed surprise, but he said nothing more as he carried the yellow pail full of soapy water out her front door.

While he was about his task, Caroline changed into deep burgundy-colored cords and a fisherman's knit sweater. She knew that with her hair she shouldn't wear colors like burgundy, but such taboos had always been mere challenges to her. How she wished she didn't have this penchant for being so contrary.

Her hair was combed and tied at the base of her neck with a pale blue nylon scarf by the time Ted returned. She followed him into the tiny kitchen and watched as he emptied the bucket, rinsed it out and placed it back under the sink. When he turned, he looked surprised to find her close.

"You might want to pack a few things."

"Pack a few things?"

"Now who's sounding like a parrot?"

In other circumstances she would have laughed, but there wasn't any humor in the look Ted was giving her.

"Why should I pack?"

"I'm taking you home with me."

"Why?" He made her sound like a puppy dog that needed a place to stay.

"Because I refuse to spend the rest of the night worrying about you." Each word was dripping with exasperation.

"It didn't seem to bother you earlier."

"It does now." Apparently that explanation was supposed to satisfy her. "Don't argue with me, Caroline. It won't do you any good."

From the scathing look he gave her, she could see that he was right. She could put up a valiant argument, but she was tired and afraid, and the truth was that she wanted to be with Ted so much it actually hurt. The lunatic on her doorstep was only an excuse for enjoying his company. She'd been bitterly disappointed when Ted had left her earlier that evening. She'd longed to spend a quiet evening alone with him. There was a peacefulness about him that attracted her, an inner strength that drew her to him naturally. Yet all she'd managed to do was offend him. She reminded herself that he wasn't taking her to his apartment to enjoy her tantalizing company but out of a sense of duty. She swallowed her pride and followed him. She was going for more reasons than she cared to analyze.

Ted's apartment wasn't anything like what she'd imagined, though she *had* been right about the fireplace, which dominated the living room, with tan leather furniture positioned in front of it. Brass light fixtures were accentuated by the cream-colored carpet. Several paintings adorned the walls. Compared to her tiny apartment, Ted lived in the lap of luxury.

"I'll take your coat."

With a wan smile, she gave it to him. He'd barely spoken to her on the way over, and she once again sought for a way to tear down the concrete walls she'd erected between them with her thoughtless accusations. "Your apartment is very nice."

He looked as if he were about to answer her when the phone rang.

Her eyes widened with apprehension as he crossed the room. His back was to her, and although she couldn't hear much of the conversation, she saw Ted's shoulders sag in defeat. She had felt as if she'd been slowly crumpling under the oppressive weight of the pressure they'd been under these last few days, but Ted hadn't once revealed in any way that the trial and its outcome had affected him, so whatever was being said now must be far worse than anything they'd experienced so far.

Replacing the receiver, he turned to her. His eyes showed both anger and defeat.

"What is it?"

He rubbed his eyes and pinched the bridge of his nose. "That was Randolph."

"And...?"

"He just wanted me to know that there's been another assault against a woman in a mini-mart."

"Nelson?"

"They don't know, but the MO's the same. Assuming our problems are tied to the trial, that can only inflame whoever's been harassing us, so he thinks it might be a good idea if we got out of town for a few days until the heat blows over."

Six

"Leave town? Whatever for?" Caroline watched with concern as Ted rubbed a hand across the back of his neck, looking as if the weight of the world were pressing against his shoulders.

"Don't you understand what I'm saying?" he barked. "Another young woman—a mini-mart clerk just like Joan MacIntosh—has been brutally assaulted. Pistol whipped in the same way as Joan, and from what Charles said, the cops are betting the same man who attacked Joan struck again tonight. And once again it was within walking distance of Nelson Bergstrom's address."

Caroline felt the strength leave her legs, and she slowly sank into a leather chair. Her voice wobbled as the tears that had hovered near the surface broke free. "And...and we set him free." Sniffling, she pressed her fingers to her eyes, but that did little good and the moisture ran unheeded down her ashen cheeks.

"We did what we thought was right," Ted countered. "We still don't know if Nelson Bergstrom is guilty or not. No one does."

"But it must've been him."

"Apparently the newspapers have gotten hold of this, and according to Randolph, the morning paper is doing a story about the mistrial in connection with this latest assault." He gave her his handkerchief and lowered himself into the chair beside hers. "Listen carefully, Caroline. The press have our names, and our addresses aren't exactly top-secret. They're going to have a field day with this, and we could be stuck in the middle of it."

"So we have to leave?"

"We don't *have* to, but Randolph advises it. I've been meaning to visit your parents anyway, and this seems like the perfect opportunity."

"We can't go see them. They've gone to China."

Ted nodded. "What about your brother?"

"No." She was just beginning to formulate her thoughts. She had a key to her parents' home. There wasn't any reason why she couldn't steal away there for a few days. "It shouldn't matter if Mom and Dad are gone. I'll take a couple of days and drive home, lounge around for a day or two, and head back. By then this thing will have been settled."

"You?" He gave her a disgruntled look. "We're in this together. Wherever *you* go, *I* go."

"You?" Caroline would have thought from the way he had been acting that the last person in the world he wanted to spend time with was her.

"Don't look so pleased," he murmured sarcastically, propelling himself out of the chair. "Believe me, I'm not all that thrilled to waste my time in *your* company, either."

"Then why do it?" she asked, feeling hurt and unreasonable. "I don't need you to escort me to San Francisco. I'm perfectly capable of taking care of myself."

"Listen, Miss High and Mighty, I had enough of you when I was fifteen to last any man a lifetime." He paused and pointed out the window. "But some loon is out there, seeking revenge because our actions set a guilty man free. You can bet that once this latest development hits the papers it's going to be more phone calls and messages smeared on doors—and maybe worse." His look cut right through her. "Now get this through that thick, stubborn skull of yours. I'm not sending you any place where I can't keep an eye on you. We're in this thing together, whether you like it or not."

Caroline had never seen Ted's eyes so flinty. Each word forced her deeper into the chair, until she felt as though she were physically embedded in the leather cushion. She crossed her arms in front of her in an attempt to ward off the hurt his words were inflicting, instead hugging the warm memory of his kiss to her heart. The burning heat from her cheeks dried her tears.

"Well?" he challenged, standing over her, apparently expecting an argument.

"When do you want to leave?"

Some of the diamond hardness left his eyes. "First thing in the morning."

"My clothes…"

"We'll pack tonight, catch what sleep we can, and leave first thing in the morning." He spoke impersonally, and Caroline had the impression that his thoughts were elsewhere. She could be a slab of marble for all the notice he gave her.

It took what felt like half the night to make the necessary preparations for the trip. Once she was packed and her apartment securely locked, they returned to his place. She offered to help and was refused without so much as a backward glance. When he went to get his things together, she sat on the sofa. She only meant to close her eyes and give them a rest, but the next thing she knew Ted was gently shaking her awake.

She sat up with a start. "What time is it?"

"Five-thirty. It might be a good idea if we left now."

"Okay." A headache was pounding at her temple, and she pressed her fingertips to it and inhaled deeply.

"There's coffee, if you'd like a cup."

She nodded, since conversation felt as if it would require a monumental effort. He stepped into the kitchen, then returned a moment later with a steaming mug. Her smile of appreciation drained her of strength, and she sagged back against the sofa cushions. He gazed at her, and she lowered her eyes, unwilling to let him see how miserable she felt. She could hear him moving around the apartment, and she took another sip of coffee, feeling the need for caffeine to inspire her to get moving.

"Here." Ted pried off the safety cap from a bottle of aspirin and shook two tablets into her palm.

"Thank you," she mumbled, accepting the glass of water he offered next. The tablets slid down the back of her throat easily. He had ranted at her earlier with an anger that had shocked her. Now he was tenderly seeing to her aches and pains. "Did you get any sleep at all?" she asked.

"No."

He didn't elaborate, but Caroline realized that, like her, he was feeling the heavy burden of responsibility for this latest assault case. Rationally, she recognized that they'd done what they felt was right by sticking to their convictions. But the fact they had felt the shadow of a doubt over Nelson Bergstrom's guilt didn't matter now. Every piece of evidence against the man had been circumstantial; they hadn't felt confident enough to hand over a guilty verdict. But this latest assault had jerked the rug out from under

Caroline's feet. In her heart, she was sure that she had set a guilty man free.

"Did—did your friend at the police station mention how badly the latest victim was hurt? I mean…" She let the rest of the words fade, not wanting to know, yet realizing she must.

"She's in the hospital. Randolph said she's in pretty bad shape."

Caroline felt like weeping again, but she managed to hold back the tears with a suppressed shudder.

Twenty minutes later they were heading south on Interstate 5. Neither spoke and the air between them hung ominously heavy and still.

"How's the headache?" Ted asked as they approached the outskirts of the state capital in Olympia.

"Better." Her hand tightened on the armrest of the car door. She doubted that the headache would go away until Nelson Bergstrom was in jail where he belonged—where she should have put him.

When Ted exited the freeway onto a secondary highway, she gave him a surprised glance. He answered her question before she voiced it.

"We're both drained. I thought we'd spend the day in Ocean Shores. I have a cabin there."

"That sounds like a good idea." She shifted to a more comfortable position in the seat, and his dark blue eyes slid briefly to her.

"When we get to the cabin we can catch up on some sleep, then leave again when it's dark and we won't be seen."

"Leave tonight? Why?" The idea of spending a relaxing day on the beach was appealing to her. She needed the peace and solitude of a windswept shore to exorcize the events of the past week from her heart.

"I thought we should probably do our traveling by night," Ted explained. "It will be to our advantage to attract the least amount of attention possible."

Staring out the window at the lush green terrain, Caroline swallowed down a ready argument. The world outside the car window looked serene and peaceful, with its pastoral farms and grazing animals. The day was glorious, especially now in the light of early morning, as they raced down the highway with the rising sun that stood boldly out to greet them in hues of brilliant orange. She didn't want to argue with Ted, not now when she felt so tired and miserable. Telling him that he'd been watching too many cop shows wouldn't be conducive to an amicable journey.

More silence followed, but it wasn't harsh or grating; it was almost pleasant. Without being obvious, Caroline studied Ted. The image of him sitting in an office all day seemed strangely out of sync. His shoulders were too broad and muscular for a man who was tied to a desk. His jawline was solid, and there was a faint bend to his nose, as if it had been broken at one time. She couldn't picture him fighting, though she was sure he would if necessary. The last few days had taught her that. Another thing that amazed her was that he had never married. Fleetingly, she wondered why. He was more than attractive, compellingly male, and he stirred her blood as no one else ever had.

"You're looking thoughtful," Ted commented, his gaze momentarily turning toward her.

Caroline continued to study his handsome profile for a thoughtful second. "I was just wondering why you'd never married."

"No reason in particular." Amusement gleamed briefly

in his eyes. "I've been too busy to settle down. To be honest, I've wondered the same thing about you."

"Me?" She half expected him to add a comment that she would be fortunate if any man wanted to put up with her. He had never seen the softly feminine part of her that yearned for a family of her own. No, he had only been witness to the shrewish part of her nature. "I've been too busy to think about a husband and home." The lie was only a small one.

"Your career is more important?"

Proving to her father that she could be the best cook in America had been more important. Her pride demanded it, but she couldn't tell Ted that. He would scoff and call her stubborn, and add a hundred other unsavory adjectives. And he would be right.

"Yes, I guess it is," she answered finally.

They didn't speak again until the road signs indicated that they were entering the community of Ocean Shores. Although she had heard a great deal about the resort town, with its rolling golf courses and luxurious summer homes, she had never been there. For herself, she would have chosen a less populated area, one with wide open spaces and room to breathe. She wouldn't want to worry about nosy neighbors or invading another's privacy. But her tastes weren't Ted's, and every minute together proved how little they shared in common.

When he turned off the main street and took a winding, narrow road that led down a secluded strip of windswept shore, then turned down his drive, Caroline was pleasantly surprised. His log cabin was far enough off the road so that it couldn't readily be seen.

He parked on the far side of the house, so that his car wouldn't be easily visible from the road, either, and turned off the engine. He rested his hands on the steering wheel for a long moment as he closed his eyes.

"You must be exhausted."

They were less than three hours out of Seattle, but it felt as if they'd traveled nonstop to California.

"A little," was all he would admit.

The fireplace was the only source of heat inside the cabin, and Ted immediately started a fire. The place was small and homey, with only a few pieces of furniture.

Caroline looked around and came up with enough odds and ends from the kitchen cupboards to fix them something to eat. They were both hungry, and ate the soup and canned fruit as if it were ambrosia. While she washed and put away the few dishes they'd used, he sat on the sofa, staring into the fire, and promptly fell into a deep slumber. For a time she was content to watch him sleep. A pleasant warmth invaded her limbs, and she yearned to brush the hair from his brow and trace her hands over his strongly defined masculine features. Finding a spare blanket, she spread it over him, lingering at his side far longer than necessary.

A walk along the deserted beach lifted her heart from the doldrums and freed her eager spirit. Even when the sky darkened with a threatening squall, she continued her trek along the windy beach, picking up odds and ends of sea shells and bits of rock. The surf pounded relentlessly against the smooth beach. Crashing waves pummeled the sand until the undertow swept it away into the swirling depths. Caroline felt her own heart being lured into the abyss that only a few hours before had seemed so frightening. She was half a breath from falling in love with Ted Thomasson, and it frightened her to death.

Ted found her an hour later, building a sand castle with an elaborate moat and a bridge made from tiny sticks.

"I wondered where you'd gone," he said, and sat on a dried-out driftwood log. "You shouldn't have let me sleep so long."

"I figured you needed the rest." She glanced up into his warm gaze. Quickly she averted her eyes.

"We should be leaving soon."

"No." She shook her head for emphasis, her cloud of auburn curls twisted with the strength of her conviction.

"What do you mean—no?"

"I refuse to run away." She leaned back, sitting on her heels. Her hands rested on her knees as she met his puzzled gaze with unwavering resolve. "I realize that I've probably had a lot more experience in dealing with guilt than you have, and the first thing I've learned is—"

"Caroline—"

"No, please listen to me. We—*I*—did what I felt was right even when the decision wasn't easy. I refuse to punish myself now because I may have made the wrong choice. If there's someone out there who wants me to suffer because of that, then I'd prefer to meet him head-on rather than sneak around in the dark of night like a common thief. I simply won't do it."

The expression that crossed his face was so like her father's when she'd utterly exasperated him that Caroline suppressed the urge to laugh.

"You know I won't leave you," Ted admitted slowly.

"I'm hoping you won't, but I wouldn't stop you," she said, feeling brave. She hadn't planned on him driving off without her—she hadn't seen the necessity. He was much too much of a gentleman.

"It would be a simple thing for anyone looking for us to learn about this cabin. Our coming here makes sense."

"Don't worry, I've got that all figured out. We'll sleep on the beach tonight."

"We'll do *what?*" he exploded. "It's cold out here."

Caroline did an admirable job of holding back her laugh of pure delight. In the last twenty hours Ted had taken great pains not to touch her. Of course, she'd asked him not to, but that shouldn't matter. If they pitched a makeshift tent here on the sandy beach, he would be forced to seek her body's warmth. Although he would have every intention of avoiding it, he would wake up holding her in his arms. The mental image was one of such delight that she experienced a tingling warmth up and down her arms.

"I'll keep you warm," she promised under her breath, smiling.

He wasn't pleased with the rest of her ideas, either, so she was astonished that he did as she asked. For dinner they roasted hot dogs on sticks and melted chocolate bars over graham crackers. By the time they'd eaten their fill, the first stars were twinkling in the purpling sky.

"I thought it might rain earlier this afternoon," she mentioned conversationally.

"If it did, maybe you'd listen to reason."

"Maybe," she said with a gleeful smile. "But I doubt it. I've always loved the ocean."

"It's cold and windy, and it's only a matter of time before everything smells like mold," Ted grumbled, tossing another dried piece of wood on the fire.

"Yet you bought a place by the beach, so you must not dislike it half as much as you claim."

His answer was a soft snort as he wrapped a blanket more securely around his shoulders. "I don't need to worry about anyone hunting me down. One night with you and I'll be dead from pneumonia."

"Stop complaining and look at how beautiful the sky is."

"Bah humbug!" He rubbed his hands together and stuck them out in front of the sputtering fire.

The pitch-black night darkened the ocean, while the silvery beams of a full moon created a dancing light on the surface of the water.

"When I was a little girl I ran away to the sea. I was utterly astonished when they told me I couldn't board the ship."

Ted chuckled. "I remember my parents telling me about that. How old were you? Ten?"

"About that. I'd pulled one of my usual shenanigans— I can't even remember what it was anymore—but I knew that once again I'd embarrassed my mom and dad, so I decided to go to sea. I'll never forget when they came down to the docks to pick me up. My mother burst into tears and hugged me close. For the first time in my life, I realized how much she loved me."

"Had you doubted it before?"

"No, I'd simply never thought about it. No matter how I tried, I could never do things right. There would always be one reason or another why my marvelous schemes failed and I ended up with egg on my face. When I ran away I thought it was for the best, so I wouldn't embarrass Mom again. That night I learned that it didn't matter how many escapades I got myself into, she would always love me. I was her daughter."

"Did you ever try running away again?"

"Never. There wasn't any need. My home was with her and Dad." She centered her concentration on the bark she was peeling from an old stick. She didn't often speak of her youth, chagrined by her behavior.

"You were marvelous, Caroline Lomax. Full of imagination and sass. Your parents had every reason to be proud of you." He spoke with such insight that she raised her head, and their gazes met over the flickering fire. The mesmerizing quality in his eyes stole her breath. Her heart pounded so loud and strong that she was convinced he could hear it over the crashing of the ocean waves. When his attention slid to her softly parted lips, she was certain he was going to reach for her and kiss her. She held her breath in helpless anticipation, yearning for his touch.

Abruptly, he stood and tossed the blanket to the sandy ground. "I've had enough of this wienie roast. You can sleep out here if you want, but I'm going inside."

She tried to hide her disappointment behind a taunting laugh. "You always were a quitter."

He ignored her derision and shook his head. "I don't have your sense of adventure. I never did."

"That's all right," she mumbled, standing. She brushed the sand from the back of her legs. "Few men do."

"You're coming with me?" He looked stunned that she'd conceded so easily.

"I might as well," she grumbled, mostly to herself. Ted helped her put out the fire, and haul the blankets and leftover food back to the cabin.

If she was disgruntled with his lack of adventure, the sleeping arrangements irritated her even more. "You go ahead and take the bed." He pointed to the bedroom, and the lone double bed with the thick down comforter and two huge pillows.

She had to admit it looked inviting. "What about you?"

"Me?" His Adam's apple worked as he swallowed convulsively. "I'll sleep out here, of course."

"But why?"

"Why? Caroline, for heaven's sake think about it."

"You can sleep on top of the covers if it will soothe your sense of propriety. I read once that if we each keep one foot on the ground, it's perfectly fine for two unmarried people to sleep in the same bed."

Clearly flustered, he waved his hand toward the bedroom. "You go on. I slept most of the day. I'm not tired."

A smile curved Caroline's full lips. She was enjoying riling him and, true to form, Ted was easy to rile. "I trust you."

"Maybe you shouldn't," he barked, and rubbed the back of his neck in a nervous gesture. "I can't believe you'd even suggest such a thing."

"Why? It only makes sense to share, since there's only one bed."

"Good night, Caroline." He crossed his arms, indicating that the discussion was closed, and turned his back to her, standing stiffly in front of the fireplace.

"Good night," she echoed, battling to disguise her amusement.

She had no trouble falling asleep. The bed was warm and comfortable, and after only a few hours' sleep the night before, she slipped easily into an untroubled slumber.

Ted woke her at dawn and brought her in a cup of coffee. "Morning, bright eyes."

"Is it morning already?" she grumbled, yawning. Propping herself up on an elbow, she brushed the hair off her forehead. "How'd you sleep?"

"Great. You were right. Spending the night on the sofa

was silly when there was a comfortable bed and a warm body eager for my presence."

She bolted upright. "You slept in this bed?"

"You're the one who suggested it."

"Here? In this bed?" she said again, too amazed to come up with anything else.

"Is there another one I don't know about?"

"You didn't really!"

"Of course I did. Honestly, Caroline, have you ever known me to tease?"

She hadn't. Her mouth dropped open, but a shocked silence followed. For the first time in recent history, she was stunned into speechlessness.

"I'd like to leave in twenty minutes," he said, and set the steaming coffee mug on the dresser top. "Will that be a problem?"

She answered with a shake of her head, still not quite believing his claim about sleeping with her. Mystified, she watched him leave the room and gently close the door, offering her privacy.

Biting her bottom lip, she cocked her head as an incredulous smile touched her eyes. Faint dimples formed at the corners of her mouth. Maybe this trip wouldn't be such a disaster. It could turn out to be the most glorious adventure of her life. Even now, she had trouble believing that she found Ted Thomasson so appealing. Would wonders ever cease? She certainly hoped not.

Oregon's coastal Highway 101 stretched along four hundred miles of spectacular open coastline. With her love of the ocean, Caroline had made several weekend jaunts to the area. She never tired of walking the miles of smooth beaches, clam digging, beachcombing and doing nothing but admiring the breathtaking beauty of the unspoiled scenery.

"We'll need to stop in Seaside," she informed him once they crossed the Columbia River at Astoria.

"Why Seaside?"

"Historians agree that the Lewis and Clark trail ended on the beaches there."

"I don't need a history lesson. Unless it's important, I think we should press on."

From the minute they'd left the beach house that morning, he had seemed intent on making this trip a marathon undertaking. He didn't want to travel the freeway, and, to be honest, she was pleased. The coastline made for far more fascinating travel, and she had several favorite spots along the way.

"It's not an earth-shattering reason," she concluded, disappointment coating her tongue. "But Seaside has wonderful saltwater taffy, and I'd like to get a box for my mother. Taffy's her favorite, and she likes Seaside's the best, so—"

"All right. We'll make a quick stop," he agreed.

"Thanks." Sighing, she smoothed her palms down the front of her dark raspberry shorts. She couldn't understand Ted. His moods kept swinging back and forth. Last night he'd been good-natured and patient. This morning he was behaving as if they were fleeing a Mafia gang hot on their tail.

When they reached Seaside, he parked along the beachside promenade and cut the engine. "I'll wait here."

"In the car?" she asked disbelievingly. "But it's a gorgeous day. I thought you'd like to get something to eat and walk along the beach."

"I'm not hungry."

Glaring at him, she climbed out of the car and closed

the door with unnecessary force. Maybe *he* wasn't hungry, but *she* was. They'd stopped for coffee and doughnuts at a gas station hours earlier, and that hadn't been enough to keep her happy. Fine! He could sit in the car if he liked, but she wasn't going to let his foul mood ruin her day. Every stride filled with purpose, she walked to the end of the street near the turnaround and bought a large box of candy for her mother. A vendor was selling popcorn, and she purchased a bag and carried it down the cement stairs to the sandy beach below.

Ted found her fifteen minutes later, sitting on a log and munching on her unconventional meal. "I've been looking all over for you," he said accusingly.

"Sorry." She offered some popcorn in appeasement, but she had no real regrets. "I got carried away. It really is lovely here, isn't it?"

"Yes." But he sounded preoccupied and impatient. "Are you ready to leave now?"

"I suppose."

Back on the highway, he turned and gave her a disgruntled look. "Is there any other place you'd like to stop?"

"Yes—two. Cannon Beach and Tillamook."

"Caroline, this isn't a stroll down memory lane. You must have seen these sights a hundred times. We're in a hurry. There's—"

"Correction," she interrupted briskly. "*You* appear to be in a rush here, not me. I explained once before that I refuse to run away. You can let me off at the next town if you insist on acting like this."

His hands tightened around the wheel until she was surprised he didn't bend it. "All right, we can stop in Cannon Beach and Tillamook, but what's there that's so all fired important?"

"You just wait and see," she said, feeling much better.

Less than a half hour later he pulled into a public parking area near Cannon Beach. While he grumbled and complained under his breath, she found a vendor and bought a huge box kite. Tight-lipped, he helped her assemble it, but then he only sat on the bulkhead while she raced up and down the shore, flying the oblong contraption. The wind caught her laughter, and she was breathless and giddy by the time she returned.

Ted gave her a sullen look and carted the kite to the car, setting it in the backseat next to the box of saltwater taffy.

Caroline wiped the wet sand from her bare feet before joining him in the front seat. Snapping the seat belt into place, she closed her eyes and made a gallant effort to control her tongue but lost. "You know, you're about as much fun as a bad case of chicken pox."

"I could say the same thing about you."

"Me?" she gasped, outraged. She was shocked at how much those words hurt. She swallowed back the pain, crossed her arms and stared straight ahead.

He started the engine and backed out of the parking space. The tension was so thick in the close confines of the car that it resembled a heavy London fog.

Thirty-five minutes later Ted announced that they were in Tillamook. She had been so caught up in her hurt and anger that she hadn't realized they were even close to Oregon's leading dairy land.

She pointed out the huge building to the left of the road. "I want to stop at the cheese factory," she said, doing her best to keep her voice monotone. She didn't bother to explain that her father loved Tillamook's mild cheddar cheese and she was planning on bringing him a five-pound block.

Ted sat in the car while she made a quick stop in the factory's visitor shop. He climbed out of the front seat when he saw her approach. She made only a pretense of meeting his cool gaze.

"Would you open the trunk, please?" she asked with a saccharine smile.

When he did, she lifted her heavy suitcase from inside and set it on the ground.

"What are you doing?" he demanded.

"What I should have done in the beginning." She opened the car door and took out the box of saltwater taffy and the kite, and sat them on the ground beside her suitcase. "This isn't working," she replied miserably. "It was a mistake to think the two of us could get along for more than a few hours, let alone a week."

He raked his hand through his hair. "Just what do you intend to do?"

She lifted one shoulder in a delicate shrug, hoping to give the impression of utter nonchalance. "The Greyhound bus comes through town. I'll catch that."

"Don't be ridiculous."

"I thought you'd be pleased to be rid of me," she countered smoothly. "From the minute we left Ocean Shores this morning, you've been treating me like I was a troublesome pest. Here's your chance to be free. I'd take it if I were you."

"Caroline, listen...."

"Believe me, I know when I'm not wanted." She'd suffered enough rejection when she was young to know the feeling intimately.

"I should have told you earlier," he said with gruff insistence, "but I didn't want to frighten you."

"I told you before, I don't scare easily."

"Do you remember when I gassed up the car this morning?"

She nodded.

"I phoned Randolph, and…" He paused, his look dark and serious. "There's no easy way to say this. Apparently there's been a death threat made against us."

Seven

"A death threat." The ugly words hung in the air between them for tortuous seconds. "Who?"

"They don't know."

"So the threat wasn't phoned into the police station? Because they could have traced it then, right? So…how—how did Randolph hear about it?" In spite of her calm voice, her heart was pounding so hard she thought it might burst right out of her chest.

"Apparently someone wrote on the walls outside my apartment, as well. This time the message was more than a few distasteful names. The neighbors phoned the police after an article came out in the morning paper."

"Your name was in the paper?" Caroline breathed in sharply and briefly closed her eyes.

"It turns out this is the seventh robbery of a minimart in which the cashier was pistol whipped. The MO's are identical in each case. The paper interviewed Nelson Bergstrom's arresting officer, and followed his case through the trial and what's happened since. The two of us aren't exactly going to be asked to run for the Seattle city council, if you get the picture."

Caroline did, in living color. "I see," she murmured, and swallowed at the lump thickening in her throat. An unexpected chill raced up her spine. "But surely whoever did this wouldn't follow us...."

"No one knows what they're capable of doing." Ted rubbed his face, as if to erase the tension lines etched so prominently around his eyes and nose. "Randolph suggested that we stay clear of your parents' place in San Francisco, as well."

She agreed with a quick nod. "Then where do you think we'll be safe?"

"Brookings. Randolph has some connections there. He's making arrangements for us to rent a secluded cottage. That way he'll know where he can reach us."

No wonder Ted had been so disagreeable all morning. Numbly, she responded, refusing to allow fear to get the best of her, "That sounds reasonable."

His rugged features hardened into glacier ice. "I'm not letting you out of my sight anymore, Caroline, not for a minute. Do you understand?" His cutting gaze fell to her suitcase.

"I wish you'd said something before now. I thought you were sick of my company."

"Never that, sweetheart, never that." He used the affectionate nickname as if it had slid off his tongue a thousand times. Then, with deliberate, controlled movements, he lifted her suitcase and placed it back inside the trunk.

"Ted?"

He turned toward her, the hard mask of his face discouraging argument. "Yes?"

"Would you...mind holding me for a minute?" For all her brave talk about refusing to run away, she was scared. Her blood was cold, and she felt weak with fright. People had disliked her over the years, but never enough to want to kill her.

Ted wrapped his arms around her and gathered her close. The warmth from his hard body warded off the icy chill that had invaded her limbs. She relaxed against him, letting her soft curves mold to the masculine contour of his body. She felt his rough kiss against her hair, the even rhythm of his pulse, and a soothing peace permeated her heart.

"Nothing's going to happen to you." His whispered promise felt warm and velvety, like a security blanket being draped around her. "Whoever comes after you will have to get through me first."

Scalding tears burned the backs of her eyes. For years she'd treated Ted Thomasson abominably. When they were younger, she'd teased him unmercifully, to the point of being cruel. Even as an adult and with the best of intentions, she'd managed to outrage him. Yet he was willing to protect her to the point of risking his own safety. She had never felt more humbled or more grateful. Frantically, she searched for the words to express her feelings, but nothing she could think of seemed appropriate.

"Would you like some cheese?"

"Pardon?" He relaxed his hold and lifted her chin so their gazes met.

"Mild cheddar," she said, and sniffled, though she managed to hold all but a few emotional tears at bay. "I... I thought you might like some cheese."

"Another time. Okay?"

"Sure." She wiped the dampness from her cheek with the back of her hand and quickly redeposited her accumulated items inside the car.

Silence reigned as they took up their journey. Finally

he reached for her hand and squeezed it reassuringly. "I should have told you sooner."

"I shouldn't have been so self-centered. Something was clearly troubling you. I was the one at fault for being so oblivious."

"Don't be ridiculous."

"Oh, Ted, how can you say that? I bought the kite just to spite you. I don't deserve anyone as good as you in my life and you certainly rate someone better than a trouble-maker like me."

"Maybe, but I doubt it," he answered cryptically.

Before this latest stop she had felt his urgency and resented it. Now the need for haste was in her blood, as well. They barely spoke after that, both of them wrapped up in the troubles of the moment. Brookings represented safety; there were people there who would help them, people who were in contact with Detective Randolph in Seattle.

"Are you hungry?" Ted asked as they approached the outskirts of Lincoln City.

Caroline was convinced he'd asked because her stomach had been rumbling, but the pangs weren't from hunger. She glanced at him consideringly. Although she'd eaten the bag of popcorn, he hadn't had anything today except coffee and a sugar-coated doughnut. A look at her watch confirmed that it was after noon.

"Maybe we should stop."

"Anyplace special?"

"No," she said, "you choose." Lincoln City was a seven-mile-long community, the consolidation of five former small cities, with a wide assortment of restaurants and hotels. Caroline had visited there often on her way to San Francisco and enjoyed the many attractions.

Ted parked in the center of the town. Eager to stretch

her legs, she stepped out of the car and lifted her arms high above her head as she gave a wide yawn.

"Tired?" he inquired, and smiled lazily.

"No," she assured him. "I'm just a little stiff from sitting so long." As she spoke, a German Shepherd approached her, his tail wagging eagerly. "Hello, big guy," she greeted him, stooping to pet his thick fur, which was matted and unkempt. "What's the matter, boy, are you lost?" The dog regarded her with doleful dark eyes. "He's starving," she announced with concern to Ted, who had walked around the car to join her.

"He probably smelled the cheese." Absently, he patted the friendly dog on the top of the head. "There's a good restaurant around the corner from here, as I recall."

"What about the dog?" she asked, slightly piqued by his indifference to the plight of the lost animal.

"What about him?"

"He's hungry."

"So am I. If he's lost, the authorities will pick him up sooner or later." A hand at her elbow led her toward the restaurant.

She resisted, shrugging her arm free. "You're honestly going to leave him here?" She twisted around to discover the dog seeking a handout from another passerby.

"I don't see much choice. A stray dog is not our responsibility."

From his crisp tone, Caroline could tell the discussion was closed. Her mind crowded with arguments. But he was right, and she knew it. Nonetheless, there had been something so sad in those dark eyes that it had touched her, and she couldn't put the pitiful dog out of her mind.

Even after they'd eaten and were lingering over their coffee, she continued to think about the lost dog. Neither of them spoke much, but the silence was companionable. When Ted stood to pay the cashier, she placed a hand on his arm and murmured, "I'll be right out front."

As she'd suspected, the German Shepherd was outside the restaurant, glancing hopefully at each face that walked out the door.

"I bet the smells from here are driving you crazy, aren't they, fellow?" She took a few scraps she'd managed to smuggle into a napkin without Ted noticing and gave them to the dog. He gobbled them down immediately and looked at her for more.

"How long has it been since you ate?" The poor dog was so thin his ribs showed. Glancing around her, she spied a food vendor down the street. "Come on, boy, we'll get you something more."

The dog trotted at her side as she hurried down the block, past Ted's parked car and toward the beach. She bought four hot dogs and found a sandy spot off the side street to feed the starving dog.

After he'd eaten his fill, she regarded the sad condition of his fur. "You're a mess, you know that? What you need is a decent bath. Someone needs to comb your fur."

A flicker from those dark eyes seemed to say that he agreed with her.

"Caroline."

Her name was spoken with such anger that she whirled around.

In her concern for the dog, she'd forgotten about Ted, and he was clearly furious. She forced herself to smile, but her heart sank to the pit of her stomach at the angry twist of his features. She hadn't meant to wander off, but she'd been so busy trying to take care of the dog that she had forgotten he didn't know where she'd gone.

"Just what do you think you're doing? You said you'd be right outside."

Responding to Ted's anger, the dog moved to Caroline's side and took up a protective stance, emitting a low growl.

"It's all right, boy. That's Ted." Caroline gave the dog a reassuring pat on the head.

"I should have known that animal was somehow involved in this," Ted snarled. "Right out front, you said. Can you imagine what I thought when you weren't there? I swear, Caroline, my heart can't take much more of this. What do I have to do? Handcuff you to my side?"

"I'm sorry…honestly, I didn't mean to take off, but I couldn't stop thinking about the dog and—"

"Just get in the car. I'll feel a whole lot better once we're in Brookings."

"But…"

"Are we going to argue about that as well?"

She didn't want any more dissension between them. "No."

"Thank you for that." He turned and headed toward the car with a step that was as crisp as a drill sergeant's.

Gently patting the side of her leg to urge the dog to follow her, Caroline followed in Ted's wake. The German Shepherd didn't need any urging and trotted along happily at her side as if he'd been doing so all his life.

When she started to open the rear door, Ted cast her a scathing look. "Now what are you doing?"

"I—I was thinking that it might not be a bad idea to take the dog with us. He's hungry and needs a home. And I bet he'd offer us a lot of protection. I'm going to name him Stranger because—"

"We're not taking that filthy dog!" Ted exploded.

"But—"

"You've already managed to accumulate a box of candy, a slab of cheese and a sackful of worthless sea shells, in addition to a man-size kite. I absolutely refuse to take that dog. The answer is no. N. O. No."

Caroline turned away. "I get the picture," she replied tightly. She crouched down on one knee. "Goodbye, Stranger," she whispered to the dog. "I did the best I could for you. You take care of yourself. Someone else will come along soon—I hope."

The car's engine roared to life, and she swallowed down the huge lump in her throat before climbing in beside Ted, who sat still and unyielding, arms outstretched, gripping the steering wheel. She closed her eyes, biting back the words to ask him to reconsider. It wouldn't do any good; his mind was made up.

"Next stop is Brookings," he said as he checked the rear-view mirror and pulled out of the parking space.

"Right," she agreed weakly.

Turning the corner, they merged with the highway traffic as it sped through town. Not wanting Ted to see the emotion that was choking her, Caroline turned and stared out the side window. A flash of brown and black captured her attention from the side mirror. Stranger was running for all his worth, following them down the highway. Cars were weaving around him, and horns were blaring.

"Stranger!" she cried, twisting around despite the seat-belt, so she was kneeling in the front seat and staring out the rear window. She cupped one hand over her mouth in horror as she watched the dog, his tongue lolling from the side of his mouth, persistently running, unaware of the danger.

"All right. All right." With a mumbled curse, Ted pulled over to the side of the road. "You win. We can take that stupid dog. Heaven only knows what else you're going to pick up along the way. Maybe I should rent a trailer."

The sarcasm was lost on Caroline, who threw open the car door and leaped out with an agility she hasn't known she possessed.

As if he'd been born to it, Stranger leaped into the open backseat of the car, curled into a compact ball and rested his chin on his paws. Still panting from exertion, he looked up at her with grateful eyes. She sniffled, and ruffled his ears before closing the back door and slipping in beside Ted.

"Thank you," she whispered brokenly to him. "You won't regret it, I promise."

"That is something I sincerely doubt."

The tires spun as he pulled the car pulled back onto the highway. Having gotten her way when she'd least expected it, she tried her best to be pleasant company, chatting easily as they continued south.

He made a few comments now and again, but his lack of attention irritated her. The least he could do was pretend that he was interested.

"Am I boring you?" she asked an hour later.

"What makes you think that? I'm thrilled to know the secret ingredient in bran muffins isn't the bran." His well-defined mouth edged up at one corner in a mirthless grin that bordered on sarcasm.

Fuming, she crossed her arms over her breasts and focused her gaze straight ahead. Ted wasn't pleased about the dog, but he didn't need to pout to tell her that. For that matter, she wasn't exactly sure what *she* was going to do with Stranger, either. But leaving him behind to face an uncertain fate was an intolerable thought. She simply couldn't do it. To be truthful, she had been shocked that he had been so heartlessly willing to leave the dog behind, though he'd redeemed himself by pulling over and letting Stranger in the car. In her own way, she'd been trying to tell him that by being chatty, witty and pleasant. She was tired of arguing with him. She wanted them to be friends. Good friends. "I won't bother you anymore," she grumbled, swallowing her considerable pride.

Ted's gaze didn't deviate from the road, and his quiet low-pitched voice could barely be heard over the hum of the engine. "Not bother me? You've been nothing but trouble from the time we met."

She forced herself to relax against the seat, refusing to trade insults with him, though the words burned on her lips to tell him that he'd been easy to terrorize. That gentlemanly streak of his was so wide it looked like a racing stripe down the middle of his back.

"Has anyone ever commented on how your eyes snap when you're angry?" he inquired smoothly ten minutes later.

"Never."

"They do—and very prettily, I might add."

"You should be in a position to know."

He chuckled and turned on the radio. Apparently listening to the farm report was more interesting than her attempts at conversation had been.

They stopped for gas in Florence, outside of Dunes City. Had things been more amiable between them, she might have suggested that they stop and explore the white sand aboard rented camels. It had always been her intention to hire a dune buggy and venture into the forty-two-mile stretch of sand, but she never had. The camels were a new addition, and she would have loved to ride one. Knowing

Ted's preferences, he would have chosen to stand at the lookout point, utterly content to snap pictures.

Thinking the situation over, it shocked her once again to realize how different she was from this man. Even more jarring was the knowledge that it would be so easy to fall in love with him.

"I might have been tempted to stop here and take a few pictures," he confessed, echoing her thoughts, "but I don't think the car is big enough to hold both a camel and a dog." Amusement gleamed in his eyes, and she chuckled, appeased by his wit. He was full of surprises. Until recently, she had thought the highlight of his week was breaking in a new pair of socks. Now she was learning that he had wit and charm, and she had to admit, she enjoyed being with him when he was like this.

They drove for what seemed an eternity. She couldn't recall ever being so comfortable with silence. He was content to listen to the radio. Stranger, who had slept for most of the journey, now seemed eager to arrive at their destination. He sat up in the backseat and rested his paw beside her headrest.

The car's headlights sliced through the semidarkness of twilight, silhouetting the large offshore monoliths against the setting sun. The beauty of the scene was powerful enough to steal Caroline's breath.

"It's lovely, isn't it?" she murmured, forgetting the reason for this exile.

"Yes, it is," he agreed softly. "Very beautiful."

Briefly, their eyes met, and he offered her a warm smile that erased a lifetime of uncomplimentary thoughts.

"We'll be there soon."

She responded with a short nod. The quiet felt gentle. She could think of no other word to describe it. A tender-

ness was growing between them. They'd both fought it,
neither wanting it, yet now they seemed equally unwilling
to destroy the moment.

"Caroline," he finally murmured, then paused to clear
his throat.

"Hmm?"

"There's something I should tell you now that we're
near Brookings."

"Yes?"

Whatever he had to say was clearly making him uneasy.
He studied the road as if they were in imminent danger
of slipping over the edge and crashing to the rocks below.

"This morning, when I talked with Randolph..." He
hesitated for a second time. "I want you to know that he
was the one who suggested this."

"Suggested what?" She studied him with renewed interest. The pinched lines around his mouth and nose didn't
speak of anger as much as uneasiness.

He ran a hand along the back of his neck and expelled
his breath in a low groan. "What I'm about to tell you."

"For crying out loud, would you spit it out?"

"All right," he snapped.

Stranger, apparently sensing the tension, barked loudly.

"Tell that stupid dog to shut up."

"Stranger is not stupid." Twisting around, Caroline
scratched the German Shepherd behind the ears in an effort to minimize the insult. "He didn't mean that, boy,"
she whispered soothingly.

"Caroline, listen, what I'm about to tell you is none
of my doing. Randolph seemed to feel it was necessary."

"You've said that twice. Would you kindly quit hedg-
ing and tell me what's going on?"

"We're going to have to pose as a newlywed couple."

"What?" she exploded, stunned.

"Apparently the people who own the cottage are old fashioned about this sort of thing, but it's safest if we stay together, so Randolph suggested the newlywed thing. I don't like it any better than you do."

A bemused smile blossomed on her lips. "Does this mean I'm going to have to bat my eyelashes at you and fawn over your every word?" She couldn't help giggling. "Will I need to pretend to be madly in love with you?" She was afraid that wouldn't call for much acting on her part.

"No," he returned sharply. "It just means we're scheduled to share a cottage."

"Oh, good grief. Is that all?"

Ted glanced at her sharply. "Well, doesn't that bother you?"

"Should it?"

"You're behaving as though you do this sort of thing often."

She decided to ignore the censure in his voice. 'I don't see much difference between sharing a honeymoon cottage and spending the night in your one-bed cabin."

"Well, you needn't worry, I'll sleep on the couch."

"Now that's ridiculous. I'm a good six inches shorter than you. If anyone sleeps on the couch, it'll be me."

"Can we argue about that later?"

Caroline released an exaggerated sigh. "I suppose."

Ten miles later she couldn't stay quiet a moment longer. "You know what's really bothering you, don't you?" There was no holding back her lazy smile.

"I have the feeling you're going to tell me." The sarcasm was back, although he tried to give an impression of indifference.

Reading him had always been so easy for her. She wondered if others could decipher him as well as she could, then doubted it. "The fact that we'll be sharing the same cottage isn't the problem here." His grip on the steering wheel was so tight that she marveled that it hadn't collapsed under the intense pressure. "What's troubling you is that we'd be living a lie. Pretense just isn't part of your nature."

"And it *is* yours?"

"Unfortunately, yes," she admitted with typical aplomb.

Her answer didn't appear to please him. "Then you should take to this charade quite well."

"Probably. For a time I toyed with the idea of being an actress."

"Why didn't you?" He tipped his head to one side inquisitively.

"For obvious reasons." Her fingers fanned the auburn curls falling across her smooth brow. "With this red hair and my temperament, I'd be typecast so easily that I'd hate it after a while."

"That's not the real reason."

His insight shocked her. "No," she admitted slowly with a half smile. "Mom didn't like the idea." It had been the only time in her life that her mother had asked anything of her. She'd been a college freshman when she'd caught the acting bug. A drama class and a small part in the spring production had convinced her that she was meant for the silver screen. As usual, her timing was off. Her mother had taken the announcement with a gentle smile, then nodded calmly at Caroline's decision to enroll in additional drama classes. But when it looked like it was more than a passing fancy, Ruth had taken Caroline out to lunch and asked her to abandon the idea of changing her major to drama. She'd given a long list of reasons, all good ones, but none were necessary. Caroline knew this was important to her mother and had forsaken the idea simply because she'd asked.

The road sign indicating that they were entering the city limits of Brookings came into view, and Ted pulled over to the side of the highway and pulled out his phone, calling up the GPS app.

"What are you doing?"

"Getting the directions."

While he punched buttons, Caroline crossed her arms and asked, "Is there anything else that was said in this morning's conversation that I don't know?"

Glancing up from the screen, Ted regarded her with unseeing eyes. "No, why?"

"You keep dropping more and more tidbits of information. Just how long were you on the phone?"

"Five minutes."

She hated being kept in the dark this way. Circumstances being what they were, she would have preferred knowing what they faced instead of bumping into it bit by bit.

After pulling back onto the road again, Ted took a right-hand turn and followed an obscure side street that led downhill as they approached the beach.

Checking the name printed on the mailbox, Ted stopped in front of a white house with a meticulously kept yard. Azaleas lined the walkway, which was illuminated by the porch light.

Eyeing Stranger, Ted murmured, "Maybe you'd better stay here."

"Of course...darling," Caroline whispered seductively and batted her eyelashes.

'Don't forget, your name's Thomasson now."

"Naturally." She couldn't resist a languid sigh.

He rubbed his hand over his eyes. "This situation has all the makings of a nightmare."

"Tell me about it," she grumbled under her breath.

She waited with Stranger beside the car, while Ted knocked on the front door of the white house. He was greeted by a short, dark-haired woman with a motherly look. She cast Caroline a sympathetic smile, and when her husband appeared and began talking to Ted, she hurried over to Caroline.

"I'm Anne Bryant. Charles phoned and told us of the unfortunate circumstances of your visit. Now, don't you worry about a thing. You'll be safe here." She smiled curiously at Stranger, no doubt taken aback by his unkempt condition. "And of course your dog is welcome, too."

"Thank you. I'm sure we'll enjoy it here." Caroline liked Anne immediately and wondered if it was because the loving concern in the older woman's eyes reminded her of her mother.

Ted and Mr. Bryant strolled toward the car, still talking. Ted introduced the other man as Oliver. Together the four of them headed down the steep bluff to the cottage, hauling the suitcases, with Stranger traipsing behind on the narrow pathway and the steep stairs that led the last thirty feet.

"We don't have many visitors this time of year," Anne explained. "And none now, so if you see anyone along the beach it might be best to get back inside. No one knows you're here except Oliver and me."

"Unfortunately there's no cell service around here, but if you need a phone, we've still got a land line," the white-haired Oliver explained.

"What a terrible thing to happen to you on your wedding day."

Ted and Caroline's stricken gazes clashed. She had thought pretending to be a loving wife was going to be so easy, but it wasn't. She hated having to lie to these nice people. Seeming to sense her unease, Ted slipped an arm around her waist and pulled her close to his side. She made the effort to smile up at him, but his mouth curved in an expression that was devoid of enjoyment.

The feel of his arm around her brought with it a welter of emotions. His touch felt warm and gentle, and caused her pulse to trip over itself. When his gaze slid to her lips, she was shocked at the desire that shot through her. She yearned for him to turn her in his arms and kiss her there and then. Mentally shaking herself, she pulled her eyes from his.

"The missus and I feel sorry that things are working out so badly for you two lovebirds."

"Yes," Ted murmured. "We're quite upset ourselves."

"Oliver and I wanted to do something special for you to make your wedding night something to remember," Anne continued. "So we spruced up this cottage and turned it into a honeymoon suite."

"Oh, please," Caroline gasped. "That wasn't necessary."

"We thought it was," Oliver said with a delighted chuckle as he swung open the door to the small cottage.

A fire burned in the fireplace, casting a romantic light across the room. A bottle of champagne rested in a bucket of ice on the coffee table, flanked by two wineglasses.

"Now," Oliver said, stepping aside, "you kiss your bride and carry her over the threshold, and we'll get out of your way."

Eight

Anne's look was as tender as a dewy rose petal when Ted slid his arm around Caroline's waist and effortlessly lifted her into his arms. His lips nuzzled her ear.

"If you ever wanted to be an actress, the time is now," he whispered.

Looping her arms around his neck, she tossed a grateful glance over her shoulder and laughed gaily. "Thank you both for making everything so special."

"The pleasure was ours," Oliver said as he pulled his wife close to his side.

"We'll never forget this, will we, darling?" Caroline batted her thick lashes at Ted.

"Never," he grumbled, then stepped inside the cottage as she waved farewell to their hosts. He closed the door with his foot. Almost immediately her legs were abruptly released. Her shoes hit the floor with a loud clump. "Good grief, how much do you weigh?"

She decided to ignore the question. "This is a fine mess you've gotten us into."

"Me?" he snapped. "I told you, I didn't have anything to do with this wedding day business."

"Whatever." As she stomped into the tiny kitchen, she was met with the most delicious aroma. She paused, closed her eyes and took in the fascinating smells before peeking inside the oven. A small rib roast was warming, along with large baked potatoes wrapped in aluminum foil. An inspection of the refrigerator revealed a fresh tossed green salad and two thin slices of cheesecake.

Silence filled the room, and the sound of the refrigerator closing seemed to reverberate against the painted walls.

A scratch on the front door reminded her that Stranger was impatiently waiting outside with their luggage. By the time she returned to the living room, Ted had let the dog inside and was lifting their luggage.

"I'll put your suitcase in the bedroom," he announced.

She was too tired to argue. As her fingers made an unconscious inspection of her blouse buttons, she said, "Dinner is in the oven."

Being ill at ease with each other was easy to understand, given the circumstances. The intimate atmosphere created by the low lights, the flickering fire and the chilling champagne did little to help.

Ted returned from the bedroom and lifted the champagne from its icy bed. A look at the label prompted his brows to arch. "An excellent choice," he murmured, but she had the feeling he wasn't speaking to her. "I'll see about opening this."

The kitchen was infinitely better lighted than the living room, and she opted to remain where she was. With the honeymoon atmosphere slapping them in the face, it would be too easy to pretend this night was something it wasn't. "Okay," she agreed reluctantly.

After turning off the oven, she set the roast out to sit a few minutes before being carved. A quick check of the living room showed Ted working the thin wire wrapping from around the top of the champagne bottle and Stranger sleeping in front of the fireplace. The dog raised his head as the cork shot out of the bottle, but he seemed to realize that he wasn't needed for anything and promptly closed his eyes.

Looking for something to occupy her time and keep her in the kitchen, Caroline turned her attention to the table. She noted that it was already set for two. She busied herself tossing the already-tossed salad and then set it in the center of the table.

Not knowing what else she should do, she stood in the arched doorway and skittishly rubbed the palms of her hands together. "Stranger needs a bath."

"Now?" Ted looked up, holding two filled wineglasses in his hands.

"Yes…well, as you may have noticed, he's dirty."

"But the champagne is ready, and from the smell of things, I'd say dinner is, too."

"I believe you also said something about me needing to lose weight. I'll skip dinner tonight," she said stiffly, her voice weakly tinged with sarcasm.

"I didn't say a word to suggest that you're overweight."

"You implied it."

"In that case, I beg your pardon because—" he paused, appraising her intimately "—you're perfect."

Her feet dragging, Caroline stepped into the living room. The fire had died down to glowing red embers, and music was playing softly in the background. She could feel the romantic mood envelop her and had no desire to fight it any longer. What puzzled her most was that Ted had fallen into the mood so easily.

"We've been through a lot together," he commented,

handing her a wineglass. "Let's put our differences aside for tonight and enjoy this excellent meal."

She stood nervously to one side. The warm, cozy atmosphere was beginning to work all too well. "It *has* been a crazy day, hasn't it?" She took her first sip and savored the bubbly taste. "This is wonderful."

"I agree," he murmured, sitting on the sofa beside the fireplace.

Reluctantly, Caroline joined him, pausing to pet Stranger.

Ted's gaze fell to the dog, and his startling blue eyes softened. "To be honest, I'm glad he's with us."

"You are?"

"Yes." He stood and added a couple of logs to the fire, then knelt in front of it, poking the embers into flames. Flickering tongues of fire crackled and popped over the bark of the new logs. He stood and turned, but made no effort to rejoin her on the sofa. "Are you enjoying the champagne?"

"Oh, yes." She hugged her arms across her stomach, attempting to ward off her awareness of how close he was to her. She was overly conscious of everything about him. He seemed taller, standing there beside her, and more compelling than she remembered. She could feel the warmth of his body more than the heat of the fire, even though he wasn't touching her.

"I don't think I've ever noticed how beautiful you are," he whispered in a voice so low it was as though he hadn't meant to speak the words aloud.

"Ted, don't," she pleaded, closing her eyes. "I'm not beautiful. Not at all, and I know it." Her hair was much too bright, and those horrible freckles across the bridge of her nose were a humiliation to someone her age. Not to mention her dull brown-green eyes.

"I can't help what I see," he murmured softly, sitting beside her at last. Gently he brushed a stray curl from her face, and then his finger grazed her cheek. Her sensitive nerve endings vibrated with the action, and an overwhelming sensation shot all the way to her stomach with such force that she placed her hand over her abdomen in an effort to calm her reaction. "I've thought so since I first met you."

"Oh?"

"You must have known." His voice remained a husky whisper, creating the impression that this was a moment out of time.

Whatever was happening between them sure beat the constant bickering. They'd done enough of that to last a lifetime. "How could I have known?" she whispered, having difficulty finding her voice. "Sometimes things have to hit me over the head before I notice them."

"I know." He bent his head toward hers, his jaw and chin brushing near her ear.

Caroline's stomach started churning again as his warm breath stirred her silken auburn curls. She gripped the stem of her wineglass so tightly it was in danger of snapping.

Ted pried the glass from her fingers and set it aside. "Relax," his soothing voice instructed. "I'm here to protect you."

She closed her eyes as if to still the quaking sensation, but the darkness only served to heighten her reactions. "Ted," she murmured, not knowing why she'd spoken. His mouth explored the side of her neck, renewing the delicious shivers over her sensitized skin.

"Hmm?"

"Nothing." She slipped her arms around him and rolled her head back to grant him access to any part of her neck he desired. He seemed to want all of it.

A soft moan slipped from her throat when his strong teeth gently nipped her earlobe. The action released a torrent of longing, and she melted against him, repeating his name over and over. If he didn't kiss her soon, she would die.

Somehow he shifted their positions so that she was sitting in his lap. "Here's your champagne," he murmured.

She looked up, surprised. She wanted his kiss, not the champagne, but when he raised the glass to her lips, she sipped rather than protesting. When she'd finished, his eyes continued to hold hers as he took a drink from the same glass. As he set the champagne aside, his smoky blue eyes paused to take in the look of longing she was convinced must be written on her face for him to see. He cupped her cheek, his fingers sliding down the delicate line of her jaw to rest on the rounded curve of her neck. Then he dipped his head and kissed the corner of her mouth. She yearned to intercept the movement and meet his lips, but she felt like a rag doll, trapped by her strange emotions.

At last his mouth claimed hers in a study of patience. Her breath faltered; she was choked up inside. The kiss was a long, slow process, as he worked his way from one side of her lips to the other, nibbling, tasting, exploring, until Caroline wanted to cry out with longing. When she attempted to deepen the contact and slant her mouth over his, he wouldn't let her. "There's no hurry," he whispered.

"So...dinner?" she mumbled, not knowing why. The only appetite she had was for him.

"More of this later," he promised, and leisurely kissed her again.

His mouth, she decided, was far headier than the champagne and twice as potent.

"You're so very beautiful," he whispered.

"Thank you," she mumbled.

He kissed her again, his mouth lingering on her lips as though he couldn't get enough of the taste of her. She didn't mind. She loved it when he kissed her. He was so gentle and caring that the emotions swelled up in her until she wanted to cry with wanting him. When he raised his head, she noted that his eyes were a darker blue when they met the troubled light in hers. He inhaled, attempting to control his desire. With unhurried ease he carefully lifted her off his lap and set her back on the couch.

"Did you say something about dinner being ready?"

Reluctantly, she glanced toward the kitchen. "It can wait a few more minutes."

"Maybe," he agreed. "But I can't. If we don't stop this soon, I'm going to carry you into that bedroom, and it won't be for sleep."

"Oh," she muttered, and twin blossoms of color invaded her cheeks. She practically leaped off the couch in her eagerness to escape. Hurrying into the kitchen, she went about the dinner preparations without thought. Thinking would have reminded her how much she wanted Ted to touch her, to kiss her. If he hadn't stopped when he did, she would have gone with him into that bedroom. Love did crazy things to people, made them weak—and strong. During all the years of repeatedly saying no to every boyfriend, she had never come so close to surrendering to a man. Heaven knew Clay had tried to get her into bed with him, and although she'd cared for him, she had never been tempted to give him what he wanted most. If he had been more subtle about his desire, she might have succumbed.

In the end, when he'd broken off their relationship, he'd used the fact that she hadn't given in to him physically as an excuse, claiming she was a cold fish, not a real woman at all. Challenging her femininity had been the worst possible tack to take if he'd still hoped to get what he wanted. If Ted had lifted her in his arms and carried her into the bedroom, she knew in her heart that she wouldn't have resisted. She'd wanted him and would have willingly given him what so many others had sought.

Ted joined her a few minutes later, standing awkwardly behind her in the close confines of the kitchen. "Is there anything I can do to help?"

For one insane moment she was tempted to ask him to hold her again, kiss her—and make passionate love to her. Thankfully, she suppressed the urge.

The atmosphere at the dinner table was strained. They ate in silence, and although the meal was wonderful, she didn't have much of an appetite.

"Caroline?" Ted said at last, avoiding her eyes as he sank his knife into the roast beef as if he wasn't sure if he should kill it before taking a bite.

"Yes?"

"You mentioned this man you were seeing recently. Did the two of you... I mean..."

"Are you asking if I'm a virgin?" She would rather swallow fire than admit that to him.

He glared at her, and she nearly laughed. "Are you?"

"That's a pretty personal thing to ask a man."

"But it's all right for a man to ask a woman?"

"In this case, yes."

Caroline sliced her meat so hard it nearly slid off the plate, but a smile hovered just below the surface. "Why do you want to know?"

"Because we nearly…"

"Did it," she finished for him. "You needn't worry, I was in complete control the entire time."

"That's not the impression I got."

She ignored that and said, "We make a good team."

"Yes, we do," he agreed, and the amusement in his vivid eyes threw her further off balance then she was already. "And you've already given me the answer to my question."

"I sincerely doubt you know what you're talking about." She swallowed and boldly met his gaze, not giving an inch.

Looking pleased with himself, he pushed his plate aside and leaned back, crossing his arms over his chest. "No woman blushes the way you do if she's accustomed to having a man appreciate her beauty, and you are definitely beautiful."

"You sound awfully sure of yourself."

"Because I am," he said with maddening calm.

Caroline took twice the time necessary to clean the kitchen after dinner. Giving Stranger a bath and cleaning the bathroom afterward took up even more time. By the time she'd finished three hours later, she was exhausted. Avoiding Ted could become a full-time occupation, she realized. But she couldn't trust her reaction to him, and being alone with him in the small cottage made the situation all the more intolerable.

He was watching television when she reappeared with a thick towel draped over her arm. Stranger traipsed along damply behind her and eyed Ted dolefully. The dog seemed to be asking him what he'd been up to while they were gone. The dog paused in the middle of the room and shook his body with such force that water droplets splattered across the room.

"Hey, what's going on?" Ted asked, brushing at the wet spots on his shirt.

"Sorry," Caroline murmured, hiding a smile.

"Things must be bad when you apologize for a dog," he teased. His eyes grew warm and gentle, and she glanced away rather than risk drowning in their deep blue depths. "You look beat."

"I am." She sat on the floor in front of the fireplace, leaned the back of her neck against the couch and studied the ceiling.

Ted didn't continue with the conversation. She supposed that he was caught up in his television program. She opened one eye, noted what was on and groaned inwardly. He was watching televised fishing—and liking it.

"Ted, since we're asking each other personal questions…"

"We are?"

"You know, like the one you asked me at dinner."

"Oh. That."

"Yes, that. Now I have a question for you."

"All right."

He was too agreeable, but she didn't want to turn around and read his expression. "Do you remember the night you dropped me off at the apartment and left because of an appointment?"

"I remember." Reluctance coated his voice.

"Were you telling the truth when you said you weren't seeing a woman?"

It took him so long to answer that she grew concerned.

Finally he said, "No, to be honest, I lied that night. I didn't have an appointment."

Caroline straightened, giving up all pretense of resting. "You lied?" She would have sworn that he was the most honest man in the world. To have him admit to lying was so out of character that it left her feeling shocked. "But why?"

A muscle close to his eye twitched as he tightly clasped his hands. "We were both feeling a bit unsure that night, and the truth is, I was afraid if I stuck around much longer, drinking coffee and sharing a meal, I wouldn't be going home until morning."

Abruptly Caroline closed her eyes and resumed her earlier position. The way she'd been feeling that night lent credence to his observation. She'd wanted him to stay so badly. "I see."

"At the time I was sure you didn't."

"I thought you preferred not to be with me."

He draped his hand over her shoulder, and she raised hers so that they could lace their fingers together. "Rarely have I wanted anything more than I wanted to be with you that night," he whispered, and bent forward to kiss the crown of her head.

Caroline's heart beat wildly against her rib cage as her brain sang a joyous song. She dared not move, fearing a repeat of what had happened earlier. The realization that Ted found her physically attractive pleased her, but he'd given no indication that his heart was involved.

"I'm going to bed," she announced on the tail end of a long and exquisitely fake yawn. She needed an excuse to leave and think things through.

"Stay," he prompted gently. "The best part of the program is coming up. In a minute they're going to show how to tie flies."

She grimaced. "Isn't that inhumane?"

"Not those kinds of flies," he chided, squeezing her fingers. He urged her up on the sofa so that she ended up sitting beside him. His smiling eyes met hers as he looped an arm around her shoulders.

To her amazement, the fly-tying part of the program was interesting. Bits of feather and fishing line were wrapped around a hook, disguising it so cleverly that she actually had difficulty seeing the hook. But finally, after a series of very real yawns, she couldn't keep her eyes open a minute longer.

"Go to bed," he urged with such tenderness that she had to fight the urge to ask him to come with her. Struggling to her feet, she paused midway across the room. "Where do you want to sleep?"

Without so much as glancing away from the television, he replied, "The better question would be where *will* I sleep?"

"All right," she whispered, embarrassed. She was infuriated with herself for the telltale color that roared into her cheeks. "Where will you sleep?"

"Here."

He was several inches too long for the sofa, but the choice was his, and she was much too fatigued to argue. Tomorrow night she would insist that he take the bed, and she would sleep on the sofa.

A moment later, sitting on the end of the mattress, she yawned again. She really was exhausted. The day had begun early, and it had been long and tiring. It didn't seem possible that so much had happened since they'd left Seattle.

After gathering blankets and a pillow, she contained a deep sigh as she walked back into the living room and wordlessly set them on the far end of the sofa where Ted was still sitting. He was so engrossed in his program that he didn't even seem to notice.

Back in the bedroom a few minutes later, after quickly washing up, she didn't waste time before putting on her nightgown and climbing between the clean, crisp sheets. Almost immediately after she rested her head on the pillow, the living room lights went out.

"Good night, Ted," she called.

"Night."

A minute later she was wandering in the nether land between sleep and reality. Then the bedroom door creaked open, and her heartbeat went berserk. Had Ted changed his mind and decided to join her? She wanted him. Oh, dear heaven, she wanted him with her. Every night for the remainder of her life she wanted him.

Her courage failed her, and she dared not open her eyes. She would play it cool, she decided, and wait until he was beside her before turning into his arms and telling him all the words that were stored in her heart. But nothing happened. Silence reigned until she couldn't tolerate it a minute longer. As she eased herself up on one elbow, her eyes searched the darkened room. Perplexed, she wondered at the tricks her mind was playing on her. She'd heard the door open. She was sure of it.

A soft whimper came from the floor and, shocked, she tugged the blanket up to her nose as Stranger laid his snout on top of the mattress, seeming to seek an invitation to join her.

"No, boy," she whispered. "You'll have to stay on the floor. This place beside me is reserved for someone else." Then she rested her head back on the thick feather pillow and promptly fell asleep.

Sunlight splashed through the window, and Caroline stirred, feeling warm and content. Long after she was awake, she lay in the soft comfort of the bed and let the events of last evening run through her mind. Ted had held her and kissed her. He'd desired her the other night when he left her, inventing an excuse because he feared he would end up spending the night with her. He'd desired her then, and he wanted her now. Knowing that was better than any dreamy fantasy.

Stranger scratched at the door, wanting out, and she tossed aside the blanket and quickly dressed. A happy smile lit up her face as she pulled jeans up over her hips and snapped them at her waist. She felt rejuvenated after a good night's sleep and was eager to spend the day with Ted. For the first time she looked forward to their time together, almost hoping that days would stretch into weeks. This picturesque cottage by the sea would become their own private world, where they would learn to overcome their differences. "Opposites attract" was an old saying, one she had heard most of her life. The strong attraction she felt for Ted was living proof. They were powerfully and overwhelmingly fascinated with each other. This time together would teach them the give and take of maintaining a solid relationship.

As she entered the living room, the happiness drained from her eyes. The cottage was empty. The blankets were neatly folded at the end of the sofa, and for an instant she wondered if they'd even been used. Then she realized that Ted wouldn't have abandoned her; she knew him well enough to realize that. His sense of chivalry wouldn't allow him to leave her alone and unprotected.

Stranger had gone to sit patiently by the front door, wanting out. Feeling hurt and a little piqued at finding Ted gone, she opened the front door. Surprise caused her eyes to widen when she realized that it had been left unlocked.

Anyone could have walked in. So this was the protection Ted offered her!

In the kitchen, she discovered that the coffee was made and had been sitting there long enough to have a slightly burned taste. A note propped against the salt shaker on the table informed her that Ted had gone grocery shopping. She knew it was ridiculous to feel so offended, but she was the one who'd gone through two years of training to become a chef. If anyone should do the grocery shopping, it was her. Or they could have had fun doing it together.

Her appetite gone, she went to try her cell and discovered that the Bryants hadn't been kidding. No bars. She pulled a sweater over her head and hiked the trail up to the Bryants' house.

Anne was outside, on her knees, pulling weeds from the flower beds. "Morning," she said cheerfully, awkwardly rising to her feet. She gave Caroline a wry smile. "These old bones of mine are complaining again, but I do so love my flowers."

"They're beautiful." One look at the meticulously kept yard revealed the love and care each blade of grass and plant was given.

"Can I help you with something? Your husband was by earlier."

For a wild second Caroline had to stop and think of who Anne was talking about. "I'd like to use the phone, if that's all right." In the rush to leave Seattle, she had neglected to make arrangements to have her mail picked up. Mrs. Murphy lived down the hall and would willingly collect it for her. They had each other's mail key for just such instances as this. Normally there wasn't much to worry about, but Caroline had filled out applications for jobs at several restaurants and was hoping employment was in the offing. The sooner she became self-sufficient, the sooner she could prove to her father that she had made the right choice. If she couldn't be reached by phone, then an employer would probably contact her by mail. At least she sincerely hoped so.

"Go right in and help yourself to the phone. It's there on the kitchen wall."

"Thanks."

Stranger followed her to the back door and stayed outside while she made the quick call. Just before she hung up, she asked Mrs. Murphy to mail a smoked salmon from the Pike Place Market to the Bryants as a thank-you for all they'd done. Mrs. Murphy said she would be pleased to do it and didn't mind waiting until Caroline was home to be reimbursed.

On her way back to the cottage, Caroline stopped to chat. Anne explained that Brookings was famous for its azaleas. The flowers were in full bloom in May, and Anne spoke with pride of their beauty. Native azalea bushes covered more than thirty acres of a state park north of town, and Caroline hoped that she would have the opportunity to see them in bloom someday.

The cottage felt empty without Ted. To kill time, she took Stranger for a long walk, trying to teach him to fetch by throwing a stick she found along the way. Anyone observing her would have found her efforts hilarious, she mused sometime later as she sat on a driftwood log, watching the waves come crashing in to shore. No matter how long she stayed, the sight would never bore her. Stranger lay at her feet, panting. Despite that, he was eager for more, as he demonstrated by offering her his stick.

When she heard her name carried by the wind, she

turned and waved. Ted jogged to her side, then sank to the sand at her feet. "You weren't at the cabin."

"Brilliant observation," she said with a hint of a smile.

"I thought I told you that I didn't want you running off?"

So they were about to start their day with an argument. She didn't want that. Their time together should be spent building a relationship.

"I didn't run off." The denial was quick, although she strove to appear indifferent.

"I couldn't find you," he returned. The words were sharp enough to sound like an accusation.

"If you were afraid the boogie man was going to get me, then you might have locked the door."

"Caroline…" He turned to her in a burst of impatience and rubbed the back of his neck. "Listen to me. I had to get out of the house this morning."

"Why? We would have had a good time doing the shopping together. I like to cook, remember? I *am* a chef, you know."

"I know." He leaped to his feet and began pacing back and forth in front of her. His steps were quick and sharp, kicking up sand. "Listen, Caroline, we're going to have to help one another. I can't be around you without wanting you. If I'm going to resist, then you'll have to help."

A warm glow of happiness seeped into her blood. "But, Ted," she whispered seductively. "Who says I wanted you to resist?"

Nine

"I wish you hadn't said that," Ted said. He stood looking toward the rolling waves that crashed against the beach. "Being together like this creates enough temptations without you adding to them."

He sounded so stiff and resolute that Caroline wanted to shake him. "So what do you want me to do?" she asked, trying not to sound too defensive. "Sleep in the car or camp out on the beach?"

"Don't be silly."

"Me be silly? I thought you knew me better than that." She picked up a handful of the sand and slowly let it slip through her fingers. The grains felt gritty and damp. She'd awakened with such high expectations for this day, and already things were beginning to fall apart.

Lowering himself onto the log beside her, he claimed her hand with his. "The problem isn't you," he admitted with a wry twist of his mouth. "I'm the one having difficulties. It's nothing you've done—or not intentionally, anyway. You can't help it if I find your smile irresistible." He bent his head toward her and tucked a strand of hair behind her ear. "And you have the most incredible eyes."

She could feel the color working its way up to her face but was powerless to resist when he lowered his head and tenderly explored the side of her neck, sending delicious shivers skittering down her spine. Her stomach was tightening as waves of longing lapped through her. Her fingers clawed against the wood as she resisted the urge to slide her arms around him and lose herself in his embrace.

"See what I mean?" he groaned. "I can't even be close to you without wanting to kiss you."

"But I want you to touch me," she whispered candidly.

"I know."

"Is that so bad?" she asked in a prompting voice, leaning her head on his shoulder. "You make me feel beautiful."

"You *are* beautiful."

"Only to you."

"Is the world so blind?"

"No," she returned softly. "You are."

His hand found her hair. Braiding his fingers through the thick length of it, he pressed her closer to him. "That's my greatest fear."

"What is?"

"That what's happening between us isn't real. I'm afraid that circumstances have put us under unnatural stress. It's only logical that our feelings would become involved."

"Are you saying that I'm not feeling what I think I'm feeling?" She cocked her head a bit and grinned. "That doesn't make sense, does it?"

"The problem is that, as a couple, *we* don't make sense."

"Oh." She swallowed down the hurt. "I thought we balanced one another out rather well."

"Maybe, but that's something we won't know until this ordeal is over. As it is, we're playing with dynamite."

"What do you suggest, then?" She was sure she wasn't going to like anything he proposed.

"No touching. No kissing. No flirting."

"Oh." She straightened, lifting her head from his shoulder as a chill that had nothing to do with the weather ran through her. "Nothing?"

"Nothing," he confirmed.

She ran her fingers through her hair, not caring about the tangles. She needed something to do with her hands.

"Do you agree?"

There was little else she could do. "All right, but I don't like it."

"Constantly being together isn't going to make this easy." He clenched his jaw and shook his head. "But that can't be helped."

Ted had made her feel lovely and desirable. When he'd held her, it hadn't mattered that her eyes were dull and her nose had freckles. To him, in those brief moments, she had been Miss Universe. Now she felt as if she had a bad case of the measles.

"I—I think I'll put away the groceries," she said, rising to her feet and pausing to wipe the sand from the back of her jeans. "Is there anything special you'd like for lunch?" She couldn't look at him for fear he would read the misery in her eyes.

"No," he answered on a solemn note. "Anything is fine."

Caroline spent the remainder of the morning in the kitchen, baking a fresh lemon meringue pie and a loaf of braided holiday bread. Heavenly smells drifted through the cottage. She loved to bake. From the time she was a child, she'd enjoyed mixing up a batch of cookies or surprising her mother with a special cake. Kneading bread dough was therapeutic for her restless mind. She thought about her relationship with Clay and was surprised to realize that the pain of their breakup was completely gone now. She was grateful for the good times they'd shared, but he'd been right—she simply hadn't loved him enough. He'd asked her to prove her love—admittedly, in all the wrong ways—and she'd balked. Her hesitation had caused the split, and for a time it had hurt so much that she had wondered if she'd done the right thing. But she had. She knew that because now she was in love, really in love, with no doubts or insecurities. But Ted doubted. Ted was filled with uncertainties. Ted wanted them to wait and be sure. How like him to be cautious, and how typical of her to be impulsive and impatient.

By evening a plan had formed. Bit by bit, day by day she would prove to him that they weren't really so different. They shared plenty of things in common, and she simply needed to accentuate those. Within a few days he would realize that she would make him the perfect wife. She would cook fantastic meals, be enthralled by what he had to say, and laugh at his corny jokes. Within a week he would be on bended knee with stars in his eyes. In fact, she was shocked that he didn't see how perfect they were together. They'd been meant for each other from the time they were teenagers. Unfortunately, circumstances had led them apart, but no longer.

Dusk had settled when Ted returned to the cottage, hauling in an armload of wood for the fireplace. She had wondered what he'd done with himself all afternoon. He'd eaten lunch with her, then left almost immediately afterward. She hadn't seen him since, but Stranger had gone with him and returned at his side now.

"Something smells good," Ted commented, setting the uniformly cut logs on the hearth.

Wiping her hands on the terry-cloth apron she'd found in a drawer, she joined him in the living room. "I hope you like pot roast in burgundy wine with mushrooms."

His brows arched appreciatively. "I don't know, but it sounds good."

"I would have attempted something more elaborate, but…"

"No, no, that sounds fantastic."

"There's homemade bread, and fresh lemon meringue pie for dessert." After days of traveling and living together, she suddenly felt awkward and a little shy. She hadn't been bashful a day in her life, so this reaction was completely out of character for her.

He didn't look any more confident about their arrangement than she felt. They stood with only a few feet separating them, both looking miserable and unsure. "I'll wash my hands if everything's ready," he murmured after an awkward moment.

"It is."

At the dinner table they sat across from each other, but neither one of them spoke. Caroline literally didn't know what to say. The silence was thick enough to taste. Again and again her gaze was drawn to him, and every cell in her body was aware of him sitting so close, and yet they were separated by something more powerful than distance. Once she glanced up to discover him studying her, and her breath caught. He looked away sharply, as though he were angry at being caught. But if he was looking at her with half the interest with which she was viewing him, then they were indeed in for trouble.

* * *

The next morning Caroline woke to find that once again Ted had already left the cottage. The pattern repeated itself in the days that followed. She could sometimes see him working in the distance, chopping wood. What else he did to occupy his time, she didn't know, and she had no idea what the Bryants thought of a honeymoon couple who barely spent time together. Evenings proved to be both their worst and their best times. Since she did all the cooking, he insisted on cleaning the kitchen. At times she was convinced he only volunteered because it limited the time they spent in close proximity to each other.

To their credit, they both did their best to put aside their almost magnetic attraction. And despite everything, there were times when she could almost believe things were natural and right between them. Ted taught her how to play backgammon and chided her about beginner's luck when she proceeded to win every game. Later they switched to chess. Oddly enough, they discovered that although their strategies were dissimilar, their skills were evenly matched. When their interest turned to cards, she insisted that he play poker with her. He agreed, as long as she was willing to learn the finer techniques of bridge. One evening of poker and bridge was enough for her to realize that cards was one area they would do better to ignore.

Some nights they read. Ted's tastes were so opposite to her own that she found it astonishing that she could love such a man. And love him she did, until she wanted to burst. Doing as he'd asked and avoiding any physical contact had proven to her how much she did care for him. He seemed so staid and in control. Only an occasional glance told her that his desire for her hadn't lessened. When he looked at her, all the warmth he had stored in his heart

was there for her to see. Some nights she wanted to cry
with frustration, but she'd agreed to this craziness, and in
time her plan would work. It was taking far longer than
she'd expected, though.

Late nights, when the cottage was dark and she lay in
bed alone, proved to be the most trying times. They were
separated by only a thin door that was often left ajar so
Stranger could wander in and out at will. Some nights,
when she lay perfectly still, she could hear the rhythmic
sound of Ted's even breathing. She wanted to be with him
so much that sleep seemed impossible and she lay awake
for hours.

Seven days after they'd arrived in Brookings, Caroline had experienced enough frustration to last her ten
lifetimes. True to his word, Ted hadn't touched her. Not
even so much as an accidental brushing of their hands. He
seemed to take pains to avoid being near her. If she was
in the kitchen, he stayed in the living room. After dinner,
he lingered in the other room so long she had to call him
into the living room for their nightly games. It was almost
as if he dreaded spending any time with her and each minute together tried his resolve. Yet in her heart she knew
that he desired her, wanted to be with her, and hated this
self-imposed discipline with as much intensity as she did.

On the afternoon of the eighth day, she was finished
baking a cake and had set it out to cool before frosting it.
Surely by now he could see what fantastic wife material
she was, she thought. If he didn't, then she would be forced
to take matters into her own hands. But she would much
prefer it if he recognized his love for her without forcing
her to resort to more...forceful methods.

The sun was bathing the earth in golden light when

Caroline pulled on a thin sweater. In moments she was on the beach, where Stranger came racing to her side, kicking up sand in his eagerness to join her.

"Hiya, boy." She sank to her knees and ruffled his ears as he demonstrated his affection. From the way he was behaving, an observer would have assumed they'd been separated for weeks.

More by accident than design, Stranger had become Ted's dog. In the beginning she hadn't even been sure he wanted the dog tagging along after him. He neither encouraged nor discouraged the dog. Stranger simply went.

What Ted did during the days was a thorn in Caroline's side. Not once had he mentioned where he went, although she had phrased the question in ten different ways and with as much diplomacy as possible. He would smile and look right through her, then direct the conversation in another direction. Her curiosity was piqued. There was nothing to do but wait impatiently for him to explain himself in his own time, which he would—or she would torture it out of him.

Petting Stranger, she noticed that he was wearing a collar. She did know that Ted had taken the dog to a veterinarian in town one afternoon and she'd been pleased to learn he was suffering no ill effects from his days as a stray. Later she'd discovered a doggie toy that Ted had obviously bought.

"Stranger," she whispered, elated, "I love him. I really do. I think it's as much of a surprise to me as anyone," she said, and ran her hand through the dog's thick fur. "You love him, too, don't you, boy?"

The dog cocked his head at her inquisitively and she thought how strange it was that she could talk so freely to him.

"Come on, let's go for a walk." Agilely, she rose to her feet. Maybe she would stumble on Ted and discover his deep, dark secret. Surely he spent his days doing more than chopping wood. By now he'd chopped enough to supply the cottage for two long winters. After an hour's jaunt up and down the sandy shore, Caroline was convinced he wasn't anywhere around.

As she started back to the cottage, Anne waved to her from the top of the bluff. The two often shared a cup of coffee in the afternoon, and Caroline waved in return and started up the creaky walkway.

"The salmon arrived this afternoon. I can't thank you enough."

"Ted and I wanted you to know how much we appreciate everything you've done."

"You're such a sweet couple. It's obvious that you two were meant to be together."

Obvious to everyone but Ted. "What a nice thing to say," Caroline murmured, glancing at the green grass between her feet.

"At first I was concerned, I don't mind telling you. It didn't seem right that a honeymoon couple spent so much time apart. Your husband painting, and you down there in that cottage cooking your heart out."

So Ted was painting. Probably helping Oliver out every day just so he could avoid being with her.

"He's so talented. When I saw the beach scene he did of you and the dog, I was utterly amazed. Oliver offered to buy it, he liked it so much. But Ted refused—said it wasn't for sale."

Caroline's head shot up. Ted was an artist! He'd never said a word to her, not a word. So that was what he did with his time. And he'd shown Anne his work, but not her.

An unbearable weight pressed against her heart, and she swallowed back the bitter taste of discouragement. "He's wonderful," she agreed weakly.

"Do you have time for coffee?"

"Not today, Anne. Sorry."

"Thanks again for the salmon."

With her hands buried deep inside her pockets, Caroline started walking along the top of the bluff. If Ted was painting, he was probably doing it from this vantage point.

"Caroline!" Anne called, pointing in the opposite direction. "Ted's over that way."

"Of course, thanks," she returned, and gave a brief salute.

Stranger raced on ahead. She rounded a curve in the windswept landscape and hesitated when she saw Ted. He was so caught up in what he was doing that he didn't notice her until she was only a few feet away. When he did see her, he glanced up and a look of incredible guilt masked his features.

"Is anything wrong?" he asked.

"No." She laced her fingers in front of her and looked out over the beach below. The cottage was in clear sight, and there was a long stretch of beach on either side, so that no matter where she walked, he could see her. "It's lovely from up here, isn't it?"

"Yes," he said and swallowed. "It is."

"I hope I'm not interrupting you," she lied.

"No, not at all." He set his easel aside and stood so that he was blocking her view of the canvas.

Caroline got the message louder than if he'd shouted it. He didn't want her looking at his painting any more than he wanted her to be there. "I just came up to say hello, and— and now that I've done that I'll be on my way."

"You can stay if you want."

She didn't believe a word of his insincere invitation. "No thanks. I've... I've got things to do at the cottage." Like count dust particles and watch the faucet drip.

"I'll be down in time for dinner."

Her answer was a hurried nod as she turned sharply and retreated with quick-paced steps that led her away from him with such haste that she nearly slipped on the path leading down the bluff to the cottage.

Stranger elected to stay with Ted, seeming to sense her troubled mood and her desire to be alone. The pain of Ted's simple deception hurt so much she could hardly bear it.

All this time that they'd been together, she'd been open and honest with him. She trusted him implicitly. While waiting for him to make his moves in chess, she'd shared her dreams and all the things that were important to her. One night in particular, when neither of them had been sleepy, they'd sat in front of the fireplace, drinking spiced apple cider. They'd ended up talking away half the night. She had never felt closer to anyone. That night had convinced her that what she felt for Ted was a woman's love, a love that was meant to last a lifetime. Unwittingly she'd given him her heart that night, handed it to him on a silver platter. Not until now did she realize that she'd been the one doing all the talking. He had shared a little about his life; he'd spoken of his job and a few other unimportant items but revealed little about himself. He certainly hadn't mentioned the fact that he painted or even that he appreciated art. She'd admired the canvases on his apartment walls and realized with a flash of renewed pain that he'd probably done those, as well. Anne was right. Ted was a talented artist.

He found her about four-thirty, sitting on the beach, looking out over the pounding surf. He lowered himself beside her, but she didn't acknowledge his presence.

"You're looking thoughtful."

"I'm bored," she murmured. "I want to go home."

He forcefully expelled his breath. "Caroline, I'm sorry, but we can't."

He'd probably been talking to Randolph again and not telling her about it. Ted liked keeping secrets.

"Not we—me! I'm the one who's going."

"What brought this on?"

Staring straight ahead, yet blind to the beauty that lay before her, Caroline shook her head. "Eight days stuck in a cottage with no contact with the outside world is enough for anyone to endure."

"I thought you liked it here," he countered sharply. "I had the impression you were having a good time."

She leaned back, pressing her weight onto the palms of her hands, and raised her face to the sky. "I told you before I was a good actress."

"So this whole time together was all an act." A thread of steel ran through his words.

"What else?" She could feel the hard flint of his eyes drilling into her.

"I don't believe that, Caroline, not for a minute."

She gave an indifferent shrug. "Think what you want, but I'm leaving."

"No you aren't."

Clenching her jaw so hard that her teeth hurt, she refused to argue. She would leave. Finding someplace else, any place away from Ted, was essential. He had discovered a place within her where only he could cause her pain. If he'd wanted to punish her for the sins of her youth, he'd succeeded. She'd never felt so cold and alone, so emotionally drained or unloved. She had given him a part of herself that she had never before shared, only to learn that he didn't trust her enough to trust her with that same part of himself.

When she chanced a look at Ted, his expression of mixed anger and bewilderment tugged at her heart. The best thing for them both would be for her to leave as quickly as possible before they continued to hurt each other.

"I'll go wash up for dinner," he announced, rolling to his feet with subtle ease.

She refused to look up at him. "I didn't cook anything."

"I'll do it, then."

"Do whatever you want, but only cook for one."

He ignored the gibe. "Come on."

"Where?"

"You're coming to the house with me."

"I thought you said you were going to fix your own dinner?"

"I am, but I don't want you out here alone."

"Why not? You leave me alone every day."

His hand under her arm roughly pulled her up from the sand. "I'm not going to argue with you. You're coming with me."

Jerking her arm aside to free herself from his touch, she took a step backward. Stranger gave the two of them an odd look, tilting his head, unaccustomed to their raised voices.

"You're confusing the dog," she said.

"The dog?" Ted shot back. "You're confusing *me*."

"Good." Maybe he would feel some of the turmoil that

was troubling her. Trying to give an impression of apathy, she rubbed the sandy grit from her hands, feeling more wretched every second.

"Good?" Ted exploded. "Why do you want to do this to me? Just what kind of game are you playing?"

"I'm not playing a game. I just want out." To her horror, her voice cracked and tears welled up, brightening her eyes. She shoved her hands in her pockets and started toward the cottage.

"Caroline."

She quickened her pace.

"Caroline, stop! You're going to listen to me for once."

"I'm through listening!" she shouted, wiping away a tear and fighting to hold back the others. When she heard his footsteps behind her, she started to run. She didn't have any destination in mind, she only knew she had to escape.

His hand on her shoulder whirled her around, throwing her off balance. A cry of alarm slid from her throat as she went tumbling toward the sand. Ted wrapped his arms around her and twisted so that he accepted the brunt of the fall. Quickly he changed positions so that she was half-pinned beneath him.

"Are you all right?"

A scalding tear rolled from the corner of her eye, and she averted her face. "Yes." Her voice was the weakest of whispers.

Gently, with infinite patience, he wiped the maverick tear from her cheek. His hands were trembling slightly as he cupped her face. "Caroline," he whispered with such tenderness that fresh tears misted her eyes. "Why are you crying?"

Unable to answer him, she slowly shook her head, wanting to escape and in the same heartbeat wanting him to hold her forever.

"I don't think I've ever seen you upset like this." He smoothed the hair from her face. "You've got to be the bravest, gutsiest woman I've ever known. It's not like you to cry."

"What do you care if I cry?" she sniffled, shocked at how unnatural her voice sounded.

"Trust me, I care."

Not believing him, she closed her eyes and turned her face away from his penetrating gaze. Her hands found his shoulders and she tried to push him away, but he wouldn't let her.

"Caroline," he groaned in frustration. "I care. I've always cared about you. I want you so much it's tying me up in knots so tight I think..." He didn't finish as his mouth crushed down on hers, kissing her with a searing hunger that left her breathless and light-headed.

"Ted," she groaned, "Don't, please don't." Having him touch and kiss her made leaving all the more impossible, and she had to go. For her sanity, she had to get away from him before he claimed any more of her. She'd already given him her heart.

"I've wanted to do that every minute of every day." Again his mouth claimed hers, tasting, moving, licking, until she feared she would go mad with wanting him.

"Ted, no...you said..." But her protest grew weaker with every word.

He cut off her protest by pressing his lips against hers, tasting them as though they were flavored with the sweetest honey. The urgency was gone, replaced with a gentleness that melted her bones. She felt soft and loved, and he was male and hard. Opposites. Mismatched. Different.

And yet perfect for each other.

But not perfect enough for him to share a part of himself, she remembered. No, he didn't need her—not nearly enough. With a strength she didn't know she possessed, she pushed against his shoulder, breaking the contact.

Stunned, he sat up, while she remained on the sandy beach, lying perfectly still. Every part of her throbbed with longing until holding back the tears was impossible. She covered her face with her hands.

"I thought you said you wanted me?"

"No," she whispered, sitting up beside him. She looped her arms around her knees and took deep, even breaths to calm her heart.

The muscles in his jaw knotted. "That wasn't the impression you gave me the other night when you invited me to your bed."

"That was the other night." Another lifetime, when she'd felt they'd had a chance.

"And this is now?" he asked with heavy sarcasm.

"Right."

"You don't know what you want, do you? Everything is a game. It doesn't matter who's caught up in your—"

Caroline had heard enough. She put out a hand to stop him from talking, and then, with a burst of energy she struggled to her feet and rushed inside the cottage. Stranger was lying beside the fireplace, waiting for her.

"You stay here with Ted," she told the dog as she hurried into the lone bedroom and dragged out her empty suitcase.

"I told you I wouldn't let you go," Ted said, his large

frame blocking the doorway between the bedroom and the living room.

"You don't have any choice. Please, Ted," she pleaded. "I don't want to argue with you over this. I'm leaving."

"But why now?" he asked firmly. "What makes today any different from yesterday?"

She could hardly tell him the truth, that her heart was breaking a little bit more every day as it became clear that he would never feel about her as she felt about him. "Because I'm bored, and if I spend one more minute cooped up in this place I'll go crazy," she lied.

Ted ran his fingers through his hair in agitation and then curled his hand around the back of his neck. "I'm sorry. I guess I haven't been very good company."

"That's not it. For Tedious Ted, I'd say you did a fine job, but I want out. Now." Delaying the inevitable would only prolong the pain. She opened the suitcase and began dumping her clothes inside.

"I'm sorry, Caroline, but I can't let you go."

"You don't have any choice." She would have thought he knew her better than to lay such a challenge at her feet.

"If I need to, I'll tie you up."

"You'll have to."

"I won't have any qualms about doing it."

Her eyes sparked with determination. "You'll have to catch me first."

Ted's gaze hardened. "I can't believe you're doing this."

"Believe it," she said, then slammed the suitcase shut and swung it off the bed.

A loud knock at the front door diverted their attention.

"Stay here," Ted commanded. He checked the window

before swinging open the door. "Hello, Oliver, what can I do for you?"

"There's a call for you. Detective Randolph."

Tossing a look over his shoulder at Caroline, Ted nodded. "I'll be right there." He closed the door and turned to face her.

"Go answer your important call."

"I want your promise you won't try to sneak out of here while I'm on the phone."

Her mouth thinned to a brittle line. "My promise?" He had no right to bring up promises. He'd said he wouldn't touch her, and then he'd kissed her until she'd thought she would die from wanting him. Childishly she crossed her fingers behind her back in an effort to negate her words.

"Caroline, promise me you won't try to leave. Either do that or I'm dragging you up that path with me."

"All right, I won't leave." Her heart ached with the lie.

His facial muscles relaxed. "Thank you. I'll be down to let you know what's happening as fast as I can."

It didn't matter, because the minute he was safely out of sight she was leaving. She didn't like breaking her word, but he had forced her into it.

Emotion clouded her eyes. Checking her purse for cash and credit cards, she decided the best thing to do was to take her chances walking along the beach. For the first few hours she would need to avoid the highway. Eventually she could find a town and rent a car.

She paused only long enough to say goodbye to Stranger and assure the dog that Ted would be good to him.

Her heart tightened as she took one last look around the cottage. She would always remember these days with Ted as a special time in her life.

She wasn't more than a few feet out of the door when a shadowy figure moved from behind a large rock.

Her heart rose to her throat, and fear coated the inside of her mouth, as the brawny, angry man she'd seen in the courtroom with Joan MacIntosh stepped directly in front of her.

Ten

Caroline felt her panic rise. She was alone and defenseless. She'd intentionally left Stranger inside, afraid that the dog would follow her down the beach. Ted and Oliver wouldn't hear her cries, and, from the size of this man, she doubted that she could outrun him. Her hands felt weak, and she dropped her suitcase to the sand.

He seemed to sense her fear and took a step toward her.

Raising her hands defensively, she met his glare head-on. "I would advise you to leave now. I've taken karate lessons," she said with as much bravado as her thumping heart would allow. She didn't mention that she'd quit after three classes. Her breathing was shallow as she edged backward with small steps, praying he wouldn't notice that she was working her way toward the bluff. If he raced after her, she would have more of an opportunity to escape. At least if she got above him, she would be able to kick at him. In addition, there was a chance Ted would hear what was happening. Somehow, some way, she had to warn him. Otherwise he would come down the bluff to tell her what was going on and walk into a trap.

The man shifted slightly, and his dark shape was outlined by the sun, making it impossible for her to see his face clearly. He looked around, but she couldn't tell what he was thinking. Why had she left Stranger in the cottage? She wanted to reason with her attacker, plead for him to understand, but alarm clogged her throat, and the words tangled helplessly on the end of her tongue.

"Where's Ted Thomasson?"

The heel of her tennis shoe hit the edge of the bottom step, and with a frenzy born of fear and determination she turned, grabbed a handful of sand and threw it in his face. Taking the creaky wooden stairs two at a time, she ran from him, screaming for Ted at the top of her voice.

"Ted! Ted!"

She heard Stranger begin barking wildly and scratching at the front door to get out.

"Caroline!" Miraculously, Ted appeared at the top of the bluff.

"He's here!" she cried. "He found us!" She was trapped between the two men, positioned halfway up the stairs. She turned toward Joan MacIntosh's companion. From this height, she could better see the bulky man. He looked surprised, almost stunned.

Ted raced down the bluff to Caroline's side. "If you've touched a hair on her head," he called to the other man, who hadn't moved, "you'll pay." He put his arm around her, his fingers biting into her side. "Are you all right?" he whispered near her ear.

"Fine, I think," she whispered back.

He attempted to step in front of her, but she wouldn't let him.

"Caroline," Ted groaned with frustration as they juggled for position. "Let me by."

"No," she argued, stepping one way and then another on the narrow stair, blocking him.

"If you two would stop being so willing to die for each other, maybe you could listen to what I've come to say."

"You listen!" Ted shouted, placing his hands on Caroline's shoulders and holding her still. "I just finished talking to Detective Charles Randolph from the Seattle police department. They've caught the man who's responsible for the attacks."

"Was it Nelson Bergstrom?" She twisted around, needing to know.

Ted didn't seem to hear her; his gaze was focused on the man below. She returned her attention to him as well.

"I know!" he shouted up at them. "I've come to try to make amends to you for everything I've done."

"You mean you don't want to kill us?" she asked, her tensed muscles relaxing in relief.

"Don't act so disappointed," Ted said in a low murmur as he smoothly altered their positions so that he stood directly in front of her.

"So you're the one who kept calling us?" Ted asked.

"Yes." The stranger laced his fingers together in front of him and looked almost boyish as his eyes shone with regret. "And I was the one who spray-painted the outside of your apartment and made those threats." He swallowed and lowered his chin. "I want you to know that I'll pay for any damage."

"We can discuss that later," Ted replied. "For now, it would be best if you returned to Seattle. I'll contact you once we return."

"I *am* sorry."

Caroline felt compassion swelling in her. "I can understand how you felt," she told him, and was rewarded with a feeble smile.

"It's the most helpless feeling in the world to have something like that happen to the person you love most in the world. However, that doesn't make up for the things I did to the two of you. Venting my anger and frustration on you was wrong."

"I understand, and I accept your apology," she said.

"Thank you for that. But I'm ready to pay for what I did, even if that means going to jail. I deserve it for having put you two through so much. If it's any consolation now, I want you to know I didn't mean any of those threats. That's all they were—empty threats."

"It took courage to come here and face us."

"I had to do something," the man continued. "You can imagine how I felt when the police contacted Joan. The attacker made a full confession. If it had been up to me, I would have condemned an innocent man."

"We did the right thing to let Nelson Bergstrom off," Ted informed her—needlessly, since she'd already figured that out.

"Oh, thank God." Relief washed through her until it overflowed. The guilt she'd experienced when another woman was attacked had been overwhelming. She'd tried to convince herself that following her conscience was the important thing. But that knowledge hadn't relieved the weight of the albatross that had hung around her neck—until now.

"I'll be leaving now. When you want to contact me back in Seattle, the name's John MacIntosh." He turned away and started walking down the beach.

"John!" Ted called, stopping him. "How did you know where to find us?"

Caroline had been wondering the same thing herself.

"Miss Lomax's neighbor told me the address."

"I see," Ted said slowly.

His look narrowed, cutting into Caroline as she searched for the words to exonerate herself. "I gave it to her so she could mail the salmon to—"

"What salmon?"

"—Anne and Oliver as a thank-you for all they'd done."

"You told someone where we were?"

"Just Mrs. Murphy, but I assumed that—"

"I can't believe you'd do something so incredibly stupid. So…insane."

"Stupid?" she sputtered almost incoherently, her temper rising. "The dumbest, most insane thing I've ever done is take this crazy trip with you."

"I couldn't agree with you more." Ted stalked down the stairs, leaving her standing there, feeling both humiliated and ashamed. All right, she would concede that giving Mrs. Murphy their address wasn't the smartest thing she'd done in her life, but it was far saner than falling in love with Ted.

He stopped outside the cottage doorway when he found her suitcase in the sand. He hesitated, as if stunned, and a renewed sense of guilt filled her.

He turned and gave her a look of such utter contempt that she knew she would remember it the rest of her life. "So you were planning to leave anyway." He stopped to study her flushed, guilt-ridden face. "Even after you'd given me your word."

"Yes," she admitted, and her chin rose a notch. "Not that it matters anymore. Now that everything's been settled, there's no reason for me to stay." Her lips trembled as she struggled to regain her composure. Without knowing why, she followed Ted inside the cottage and watched as he took out his own suitcase and began to pack. His movements were short and jerky, as if he couldn't finish the task fast enough. He was normally so organized and neat, but now he merely stuffed the clothes inside, then slammed the lid closed.

"I'll tell the Bryants we're leaving."

"Not together we're not," she corrected him briskly. "I'm not going back to Seattle."

"Just where do you plan to go?"

"San Francisco." The name came from the top of her head. Her parents' house would be empty and cold, but she couldn't remain with Ted. She had too much pride for that, and too little self-control. He had to know she loved him. She'd done everything she could to prove she wanted to be his—everything except propose marriage. From the things she'd realized lately, she recognized that he simply didn't want her. The knowledge seared a hole into her heart. She would recover, she told herself repeatedly as she picked up her suitcase and followed him up the creaky old stairs. But her heart refused to listen.

Caroline had assumed that familiar surroundings would lessen the void in her soul. She was wrong. A three-day stint alone in San Francisco had taught her that she couldn't return home like a little girl anymore. She was a woman now, with a woman's hurts. She'd wandered aimlessly around the empty house, and all she could think about was Ted.

He had dropped her off at the airstrip in Brookings and left almost immediately afterward, with Stranger looking forlornly at her from the backseat of the car. She hadn't heard from him since, not that she'd really expected to.

Her return to Seattle a couple of weeks ago had been un-eventful. She found part-time employment the first week. Having a job lent purpose to her days and proved to be her salvation.

Her mother telephoned, full of enthusiasm after they re-turned from China, but for the first time in her adult life, Caroline couldn't bare her soul to her mother.

"For a minute when I walked in the door, I thought you might have come for a visit."

"I *was* in San Francisco, Mom."

"When? Why?"

"It's a long story."

Her mother seemed to sense that Caroline wasn't eager to share the events of her latest escapade. "You don't sound like yourself, honey. Is something wrong?"

"What could possibly be wrong? I've got the very thing I've always wanted. I'm working as a chef and loving it."

"But you don't sound happy."

"I'm…just tired, that's all."

"Have you seen any more of Ted Thomasson?"

The pain was so intense that Caroline hesitated before speaking. "No, not for a couple of weeks now." Two weeks, four days and twenty-one hours, she mentally calculated, glancing at her watch.

An awkward silence followed. "Well, I just wanted you to know that your father and I arrived back home safely, and that China was wonderful."

"I'm pleased you're home, Mom. Thanks for calling. I'll give you a ring later in the week."

"Caroline, don't you want to tell your father about your job?"

"You can go ahead and tell him, if you want to."

It wasn't until she hung up that she realized her mistake.

At any other time in her life, she would have been puffed up like a bull frog at having achieved her goal of working in a restaurant kitchen. Now her profession was nothing more than a means to fill the empty days.

She'd barely finished the conversation with her mother when a hard knock sounded against her front door. She glanced at it, inexplicably knowing in her heart that Ted stood on the other side. The entire time she'd been back, she had subconsciously been waiting to hear from him. Now, like a coward, she waited until the hard knock was repeated. Forcing a brittle smile to her lips, she finally turned the lock and opened the door.

"Hello, Caroline." His eyes caressed her like a warm, golden flame.

"Hello, Ted. How are you?" Pride demanded that she not reveal any of the emotional pain these weeks apart had cost her. He looked wonderful. Everything she'd remembered about him seemed even more pronounced now. His features were even more rugged and compelling. His eyes were an even deeper shade of blue, if that were possible. The strong, well-shaped mouth that had shown her such pleasure slanted into a half smile.

"I brought your kite and your other things."

The instant she'd seen what he was carrying, she had realized with a sinking heart that the reason for his visit wasn't personal. "How's Stranger?"

"Fine. My apartment doesn't allow pets, so I had to find a home for him."

"You gave Stranger away?" She breathed in sharply, unbelievably hurt that he would so callously give up their dog.

"Could you take him?"

Her apartment building had the same restriction. "No,"

she admitted, subdued. "You…did the right thing. Is he happy in his new home?"

"Very."

Her smile wavered, and she murmured with a breathless catch in her voice, "Then that's what counts." Realizing that she had left him standing in the doorway, she hurriedly stepped aside. "Come in, please."

"Where do you want me to put all this?"

"The kitchen counter will be fine. Thanks." She threaded her fingers together so tightly that they ached. She knew her features were strained with the burden of maintaining an expression of poise. She tried unsuccessfully to relax.

"Do you still make that fancy coffee?" he asked softly.

"Yes…would you like a cup?"

"If you have the time."

Time was something she had plenty of these days. Time to remember how his mouth tasted on hers. Time to recall the velvet smoothness of his touch and how well their bodies fit together. Time to compile a list of regrets that was longer than a rich kid's Christmas list.

Their gazes held for several seconds. "Yes, I have the time," she murmured at last, breaking eye contact.

He followed her into the kitchen. "How have you been?"

"Wonderful," she lied with practiced ease. "I have a job. It's only afternoons for now, but I'm hoping that it'll work into full time later this summer." Actually, she'd taken the first job that was offered, even though she would have preferred a regular forty-hour work schedule. But anything was better than moping around the house day after day.

"I'm pleased things are working out for you."

"What about you?" She couldn't look at him, knowing it would be too painful.

"I've been fine," he supplied, leaning against the kitchen counter.

She put as much space between them as possible in the cozy kitchen. Her gaze centered on the glass pot, praying the water would boil quickly.

"We need to talk," he said quietly. "You know that, don't you, Caroline?"

She gripped the counter so hard it threatened to break her neatly trimmed nails. "About what?" Wildly she looked away as her heart jammed in her throat.

"About us."

"Us?" She forced a laugh that sounded amazingly like a restrained sob. "Within two hours we were at each other's throats. How can you even suggest there's an 'us'?"

"That's not the way I remember it."

The minute the coffee finished brewing, she filled two cups and handed him one. He immediately set it on the counter. "Coffee was only an excuse, and you know it."

She took a quick step away from him. "I wish you'd said something before I went through the trouble of making it."

"No you don't."

Without her noticing, he had moved closer to her, trapping her in a corner. Mere inches separated them. Her breathing had become so shallow it was nearly nonexistent.

"I thought I'd give myself time to sort out my feelings." He lifted the luxurious silky auburn curls away from the side of her neck. Her pulse hammered wildly as his thumb stroked her skin. "Every time I was close to you, I had to fight to keep myself from kissing you."

Magnetically, Caroline's gaze was drawn to his eyes. "It's only natural that under the circumstances we—we feel these—these strong physical attractions."

"Problem is," Ted said softly, his breath caressing her

face, "I'm experiencing the same things now, only even more powerfully, more intensely, than ever."

"That can't be true," she insisted, too afraid to believe him and seeking an escape. Abruptly she turned and reached for her coffee, nearly scalding her lips as she took a sip. She clenched the mug with both hands. "What we had on the beach wasn't real," she said in a falsely cheerful voice. "You warned me that things would look different once we returned to Seattle, and now I'm forced to admit that they do."

"Caroline," he said her name with a wealth of frustration. "Don't lie to me again."

"Who's lying?" Her voice cracked, and she struggled to hold back stinging tears as she chewed on the corner of her bottom lip.

"Is your pride worth so much to you?"

Unable to answer him, she stared into the black depth of the coffee mug.

"Maybe we should experiment."

"Experiment?"

"Let me kiss you a couple of times and see how you feel." He took the mug from her hands and set it on the counter.

"There isn't any need. I know what I feel," she argued, knowing that if he touched her, she would be lost. With her hands behind her, guiding her, she edged her way along the kitchen wall.

"It may be the only way," he continued, undaunted. "It seems that we've come to different conclusions here. There's too much at stake for me to let you pass judgment so lightly."

"I know how I feel."

"I'm sure you do." He cupped her shoulders with his

hands, halting her progress. "I just don't think you're being honest with yourself—or me—about your feelings."

"Ted, please don't."

"I have to," he breathed, bending toward her.

She averted her mouth, so that his lips brushed her cheek. "Please," she whispered. "It won't do any good."

His hands slid from her shoulders up her neck to her chin, tilting her face to receive his kiss. The pressure of his mouth was as light as the morning sun touching the earth. Soon the magnetic desire that was ever-present between them urged their mouths together in a kiss that left Caroline clinging to the counter to stay upright.

"Well?" he asked hoarsely, spreading kisses around her face, pausing at her temple.

She kept her eyes pinched shut. "That was...very... nice."

"Nice?" His hands slid around her waist, bringing her to him until she was pressed hard against his chest. "It was more than nice."

"No," she offered weakly, pushing against him.

He kissed her again, only this time his lips stayed and moved and urged and tested. Caroline was lost. Her arms rose from his chest to link around his neck, so that she was arched against him. Softly, she moaned, unable to hold back any longer, clinging to him, weak with longing and desire. Again and again his mouth met hers, until she saw a glimpse of heaven and far, far beyond.

When he broke the contact, she buried her face in the curve of his neck. The irregular pounding of his heart echoed hers.

"Does that convince you?"

"It tells me that we have a strong physical attraction," she answered, breathless and weak.

"More than that. What we share is spiritual."

"No." She tried to deny him, but her feeble protest was broken off when he raised his mouth to hers and kissed her again. The kiss was tempestuous, earth-shattering.

"Don't argue," he said with a guttural moan. "I love you, Caroline. I want us to marry and give Stranger a home."

"I thought you said you gave him away." It was far easier to discuss the dog than to think about the first part of his statement.

"No, I didn't." Tenderly he kissed the bridge of her nose, as if he couldn't get enough of the feel of her. "I said I found him a home. And I have. Ours."

"Oh." She pressed her forehead to the center of his chest as she took in everything he was saying. She loved him. Dear Lord, she loved him until she thought she would die without him. But sometimes love wasn't enough. "I—I don't think anyone should base something as important as marriage on anything as flimsy as making a home for a stray dog."

"I love you," he whispered against her hair. "I think I've loved you from the time I first saw you."

Slowly she raised her eyes so that she could see the tenderness in his expression and believe what he was saying. Her fingertips traced the angular line of his jaw.

"Why didn't you tell me?"

"That I loved you? Honey, surely you can understand why, given the—"

Her fingers across his lips stopped him. "You're an artist, aren't you?"

He blinked and captured her hand, then kissed it. "So that's it." He forced the air from his lungs. "I should have told you, but to be honest, I was wary. I was afraid that if you saw my work, you'd think it was another one of my interests, like dancing lessons, that always made you think less of me."

"You thought that of me?" she asked, forcibly trying to break free. It hurt to believe that he saw her as so insensitive.

"Listen to me." His hold tightened, not allowing her out of his embrace. "That was only in the beginning, before I realized how much you'd changed. Later, I thought I'd surprise you with the painting and make it a wedding gift."

"That's why you didn't want me to see it that day on the bluff?"

He wove his hand into her hair, running her fingers through her curls. "The only reason."

"Oh, Ted." She pressed her head over his heart, hugging him hard. "I was so hurt… I'd talked for days and days, sharing the most personal parts of my life with you. And when…when I saw that there was a part of yourself that you hid from me, I felt terrible. I lied about being bored. I loved being with you every minute that we were together. It nearly killed me to leave you."

"I knew you were lying all along. What I couldn't figure out was why."

"I lied because I thought you didn't care. But…how did you know?" She had thought she'd given an Academy Award–winning performance.

"No one could shine with as much happiness as you did and be faking it," he replied, smiling tenderly.

She closed her eyes, holding on to the rapture his words spread through her soul. "You're sure you want to marry me? I'm stubborn as a mule, contrary, proud—"

"Headstrong, reckless and overbearing," he interrupted with a chuckle. "But you're also warm, loving, creative and so many other wonderful things that it will take me a lifetime to discover them all."

"I'll marry you, Ted Thomasson, whenever you want."

His gaze took in her happiness. "We're going to have some fantastic children, Caroline Lomax."

They kissed lightly, and Caroline grinned. "I think you may be right," she whispered, bringing his mouth down to hers.

* * * * *